THE THIRD GUN

The Korean unfolded the stock of the MAC–10, put it to his shoulder and aimed down at Lake.

Sparks flew off the concrete floor. Lake rolled and looked up, spotting the muzzle flash of a weapon being fired up on the south wall. The Korean who had been about to shoot Lake rolled right, out of the way of the unexpected firing. Lake didn't stop to savor his reprieve. He scuttled on his back, the concrete ripping through his shirt. Whoever the gunman on the wall was, he had a perfect shot at him. But he'd had a perfect shot at Lake earlier, and hadn't taken advantage of it.

The Korean let loose a sustained burst of fire up at the wall, but the man was firing blindly. The gun battle was eerie, played out in almost total silence, only the flaming strobe of the muzzle flashes and the sparks of rounds ricocheting giving any hint as to what was happening. . . .

St. Martin's Paperbacks Titles
by Bob McGuire

THE LINE
THE GATE

THE GATE

BOB McGUIRE

St. Martin's Paperbacks

THE GATE

ISBN: 0-312-96278-9

Printed in the United States of America

St. Martin's Paperbacks edition/September 1997

St. Martin's Paperbacks are published by St. Martin's Press, 175 Fifth Avenue, New York, NY 10010.

10 9 8 7 6 5 4 3 2 1

THE GATE

PROLOGUE

HUNGNAM, NORTH KOREA
FRIDAY, 3 AUGUST 1945
5:24 A.M. LOCAL

"Quickly!" The officer barking the orders wore the white uniform of the Japanese Imperial Navy, but the tunic was stained with sweat and dirt. The reason was obvious as he added his strength to the work party, fastening the large crate in the back of the truck to a crane's hook.

A man standing on the deck of the submarine echoed the naval officer's words. "Quickly!" This man did not wear a uniform, but his demeanor brooked no argument. His eyes blazed darkly at the workers and a long, straight scar ran down the right side of his leathery face, disappearing under the collar of the black shirt he wore. Through a tear in the shirt, the officer could see part of a tattoo that covered the man's chest. Large, black ominous waves were etched into the skin with the red orb of a sun looming behind them.

The man was standing next to a midget submarine which was bolted to the deck, just aft of the conning tower. Behind the midget sub, a special sled rested on a cradle. The sled was designed to fit the rectangular crate. The cradle had been hastily welded to the steel deck, the work finished just moments ago. Cables were lying on the deck, waiting to join the sled and crate to the submarine.

The officer cast an anxious glance to the northwest, up the long valley floor. In the dim light of early morn, he could see the flash of artillery and he knew that it wasn't Japanese tubes firing the rounds. They could all hear the rumble of nonstop heavy firing echoing off the tall mountains that framed the broad river valley.

It was the Russian way to use a sledgehammer to open a walnut. The Germans had been experiencing it for years on the eastern front and now it was Japan's turn. There had been no formal declaration of war yet. The Russian bear had not officially joined the American eagle to pick over the remains of Japan's Greater East Asia Co-Prosperity Sphere, but the officer knew the Russians weren't fools. They wanted what was in this valley, most particularly what they were currently loading onto the submarine, and a trivial thing such as declaring war wasn't a factor. The Kremlin could always do that later. Just as the Russians had gobbled up as much of Eastern Europe as possible before the end of hostilities in the West, they were doing the same here.

There was little in the valley to stop the Russians. Forces had been stripped down to the bare minimum in Korea. The greatest need for men was in Japan, to await the impending American invasion of the homeland and farther north in Manchuria. The officer had even heard rumors of desperate negotiating by Japanese officials with the Russians in an attempt to form a last-minute alliance. Obviously, from the sound echoing down the valley, the Russian bear wasn't biting the offered bait. In fact, if the crate had been one of the bargaining chips put on the table in those negotiations, that offer might have precipitated this assault. The officer knew much of what was at stake and he could tell none of the enlisted men working for him. They would find out shortly.

The officer had been here for two years and he knew that not only the crate but the entire area was enticing bait for the Russians. Hungnam was an industrial city with a river running through it opening onto a small harbor facing the Sea of Japan. The river formed a valley sided on both the north and south by very steep mountains. Farther west, where it sounded like the Russians now were, this river and others had been damned to form hydroelectric plants to run the numerous factories dotting the valley floor. The landscape was bleak, almost all the trees cut down, a result of a deliberate program begun by the Japanese when they occupied Korea in 1904 to denude the entire Korean peninsula so guerrillas would have no place to hide. It was a dark landscape, made even more so by the filth pouring out of smokestacks and the piles of debris and rubble that the factories discarded. The Japanese occupiers had no use for the land other than what it could produce to support the Empire.

"Carefully!" the officer exclaimed as the crate lifted off the floor of the truck. He put a hand on it, helping to guide it across the dock. The crate went over the edge of the pier and then was slowly lowered down. It slipped between the waiting arms of the sled. The man on deck quickly ran chains over the wood, securing the item inside. He then attached two cables from the back of the midget sub to the front of the sled the crate was on. There wasn't a single member of the crew in sight; all were below decks, anxiously waiting to get underway and get out to sea.

Hooking the edge of the chain over a bolt and securing it with a lashing of rope, the man quickly walked forward to the conning tower and climbed up the external ladder. He turned and looked at the officer and briefly raised an arm in salute. Then he was gone, the *clang* of the hatch closing overlaid on the sound of the Russian ordnance coming closer.

The submarine immediately began moving, heading out into the harbor. The officer had no time to wait. Another truck with a similar crate slowly rolled up in a swirl of dust. An open-bay landing craft pulled into the slot the submarine had filled. The officer began barking orders, getting the crane hooked up to the crate. As it was being lowered into the waiting boat, the officer spared a glance toward the mouth of the harbor. The conning tower of the submarine was slipping underwater and disappeared as he watched. Perhaps it would beat the Russian ships that were coming to seal off the exit. He turned his attention back to the task at hand. The landing craft settled a foot deeper in the water as the weight of the crate came to a rest on its floorboards.

The officer heard the drone of airplane engines. He turned landward. A Mitsubishi "Betty" bomber, converted into a cargo plane, labored up into the early-morning sky and skittered to the north, barely fifty feet above the dark wavetops. Damn those scientists, he cursed to himself. They were running. But there was no way the men inside that plane could be taken by the Russians. Death was a good option, but the knowledge the men on board that plane held could still be useful so they were being taken away. The plane disappeared around the shoreline to the north.

"The other boxes!" the officer ordered.

The men didn't need to be told to handle these smaller crates gingerly because they could all read the markings on the outside: high explosive and detonators. They formed a human chain, passing the munitions down into the launch.

As soon as the last box was in place, the officer jumped down and cast off the bow line as a seaman cast off the aft. The officer didn't spare a second glance at the work crew and soldiers left behind on the shore.

"Go!" he ordered the coxswain.

The launch slowly picked up speed, heading into the harbor. The officer looked up as a pair of planes roared by overhead. It was now light enough to see the red star painted on their wings. The officer cursed his own pilots and his own leadership. This should have been the number one priority for protection, but they were practically defenseless.

The Russian planes banked and leisurely began strafing the shore, firing into the work party which was scattering. The officer knew there were Russian ships coming. That was the only reason the pilots were ignoring the launch. When the submarine had come in just after midnight, the captain had told him that Hungnam Harbor would shortly be cut off by sea.

The submarine could only fit the one crate on deck. There was no plane with enough power to take off with the second heavy crate even if they could get past the Russian fighters. There were no options left except this last one. The officer pounded a fist onto the side of the crate, ignoring the splinters and the blood that ran forth. If only they'd had more time! But there was still hope, the officer reminded himself. He thought of the last glimpse he'd had of the submarine. There was also the plane that had left earlier and the knowledge that was on board it. There was always hope.

He turned his attention from the fighters to the course ahead. Two thousand meters from the dock there was a small, rocky islet in the middle of Hungnam Harbor. It had a pebble beach on the landward side, the rest of the island being a pile of rocks with only a few lonely birds as inhabitants. It was toward that beach that the officer directed the nervous and confused coxswain. The crew could see the explosives piled on board. The officer knew their first guess had been that he was going to use the launch in a kamikaze attack against the Russian ships at sea. This beaching was an unexpected turn of events and they were uncertain as to whether it was a good turn or not.

The officer would have liked to go out among the Russian ships. But he could not take the chance that the project would not work and the crate be captured. He also had to give the submarine a chance to make it clear. Everyone's heads snapped up as a very loud and much closer explosion reverberated across the water. On the side of the near mountain on the south side of the valley a large cloud of dirt and rock bellowed into the air. The cave from which they had taken the two crates earlier this morning was now sealed. Secondary explosions followed, destroying the road carved into the side of the mountain that had been the only access to the cave, further isolating the site.

The officer nodded and whispered a swift prayer for those who had just died. His military staff was dead, and that secret was safe, at least. He felt no sympathy toward the men now entombed in the mountainside. They had done their duty; now he was doing his.

The bow of the boat grated on the pebbles and they were beached. One of the Russian fighters flew over to investigate, its pilot leading the way with a barrage of bullets from the machine guns in the wings. The bullets churned up water then onto the beach, only a few hitting the boat. Two sailors fell wounded and miraculously none of the explosives' boxes were hit.

The officer ignored the screams of the wounded men as he ripped off a piece of wood on the side of the crate. He reached in and began working, his fingers following a procedure he had memorized over the past week under supervision of the scientists.

The fighter made another pass, then, confirming that the launch was beached, left to pick more lucrative targets in the valley. They were leaving the launch to the ships that were coming.

The officer had a small electric wire on a reel. He attached one end to the object inside. With that, the officer was done with the crate. He quickly had the surviving crewmen stack boxes of explosives around it, wiring each box for detonation as quickly as it was stacked.

He connected all the firing wires, then unreeled a length of detonating cord up over the edge of the boat, onto the shore, while also unreeling the electric wire. He moved back fifty meters, the other sailors joining him. He wired the detonating cord into a firing box. Only he knew the explosives were the backup. If the object inside failed, he had to ensure that the crate would not be found intact.

The officer hooked the electric wire into a small hand-cranked generator. He checked to make sure the generator functioned and all was ready. The sun had now cleared the horizon.

The officer turned to the east, the direction of the Emperor, and bowed. Then he cranked the small handle. In the microsecond before he was consumed by the flash, the officer rejoiced. It worked and there was still hope! Then he, and all in a half-mile circle, were gone, obliterated by the blast.

In the skies above, the planes were consumed by the fireball. Out at sea the Russian Admiral in charge of the flotilla steaming for Hungnam at flank speed was left to wonder at the mushroom cloud that rose up over the shore.

CHAPTER 1

SAN FRANCISCO
SUNDAY, 28 SEPTEMBER 1997
4:12 A.M. LOCAL

"Just like in the Cav, man. Locked and loaded. Ready to rock-and-roll and waste some motherfuckers." Preston smiled, the gap between his middle teeth showing clearly. His skin glistened with sweat inside the stuffy interior of the van. He held up the AR-15 that Lake had modified three days earlier. "I hope we run into someone," he continued. The rubber gloves he wore squeaked as he patted the weapon one more time.

"Not before we put the device in place," Starry said. "Keep the operational priorities straight in your head, Preston."

"Sure, Top, sure," Preston said. "That's cool."

Lake was seated in one of the captain's chairs in the back of the van, watching Starry work on the "device." This was the first he'd seen of the machinery and he had a very good idea what it was: an industrial high-pressure paint sprayer. The problem was, Lake didn't know why they had it in the back of the van. He also didn't know what the operational priorities were that Starry kept talking about. Lake's initial job with the two had been acquiring and modifying their weapons. Now he was providing security.

Lake ran his hand along his AR-15. Actually, technically speaking, it could now be called an M-16 since he had modified the inner workings to allow the commercially sold single-shot assault rifle to be fired on full automatic. He also wore gloves. He'd been handed them before entering the van and that told him that whatever they were going to do was illegal since Starry didn't want any prints left. Actually, Lake reminded himself, the fact that they had the automatic weapons in their hands already put them on the wrong side of the law, not that he had expected anything else. In fact, Lake would have been disappointed if his new partners had stayed inside the confines of the law.

He continued to watch as Starry carefully read instructions, completing the preparation of the sprayer. One thing Lake had learned in the past three weeks working with them was that although neither man would qualify as a rocket scientist, they were very thorough and well trained on security. They had never discussed their plans around Lake. They'd simply given him orders and told him when and where to be.

Lake knew they didn't totally trust him, but they'd needed him for the guns after the ATF had raided a "Patriot" compound in Oregon last month and seized the weapons they had planned on using. And there had been Lake, three days later, attending a Patriot rally and letting it be known to a few of the people there that he had access to weapons. And five days later he'd been contacted by Starry at the cabin he'd been hiding out in the shadow of Mount Hood. And now he was in San Francisco. Lake knew that to Starry his presence and access to weapons was a fortunate coincidence. Lake also knew that in this business coincidences didn't happen. He wasn't quite sure how aware of that Starry was. Their lack of trust in revealing plans showed some degree of awareness.

They'd driven south from Oregon the previous day and stayed in a seedy motel in Novato, just north of the city.

Peeking out the window of his room, Lake had watched Starry and Preston drive off in the van several hours ago and return just a few minutes ago. He'd jumped back in bed and pretended to be asleep when Preston had opened his door, telling him to grab his stuff and get ready to move.

Lake knew better than to ask too many questions. Paranoid didn't quite apply to these people. When a person implicitly believed that the UN was going to take over the United States with the blessing of those in power in Washington, that person's reasoning abilities were difficult to rationally analyze. Lake found that particular fear quite humorous. He'd personally seen that the UN couldn't keep its own soldiers safe in Bosnia and other places around the globe, so how was it going to take over the United States? And why would it want to? But that larger reality was not the issue right now. This sprayer was the current reality that he had to keep his focus on.

Starry was done with the equipment. He was a big man. He didn't say much about his past, but Lake guessed that he was a former noncommissioned officer in the army. The way Starry spoke made it seem like he'd been officer but Lake could tell the difference. A wannabe. Lake had met many. Pretending to be something they'd never been. Maybe a platoon sergeant, was Lake's best guess as to Starry's past. Preston's calling him "Top" indicated he might even have been a first sergeant.

Lake did know that Preston had been a staff sergeant. That is until he'd let his little head do his thinking for him during a tour as a drill instructor at Fort Dix. It didn't matter that the female trainee had been more than willing. Preston had had his career abruptly ended, and that was all his simple mind could focus on now. It just wasn't fair! How many times had Lake heard that cry from people who had brought their own misfortune down on themselves? Preston was from the South, one of those who'd run away from the farm and found a pair of shoes and a home in the army, except he'd lost the latter and he really wasn't trained or schooled to do anything else. He had reason to be mad at the government, or at least he felt he did.

Preston didn't worry Lake. Starry was the one who was getting instructions from somewhere and had enough smarts to carry those instructions out. Lake knew the two didn't think of this—whatever this was—on their own. The question for the past several weeks had been which would come first: finding out who was giving the orders or the arrival of orders precipitating an action that would force Lake's hand. This morning it seemed the latter had come to pass.

Preston giggled as Starry opened a large hard-plastic case that had not been in the van on the drive down. The sprayer had been, but in pieces, hidden under a tarp that Lake hadn't had the chance to investigate. One thing Lake had noted immediately was the small written label on the side of the machine: MADE IN JAPAN.

Starry removed a large glass jug from the foam rubber interior of the case. Lake estimated the jug could hold about five gallons. The outside was painted bright red and had Japanese characters stenciled on it. The way he handled it told Lake that whatever was inside the glass scared Starry. That bothered Lake because he sensed Starry didn't scare easy. Starry placed the jug onto a platform on the side of the sprayer, then levered down a steel hose that had a pointy spout until it rested just above the metal lid. He locked the jug in place, then suddenly looked up at Lake.

"You said you're airborne qualified, right?"

"Eighty-deuce at Fort Bragg," Lake replied. He mustered a semblance of enthusiasm. "Airborne all the way!"

Starry wasn't impressed. "Uh-huh." He flipped open the lid to another crate that Lake hadn't been able to look into. "Here. Put this on."

Lake stared at the MC-1B parachute that Starry had handed him. Even though he knew better, Lake had to ask. It would be too far out of character not to. "Are we going flying?"

"Just put the chute on. And this," Starry added, handing him an inflatable set of water wings that would fit around the parachute rig.

Lake pulled out the waist strap of the parachute and unbuckled the leg and chest snaps. He checked the sizing on the harness. It was a large, which was fortunate because he knew from experience a medium would be a tight fit.

Lake was a big man, not so much in height—although he did top out at six feet, one inch—but in width. His shoulders were broad, his chest well muscled from daily workouts. His body didn't taper in to the waist, but just continued in straight lines down to his thick legs. His stomach was smooth and flat, not rippling with muscles like those male models who spent their life doing crunches in pretty gyms, but solid from time spent working in the outdoors. Lake was thirty-eight and his face indicated many of those years had been spent out in the elements—and not the gentle elements of California. His face was dark, the skin creased. Rough lines flowed from around his eyes, intersecting with those coming up from his mouth and jaw. His dark hair was cut short except for a small wave of curls in the back and liberally peppered with gray. His green eyes were the best feature in the beaten face.

As Lake shrugged the parachute rig over his shoulders, settling it in place, the bandana that he normally kept tied around his neck slipped, revealing old scar tissue encircling his throat like knotted red rope. Starry and Preston had seen the scar before and they hadn't asked in the way that men avoided the uncertain obvious when gathered together. Not that Lake would have told them.

Starry walked behind Lake and reached. "Left leg," he said, passing a strap between Lake's legs. "Left leg," Lake instinctively replied, taking the strap and hooking it in place. "Right leg." They repeated the process.

"No reserve?" Lake asked as he squatted and pulled the straps as tight as he could make them.

Preston giggled again. "Won't need one, man, if that

main don't open. Ain't no time for a reserve.''

Lake ignored Preston, pulling the waistband tight and making sure he had a quick release in it. He put the water wings on and sat back down, watching Preston and Starry rig each other.

The scenario didn't fit, and that bothered Lake. These two were still one step ahead of him. The chute indicated they were going up high. Lake ran through the options. They could go to an airfield and get on a plane, but then why had Starry already rigged the jar on the sprayer in the back of the van? Unless they would get on a plane after leaving the van and use that route to escape. Fly, put the plane on autopilot, jump, and let the plane crash. Not bad, Lake thought, but also not likely. It was too complicated and men like Starry and Preston needed simple plans.

There were places to jump from other than a plane, Lake knew. Maybe the Transamerica Pyramid in downtown San Francisco? But why the water wings then? San Francisco was surrounded on three sides by water, but even if they jumped off the top of the Pyramid, it was less than a thousand feet high. There would barely be time for the chutes to open, as Preston had indicated, never mind float over to the harbor.

And why were they rigging now? They certainly wouldn't be inconspicuous getting to the top of a building wearing the parachutes. And again, Starry had already set up the sprayer in the van. And the Japanese angle, not just the label on the sprayer and jar, but Lake had seen a bilingual map—English and Japanese—of San Francisco in the front of the van. What was that for? Lake took the pieces he had: the van, the sprayer, the parachutes, the water wings, and slithered them through the recesses of his brain, trying to think nasty thoughts.

Then Lake had it. The whole plan was laid out in front of him in his mind, except of course for some of the details that would develop, but he knew exactly where they were going and pretty much what they would be doing. He still needed to know who was pulling the strings on this, though, and for that he would have to play it cool. Also, the Japanese angle didn't quite fit, but that wasn't important right now. Maybe somebody would let something slip.

"Passenger seat," Starry ordered, pulling aside the curtain. Lake squeezed through and took the seat while Starry took the wheel. Preston remained in the back. Starry started the engine and they rolled out of the parking lot. Lake sat back and relaxed as much as the parachute on his back would allow as they turned onto Route 101 and headed south toward San Francisco.

It was early Sunday morning and they made good time, passing the last exit north of the Golden Gate Bridge at a quarter to five by Lake's watch. There was no toll for southbound traffic and that explained why they'd stayed on the north side of the city last night.

Starry's head was swiveling, checking the rearview mirror constantly, looking out and up through the open side window, as if he expected helicopters to be hovering overhead.

Starry was in the right lane and at exactly the midpoint of the bridge, 260 feet above the water, he stopped the van, and turned on the blinkers. "In the back," he ordered Lake, who was not surprised in the least at this course of events.

Lake slid into the rear. He noted that Preston had already hooked his parachute static line into a large eye bolt in the roof of the van, just in front of the two back doors. Preston kicked the doors open and stepped out, weapon at the ready. "Hook up there and join Preston on security!" Starry yelled.

Lake did as he was ordered, slipping his static line hook over the eye bolt and insuring it slid shut, pushing the safety wire through the small hole in the hook and bending it over to make sure it couldn't open. He carefully stepped out, making sure his static line wasn't tangled, and joined Preston. A few cars drove past, but the drivers didn't seem interested in checking out the van with two armed men standing behind it. Somebody might be making a cellular call to the cops, but they would take a while to respond. Too long, based on how quickly Starry was working.

Lake knew Preston and he were here on the off chance a police car happened by. But he knew that wasn't going to happen. He glanced behind. Starry was extending the large nozzle of the sprayer up and out, over their heads, tilted toward the center of downtown San Francisco two miles to the southeast.

As Starry reached over and lowered the pointy spout to puncture the metal top of the glass jar, Lake shot him with the M-16, the high-velocity bullet entering in a tiny black dot squarely between Starry's eyes, and taking with it most of the back of his skull on the way out along with assorted brain matter and blood.

"What the fuck—" Preston began as he spun about.

Lake used his left hand to simply snatch Preston's AR-15 right out of his hand just like a drill sergeant would take a rifle out of a trainee's hands for inspection, which Lake found ironic as he tossed the weapon into the rear of the van on top of Starry's body. Preston's AR-15 wouldn't have fired anyway, as Starry's wouldn't have, but Lake didn't have time to play around. He jammed the muzzle of his own weapon into the soft spot under Preston's jaw, twisting about so that the back of Preston's legs were against the bumper of the van.

"Who's paying for all this? Who's giving you the orders?"

Preston was shaking. The man had sat in on all the meetings in dirty halls and campsites and raised his open right hand in the hard-core Patriot salute. Probably even stomped a Jew or a black in some dark alley in the company of others of his kind, but Lake doubted that he'd ever seen someone's brains blown out or had a gun shoved up against his chin and had to face someone down while all alone.

"Talk or you're dead," Lake said.

''What are you doing, man?'' Preston's voice quivered. ''Why'd you do that to Starry?''

''I'm asking the questions,'' Lake said, emphasizing that by a sudden shove of the barrel. He could hear Preston's teeth clash together. ''Who gave you the orders to do this?''

''I don't know. Starry didn't know either, man. We got it off the web. The money followed. Then we were told where to pick up the gear.''

''You did all this just cause someone on the Internet told you to?'' Lake asked.

''They were with the cause. There was a notice, man. Four months back. On the Patriot newsletter, looking for volunteers for a special, secret mission. We responded. I don't know why we got picked.''

Lake wanted to rub his forehead. He'd hoped that the orders had come from the Patriot organization in California. But he believed what Preston was saying and not simply because he was holding a gun on him. The Patriot movement was very fragmented and paranoid. There was no overall leadership and each group did its own thing. If there was one thing that held it together, it was the Internet. At least he could try to follow this lead on the Internet website where the Patriot filth piled up and fermented.

''What happens below?'' Seeing the confusion in Preston's wide eyes, Lake amplified the question. ''After we jump. What happens?''

''Boat picks us up. It's supposed to be waiting. That's what Starry said. I don't know nothing else, man.'' Preston blinked. ''Why'd—''

He never finished, as Lake squeezed the trigger. He'd fine-tuned the trigger tension. He'd had nothing else to do for the past couple of days and it didn't take much work. The top of Preston's head mingled with the gore inside and the body flopped back. Lake threw the legs up and tossed the AR-15 on top of the two bodies, then wedged the doors almost all the way shut. His static line kept them from latching.

He then pressed a button on the side of his watch, checked to make sure the pager had activated, then he stepped over the railway onto the walk. He reached inside his shirt, ensuring the High Standard silenced .22 was secured in the shoulder holster, then crossed the walk. He made sure his static line was clear as he stepped up on the outer railing, balancing himself with one hand on a steel cable. The water below was a sheet of black. There was a stiff breeze in his face, something he knew that Starry's plan had called for to carry the contents of the glass jar toward the city.

Lake paused as tires squealed and two blue vans with dark tinted windows screeched to a halt, one behind, one in front of the parked van. Men in black combat gear flowed out of the vehicles, weapons at the ready, the red dots of their laser sights flickering over the scene, a pair fixing on Lake's head.

Lake kept his grip on the cable and his other hand away from his side. "I'm Lake. Two bodies inside," he called out. "Their getaway boat is below. I'm going down to take it out."

A thin old man dressed in a long black raincoat stepped forward. "Lake, hold on—"

Lake pointed with his free hand. "I think they have bio-agents in the glass jar in the sprayer inside, so don't break it, Feliks. I'll meet you at the Coast Guard station on the south shore."

"Lake!" Feliks' voice threatened. "Take backup."

"They'll just get in the way." Lake threw himself out into space, then immediately tucked into a tight body position as he'd been taught on the thirty-four-foot towers at Fort Benning what seemed like a lifetime ago.

Lake counted, knowing it would take longer because he didn't have the added speed of an airplane to get to the end of the static line. One thousand, two thousand. At five thousand he felt a tug, then a jerk as the chute blossomed open. Just in time as he hit the water three seconds later, still pulling the quick release he had put into the waist belt.

The shock of the cold water caused Lake to gasp, expelling what little air he had in his lungs. He didn't panic even though he was completely submerged. He'd been in this situation in the past and he calmly felt for the small knobs for the water wings. Locating them, he pulled and they inflated, popping him to the surface. The chute settled down into the water off to the side and Lake struggled with the chest release, then each leg release.

Lake kicked to get away from the chute and was promptly entangled in the web of parachute line. He immediately stopped kicking. Drawing a knife from inside his left boot he carefully began cutting the 550 cord to clear himself before the chute became soaked and sank.

As he was doing that, he heard the mutter of a boat's engine. Small, maybe sixty-horsepower, Lake estimated from the sound. It was coming from the southwest. He cut through the last line as the sound of the boat came very close. He kicked as a wave rose him up and looked. The silhouette of a zodiac with a man in it was about forty meters away. Good thing there wasn't much of a swell, Lake thought, or that zodiac would be in trouble. He glanced up. The current had already pushed him well away from the bridge toward the ocean.

"Over here!" Lake yelled.

The zodiac turned head on and slowly puttered forward. Lake grabbed the safety line rigged around the forward pontoon and pulled himself up as a swell helped lift him. He rolled into the bottom of the zodiac.

"Where are the others?" the man running the engine hissed, as if his whispering negated the sound the engine made. The man was holding a large pistol, one Lake knew he hadn't worked on. He couldn't make out the man's features in the dark. It had only been Starry and Preston for the past several weeks, so this man was a new factor.

"They're coming," Lake said as he pulled off the water wings.

"You were all supposed to jump together! I only saw one chute." The man looked up, over Lake's head toward the bridge. Lake dropped the water wings into the bottom of the boat. As he did so he saw the man bring the pistol up level, muzzle pointing at Lake's chest.

Lake rolled right along the rubber bulkhead, drawing his High Standard as he moved. He heard the sound of a gun going off and the flat crack of a bullet. Coming to a halt against the right pontoon, Lake fired twice, aiming for the man's gun shoulder.

The man was startled by the impact, not sure what had happened as the slight sound of the receiver working on Lake's gun was easily muffled by the engine. He looked at Lake, who immediately knew he was in big trouble. Either the small-caliber rounds hadn't hit anything important enough to immobilize the arm or the man was wearing a vest. Those thoughts flashed through Lake's brain as the man brought the pistol to bear again.

Lake swiftly fired two more shots, directly into the man's right eye socket. There was no exit wound this time. Lake's homemade .22 shells mushroomed upon passing through the eye socket into the man's brain, making jelly of the gray matter. The gun fell to the floorboards with a clatter, and the man slumped over.

"Fuck," Lake quietly cursed. He checked the body and found that the man was indeed wearing a bulletproof vest. The .22 slugs had barely cut through the cloth on top of the armor. He looked at the face, ignoring the bloody eye socket. The man had slightly Asian features. Lake patted him down. No ID. Nothing other than the gun and the clothes.

Lake pushed the body aside and took the engine handle. He opened the throttle and headed for the Coast Guard station on the south shore. The engine fought hard against the strong seaward current, but Lake kept on course, guiding off the massive south pier of the bridge, which he knew was over a thousand feet from the south shore. He passed the tower by, just to his right, then headed in to shore, angling against the current.

On the jetty for the Coast Guard station, Feliks was waiting for him with one of the blue vans and several of his men. The men secured the line Lake tossed them, then grabbed the body, taking it into the van. They hauled the boat up onto the jetty and began deflating it.

As they were doing that, Lake held out a hand to Feliks. The older man reached into a pocket of the raincoat and pulled out a cigarette case. He handed it to Lake. Lake snapped open the battered metal top and pulled out a cigarette. Feliks lit it for him. There was a crest on the case. Lake had seen it the first time Feliks had given him a cigarette several years ago. He'd checked the crest and found out it was from the OSS, the Office of Strategic Services, the World War II predecessor of the CIA.

Feliks had white hair and appeared to be in his mid-sixties, but Lake didn't know for sure—the man could be a dozen years either way. Lake didn't know much about Feliks other than the cigarette case. No one at the Ranch did. Feliks was as tall as Lake and his skin was very white, as if he spent little time out of doors.

The first question Feliks asked was the one Lake knew he would ask. "Do you believe they were on their own?"

"No."

"Why not?"

"Those bozos couldn't plan a trip to the bathroom," Lake said. "They also had plenty of money to spread around. You knew that when I picked up the weapons and sold them. Someone was financing them and making the plans. Before he died, Preston told me they were recruited over the Internet. Their specific instructions and money probably went directly to Starry in a dead drop."

Feliks nodded. "The Internet's an avenue we can check. The FBI has been monitoring that and has records. What about the Japanese evidence planted in the van?" Feliks asked.

"I don't know. Probably put there to throw the FBI off track when they found the van, I suppose."

"There's a lot of people who'd like to whip up a little hatred for the Japanese," Feliks noted.

"Yeah." Lake pulled off his soaked clothes and slipped on the one-piece coverall one of Feliks' men had brought over. "Take a look at the body I brought in." He smoked his cigarette while Feliks walked over, then came back.

"Doesn't look like good Aryan Patriot material," Feliks noted.

"Nope. And he tried to shoot me as soon as I was on board. I don't think he was down there to rescue us. I think he was down there to close out the loose ends."

Feliks was an unmoving figure as Lake continued.

"Like I said, those idiots were just doing what they were ordered. They might have had their own thoughts as to why they were doing it, but the people giving the orders probably had different ones. That's one of the curses of being a peon," Lake added, giving Feliks a hard stare. "You never know what's really going on."

Feliks returned the look. "And?"

"And what?" Lake was tired. He'd been up all night. The adrenaline rush was gone and the nicotine didn't quite make up the gap.

"Any idea who the mastermind is?"

"No." Lake handed the cigarette case back to Feliks.

"Well, we certainly can't ask anyone you ran into, can we?" Feliks said sarcastically. "You couldn't take him alive?" he asked, pointing at the van where the boat driver's body had been taken. "You couldn't take *anyone* alive?" Feliks amended the question.

"Starry was getting ready to let whatever was in that glass container loose when I shot him. I don't think the citizens of San Francisco would be too happy if I'd let him live another two seconds."

Feliks nodded. "Randkin's with the van. He thinks it might be anthrax, but he'll have to take it back to the Ranch and test it to make sure. One of my other operatives has a line on someone who might be working for the Patriots making biological agents. We'll have to see if we can connect the dots, then roll up the puzzle.''

''The jar had Japanese markings,'' Lake repeated.

''Yes. I saw it. But we know that the men were Patriots,'' Feliks said. ''I really doubt the possibility of a link between the Patriots and the Japanese. That would be like the FBI and the CIA sharing information.''

''The Patriots could be getting used,'' Lake noted. ''It's happened before. The guy in the boat had to be from somewhere.''

''Even the Patriots can tell Japanese markings,'' Feliks said. ''They wouldn't use that stuff unless they had a reason.''

Lake continued his report, not wanting to discuss theory with Feliks. ''The other man, Preston, didn't know shit and taking him alive would have made a scene on the bridge. I wasn't exactly very mobile in my parachute rig.''

''And . . .'' Feliks nodded at the van again.

''I don't know who he is. Never saw him before. I tried to take him alive, but he was wearing a vest and it came down to him or me.'' The cigarette burned bright as Lake turned toward Feliks. ''And you do prefer that it was me, don't you?'' His tone was light, but there was an edge to it.

''Of course, of course,'' Feliks said. ''You did well. But this is very serious. Beyond what they planned to do, we don't have a clue who wanted this done. And the body from the boat complicates matters. This might not be a simple Patriot plot.''

No shit, Sherlock, Lake thought, but he kept the words to himself. Feliks seemed worried, which was a first in the years they'd worked together. Lake rubbed his forehead. ''There is an advantage to them all being dead.''

''There is?'' Feliks waited.

''My cover is still intact.''

"Ah, yes." Feliks smiled without any humor. "And, of course, our three friends have just vanished off the face of the earth, correct? Or perhaps they should be in an accident? The van perhaps?"

"I think disappearing would serve better," Lake suggested. It was the way they worked. Outside the law. Even if he had taken any of the three alive, Lake knew from experience that the man would never have seen the inside of a courtroom. And the people of San Francisco would never know how close they had come to disaster.

"Starry and Preston were supposed to disappear," Lake added. "The guy in the boat not coming back is the one that's going to rattle someone's cage."

Feliks touched Lake's arm and indicated that they should walk over to the van now that everything was loaded. "And? With your cover intact? What then? Can you find out whose cage is getting rattled?"

"I'll try."

"You have any leads?"

"I don't know," Lake said. "I've heard rumors."

"You don't know. Rumors," Feliks repeated. "That's it?"

"That's it."

"All right. You have two weeks."

CHAPTER 2

HUNGNAM, NORTH KOREA
MONDAY, 29 SEPTEMBER 1997
2:47 A.M. LOCAL

"The helicopter cannot take off," Nagoya said, removing the earplug for the satellite radio.

Nishin simply looked at his partner, waiting for an explanation. The two men were crammed into a niche two-thirds up the side of a six-thousand-foot mountain. The only thing keeping them from tumbling down to the valley floor below were snap links hooked into ropes attached to cams they had lodged in small cracks farther in the niche. It had taken them four days of climbing, all done at night, to go over the top of the mountain and make their way down to their present position. They'd been here for six hours, watching and waiting for the final word.

"The North Koreans have spotted the ship and are shadowing it," Nagoya explained, carefully coiling the earplug cord.

Getting in was always easier than getting out, Nishin knew. Getting in they'd been flown on a CH-47 Chinook helicopter to a point forty miles off the North Korean coast. The entire flight had been made barely ten feet above the wave tops to avoid radar. Then the helicopter had slowed to a forward speed of ten knots, the back ramp had been lowered, and a rubber boat had been pushed off the rear, Nishin and Nagoya following right behind in their wet suits.

They'd used the engine to get within a kilometer of the shore just south of Hungnam Harbor, checked their position, and then sunk the boat, swimming the rest of the way. Then across the rocky shore, to the base of the mountain, over the mountain, and now here overlooking the valley.

They both knew the ship could not launch the recovery helicopter with the North Koreans watching. It would be like turning a spotlight on the entire mission.

"What did Nakanga say we should do?" Nishin asked, looking into the valley. Smokestacks billowed black smoke filled with sparks into the night. With almost unlimited power fed to it from reservoirs such as Chosin, the Hungnam valley was one of the manufacturing centers of North Korea and had been so for over sixty years, ever since an enterprising Japanese industrialist had first spied the valley's potential in the decade before the Second World War. It was one of the spinoffs of that industrialist's efforts and vision so long ago that had led to the two men clinging to the side of this mountain on this early fall night.

"The mission must go," Nagoya said.

Nishin's face didn't betray any reaction, even though he knew Nagoya's statement was a death sentence. He peered down the rocky slope. A hundred feet below them arc lights brightly lit the mountainside. A new path from the valley floor had been cut with great effort into the rock, switching back and forth up to an opening in the side of the mountain. It was impossible to get heavy equipment up the slender path. So a line of men slithered into the opening every day with shovels and picks, carefully unearthing what had lain hidden inside for the past fifty-two years.

At night there was a squad of guards protecting the dig, their main post on the path itself. The guards would not be a problem, Nishin knew. The men were oriented toward the road and downward. The guards did not suspect that someone would come from above. As far as the North Koreans were concerned the mountain was impassable. In fact, they probably were not expecting anyone since Nishin had no doubt that they did not know what they guarded. He himself did not know exactly what the cave held. He only knew that whatever was in there must be kept in there.

The site could not be spotted from the air. Camouflage nets draped over the cave mouth and the vertical slope prohibited that. If Nishin and Nagoya had not been given the exact location during the mission briefing they would have never found it. He briefly wondered if Nakanga, the man who had briefed them on the mission and given them their orders, knew what was so important. It had to date back to the war. Of that Nishin had no doubt. He also wondered how Nakanga knew the cave had been opened if it couldn't be seen from the air. Information did not flow freely out of North Korea.

Why now, why here? These were questions Nishin accepted he would never know the answer to. Nagoya was checking the charges one last time. They were a powerful new explosive, each containing three kilograms of liquid in a thick rubber container shaped like a large sausage. The fuse was built into the end of the container and Nagoya was checking the connections. They had twenty-four of the charges, twelve each, and Nakanga had assured them it would be more than enough to take down the mountainside around the cave.

"Now that we have made it this far, I can plant the charges myself," Nagoya said, not looking up from his hands, the delicate fingers tracing wires in the dark.

"Without the helicopter . . . ," Nishin began.

"You can head back up as I start down," Nagoya said. "I will give you enough time to get over the top of the mountain before I proceed. They will find my body among the rubble, but that will not be a problem and it should make any further search less intensive as they will think they have found the infiltrator. You can also remove all signs of us having climbed down as you go back over. It will confuse them greatly. They will suspect a traitor in their own ranks."

Nagoya was half-Korean. His mother one of the many women who came over to Japan in the sixties to do domestic work and his birth was never legitimized. If his father had not been a member of the Society—and Nagoya's loyalty tested on several missions—Nishin would have had his own doubts about the man and the new course of action he was proposing. But he knew Nagoya was true.

"If they find *your* body, that will not be good," Nagoya continued. There would be no denying Nishin's racial makeup. He was pure Japanese. "You must escape or, at the very least, your body must not be found. You can make it to the ocean. Swim out and activate your beacon. Maybe you will be picked up. If not, you must make sure you puncture your life vest so that your body sinks."

Nagoya's logic was cold and practical, something Nishin could appreciate. The other man was not suggesting he plant the charges alone out of some sense of misguided heroism. It was what would be best for the mission, and the mission always came first. Nishin did not consider the new course of action in terms of his own survival but in terms of mission accomplishment. It would be best.

Nishin grunted his assent. He pulled his pack off and passed it to his partner.

"You must go now," Nagoya said. "You must be at the ocean by dawn."

Nishin stood and looked up.

"For the Emperor and the Sun Goddess," Nagoya said, his face pointed down at the explosives.

"For the Emperor and the Sun Goddess," Nishin repeated. He reached up and his hand curled around a knob of rock. He began the climb.

* * *

Two hours later, Nishin's fingers were torn and bleeding but he hardly felt the pain. He was at the crest of the mountain. It was downhill from here to the ocean.

He swung his head to the side as he heard the faint crack of gunfire. Looking, he could see a line of green tracers far below. The firing lasted for almost a minute and then the side of the mountain erupted. The charges had worked even better than Nakanga had promised from the way the earth shook underneath Nishin's feet.

Nishin stuffed his climbing gear into his backpack and continued on.

SEA OF JAPAN
WEDNESDAY, 1 OCTOBER 1997
3:22 P.M. LOCAL

Nishin's eyes were swollen shut from exposure to saltwater and the sun. The life vest he had inflated on entering the ocean two and a half days ago kept him on the surface, but the way it was designed, it also kept his face turned up to the sky and there was no way to avoid either the harsh rays of the sun or the waves that broke over him every few seconds. He would suck in a mouthful of saltwater and spit it out the side, gasping in air before the next wave repeated the process.

After swimming out for an hour, the current had taken hold, and his best guess was that he was somewhere to the north of Hungnam in the Sea of Japan. Just before his eyes had swollen shut completely, yesterday morning, he had waited until he'd ridden to the top of a swell and then kicked vigorously, rising out of the water as far as possible and looking about. Nothing but sea.

He remembered Nagoya's words in the crevice. The vest would keep the body afloat, but the ocean and sun were draining the life out of him. If he was not careful, he would lapse into unconsciousness and then death would come while he was still afloat. That was not acceptable.

His waterlogged hand slid down his side, feeling for the knife hung on his harness. With great difficulty, his fumbling fingers flipped open the clasp on the sheath and pulled the knife out. The cuts in his hands from climbing the mountain were invaded anew by the saltwater as scabs ripped open. Pain ripped into his brain, shocking him into consciousness as he grasped the knife tightly.

Using his free hand to aim it, Nishin placed the tip of the knife against the flotation device. He knew there were two chambers. First the left then the right. It would be over in a little while. He just needed a second of rest before he pressed the blade home.

Nishin came awake. He did not know how long he had slept. He panicked until he realized the knife was still in his hand. His training had worked when his mind wouldn't. He had even been able to breathe and spit out water while unconscious so used to this he had become.

Nishin shifted the point until it was pressed against his neck. Would it be better to end it quickly? his feverish mind thought. No. That was stupid. His body would then continue to float and be found. No matter what, he must cut the vest first. He guided the blade back lower and pushed.

Air hissed and Nishin felt his body tilt to the left. A wave, larger than what he had been experiencing, washed over him and he was completely submerged. He instinctively kicked furiously and broke through to the surface, gasping for air.

He laughed, it coming out more as a rasp as the sound passed his dehydrated mouth and lips. He was going to die, but he still wanted to live. He had wondered what this moment would be like. The nature of his job and his life had caused him to reflect on this often.

He must puncture the other chamber of his vest. He shifted the knife to his left hand. There was a strange noise, then another large wave slammed into and over him. Nishin flailed about, uncertain in his blindness and exhaustion which way the surface was. The hand with the knife slammed into something solid and the shock tore the knife from his fingers and it disappeared into the depths.

He reached out, lungs bursting and felt what had knocked the knife free: a metal wall!

Hands were grabbing him, pulling him. He broke the surface, again gasping for air and felt a line being put over his shoulders and cinched about his waist. Then he was being hoisted up, clear of the water, sliding along the metal wall he had felt.

As he was set down on a deck, he twisted his head and reached with his teeth for the small capsule sown into the right shoulder of his wet suit.

A hand slapped his face. "No!" a voice called out in Japanese and Nishin finally allowed himself to collapse into unconsciousness as he recognized Nakanga's voice.

SAPPORO, HOKKAIDO, JAPAN
THURSDAY, 2 OCTOBER 1997
9:00 A.M. LOCAL

The swelling in his face had gone down enough so that Nishin could see—just barely. His hands were wrapped in gauze and they had only removed an IV from his arm fifteen minutes ago. He was seated on a hard iron chair on the balcony of what had once been a Buddhist temple. The building was perched on the side of a pine-covered hill. Below, the view encompassed rice paddies as far as the eye could see, lit by the sun rising slowly in the east. Behind the temple, mountains ranged up, their slopes bathed in the morning light.

It was a beautiful location and Nishin could well imagine the monks who had once inhabited the temple sitting cross-legged on this very spot, meditating. The wood floor was polished smooth by generations of bare feet, and the thick stone columns holding up the roof to the balcony were painted with intricate religious scenes. To his rear a room that had once been the main room of the temple was separated from him by an opaque curtain covering heavy metal doors of modern design.

Nishin twisted his head as he heard a noise. The doors slid open on smooth bearings. Someone was moving in the darkened room. He made out the silhouette of a man pushing another in a wheelchair. The pair halted, then the first man walked forward and through the curtain. It was Nakanga.

Nishin got to his feet and stood at rigorous attention, ignoring the pain. Nakanga stood, arms folded across his chest, staring hard at Nishin.

Nishin bowed his head. Nakanga was the right arm of the Genoysha, the head of the Black Ocean Society, and as such he held the power of life and death over all members. He was also the voice of the Genoysha since no one other than Nakanga, as far as Nishin knew, had ever spoken to the Genoysha. As such he was known as the Sensei of the Society. He issued the orders to the most trusted agents of the Society of which Nishin felt honored to count himself one.

"Ronin Nishin," Nakanga said, greeting him in the traditional form.

"Sensei Nakanga," Nishin replied in return.

"Sit down," Nakanga said. "I have listened to your after-action report again and played it for the Genoysha."

Nishin's eyes involuntarily flickered to the shadowy figure inside the room and he felt his heart pick up pace. No one he had ever met, other than Nakanga, had ever seen or met the Genoysha in person. He carefully sat down.

Nakanga had questioned Nishin on the submarine that had picked up the signal from the transponder Nishin had activated once he was in the ocean. Even before the ship's doctor had been allowed into the small cabin to tend to him, Nishin had been questioned in detail about the mission, a small tape recorder taking down his words. The submarine's crew were dressed in a strange uniform—not that of the Japanese Maritime Self-Defense Force. Nishin had not known that the Society controlled its own submarine, but it did not surprise him. After all, the company that built submarines for the Self-Defense Force was owned by the Society as so much else of Japan's small but very efficient military industrial complex was. The wealth of the Society was greater than that of many countries.

"It is unfortunate that the helicopter could not take off," Nakanga continued. "Our sources say that the North Koreans are puzzled. They have Nagoya's body, but it tells them nothing. Certainly they may have suspicions, but they have proof of nothing. The cave has been destroyed."

Nishin waited, perched on the edge of his seat. He knew the first sentence was all Nakanga would say about the lack of exfiltration that had left Nagoya and he stranded. From the rest of what Nakanga said, it appeared that the mission had been a success. But then why was he talking to him? And why was the Genoysha listening? For there was no doubt in Nishin's mind that the man in the wheelchair was the head of the Black Ocean Society. And what suspicions could the Koreans have?

Never before had he been in the Genoysha's presence. In fact, he had not expected to be in Nakanga's presence again so soon. Success on a mission was considered the standard. If Nishin had ever failed on an assigned mission he would not be here. He'd be dead. He watched carefully, waiting.

Nakanga's face was devoid of expression. His skull was completely devoid of hair and on the left side, behind his ear, there was a jagged scar, starting at the top and working its way down, disappearing into the neck of the traditional robe he wore. From his chest, flowing up his neck and out over his face, were the bright red tendrils of sunlight, an extension to the same tattoo that was on the chest of senior members of the Society. Nakanga could never go in public unnoticed with the intricate needle work on his face, but since having it placed there, on the day he was chosen as First Sensei to the Genoysha, he had never gone out of the temple except on special missions as the personal envoy of the Genoysha. At such times the tattoos served a purpose by showing all he met who he was and the power he represented.

"Do you have any idea what was in that cave?" Nakanga asked.

"No, Sensei."

Nakanga's dark eyes turned away from the balcony and peered at the countryside. "Unfortunately, it is not finished. There is more work to be done."

Nishin waited.

"The North Koreans are making trouble. They will dig into the mountain again, but we believe that this blast finished a job that should have been done better long ago. The problem is that we do not know what they found prior to your mission. We only knew that they had found the cave when they made a discreet, for them at least, approach to a government official in Tokyo.

"They are very primitive people, the Koreans. They would still be living in caves if we had not pacified them so many years ago. But do they show any gratitude? No. They act like gangsters, trying to blackmail our country and our Emperor."

"Blackmail, Sensei?" Nishin was surprised. What had been in that cave?

Nakanga continued, almost speaking to the man inside the room. "We are walking a very thin path that is fraught with dangers on both sides. There can be no allowance for further trouble. We must make our path and not allow others to dictate it. Our past is haunting us and if it is revealed it will be devastating to our interests and the country's interests. It will change history, which will change the present.

"The current situation between our country and the Americans is very tense but also filled with great opportunity. There are many who do not see the parallels between now and the late nineteen-thirties, but they are there. Except now the roles are reversed. We hold the economic power and the Americans are squirming under the imbalances.

"Unfortunately," Nakanga continued, "one factor that remains the same is that the Americans still have the more powerful military and a country full of natural resources, neither of which we had then or have now. What we must insure is that they do not have reason to use their military as we degrade their economic capability. This is a path we have tried to walk for many years now, but it is a path that is threatened by the North Koreans." Nakanga's voice strengthened. "What I tell you now goes to your heart."

Nishin knew that meant as long as he lived he could never repeat it.

Nakanga waved a wrinkled hand. The skin was covered with small black waves, flowing toward the fingertips like black fish scales. "This started many years ago. Before the war. And it did not start in Korea. It began here. What I tell you I only know from the mouth of the Genoysha. All written records of the Society were destroyed just before the occupation at the end of the war. And the Genoysha only knows what he saw and was told by his predecessor. There is the possibility that some information was lost with the death of the previous Genoysha and the destruction of all records. And there are some aspects of this that died with those involved and no one alive knows about."

Nishin listened raptly. He had never heard Nakanga speak so many words. And for him to repeat the words of the Genoysha! The Genoysha's mind was the true record of the Black Ocean Society. But what Nakanga said next dumbfounded Nishin.

"In the autumn of 1938 the first atom was split in Germany," Nakanga continued. "That is common knowledge. What is not common knowledge is that a member of our society was immediately sent to Germany to study at the Kaiser Wilhelm Institute where this event took place. He was a scientist. A young man named Kuzumi who saw the potential in this event just as a few other scientists in Germany, England, and the United States saw it.

"Kuzumi learned as much as he could from the German scientists. Then he returned by way of America. His mission there was to see where that country stood in the field of atomic research. Even at that time, well before the United States was at war with us, the Americans were beginning to classify all atomic research. They were preparing for their war against us years before they forced our hand, yet they cried so bitterly after Pearl Harbor.

"Besides being a scientist, though, Kuzumi was well trained as a spy by the Society. He learned enough to believe that the Americans were looking at the potential of the atom as a weapon. He returned here and made his report. We dutifully sent it to the military authorities to warn them and also to show them the potential of such a weapon."

Nakanga made a sound of disgust. "The fools scoffed. The young ones had taken over." Nakanga glanced at Nishin. "You know the history of that time. There was much turmoil in the government and the military. The report disappeared. But the Genoysha at the time saw the potential in what Kuzumi had reported. He ordered Kuzumi to begin work to see if this thing was truly possible. Much money and resources from the Society were allocated.

"On the first of October in 1941, Kuzumi presented a report on his own research. The conclusion he drew was that an atomic bomb was feasible but would require much work to move from theory to reality. Again the military was informed. This time some more attention was paid, but only because the external situation was growing more dangerous. The United States was economically trying to destroy Japan. Not unlike certain events in the present," Nakanga said. "Pearl Harbor was only two months away and far-thinking minds were beginning to see that the war we were already fighting for our survival was going to expand.

"A pact was made between the Genoysha and the head of the Imperial Navy to continue Kuzumi's work. The Army also showed interest and started their own project, but they were very far behind ours and the Navy's project because we had Kuzumi and his experience and knowledge. The project was originally based outside of Tokyo in the Rikken."

Nishin knew that was the name for the old industrial research arm of the government.

Nakanga paused, then continued. "As I said, there is much information that has been lost. Suffice it to say that the project was a difficult one and work proceeded very slowly. It took the Americans, with more resources and expertise, until 1945 to complete their Manhattan Project. Kuzumi worked miracles with what he had, but as the war turned against us, he was forced by the American B-29 bombings to move from the home islands. He lost much time in making this move. Perhaps a fatal amount for our country."

Nakanga's dark eyes focused on Nishin. "Seeking a more secure place that could also supply him with the necessary amount of power he would need to complete the work, Kuzumi moved the project, named Genzai Bakudan, to Hungnam."

Nishin bowed his head. He now had some of the answers he'd never thought he'd get.

"We had much industry there. Most of it owned by the Genoysha who had seen the potential of the valley and its resources early in the nineteen-thirties. It was out of the way of the American bombers. Kuzumi continued working even as the Americans came closer and closer to the homeland, island by island.

"At the end . . ." Nakanga's shoulders moved under his robe in what might have been a shrug. "I do not know exactly what happened. The Genoysha told me that he was informed that Kuzumi succeeded. That he and those who worked with him actually made a prototype bomb. But it was too late. The Russians were close to the project, perhaps even trying to capture it for their own purposes. They were like scavengers invading Manchuria and Korea as they saw the end of the Empire coming. As you know, they still hold the Kuril Islands as a result of the war.

"The cave you were sent to reclose housed the assembly portion of the Genzai Bakudan project. It was sealed before the Russians arrived. It was reported that the prototype Genzai Bakudan was taken out into the harbor of Hungnam by the ranking naval officer and detonated, destroying the last evidence. There is no way to verify this. In fact, it is not something we ever wish to have verified."

Nakanga fell silent.

"Sensei?" Nishin prompted.

"Yes?"

"What happened to Kuzumi?"

Nakanga glanced toward the figure in the wheelchair, then sighed. "I was told he was in Hiroshima with his family when the American bomb came down. He died there."

Nishin frowned. Why had Kuzumi not been in Hungnam working on the bomb until the very end? That was his duty, and as Black Ocean, duty would have come first. But this was not the time to ponder that question of the past. There were more immediate concerns in the present. "You say we still have a problem, Sensei. Did the Koreans recover something out of the cave before we were able to close it again?"

"I believe so," Nakanga said. "At the very least they are pursuing a new direction. Our sources tell us that four days ago North Korean agents left their country by ship. They are going to San Francisco."

"San Francisco, Sensei?" Nishin frowned. Four days ago? That was when Nagoya and he had been at Hungnam.

Obviously they had been too late. "What is in America that they seek?"

"As I told you, all documents about Genzai Bakudan were destroyed here in the Society. The site in Hungnam was destroyed, or at least we thought it was. But remember I also told you that the Imperial Navy was involved in the project. They had their own records. We thought they too had been destroyed. But that thinking is being re-evaluated in light of this new development.

"When the Americans occupied us after the war, their intelligence services seized much information in the form of documents and they also debriefed many officers and men of the Imperial Navy. That information was returned to the United States. We believe that the North Koreans learned something from the cave. Perhaps they recovered a radio message log. That would point to other documents that the Americans might have in their possession."

"But surely, Sensei," Nishin said, "the Americans would have made public any information they had about our having had an atomic bomb program if they had it in 1945!" Nishin could now well imagine what Nakanga had meant earlier about the importance of what they were discussing. Such a disclosure would have been fantastic back then and would most certainly have changed the course of the next half a century. It would be just as disastrous now, especially with tensions between Tokyo and Washington so strained over the trade imbalance. Such a discovery would give the Americans a moral club almost as powerful as the surprise attack on Pearl Harbor had so many years previously. It would be devastating to the national psyche of the Japanese people."

"If they knew what they had," Nakanga agreed, "I believe they would have made it public. But the Americans seized so much material. It is very possible they simply placed such documents in boxes that have never been looked into. Or, if looked into, the significance of the material was not recognized because little word of the Genzai

Bakudan program has ever been made public before.

"There was a newspaper report in a minor American newspaper after the war about Hungnam and a Japanese atomic bomb project. But since the Russians occupied North Korea, little was made of the report and the Genoysha also worked then to ensure nothing more was said. As we must work now," Sensei Nakanga concluded. He turned and looked out over the valley for a few moments.

Nishin waited for his orders. He was acutely aware of the presence in the darkened room. He could feel the Genoysha as if the man were a shadow looming over the sunlit porch. A thrill of dedication ran down Nishin's spine as he realized he was part of perhaps the most important thing happening right now in the Black Ocean. Something so important that the Genoysha himself would listen in. There was only one being on the planet higher than the Genoysha in Nishin's mind and that was the Emperor.

Nakanga turned back. "The North Koreans are amateurs at overseas operations. However, we suspect that they might pose as South Korean agents and recruit assistance from the large population of South Koreans in the San Francisco area. In the same manner, you will be able to operate there. We have contacts among the Yakuza in San Francisco. I have already made contact with the local Oyabun."

The Yakuza was the Japanese equivalent of the American Mafia. It operated here in Japan and had branches overseas, wherever there was a Japanese subculture. Nishin knew that the secret societies and the Yakuza were not unaware of each other's presence and on occasion worked together when the objectives met both organizations' goals. They also clashed on occasion when the objectives did not concur. Nishin had blooded himself several times in such clashes. The thought of rubbing shoulders with Yakuza, especially American Yakuza, bothered him, but he dared not let it show in front of Nakanga and the Genoysha.

"The government," Nakanga continued, "is also on alert. Ever since those fools gassed the Tokyo subway every organization, even one as old and venerable as ours, has been under constant surveillance by Central Political Intelligence. You must be careful not to be tracked by CPI to the United States."

Nishin was glad he had had a good night's sleep and had recovered as far as he had from his injuries. The information he had just been given and the task assigned seemed overwhelming. CPI was a secret arm of the Japanese government that battled the secret societies and the Yakuza by any means possible. Nishin had run into CPI agents while on mission and he respected their dedication and most especially their technical expertise. Given that they had access to the best electronic equipment in the world, CPI agents were masters of surveillance. Unfortunately for them, and fortunately for Nishin, CPI agents usually lacked the ruthlessness needed to complete missions. They were limited by the laws and regulations placed on them by the government.

"Arrangements have been made for your travel." Nakanga held out a large brown envelope. "I have your cover documents ready: passport, driver's license. All that you will need. Also a sufficient sum of money to allow you to do your job. Memorize the contact plans and procedures. You will leave this evening."

Nishin stood and took the envelope. He froze when a voice spoke from the shadows.

"You must not allow the secret of Genzai Bakudan to be revealed," the man in the wheelchair rasped. "Use whatever means necessary."

Nishin inclined his head, indicating he understood, afraid to say anything. When nothing more was said, he quickly left the deck.

Behind, standing alone, Nakanga looked at the entrance to the room, waiting.

"Leave me," the Genoysha ordered.

"Yes, Genoysha Kuzumi."

As soon as Nakanga left, Kuzumi slowly pushed aside the curtain and rolled onto the balcony. It was his favorite place to think. It was also the only place where he was ever out of doors. Nakanga's words rang in his ears, as did Nishin's questions. They raised disturbing thoughts like a dust cloud on an old road.

Lies, deception, and double and triple dealing were the way of power, Kuzumi knew, but Nakanga's answer to Nishin's question about his location at the end of the war brought forth a double-edged sword of deception that cut deep. I did not die in Hiroshima, Kuzumi bitterly knew. Late at night when he was alone lying on his mat he often wished he had. Sometimes he wondered if memories and nightmares were all he had other than his duty to the Society.

At least everything else Nakanga had told Nishin was true. What bothered Kuzumi as much as anything else was the fact that the part about *not* knowing the full story was also true. Kuzumi had been high in the Society by the end of the war, but only the Genoysha at the time, Taiyo, had known all that was going on. As only Kuzumi knew all that was presently going on within the many tentacles of the present-day Black Ocean society so Taiyo had ruled and plotted. What concerned Kuzumi was whatever had grown from those unknown past seeds that had been scattered at the end of the war.

Naturally, he was concerned about Genzai Bakudan being found out. More specifically about the Black Ocean's role in developing Genzai Bakudan. But when he had learned that the North Koreans were heading to San Francisco his blood had run cold and more ghosts had arisen to swirl about his consciousness. There were a few things that Kuzumi knew from that time that Nakanga himself did not know because Kuzumi had not informed him.

But it was years before that desperate time when the war closed in on the homeland that Kuzumi's mind wandered to now on the balcony. Seven years earlier to be exact, before the entire world had turned black with war.

Unlike his present situation, in the late thirties Kuzumi had traveled the world. He had been in Germany right after fission had been discovered in 1938. He had earned his degree in the fledgling science of atomic physics at the University of Tokyo the previous year, so he had understood the importance of what had just occurred. As a member of the Black Ocean, which had funded his education, Kuzumi had informed his superiors and they had sent him to the Third Reich.

So strange that the Germans, who had first discovered fission, would lag so far behind in their development of an atomic bomb. But Kuzumi knew the main reason for that. Hitler. The crazy man had not trusted discoveries uncovered mainly by Jewish scientists. He had also run away most of his prominent physicists for the same reason. Run them right to his enemy in America. The German program had lagged and then the British had sent a suicide commando mission to destroy the heavy-water plant in Norway in 1942 to dash any possibility of the German scientists achieving success. The raid was something a Japanese would have done.

Leaving Germany in 1939 after learning all he could, Kuzumi had gone to the west coast of the United States. It was at the University of California at Berkeley that he had studied under Professor Ernest O. Lawrence, who won the Nobel Prize in physics that same year for inventing the cyclotron a few years previously.

A circular accelerator capable of generating particle energies, a cyclotron was essential for developing the theoretical groundwork in the growing field of atomic studies. Lawrence had built the first one, four and a half inches in diameter, at UC-Berkeley in the early thirties. By the time Kuzumi was in California, the Japanese had one thirty-nine inches in diameter. The Americans had built even larger ones and were beginning to classify much of their work in atomic physics.

But as a young exchange student Kuzumi had learned much about atomics in the relaxed atmosphere of the university. He had also learned something that no amount of schooling could have prepared him for.

Kuzumi looked over the valley and beyond, his eyes soaring through his memory in both time and place. Berkeley, 1939. The campus was in the bloom of spring and Kuzumi's mind had been on atoms and international intrigue. There was war in Europe and his own country was at war in China. The United States was a tranquil island in the middle of the death raging elsewhere.

Perhaps that was what had lulled him. His old hands strayed up to his neck, feeling the absence of the locket that had hung around his neck for six years. He had passed it on in 1945 and it had been destroyed at Hiroshima along with much else that was precious to him.

San Francisco. Damn those North Koreans. Damn that old cave. What had they uncovered there? Kuzumi shook his head. How had the North Koreans found out about the cave? From the Russians? From someone simply stumbling over it?

There was more at stake than even Nakanga knew. Kuzumi could take no chances. He pressed a button on the side of his wheelchair and waited for the person he had summoned to appear.

CHAPTER 3

SAN FRANCISCO
FRIDAY, 3 OCTOBER 1997
12:27 A.M. LOCAL

''I need a Hush Puppy,'' Lake said.

The man across the table from him whistled. ''That'll cost you big. What do you need the Puppy for? You got the High Standard I sold you, right? Or did you resell it?''

''I still have the High Standard,'' Lake confirmed. ''But I don't like it, Jonas. Too light. That .22 bullet couldn't hurt a rabbit.''

''It can kill you if you put the bullet in the right place,'' Jonas said. ''I remember . . .''

Lake pretended to listen as Jonas told his war story. The bar they were in was named Chain Drive, but that was a relic from its days when bikers had haunted the imitation-leather booths and rickety wooden tables. The bikers were gone now and the Patriots had taken over.

As he leaned back against the back of the booth, it occurred to Lake that he would have preferred dealing with the bikers. He'd been working the Patriots since they'd changed their name two years ago. Previously they'd been known as Militias, but the Oklahoma bombing had made that name a disadvantage. Some smart guy had come up with the new name, and because the group used the Internet for much of its communications, the name had caught on within two months.

The best estimate the Ranch had was that there were over a quarter million members of various Patriot groups around the country. Contrary to the claims of the media, though, Lake knew that most of those were law-abiding citizens who simply felt that the federal government had overstepped its bounds and they were exercising their freedom of speech. It was the handful of extremists among that quarter million that worried everyone.

The Ranch had put its focus on the Patriots six months after the Oklahoma bombing when the FBI, the ATF, the DEA, and the rest of the alphabet soup failed to agree on how to combat domestic terrorism. The President had grown tired of the infighting and pulled the entire problem away from all of them without them even knowing it had been pulled away. As the agencies *still* were working on a joint task force, the Ranch had been given a highly classified presidential directive. It was covered by Section 180102 of the Omnibus Crime Bill which allowed "Multi-jurisdictional Task Forces" to be funded by "assets seized as a result of investigations."

As far as Lake knew, the Ranch had been in existence for a long time before the problem of the Patriots or Militias, or whatever they wanted to call themselves, had arisen. Over half a century at least as Lake had heard references to competition with the OSS, Office of Strategic Services, during World War II for personnel. The OSS, and its follow-on, the CIA, had been the public front. The Ranch was the hidden part. Perhaps the Ranch had once been part of the OSS, if Feliks's cigarette case was to be believed as being his, and then had split off sometime during World War II.

Lake found it amazing that it never really occurred to Congress, or the general public for that matter, that there simply *had* to be a covert government agency that no one had ever heard of, that conducted missions that could not be done by an organization open to public or congressional scrutiny. The CIA, no matter how covert its covert wing tried to operate, was known to the public and that meant that conflicting priorities and a lack of secrecy were built into the organization. It was only natural when the President ran out of other options that he picked the Ranch to delve into the problems of the right-wingers. The Ranch was where the buck always stopped.

Feliks was the leader of the Ranch. Had been ever since Lake had been hand-picked to join it five years ago. From what Lake could gather whenever he went to the Ranch, Feliks had been in charge for decades. Lake actually had no idea of the extent of the organization or how many people worked for it, such was the extent of the compartmentalization that Feliks imposed. In fact, Lake wondered if Feliks truly was the head of the organization. For all he knew, Feliks was just a section chief, although the man never seemed to have to defer his decision making to anyone else.

Lake had never met any of the other field operatives. Whenever he went back to the Ranch, located outside Las Vegas at a secret Air Force base that had been used for such things as testing the Stealth Fighter and other classified aircraft, he dealt only with Feliks or support personnel. His training had always been one-on-one with the instructors, all of whom were the best in their specialties.

Lake had been well-qualified in the field of special operations before being recruited and, with the Ranch training, he knew he was among the best in the world. But as events just a few nights ago had proven, even the best could get killed when things didn't quite work like they should. James Bond looked very good on the screen, but one thing Lake knew was that real life was full of screw-ups and human foibles. Training didn't make him perfect but it did give him a leg up on other, less well-trained personnel.

Beyond the organizational security, there was a level of

personal security that was extremely strict, for two reasons, one obvious, the other not so obvious. The first reason was to allow operatives to go deep undercover, something that was essential for the w$ork to be done. On this operation, Lake had now been under for sixteen months, which was unheard of in law enforcement or even intelligence circles inside the United States. The reason it was unheard of was not only the psychological strain on the undercover person, but the fact that anyone under that long on the wrong side of the law in the States *had* to end up breaking the law in order for the cover to remain valid.

And Lake did break the law. That was the second reason for the tight security because, even with the presidential directive reference the Patriots, the Ranch operatives were committing crimes up to, and including, murder. Taking out the three men the other night wasn't the only law Lake had broken. He broke the law every time he sold illegal automatic weapons and ordnance. But it was because he sold that gear and broke the law that criminals like Jonas trusted him as much as they were able to trust anyone they hadn't grown up with.

Lake knew he had added three counts of murder to his list of felonies the previous evening, although he supposed a lawyer could make a good case for self-defense and a high degree of justification for action. Still, he hadn't read anyone their rights or given them the option of surrender.

That thought made Lake smile, the gesture lost in the darkness of the booth. Lake wasn't a cop. Never had been. That wasn't what Feliks looked for at the Ranch. People in power were scared, and when people were scared they went for the best. And the Ranch always got the pick of the crop, even when people weren't scared.

Lake knew another fertilizer bomb wasn't what scared the piss out of everyone from the President on down. Something like the biological agent Lake had just stopped on the Golden Gate was the real fear. The amount of fissionable material floating out of the former Soviet Union was another source of fear. The potential for a nuclear, chemical, or biological weapon of mass destruction being unleashed was no longer a question of if, but more one of when.

And that "when" occurred about every five or six months. So far the Ranch operatives had a perfect record against the Patriots and other terrorist organizations, covering four different attempts at domestic terrorism. Five, Lake reminded himself, after the events of the previous evening. Of course only Feliks and the President knew that.

"Can you get me a Hush Puppy?" Lake finally asked as Jonas's story wound to a close somewhere in the jungles north of the DMZ in Vietnam, over thirty years ago.

"You don't get a Hush Puppy to *use*," Jonas said. "It's a fucking piece of history. A goddamn classic."

Lake's expertise was weapons, but he didn't look at them as stamps to be collected like many people did. They were tools. A great violinist didn't buy a Stradivarius to hang it on the wall in a glass case and be looked at. He bought it to play it. Lake needed a new instrument. The .22 High Standard bullets had bounced off the man in the boat's vest. The Ranch ordnance department had provided the High Standard and Lake had used it. Lake allowed himself only one mistake and he wouldn't use it again. The only advantage the gun had was it could be fired repeatedly without recocking, unusual in a silenced semiautomatic weapon. In the future, Lake simply wanted one bullet that would do the job instead of two that wouldn't.

A Hush Puppy was a Smith & Wesson Model 99, 9mm automatic pistol specially modified with a silencer. Because of the modifications, it had been officially designated the Mark 22 Mod O pistol with a Mark 3 Mod O silencer attached to the barrel. The gun had been developed during the Vietnam War for use by the Navy SEALs. The stated purpose was to kill enemy sentry dogs, thus the nickname. The next time Lake shot someone with a silenced weapon, he wanted a bigger bullet. One that could cut through a vest if the round was specially modified, and Lake knew how to modify bullets.

There were drawbacks to the Hush Puppy. It had a lock on the slide, to keep the slide locked closed when it was fired. This prevented metal on metal noise. But it also prevented the gun from ejecting the spent round and chambering a new one, unlike the operation of the High Standard. The Hush Puppy had to be manually unlocked and a new round chambered each time it was fired. That could take a trained man almost a second, a very long time when bullets were flying.

The Mark 3 silencer consisted of a hollow tube screwed on the end of the barrel. Inside the tube was a disposable insert that suppressed sound. The insert was a cylinder holding four quarter-inch-thick plastic disks with a small hole in the center. The disks slowed down the escaping gasses which in guns makes most of the noise of firing. Each insert was good for two dozen rounds. Combining the Mark 3 with specially developed subsonic ammunition and the slide lock, the gun was practically noiseless.

"I'll give you three thousand, cash," Lake said.

The museum curator vanished and Jonas the wheeler-dealer was back. "You got it. Tomorrow soon enough?"

"Yeah." Lake tapped the fat man on the arm. "And make sure I have a good Mark 3 with two new inserts."

Jonas smiled. "You do know your guns." He signaled and the bartender came over with two more beers. "I heard you were with that Starry fellow."

Lake took a deep slug. "Yeah. Him and Preston."

"Nobody's seen them for a few days. I heard someone was looking for them," Jonas said.

"Who's looking?" In the dim light of the bar, Lake was studying the poster behind Jonas's head. It showed Hitler, his arm raised in the Nazi salute. Below it was written in large letters: EVERYONE IN FAVOR OF GUN CONTROL RAISE YOUR RIGHT HAND.

Jonas didn't answer his question. "You know where they're at?"

"I know where they were at," Lake said. "We split in Novato a few days ago. They said they had a job to do. I got them the guns they needed and I guess they didn't want me in on the action. They paid so I don't care where they went."

"Can you get in contact with them?"

"I don't have any plans to get in contact with them, so, no, I couldn't get in contact with them," Lake said. "But if they get in contact with me, I'll let them know you're concerned."

"Heard the ATF grabbed some of their buddies up in Portland," Jonas said, changing the drift of the conversation.

Lake shrugged. "Hell, the goons raided Starry twice. The first one was why they came to me; they lost all their automatic rifles. On the second raid they grabbed some of Starry's people on charges drummed up from what they seized on the first raid."

The second ATF raid had been set up by Feliks to give Lake a way into Starry's group after supplying them with weapons. The first raid had been a setup months ago to get Lake into position to sell the weapons. It was all complicated and took a long time to work and the ATF didn't have a clue that they were being used by the Ranch. They thought the raids had been legitimate, which meant the Patriots also thought that. Which meant Lake *was* legitimate as far as the criminal element was concerned. In a strange way, Lake normally stayed on the wrong side of the law, only going on the right side when the stakes were raised high. That's what made him so good.

Lake knew Jonas was fishing. Starry, Preston, and the third man simply disappearing off the face of the earth had to have jerked someone's chain. Now he was hearing the rattle. Of course, Jonas hadn't mentioned the third man.

"You haven't heard from Starry?"

That was too blunt. Lake put down the beer. ''Maybe Starry don't want to be heard from. I just told you I don't know how to get a hold of them. Last I saw of them, it looked to me like they were on a mission and they might not like me saying anything about their movements. I've learned to mind my own business.''

''Hey, chill, man. I know that. But information's my business. I wouldn't betray the cause. Just some people asking.''

''What people?'' Lake asked.

''People,'' Jonas repeated vaguely.

''Those people need any guns?'' Lake asked. ''That I can help you with. Starry, I can't. And I don't answer questions for people when I don't know who they are. These people talking to you might be feds.''

''No, these people aren't feds and they don't need guns,'' Jonas said. ''At least not right now. They're cool, man. Just some of Starry's and Preston's buds in the movement.'' He finished his draft with one long gulp, then patted down his long flowing gray beard. ''Hey, but there are some people asking around for some firepower.''

''People?'' Lake repeated. ''Not with the cause?''

Jonas laughed. ''No, these people aren't with the cause.''

''What kind of people?'' Lake asked.

''Foreigners. Slopes. Asking around.''

''What kind of slopes?'' Lake thought of the Japanese information planted in the van. Maybe it wasn't a plant. Maybe Starry had gotten the glass jar from someone foreign that morning. Maybe even from the man in the boat.

''I don't know. They all look alike to me. Japs, I guess. Maybe Chinese. Who the fuck can tell?''

I can, thought Lake. As can anyone who gave a shit. ''What are they asking about?''

''Looking for automatic weapons with some special adaptations. Silencers.''

''Here?'' Lake asked, surprised. This bar was the last place he'd expect a Japanese person to be searching for weapons. Besides hating the government, the Patriots hated foreigners, particularly Japanese. And Jews. And Blacks. And Hispanics. And just about everyone who wasn't them.

"No, not here. On the street. But word gets back. The city's not that big."

"They can get all the firepower they need over in Jap-town," Lake said. "The local U.S. branch of the Yakuza has the market there."

"Maybe they ain't Japs, then," Jonas said. "Or maybe the Yakuza don't like them. That old man who runs the Yakuza is real particular about people horning in on his turf. He's a badass dude and I wouldn't want to cross him."

"The Yakuza would still know," Lake mused out loud. "But maybe they aren't Japs. Might be Chinese, but if they're chink then they can go to the Triads," Lake added, feeling uncomfortable using the racial term.

"Hey," Jonas said, misinterpreting his discomfort. "I don't know who the hell they are. I just heard a whisper here, a whisper there. What the fuck you getting so riled about?"

"I don't like slopes," Lake said, idly rubbing his neck.

"Hey, I don't like 'em either," Jonas said. "I lost a lot of good buddies back in the 'Nam."

"Can you set up a meet?" Lake asked.

"What?" Jonas said. "With who?"

"The slopes," Lake said, clenching his jaw. "I've got guns."

"I thought you said you didn't like slopes?"

"I don't. But I do like money."

SAN FRANCISCO
FRIDAY, 3 OCTOBER 1997
10:20 P.M. LOCAL

Getting a person into the United States required the proper documentation and the Black Ocean Society had handled that for Nishin with no problem. But getting weapons in was a different story, and instead of the hardware, Nakanga had given Nishin a place and a name to be memorized to take care of that logistical problem.

As he got closer to the designated place, Nishin felt more and more as if he were back in Japan. Very strange, considering he was less than two miles from the corner of Haight-Asbury, a place that had symbolized all the decadence of America during Nishin's teenage years.

Japantown is an approximately twenty-block section of San Francisco that has a concentration of Japanese-Americans living there along with all the trappings for tourists to get a taste of the Asian homeland. The area is bordered on the south by the Japan Center, a five-acre shopping center designed as a small Ginza. The two-level area encloses various shops, restaurants, galleries, and Japanese gardens. This time on a Friday night it was packed with people and well-lit. Not exactly what Nishin had expected or desired in a covert meeting place.

He checked the directory for the center and found his destination. The Yotoku Miyagi bookstore contained the city's largest collection of books in Japanese. Therefore it was not strange at all when Nishin walked up to the register and made his request in his native tongue, naming a specific book he was looking for.

The response of the young woman standing behind the counter was not normal, though. Her eyes flickered back and forth, then lowered.

"You must go to the Morikawa Restaurant," she said in a low voice. "Down the stairs directly across from the door you came in. Turn left. Two hundred meters. On the right. They will expect you."

Nishin turned and departed, glancing over his shoulder as he pushed open the door. The woman was on the phone, but she still was avoiding looking at him.

He followed the instructions. The Morikawa was darker than the bookstore and there was a queue of people outside.

Nishin bypassed the line. A thin, Japanese man in a very expensive suit stood next to the maître d', his eyes watching Nishin's approach. He took Nishin's right elbow in his hand. "This way," he said in Japanese.

Nishin felt the man's thumb press into the nerve junction on the inside of his elbow, effectively paralyzing his right hand. They wove their way through the darkly lit bar, then through a swinging door. Another man sat on a stool in the small corridor, a raincoat folded over his lap. The two men nodded. Nishin heard a distinct click, a door unlocking. They passed the second man, going through another door. It swung shut behind them with another click. Two men stepped forward and Nishin's guide let go of his arm. They were in a short corridor with walls of some dark material that Nishin couldn't quite make out. The lighting was also strange.

"Hands out."

One of the men ran a metal detector carefully around Nishin's body. The other then patted him down, double-checking. Then one on either side, they escorted him to a set of metal stairs. Their shoes clattered on the steel as they went up. A door opened and Nishin blinked. They were on the top of the Center in a glass-enclosed room about sixty feet long by thirty wide. The room was dimly lit by the reflected light from the surrounding city and the sky overhead. A dozen tables were spread out on the roof and the two men led him to one separate from the rest where several men dined.

Nishin was brought to a halt facing an older Japanese man who sat at the head of the table. Nishin could see that the man's skin was covered in various tattoos, the signs of his Yakuza clan. Serpents disappeared into the collar of his gray silk shirt and dragons peeked out from his shirtsleeves. His fingers were covered with gaudy gold rings, jewels sparkling in the street lights. Nishin shifted his gaze about, checking out the roof.

The old man laughed. "The glass is specially made. It

can take up to a fifty-caliber bullet. If my enemies wish to use something larger than that, then nothing much will stop them. It is also one-way. We can see out. Those on the outside see only black, making it also rather difficult for a sniper.''

Nishin returned his eyes forward and waited.

''I am Makio Okomo. Oyabun of all that you see. I received a message from your Sensei Nakanga,'' the old man said. ''I do not need such messages. You and your friends are out of date.'' He waved a hand, taking in the Japanese Center. ''My way is the new way. You fools waste much time and energy living in the past.''

Nishin remained silent.

Okomo leaned back in his seat. ''What do you need?''

''Weapons. Information.''

Okomo's hand slapped the table top. ''This is *my* city. You are not in Japan now. You show me respect.''

Nishin stood still.

''I could have you killed and no one would ever hear from you again.'' The old man gestured and the guards pulled Nishin's jacket down around his shoulders. One of them flicked open a knife and with a single slash cut through Nishin's shirt, the blade grazing the skin without leaving a mark. They pulled the cut shirt apart, exposing Nishin's chest.

''You do not have the Black Ocean tattoo,'' Okomo said, turning back to his meal. ''Kill him.''

''Operatives of the Black Ocean do not have the tattoo . . . Oyabun,'' Nishin said as one of the guards pulled out a pistol and placed it next to his temple. The last word rolled off his tongue with difficulty. Showing any sign of respect for such a man distressed Nishin. ''Only those who have been accepted into the inner circle have that honor. I am only a ronin of the Society.''

''And that is why you are cowards,'' the Oyabun snapped. ''Afraid to show who you are.'' He held his arms out from his sides and the tattoos on them rippled in the reflected light. "My lowest man has no fear of showing who he is or that he belongs to me. He is proud of his marks!"

"The Sun Goddess knows who we are and what we do," Nishin replied, holding his head up high.

Okomo's mood changed and he laughed. "Ah, yes, you are Black Ocean. Only one of their fools would believe that. The Sun Goddess? The Emperor? Sheer stupidity." He gestured and the two guards let go of him, the pistol disappearing.

Nishin shrugged his jacket back up over his shoulders. One of the guards put a metal briefcase at Nishin's feet.

"Your weapons are in there." Okomo raised a white eyebrow. "As Nakanga asked." He gestured for Nishin to leave and picked up his chopsticks.

"There are North Korean agents in this city," Nishin said. "I need to find them."

The sticks poised. "Why are they here?"

"I do not know. That is why I need to find them."

Okomo chuckled. "The dog is chasing its own tail. Political games don't interest me." He stuffed food in his mouth and chewed. "I will inform you when I have something to inform you of. My men will find you. Do not come back here."

Nishin picked up the briefcase and followed the two guards back to the stairs.

Behind Nishin, Okomo waited until the Black Ocean agent was gone, then the old man stood. He quickly walked to an elevator, a pair of guards surrounding him as he moved. He stepped in, leaving the guards behind. It whisked him down over a hundred and fifty feet, through the Japan Center to a level four floors below ground. When the door opened again, Okomo stepped forward into a large room, then bowed toward a figure behind a desk twenty feet in front of him, hidden in the shadows cast by large halogen lamps on the far wall. Okomo spoke from the bow, his words echoing off the heavily carpeted floor. "The

Black Ocean agent is here. I gave him the weapons. He has asked for information about North Koreans in the city. It goes as you said it would, Oyabun."

When there was no reply, Okomo turned and reboarded the elevator to go back to his public role.

Two blocks away a man on a dark rooftop fiddled with the controls on the small laptop computer and continued to listen to the voices from the top of the Japan Center through the headphones he wore. In front of him a black aluminum tripod held what looked like a camera. Actually it was a laser resonator. It shot out a laser beam that hit the black glass on the top of the Japan Center. The beam was so delicate that it picked up the slightest vibration in the glass. Reflecting back to a receiver just below the transmitter, a computer inside interpreted the vibrations into the sounds that caused them.

It had not taken the man long to tune out the background noise and get the computer to pick up the voices inside. He'd heard the entire exchange between Nishin and the old man. Satisfied that Nishin had left the room, he quickly broke down the laser and placed it into a backpack along with the computer. Within thirty seconds he was gone from his perch.

In the small room he'd rented, Nishin opened the aluminum case. The packing held specially cut slots for the weapons stored inside. Nishin pulled out a specialized Steyr AUG. The Yakuza had done well, Nishin reflected as he checked out the weapon. He'd used one before, as he'd used almost every weapon on the world's arms market.

This AUG was a smaller version of the rifle that saw service in numerous Western countries. The magazine was fitted behind the trigger assembly which contributed greatly to its shorter length. A telescopic sight and laser designator was fixed on top of the barrel assembly. Nishin aimed, watching the red dot sweep around the dingy room. Very nice. There were six 30-round magazines of 9mm ammunition. The magazines were clear plastic, which allowed the firer to keep track of expenditure without having to remove the magazine from the weapon.

There was a safety, but no selector lever such as the M-16 or AK-47 had. The AUG was designed for a more professional shooter. A slight pull on the trigger fired one round. Pulling the trigger all the way to the rear fired the weapon on automatic. A stubby suppressor was fitted on the tip of the barrel that extended forward of the front plastic grip. Nishin had to trust that the 9mm ammunition was subsonic, otherwise there would be no reason for the suppressor. Nishin carefully disassembled the gun and checked every piece to make sure it was functional. He would not put it past the Yakuza to give him a gun with a filed-down firing pin. Satisfied that he could find nothing wrong, he reassembled the gun. Then he inserted a magazine and pulled back the charging handle. He fired a shot at the wood frame around the closet. A round splintered the wood, the gun making just the slightest sound. Nishin took the magazine out, cleared the chamber, and put the gun back in the case.

A Browning High Power 9mm automatic pistol, along with a shoulder holster, was also in the case. A reliable pistol. After checking it as he had the AUG, Nishin strapped the holster on, then slipped his jacket over it. He slid the case with the AUG under the bed.

The room was on the second floor of a six-story hotel. Nishin had picked it as he'd been taught in the terrorist camp in the Middle East so many years ago for its transient and illicit clientele, mostly prostitutes and drug addicts. He hadn't even had to say a word when getting the room. He'd shoved two hundred-dollar bills at the clerk and received a key in return. Very convenient and inconspicuous, just as he'd expected.

Of course, if pressed, Nishin could have spoken in English and presented all the proper documents to prove he was an American. Nishin was no stranger to America or this type of work. The Black Ocean Society had seen to that and his present cover.

Nishin did not know where he had been born or who his parents had been. His earliest memories were of the Home-place. It was where the Black Ocean Society raised its operatives. Perhaps he had been sold to the Society by a family with too many mouths to feed. Perhaps he was an orphan whom the Society had taken under its wings. He didn't know, they had never told him, and he didn't care.

He'd been cared for and schooled by the Society from the very beginning of his memories. Trained in foreign languages, martial arts, weapons, covert operations, communications—all the black arts. And above all was loyalty to the Sun Goddess, the Emperor, the Genoysha and the Society, the last two being one in the same in his mind.

When he was sixteen he had begun his fieldwork. There was always some group somewhere, protesting something. The only requirement was that the group had taken up arms and were willing to use them. The Black Ocean Society sent its operative students to such overseas groups, regardless of the group's cause. The key was to learn and gain experience while staying away from the eye of Japanese law.

Libya. Lebanon. El Salvador. Yugoslavia. A short stint in Mexico with the rebels in the south when they rose up, then slipping away when a deal was struck with the government. Then to Chechnya. Nishin had been in on the planning of the raid into Russia and the seizing of the hostages that had changed the course of that war.

Just two years ago, after Chechnya, the Genoysha had finally ruled that Nishin was able to do Society work and would no longer be risked getting experience. Only one in twenty of those Nishin had grown up with made it to that level. Many died gaining their experience, others simply weren't good enough and were slotted elsewhere in support positions.

Putting aside memories of the past, Nishin left the room to take care of other preparations. He felt the soreness in his limbs as he walked the streets. He wasn't one hundred percent recovered yet from his ocean experience. Someone else should have been sent, except for two things: he had been briefed on what was in North Korea, and he was one of the few operatives the Society had with field time in America. Despite its apparently open society, America was actually a very difficult place for covert, foreign operatives to work. The American intelligence agencies were more proficient than the media reported.

An all-night supermarket beckoned. Nishin walked in and wandered the aisles until he found the three items he was looking for. He paid and returned to the motel by a different route, occasionally backtracking to make sure he wasn't being followed.

Back in the security of his room, Nishin removed the objects from the bag: a clear Plexiglas ice scraper with a rubber handle, a file, and a roll of medical tape. He began filing down the ice scraper. After an hour he had turned the wide edge into a single point. He took the newly formed weapon and used the tape to secure it vertically to his stomach, above his waist; the one place the man who had patted him down had not checked. The plastic would not be picked up by the metal detector.

The next time Nishin had to visit the Yakuza, he would be ready. If action was necessary. He thought of the old man and the smile on Nishin's face was not a pretty sight.

Nishin turned off the light and lay down on the floor next to the bed. The AUG was locked and loaded next to him, his right hand lightly curled around the pistol grip.

A block away, the man who had been listening to Nishin's Yakuza meeting lowered the lid on the metal case that held the laptop computer. He slid through a curtain to the front of the rental van. He drove to the hotel he was staying at. It was much nicer than Nishin's. He parked in the garage and retired to his room.

CHAPTER 4

SAN FRANCISCO
SATURDAY, 4 OCTOBER 1997
2:37 A.M. LOCAL

"I got your message," Lake said to Jonas. A group of men wearing camouflage pants, brown T-shirts, and hats with various Patriot logos on them were sitting at a table on the main floor of the bar, arguing loudly and drunkenly about what had happened years previously in Waco and Ruby Ridge and the last year in Montana. There was no disagreement about ideology, just the basic manly desire to be more outraged than the fellow sitting next to you. If they'd been talking about the World Series it would have been no big deal, but they were talking about bombs and guns and hate, and that made it more than just idle talk.

Lake had heard it all so many times before and he'd even said it all when required. The party line was easy. He assumed that was why it was a party line. Check your brains at the door, no thinking required. But somebody was doing some thinking, that was for sure, as events of the previous week on the Golden Gate Bridge had shown him.

"I got a list of exactly what they want," Jonas said, echoing the message that he'd given Lake over the phone. They were seated in their usual booth. Lake had met Jonas thirteen months ago after he'd begun working the west coast. The Ranch had access to all FBI and ATF records and from those Lake had managed to get a very good idea of where to go and who to see. The other agencies couldn't arrest a lot of the people in their files because the evidence wouldn't stand up in court. The Ranch could use the people in those files to run their operations and did so without a second thought.

Lake had used Jonas as a broker in three weapons deals so far and since Jonas hadn't been arrested and the weapons were still out on the street, he had the man's conditional trust. That was something a normal federal agent couldn't do.

"That was quick," Lake said.

"They're rookies at the game and they're in a rush," Jonas said. He frowned. "But I wouldn't want to double-cross them. These slopes are hard-looking people. Almost . . ." Jonas paused.

"Almost?" Lake prompted.

"Almost like they're military types. Soldiers."

"Probably are ex-military," Lake said.

Jonas frowned. "No, I get the feeling like they're still military, like they're a unit that's trained together. Like you'd feel being around a Special Forces A-Team. Plus, the weapons they want are unique."

"Why do they want the weaponry?"

Jonas gave Lake a look. "Come on, you know I ain't about to ask them that. Like I said, though, they're in a hurry and because of that I did tell them they'd have to pay more."

"How'd you get a hold of them?" Lake asked. He knew Jonas didn't like the question, but he needed as much information as he could get.

"They told me they would call back and they did," Jonas said.

"How'd they get a hold of you in the first place?"

Jonas frowned. "I don't know and I didn't fucking ask

them. You want this deal or not? You aren't the only dealer in town."

"Let me see the list." Lake took the Post-it note from the other man and scanned it. He saw what Jonas had meant by "unique."

"Can you do that?" Jonas asked.

"Ingrams with suppressors are hot items," Lake said. He looked up. "When do they want it?"

"Monday. They said they'd get back to me with a time and place."

"I'll have it Monday. Tell them eight hundred for each Ingram. That's six thousand four hundred; five hundred a suppressor, four thousand; and a thousand per each six magazines, since I'm going to have do subsonic rounds. Total, sixteen thousand, four hundred."

"My commission is ten percent," Jonas noted. He slapped a bundle of money down on the table. "Earnest money. Five grand."

Lake tucked the list into his breast pocket. He peeled a thousand off the roll, handing it to Jonas. "Okay, charge them twelve thousand beyond the down payment and you keep another grand when we finalize the deal."

Jonas nodded and leaned back in the bench.

Lake stared at him, waiting.

Jonas slapped his forehead. "Oh, yes. Your gun." He reached down under the table and pulled up a paper bag. He started to slide it across, but froze as the door to the bar opened and three men walked in, dressed in black pants and windbreakers. "Shit," Jonas muttered, leaving the bag sitting in the center of the table, between him and Lake. "Federal Task Force. They're not supposed to come here. I'm fucking protected."

The three men sauntered around the table of Patriots and came straight to the booth. "Hey, Jonas," the leader said, leaning over the table. "What do you have in the bag?" He was a large man, hard-eyed in the way cops who'd spent a long time on the street were.

"It's mine," Lake said, pulling the bag over to his side. He checked out the other two agents: younger, college types who were following the other's lead out of respect for his experience and age. Lake could sense the high testosterone level coming off the three agents. They were pumped and ready for action.

One of the younger men stepped up. He wore expensive glasses which didn't match the black outfit. "And who the fuck are you?"

"Who wants to know?" Lake's voice was flat.

The leader's eyes narrowed, but he didn't intervene, waiting to see how both sides played it out.

"Federal Task Force," Glasses said, holding up an ID.

"I can buy one of those in any surplus store in town," Lake said. "And you have a foul mouth for a peace officer."

"The badge is real," Glasses said. "You want me to imprint my number on your fucking forehead," he added, holding the badge close to Lake's face.

Lake didn't move. "I'm not impressed."

"What's in the bag?" the leader cut in.

"My dick," Lake said. "Want to play with it?"

The Patriots at the table burst out laughing. They began making oinking noises.

"I'll put your dick in the goddamn bag." Glasses put his badge away and pushed up against the edge of the booth inside Lake's personal space. He was too close, a result of poor training, Lake idly thought.

"Do you have a warrant?" Jonas had finally recovered.

The leader was tired of the game and he knew, as Lake knew, that Glasses had made a mistake. "Open the fucking bag, asshole."

Lake sighed as he slowly stood, his shoulder brushing lightly against Glasses's chest. "I don't think so."

The leader went for his piece instinctively and Lake's movements went into hyper-speed. Glasses didn't know what hit him as Lake's left hand hit his chest, knocking the wind out of his lungs and toppling him backward. Lake was moving, following the strike, his right hand extended, grabbing the leader's gun hand as it cleared the shoulder holster. He squeezed hard and the gun dropped back inside the jacket, the man hissing with pain. Lake's left hand slammed the man's jaw, teeth smashing together with a sound heard throughout the bar, wiping the surprised look off the face. The leader went down, out cold.

The third agent was frozen at this unexpected turn of events. Lake spun, the back of his right foot catching the man on the side of the head and dropping him. The first man he had hit was still trying to catch his breath. Lake stepped over him and knelt on his chest. "You serve the people," he hissed. "We don't serve you." He pulled the man's gun out and tossed it away, then stood. "Next time, watch your language." Lake sharply tapped him on the side of the head with his hand, middle finger knuckle extended, and he was out like a light.

Lake reached into his pocket and peeled off three thousand dollars. He slapped them on the table in front of Jonas.

"What did you mean you were protected?" Lake asked.

Jonas was staring at the three agents, then slowly swiveling his large head to look at Lake. "You're fucking crazy, man."

"What did you mean about being protected? From the feds?" Lake asked again.

"I got friends," Jonas said vaguely. "Special friends who make these guys look like nothing."

One of the other agents was beginning to stir and Lake decided he would have to delve into things at another time. "Later," he said to Jonas as he picked up the bag and headed to the door, leaving those still conscious in stunned silence. As he walked out the door a couple of the Patriots began cheering and clapping. The smart ones followed Lake out the door and disappeared into the darkness.

Lake walked steadily, heading east, then north, for several miles, the pavement flowing under his stride until he hit the Embarcadero. The cool night air coming off the water slowly seeped into him, throttling back the adrenaline flowing in his veins. He could have gotten the Hush Puppy from the Ranch supply without any problem, but getting it from Jonas helped his position with the man. Ideology aside, most people looked more favorably upon those they could make some money off of once in a while. Plus Lake wanted a gun that the Ranch didn't know he had. He couldn't explain that desire, but he had learned a long time ago to trust his instincts. Lake followed the waterfront street until it passed under the ramp for the San Francisco–Oakland Bay Bridge.

A figure came out of the dark, wrapped in a long raincoat. "I don't have much time. I have a plane to catch."

"Nice to see you too," Lake said. Randkin was the science expert for the Ranch. He was a short, compact man who moved nervously. He had long blond hair and wire-rimmed glasses that framed a pinched face. Randkin always looked to Lake like he was constipated. He imagined having to work at the Ranch with Feliks looking over his shoulder all the time contributed to that.

Randkin ignored the barb. "There was a virus in the glass jar. But it wasn't lethal."

That was Lake's first surprise of the evening. "What?"

"It would have made a bunch of people sick. Maybe even killed a few people here and there who had other physical problems, but it was basically a non-lethal virus. That's why Feliks sent me to meet you."

Lake rubbed his forehead. "I killed three men over that virus."

"You didn't know that it wasn't lethal," Randkin said. "No reason to. Your wet work was justified."

"That's not the worry," Lake said. "What concerns me is that maybe this was a test-run and I shot up my only link in the chain. Maybe somebody wanted to see if it was possible to get some dumb-shit Patriots to do this sort of thing.''

''Feliks did express some concern about the same thing,'' Randkin dryly noted. ''But there might have been another purpose to the entire episode.''

Lake had been considering the situation. ''To make the attack public and point the finger at the Japanese without causing a major disaster, but hinting at one.''

''Correct.''

''And the Patriots would love that,'' Lake noted.

''Not just the Patriots,'' Randkin said. ''The automobile industry. The entire Republican Party. The American Legion. Wall Street. There're a whole lot of people in this country right now that are just itching for an excuse to go after the Japanese. The sanctions Clinton started and this administration picked up have backfired and we aren't winning this trade war. The Japanese aren't winning either, which in a way makes it worse all around. The Tokyo market crash last year shows that, but the man on the street doesn't care about what's happening in Japan. He only cares about what's happening in his home burg.

''So we know it was a setup,'' Randkin concluded. ''We just don't know who was behind it.''

''And Feliks wants a name,'' Lake said.

''Correct. Feliks also is concerned about the third man. We checked him out. Fingerprints weren't on record. His image isn't on record either. We don't have a clue who he is. Genetics indicates he has Japanese ancestry. That doesn't jive with a Patriot operation. You never saw this guy before?'' Randkin asked, holding out a morgue photo of the man from the boat.

''I told Feliks that,'' Lake said, taking the photo.

''Feliks told me to double-check.''

''You've double-checked,'' Lake said.

''Hey, don't jump my case!'' Randkin looked around nervously. ''Hey, Feliks is upset about something. Some weird stuff is going on, so everyone's a little uptight.''

"What kind of weird stuff?" Lake asked.

"If I knew, it wouldn't be weird," Randkin said. "I just wouldn't want Feliks after my ass. Some of the stuff I've heard about him . . ." Randkin paused, then shrugged. "Anyway, one more thing about our friend there," he said.

"Yes?" Lake asked irritably. He didn't like being drip-fed and Randkin's vague comments bothered him.

"He had a tattoo removed shortly before this operation." Randkin handed over another photo. It showed a large patch of pink skin on the man's upper right arm.

"Any idea what the tattoo was of?" Lake asked.

"No, but the fact it was removed could—"

"I know what it could mean," Lake snapped.

"I'm just trying to be helpful," Randkin sniffed. "Feliks is *very* concerned about this whole situation."

"Why?"

Randkin blinked. "What do you mean why?"

"I've been working for Feliks for a long time," Lake said, "and on cases that looked bigger than this. He never showed as much interest as he is in this one."

"A biological agent attack on San Francisco is serious," Randkin said, as if speaking to a two-year-old.

Lake wasn't happy. There had been no need for Feliks to be in San Francisco the other night and there was no need for Randkin to be here to give him information that they could just as easily transmit to him over the phone. Then there was Randkin acting strange.

"What about the Internet?" Lake asked. "Anything on the recruitment message that hooked Starry and Preston?"

"We're running it," Randkin said. "There's so much crap that's been on the Internet in the Patriot part of the Web that it's taking longer than I thought it would. As soon as we get it, we'll send it to you."

Then what are you doing here, Lake thought. "Get this in the works," Lake said, handing him the weapons list. "I need it in my drop by tomorrow evening."

"A lead on the van people?"

"Maybe."

"Feliks won't accept a maybe." Randkin looked at the piece of paper. "And he won't give this hardware away to just—"

"I stand on my record," Lake cut in.

"You may, but I have to go back to Feliks and I don't want your record standing on my shoulders when the ship goes down."

"The people who want those weapons are Asian," Lake said, noting that he'd given Randkin his surprise of the evening.

"Japanese? Going to the Patriots for guns?"

"I don't know," Lake said. "I'll know when I see them and give them their guns. Maybe they have tattoos on their upper-right arm. How the fuck do I know until I get the guns? I got the order through a Patriot cutout, which is kind of different by itself. So maybe there's something here."

Randkin fingered the note, then put it in his pocket. "You didn't have to be so hard on those feds. They were just doing a job. They didn't know they were bait in your game to keep your cover floating."

"Maybe they'll treat citizens like citizens next time they go on the street."

"Yes, and maybe next time they'll bust someone's head."

"Lots of maybes in the world," Lake said. He walked back off to the south, his mind full of troubled thoughts.

SATURDAY, 4 OCTOBER 1997
1:12 P.M. LOCAL

The phone rang, shattering the silence of the room. Nishin stared at it. No one knew he was in here. Perhaps a wrong number. It rang six times, then stopped. He went back to doing elevated push-ups, feet up on the bed. He was working out the soreness accumulated on his last mission. The pain felt good.

The phone rang again. Nishin stopped and hopped to his feet. He walked over to the cheap table next to the bed and stared at the ancient black instrument. On the fourth ring he picked it up and held it to his ear without making a noise.

A voice spoke in Japanese. *"Senso to Kyonsanshugi. By Takeo Mitamura."* The phone went dead and Nishin slowly lowered it back onto its cradle.

He taped the Plexiglas knife to his stomach, then strapped the Brown High Power on, putting a short blue windbreaker on over the gun. The AUG was in its case and he took that with him. The rest of his meager belongings went into a gym bag. He wiped down the room. By the time he was done there was no sign he had ever been there. He jammed a chair up against the door. Someone would really have to want to get in to open that door. It might gain him a couple of days.

He took the fire escape down to the back alley. Six blocks away, he checked into another flophouse, reserving a room for a week. He went upstairs, deposited the AUG case and the gym bag, then left, this time by the back staircase.

His new hotel was three miles from the Japan Center and he made it almost twice as long by zigzagging and occasionally doubling back on himself.

He knew where the Yotoku Miyagi bookstore was, but he approached it slowly. He sat for a half-hour a block away, watching customers going in and out. Finally he went into the store. The young woman from the previous evening was not there. An older man stood behind the counter. Nishin gave him the book title and author in Japanese.

The old man nodded. "Yes, sir. We have your special order. It just came in." He reached under the counter and handed Nishin a hardbound book. The old man pulled a receipt out from the inside cover. "It is already paid for."

Nishin thanked the man and tucked the book under his arm. He took an even more roundabout route back to his new nest. By the time he arrived it was getting dark. He locked himself into the room and finally took a look at the book. It was old. The copyright information said it was published in 1950 by a press in Tokyo.

The book was only the wrapping, though. Tucked inside was a map of San Francisco. Nishin scanned it. A pier on the northeast side of the San Francisco peninsula off the Embarcadero was circled in red.

Nishin put the map in his shirt pocket. He opened his gym bag and pulled out a sweater. It was foggy out and would get chilly before dawn. He put the sweater on, re-strapping the shoulder holster on over it, then the wind-breaker.

The phone startled him. He stared at it, then reluctantly picked it up.

A voice on the other end laughed, then spoke briefly in Japanese. "This is my city, remember that." Nishin recognized the voice: it was Okomo, the Oyabun of the San Francisco Yakuza. The phone went dead.

Nishin put the phone down. Before he picked up his gym bag and the AUG case, his hand strayed to his stomach and tapped the knife strapped there.

A half a mile away the same man who had been on the roof the previous night had Nishin's travels of the day overlaid on a computerized map of San Francisco. He was sitting in the driver's seat of his white rental van, a laptop computer wedged up against the steering wheel. He started the engine when the computer told him Nishin was moving again.

A freighter and a fishing trawler were docked in the berth that had been circled. Nishin knew which was his target immediately. The freighter flew a Panamanian flag, the trawler the flag of South Korea. He found a large crane that looked like it wasn't used much and climbed up to the control booth so that he could overwatch the trawler. It made perfect sense that the North Koreans would infiltrate using a fishing boat flying the South Korean flag as their cover.

Now it was a waiting game and Nishin had never lost a wait. First, though, he needed to check in. He went to a pay phone and called in a report to Nakanga, then he returned to the crane.

The man in the van also waited as the sun came up. Nishin didn't move from his perch. The man had seen the bag and metal case Nishin carried, which indicated he wasn't going back wherever he'd come from. The man typed commands into his computer tracker. It was now set on alert. If Nishin moved it would come alive and beep him. He headed back to his hotel room.

SAPPORO, HOKKAIDO, JAPAN
SUNDAY, 5 OCTOBER 1997
10:00 P.M. LOCAL

Nakanga had just reported to Kuzumi that Nishin had located the North Koreans on their ship. Kuzumi did not acknowledge the report. If it was spoken in his presence, he heard it. Acknowledgment was a waste of time and energy. It was a trait he had used since first graduating the university over six decades ago. His Sensei departed the room, leaving him in peace.

Kuzumi's office was on the top floor of the temple. There were no windows and the walls were hung with tapestries, muting the hard armored walls underneath. Kuzumi's desk was a massive semicircular piece of highly polished dark teak. On the wall to the left were a bank of TVs tuned in to various channels around the globe. The sound on all of them was currently muted. A small box on the left side of the desk controlled all the TVs and a computer sat there awaiting his instructions. Several phones were on the right side of the desk. Behind the desk, a three-drawer file cabinet squatted beneath a large painting. The painting depicted the same tattoo that was on Kuzumi's chest, in startling, brilliant colors.

It had been a long day for Kuzumi. There were always deals to be made, information to be absorbed, people to be dealt with, plans to be made. The last was always the most difficult. Kuzumi often felt like those chess champions who played in a large room against multiple opponents, moving from table to table, remembering the setup of each one. Except his stakes were much higher than simply losing a game. Kuzumi dealt in life and death and fortunes and the future of his country.

The Black Ocean was a legitimate organization most of the time, although Kuzumi saw the law as simply a set of rules the government had to abide by, not the Black Ocean. If he had to break it, so be it. He answered to a higher authority than words written by men in a book.

The Black Ocean controlled a vast amount of industry and land, both in Japan and overseas. What caused the government to cast a suspicious eye on it and the other secret societies was the fear of history repeating itself and the simple fact that the societies represented power. Any government with half a brain would keep an eye on the powerful organizations that existed within its borders and weren't directly under its control.

Kuzumi had become Genoysha in 1968. He had done so primarily because of his strength in the scientific and manufacturing field. He was one of the key architects, through the Black Ocean, in helping rebuild Japan from its wartime wreckage into the powerful economic juggernaut it currently was. Kuzumi being chosen by Genoysha Taiyo to be his successor was an indication of the appreciation of the role he had played in Japan's economic rebirth. Always before, the Genoysha had been selected from among the field operatives. A man of unquestioning loyalty and proven ability to fight for what the Society stood for. Kuzumi's field record was weak, but Genoysha Taiyo had done his job correctly, seeing the direction that Japan was heading in and picking the right type of leader the organization needed to change with the times. When the cancer that had been eating his insides finished Taiyo in 1968, it was Kuzumi's destiny to get the tattoo of Genoysha of the Black Ocean.

Kuzumi had wielded the power for the past thirty years, keeping the Black Ocean on a narrow path between the government, the people, the influence of other countries, and the Yakuza. There was no doubt he had succeeded so far in that he had much more influence among those other groups than they had with him. The Society controlled more wealth than many countries. It employed more people than most major corporations, although many of those who worked for it were unaware of the exact nature of their employer. But wealth and power was not the ultimate goal of the Society. The glory of Japan, and beyond and above Japan, the Sun Goddess and Emperor were.

Japan was the center of the world and as such all events must turn in the direction that benefited the islands. The Black Ocean and the other societies existed because the government and the people often lost their way and a steady hand behind the scenes was needed. It was Kuzumi's job to exercise that steady hand here and abroad.

That thought drew his mind to the west. San Francisco. The name of the city brought conflicting emotions. He turned his wheelchair to the file cabinet behind him. The metal it was constructed of was the same used to line jet engines, impervious to heat and blast. The lock could only be activated by his retina placed up against a scanner at his eye level on top of the cabinet. Anyone else attempting to open the cabinet would set off a thermal charge on the inside, destroying the contents.

Kuzumi leaned his forehead against the scanner and the

laser flickered across his eyes. With a loud click, the locks withdrew. Kuzumi opened the bottom drawer and drew out a small, intricately carved wooden box. He turned back to the desk, the box in his lap. He turned the small clasp and opened the lid. Tenderly he drew out a black-and-white photograph that lay on top of other documents. The picture had been folded and the paper was worn around the edges.

He had not looked at this for over twenty years. He blinked, then refocused his eyes. There was a very young woman standing with a baby in her arms. Behind her the Golden Gate Bridge arched over the water. The woman appeared to be part Caucasian, part Japanese, the blend mixing together to form an exotic beauty. She was tall and slender, the Western-style dress clinging to her body. Her hair was jet black and very long with edges of it framing her waist. Her skin was dark and her eyes coal black. The slant to them wasn't strong enough to pass in Japan but too far to pass as white in the West. Today he knew she would be considered beautiful, perhaps a model, but back then she was simply a half-breed.

"Nira," Kuzumi whispered, slowly putting the photograph down on his desk. Nira Foster. The name was strung like a harp string inside of him. A string that he had long ago thought he had put away by sheer force of will. Over half a century before that string had played hard and loud.

It was her beauty that Kuzumi had not been able to resist at first. That she was Dr. Lawrence's primary undergraduate assistant made her that much more attractive. She knew all that Lawrence did. Kuzumi had used that as a justification to get closer to her, not admitting the real reason, even to himself for a long time. That she had returned the attraction had not surprised him. She was half-Japanese and in those days there was much prejudice against Asians in California. She was also a budding physicist and Kuzumi represented the cutting edge of international study. He'd been published and she'd read his articles even before he'd arrived. He was three years older and had traveled the world. And, most importantly, he was the first true Japanese she had spent much time with.

Nira's father had been a petty officer in the American Navy. She didn't know her mother. Her father had dumped her in the care of a convent when she was two. She'd seen him several times over the next decade when he happened to be in port, but then he'd disappeared and she'd never heard from him again. He had never told her about her Japanese mother or where she had been born. There were no records at the convent other than the papers her father had signed to get her into it.

She'd done well on her own and the nuns had given her a good enough education to get a scholarship to UC-Berkeley, but there was a glass ceiling waiting for her and she was smart enough to know it. Her ethnic background and her gender limited her options in the United States. That intellectual awareness didn't temper her pain and anger, though.

Their first talks had been of atoms and particles and cadmium and all the other subjects that made up the burgeoning science they both were immersed in. Kuzumi could not recall when the talk had changed. He did remember the first time they had slept together. For two reasons. First, of course, was the experience itself, passionate and exciting beyond anything he had experienced before. But of more consequence was the fact that in his next message to be sent back to the Society through the Japanese Embassy pouch, he reported that he was involved with her, as was required by his standing orders.

He had been half-afraid he would be ordered to stop the relationship. What happened was worse. His instructions were to continue, build it, make it stronger. Then he was to recruit her. Kuzumi knew he would have to return to Japan soon to begin work on Genzai Bakudan. The Society wanted Nira to stay at UC-Berkeley and keep an eye on Lawrence and his work. They knew that Lawrence would undoubtedly be part of any atomic project the Americans developed and being an American citizen Nira was the perfect spy. Because of her father's abandonment, she hated the United States deep inside and it wasn't hard for Kuzumi to tap into that. He told her stories of a Japan she'd never seen and the different life she'd have there. They kept the relationship a secret so that there would be no stories of her liaison with Nishin to filter back to the FBI.

At first it had been easy to work Nira as an agent and to be her lover. Another part of the job coupled with certain distinct advantages. But the more he spent time with her and talked, the more Kuzumi realized he wasn't being honest or fair with Nira. He knew her Caucasian blood would keep her from being racially accepted in Japan. In fact, to be honest, he had to admit that she was treated better in the United States than she would be back in the Islands. And there was no doubt she could not study atomic physics in Japan. There were no women in the higher scientific fields. She would have to be a wife, but no true Japanese man would take her as wife because of her Western blood.

Kuzumi knew he could not take her back when he left and the orders of the Black Ocean reinforced that. She understood. As she understood everything about her situation. Her understanding disconcerted Kuzumi for a while until he realized it was because she was acting like a man would. Accepting reality stoically and with a sense of duty.

But she was still a woman, Kuzumi reminded himself. He should have remembered that. He looked at the picture again and the child in Nira's arms. He had left in the fall of '39, unaware of her condition. And she did not even tell him in the letters she sent, forwarded through the spy network the Society had tapped into. He was informed by his Sensei in the Black Ocean. They kept track of all their people and Nira could not hide the birth and the child from the spies who spied on the spies.

By then Kuzumi was wrapped up in Genzai Bakudan. As Nakanga had briefed Nishin, the government and military in Japan had not been impressed with the potential of the atom that Kuzumi had put into his report upon his return to Japan in 1939. But the Genoysha Taiyo had given him the go-ahead with all the resources of the Black Ocean to support him. "We do not have the time to wait on those fools," had been Taiyo's explanation. "They drive the country to war but they realize not how to negotiate the path. You have seen the beast we must fight. The United States will not break as easily as the General Staff thinks. We must have a weapon that will break them."

Kuzumi had to agree with that. Crossing the breadth of the United States by way of New York to San Francisco coming from Germany he had been numbed by the sheer vastness of the country. The industrial might and the numbers that the country could throw against Japan were chilling. But Kuzumi had understood something even more profound, something he had not shared with anyone. His relationship with Nira had shown him something, a paradox. Although Nira was not treated as equal, she *was* American. All Americans had come from other places at various times. To believe that the national psyche could be encapsulated so easily into a caricature of a weak-willed white man as the military would like was foolish. Kuzumi believed there was much more to the people across the great ocean, and he knew that to defeat them Japan would need more than it presently had.

Kuzumi was working at the Rikken, the national laboratories, when his Sensei told him of the birth of his son. In the same telling, he had been informed that nothing would be done. Nira was to stay in San Francisco and continue her duties. Kuzumi was to continue with Genzai Bakudan. And the boy, the boy was just a baby for now and not a factor to be considered yet.

Those were the exact words: "Not a factor to be considered yet." Kuzumi ran a liver-spotted finger across the picture. Nira had named him James and kept her American family name. James Foster. Strange for a child so clearly of Japanese ancestry. Her unmarried status piled another boulder on top of the many she had to shoulder. But she continued to work at UC-Berkeley and she continued to spy for the Society. And Kuzumi, well, he received this one photo at least in the beginning.

Genzai Bakudan. Nira. San Francisco. Kuzumi pressed his hands against the arms of his wheelchair. What were the Koreans up to? What had they discovered and what were they looking for? How had they found the cave? What had they learned about San Francisco and what were they looking for there?

This whole thing was making Kuzumi search memories he had long hoped had disappeared from his mind. A light blinked to his right. A line to his high-ranking contact in the Parliament. Another fire to be put out, probably something to do with the trade war being waged with the United States.

Kuzumi put the picture away and picked up the phone.

CHAPTER 5

SAN FRANCISCO
SUNDAY, 5 OCTOBER 1997
9:14 P.M. LOCAL

Lake watched the figure in the mirror. Muscles flowed as the legs and arms performed one of the required movements of a fourth-degree Aikido black belt.

''Kai!'' Lake yelled, his fist halting a millimeter from its reverse image. He slowly pulled the fist back as he returned to the beginning stance. The windows in the one-room efficiency were open and the chill night air hit the sweat pouring off his bare chest, creating a thin layer of steam. He wore only a pair of cutoff white painters' pants. His feet slid across the floor as he began another formalized kata. The calluses that years of working out had built up made little notice of the rough wood floor.

The room was empty except for his clothes hung and stacked in the closet. A bed sat near the window but Lake had never used it. He slept on a thin mat, moving its location on the floor every night. Sometimes he slept right under the window; sometimes just behind the door; sometimes he folded his body into the scant space in the bathroom, a gun always laying close at hand.

Lake's leg snapped up high: front kick to the face. He

froze for a second, then slowly lowered the leg, his head canted to one side. A phone was ringing down at the end of the hallway. A door slammed. Footsteps. Lake reached down and picked up the Hush Puppy, pulling the slide back and taking it off safe.

"Hey, man," a voice outside his door yelled. "You got a call."

"All right."

Lake waited as the footsteps retreated and the door slammed shut. He threw on a T-shirt and tucked the gun into the waistband of his shorts, making sure the shirt covered the handle. He checked the peephole, then pulled the chain off. He quietly walked down the hall and picked up the receiver on the battered pay phone.

"Yeah?"

"Hey, it's me." Jonas's voice was surprisingly clear. "I asked for the room number like you said. Man, when are you going to upgrade your facilities?"

Lake didn't feel like chatting. "What do you have?"

"They want their shit tonight."

"I said Monday night."

"Yeah, well, change of plans. They're throwing in an extra five grand for early delivery. And no deal if you don't deliver tonight."

Lake closed his eyes briefly, then they snapped open. "When and where?"

SUNDAY, 5 OCTOBER 1997
10:27 P.M. LOCAL

Two and a half miles away from Lake's hide, the computer awoke with a chime. The man had been reading a newspaper which he carefully folded before flipping open the lid. The display told him Nishin was moving. He shut the lid and gathered his equipment.

* * *

Nishin was indeed moving. He was following four North Koreans who had just left the ship. Two of the men carried duffle bags, but the ease with which they carried the folded bags told Nishin there was nothing in them.

Once they were off the pier he slithered down and followed, staying in the darker shadows, blacker than the night sky. The Koreans made little attempt to lose a tail, which Nishin had expected. They were not spies. They were soldiers.

North Korea's idea of covert operations was to take the uniforms off some soldiers and send them to a foreign country with specific orders on the mission to be accomplished. Subtlety was not a prized trait, as the North Koreans had demonstrated time and time again in their operations. Being on the other side of the Sea of Japan from the Korean Peninsula, Nishin was familiar with their operations. On top of that, his preparations for the mission into Hungnam had required intelligence preparations that had updated him on his potential foes. He had to know their history to know what they could be capable of in the present.

History said the North Koreans were direct and to the point when it came to taking action. In 1968 thirty-one North Korean soldiers had infiltrated across the DMZ and made their way down to Seoul to raid the Blue House, the home of the South Korean president. The mission had failed, with twenty-eight men killed, two missing, and one captured.

Shortly after that attack, on 23 January 1968, North Korean Special Forces men in high-speed attack craft seized the U.S.S. *Pueblo* with highly publicized results. Later that same year, a large North Korean force of almost a hundred men conducted landings on the coast of South Korea in an attempt to raise the populace against the government. It failed, but such failures didn't daunt the North Korean government. In 1969, a U.S. electronic warfare aircraft was shot down by the North Koreans, killing all thirty-one

American service members on board. To these transgressions it looked like all the outside world could do was sputter in indignation. World opinion meant nothing to Pyongyang.

The Korean DMZ was the hottest place on earth, and contrary to what most people believed, Nishin knew it was active with both sides probing the security of the other side. People died there every year, but usually they were only Koreans, and Nishin was worldwise enough to know that in the West that didn't mean much. When an American officer was beaten to death in the same place by North Korean guards with ax handles—now that was news over here.

As security stiffened in South Korea over the decade of the seventies, North Korea moved its attentions overseas, not caring about the international effect. In 1983, three PKA officers planted a bomb in Rangoon in an attempt to kill the visiting South Korean president. That mission also failed, although of course there were those in the way who died. Later in 1983, four North Korean trawlers—similar to the one Nishin had been conducting surveillance on—infiltrated the Gulf of California to conduct monitoring operations against the United States mainland. One of the ships was seized by the Mexican authorities, but that didn't prevent the North Koreans from continuing such operations.

The breakup of the Soviet Union had never been acknowledged by Pyongyang, except in cryptically worded exhortations to the people, telling them they were the last bastion of communism in the world. The North Koreans truly believed they were part of the final line in the war against Western imperialism, especially with Cuba crumbling around the edges.

Nishin had never heard of the North Koreans conducting an active covert operation on American soil, but he also had never heard of the Genzai Bakudan project or Hungnam before this month. With stakes this high, who knows what they were capable of? That wasn't the question that concerned Nishin, though. The question was what were they here for? What evidence of Genzai Bakudan was here in San Francisco? Nishin hoped he would soon find out and leave this country of no values.

The Koreans continued up the Embarcadero, through the center of the waterfront tourist district. It wasn't hard for Nishin to follow. He made sure he was inland of them, prepared if they turned in the only other direction they could go. After twenty minutes they passed Fisherman's Wharf. They circled around Fort Mason, moving purposefully and ignoring all other pedestrians. As they passed the marina, there were less and less people around. Then they were into the Presidio, the former army post that had been turned over to the National Park Service.

First established in 1776 by Spanish explorers, the Presidio evolved into a military post for the area. Covering sixty-eight square miles of land at the northern point of the peninsula, the terrain that didn't hold former military buildings was covered with pine and eucalyptus trees, making it an ideal site for covert operations at night, Nishin knew. In 1993 as part of the base-closings trend the post had transitioned from the military to become the Golden Gate National Recreation Area, which removed the gates and the military police that used to patrol the area.

Nishin looked up. The Golden Gate Bridge was close now, straddling the horizon north of the hills of the Presidio. He felt more comfortable in the park. There were very few people about and there was foliage that he could melt into. The Koreans were more at home also. They left the paths and moved cross-country, spreading out like an infantry squad approaching an objective.

Nishin followed until they reached their destination, underneath the arch of the bridge itself. He watched as they slipped into the front entrance of Fort Point, one of the men breaking open the lock that closed the large metal gates. Nishin stayed to the side of the parking lot to the south, considering the situation. He knew this area based on the study he had made of San Francisco on the flight over.

The fort was old, having first been built in 1854 and completed in 1860, just in time for the American Civil War. For over seventy years it had been the dominating man-made feature on the southern land tip of the narrowest part of the Golden Gate. The fort itself was made of brick like a cousin on the east coast: Fort Sumter, which didn't fare very well against the advent of rifled cannons. But although the brick walls would have quickly crumbled under the cannonade of modern weapons developed shortly after the fort was constructed, in the 1930s the unique construction—for San Francisco at least, a mostly wood and concrete town—saved it, because in 1938 a more spectacular man-made feature made its appearance on the point. The fort was in the way and initial plans for the Golden Gate Bridge called for it to be torn down. Only a strong protest by locals prevented the dismantling of the fort during the building of the bridge. So now the first southern arches of the bridge swoop over the fort, leading out to the south tower.

Nishin knew there was a museum inside the fort. Were the Koreans breaking into that? Was there some document or artifact in the museum that referred to Genzai Bakudan? And what were the duffle bags for? Setting his bag and case down, he opened the latter and pulled out the AUG and made sure he had a round in the chamber, then settled in to wait uphill from the fort, with a good view of both the open courtyard inside and the parking lot in front.

A faint noise up in the hills caught Nishin's attention. It sounded like a car engine, but the noise was gone as quickly as it had come. He focused on the fort.

The time switch from the following night to this evening was something Lake would have done himself. That set him on edge because it meant the people he was meeting weren't stupid. The lack of time meant several things. First, he had to rush to the drop site to pick up the weapons.

Second, he would not be able to put the meet site under surveillance. Third, any backup team he might request from the Ranch would not be here until tomorrow morning. As he had been working out, he had been mulling over whether he should call the Ranch and ask for help or if he would do this alone. He had pretty much decided to run this op solo and this phone call sealed it. There was no way he could get local backup, which was one of the disadvantages of his deep cover.

Lake also knew that Ranch standard operating procedure required that he not make the meeting. Without backup standing by just in case he would be in a precarious situation, especially since the Ranch didn't know he was doing the meet this evening. He had told Jonas the meet would be the following night and he should stay with that. Use his leverage as possessor of the weapons to make the buyers stay with the original agreement. But there was also the possibility the buyers might get spooked and go elsewhere. The mysterious Japanese–Patriot connection was too strong of a lure for Lake.

The drop site was in a storage unit. Lake unlocked the combination lock and pulled up the door. Two crates and one small box lay just inside, in front of other boxes containing various equipment. The Ranch was anything but inefficient. He didn't know who had put the guns in there and he was sure that that person didn't know he was taking them out. The storage unit was a good cutout between operatives and support personnel.

Lake uncrated the eight Ingram MAC-10s and the ammunition. The MAC-10 was American made and very popular with the drug underworld. It was made of stamped metal and very small, easily concealable under a jacket. These were longer than normal because of the requirement to have a suppressor on the end of the short barrel, which more than doubled their length to almost eighteen inches. The stock was made of metal and folded up along the body of the weapon.

The ammunition in the small box was also special, which explained why Lake had charged so much for the 9mm rounds. They were subsonic bullets, designed not to break the speed of sound; they worked in conjunction with the suppressor. The firer lost some power and range with the adapted bullets, but they made hardly any sound at all when fired, just like the ones he had loaded in his Hush Puppy. Because the weapon was automatic, though, the metal-on-metal sound of the bolt working and rounds being ejected would make a sound, but very little when compared to the normal sound of a gun being fired.

Lake worked on one of the Ingrams, secreting a small transmitter underneath the small plastic piece on the back of the pistol grip; a place no one would have any reason to look. He tied the submachine guns together, then wrapped plastic bags around them, waterproofing both them and the ammo. The package was bulky, but he managed to stuff it into a large rucksack.

Lake relocked the door to the bin. He had time to make it to the designated meet site, just barely. He put the rucksack on the passenger seat of his old Bronco II and began driving through the streets of San Francisco.

As he drove, Lake put the finishing touches on the story he would have to give Feliks for breaking Ranch SOP. He considered the upcoming situation, but he knew he would have to play it by ear when he arrived since he knew nothing of the people he was to meet.

By the time he arrived in the Golden Gate National Recreation Area, he was shifting into his action mode. He continued down Marine Drive toward the fort. There was no sense trying to sneak up on the meet site since the other party held the advantage of time and place. Lake parked at the far end of the parking lot from the fort. Taking the rucksack, he left the truck.

The gates to the fort were wide open. Lake felt naked walking across the parking lot and he knew that he was being watched. He noted that there were no other vehicles about. As he entered the brick archway he sensed someone behind and spun about. Two dark figures stood there, blocking his way out.

"Come in!" a heavily accented voice echoed in the courtyard. The voice was high-pitched, which fit Jonas's description of Asians. Lake turned and walked forward. The courtyard was surrounded by the fort's walls, three stories high on all sides with brick arches opening to the mezzanines. Several cannon were mounted for display on the concrete floor. Lake couldn't see who had called out. The voice could have come from one of dozens of arched openings on any side, from any floor.

Lake walked directly to the middle and put the rucksack down. He folded his arms over his chest and waited. The two men who had followed him were standing on the inside of the entrance, also waiting.

A slight shuffle caught his attention and Lake turned. Two other men were walking out of the shadows from the north wall.

"You have the guns?" the man on the right asked. As he cleared the shadows, Lake finally got a good look at his face. Korean. There was no mistaking the facial features.

"We weren't supposed to meet until tomorrow night," Lake replied.

"You have the guns?"

"I have them."

The leader gestured and the man at his side came forward and opened the rucksack, checking the weapons and ammunition.

"The money?" Lake asked.

The man was breaking down one of the weapons, his hands moving expertly over the metal pieces despite the lack of light. Jonas was right; these men had the look of professional soldiers.

"It is functional," the man called out to his leader in Han Gul, the language of the Korean peninsula. Lake assumed that the Koreans didn't know he understood their

language and he wanted to keep it that way until he was forced to disclose his knowledge.

"The money?" Lake repeated.

"You will be paid," the leader said. *"Kill him,"* he called out in Han Gul to his men. Lake's language ability had remained secret for all of ten seconds.

The man with the Ingrams near Lake was sliding a magazine into one of the weapons. Lake had always considered it a fundamentally unsound business practice in the arms trade to be killed by your own merchandise. He turn-kicked toward the man with the MAC-10 only to have the man sidestep the strike, grab his leg, and twist, dumping Lake on his back. The Korean unfolded the stock of the MAC-10, put it into his shoulder and aimed down at Lake.

Sparks flew off the concrete floor near the Korean and Lake could feel the presence of bullets flying by, although he heard no sound of firing. He rolled and looked up, spotting the muzzle flash of a weapon being fired high up on the south wall. The Korean who had been about to shoot Lake rolled right, out of the way of the unexpected firing, grabbing the duffel bag with the other weapons and getting under the cover of one of the large cannons.

Lake didn't stop to savor his reprieve. He scuttled on his back, the concrete ripping through his shirt, getting behind the cover of a large pyramid of cannonballs. At least covered from the Koreans, Lake realized as soon as he was there. Whoever the gunman on the wall was had a perfect shot at him, but whoever it was had had a perfect shot at him earlier and hadn't taken advantage of it.

The Korean let loose a sustained burst of fire up at the wall, but the man was firing blindly, not sure where his target was. The gun battle was eerie, played out in almost total silence, only the flaming strobe of the muzzle flashes and the sparks of rounds ricocheting giving any hint as to what was happening.

Lake drew his pistol and waited, peering around the cannonballs. The Korean leader had joined the gunman. While one provided cover, the other ran with the duffel bag toward the archway where the other two waited. Lake got a perfect sight picture on the back of the running man and his finger began to bear down when he halted. He remembered what had happened on the bridge. He relieved the pressure on the trigger and watched as the man made it to the safety of the entrance arch. The three men there then provided cover as the leader joined them. Whoever was on the wall had not fired again since the initial bursts. Lake assumed that the gunman was gone.

Silence reigned and Lake did nothing to break it. He gave the Koreans plenty of time to escape, then stood. He didn't hear any sirens. Time to be going. Lake cautiously made his way to the entryway and slipped through. He chose the quickest way across the parking lot to his truck. Throwing it in gear he got away from the fort as quickly as possible.

Nishin watched the weapons dealer leave. When Nishin had seen that the man carried Ingram MAC-10s, he'd known that this meeting was not what he was after. He would have let the North Koreans kill the man except for the fact that it would have drawn unwanted attention from the American authorities. The Koreans were so obtuse at covert operations that they didn't understand the consequences of such actions. Nishin knew they would just assume his firing to be part of the man's backup, so he had not tipped his hand there.

What Nishin wanted to know was what did the Koreans need weapons for? What did they have planned next? To find that out, he would have to go back to his perch near the dock. Nishin faded away to the southeast.

Which left only one man in the area. The last watcher wasn't worried about where the Koreans went because he knew that Nishin would stay with them and he had the computer which would tell him where Nishin was.

The weapons dealer didn't concern him either. Guns were a part of the American culture and this man was of no concern. The last watcher had the same questions as Nishin. He packed up his night-scope and went back to his van.

SAPPORO, HOKKAIDO, JAPAN
MONDAY, 6 OCTOBER 1997
9:00 P.M. LOCAL

"Weapons?"

"Yes, Genoysha," Nakanga said. "That is what they wanted."

Kuzumi sighed. Still no idea what the Koreans were up to. "Anything else?"

"No, Genoysha."

Kuzumi turned his wheelchair away from the desk. He heard the pad of Nakanga's feet across the wooden floor, then the door shutting. He pressed up against the eye scanner and opened the file cabinet. Again he pulled up the wooden box. He turned back to the desk, putting the box on top. He opened the cover and took the picture out. He carefully unfolded the paper and leaned it against one of the phones, angled so he could see it.

He had looked at the picture every day for eight years in the same manner. Except then it was leaned up against the pitted concrete wall of his cell. When they came for him each day, he would fold it and put it back in the breast pocket of his prison shirt.

Other than the clothes he wore, it had been the only personal thing he had with him when he'd flown out of Hungnam on the third of August in 1945. By orders he had had to leave everything else in the assembly cave.

Kuzumi rubbed his left temple as he remembered the crowded cargo airplane. There were no seats and all the senior scientists who had worked on Genzai Bakudan were seated on the bare metal floor of the converted bomber. They were heading back to Japan, but not directly. They knew the Russians would be waiting in the Sea of Japan and there wasn't enough fuel anyway to make the hop directly. So they flew north, along the coast of the Korean peninsula. They would refuel at an air force base in Manchuria, then make the shorter hop across the sea there to the northern island of Hokkaido and the home of the Black Ocean.

They were excited, staring out the windows, back toward Hungnam. The flash of the bomb going off had come on the horizon less than twenty minutes after they'd departed. They'd celebrated, slapping each other on the back. It worked! There was hope that all could be changed!

An hour later the pilots climbed over land again, crossing the mountains on the shore and then quickly dipping down toward the airfield. They were just about on the ground before anyone realized something was wrong. The large white pieces of cloth scattered around were parachutes. A machine gun at the end of the runway opened fire. Planes with the red star descended out of the clouds like wolves after a rabbit.

Kuzumi could see Russian paratroopers firing their rifles at the plane as the pilot desperately tried to pull up. A stream of bullets tore through the fuselage and men screamed as the large-caliber bullets found flesh. The plane tipped over and slammed into the ground.

Kuzumi woke up in agony, pain spiking through his back. He was in the back half of the plane, he could tell that, but there was no front half. Daylight streamed in. He could hear voices yelling in Russian. He reached down his side and with difficulty flipped open the holster holding his Model 94 pistol. For some reason he was having great trouble moving his arms. He pulled the pistol up and put the muzzle to the side of his head as he saw a Russian officer climb into the wreckage. Kuzumi pulled the trigger.

Nothing.

He pulled again, then remembered he had not pulled back the slide to chamber a round. He reached to do it but a jackboot slammed down on his right hand, pinning it to the floor of the plane. Kuzumi could feel bones crack in his hand.

The Russian officer stooped over and took the pistol. The man laughed and shook his head as he tucked the souvenir into his belt. Then he spit in Kuzumi's face as other soldiers clambered into the wreckage. They dragged Kuzumi out of the remains of the plane. He spent a few days trussed there at the airfield, lying in his own excrement and in agony before a senior officer arrived. They cleaned Kuzumi up and took him on a Russian plane to a camp in the middle of Siberia. Kuzumi had only a glimpse at it as they dragged him off the plane to the prison building. He didn't see the world outside that building for eight years.

Kuzumi looked down at his right hand. The fingers had never healed properly. Nothing had. The Russians had used every injury he suffered in the crash for their torture and then made new ones.

Eight years. Eight years of needles directly into his spine where the bone had been broken. The nerves manipulated to bring forth pain. Eight years of the fingers being bent back again and again and again. The drugs, the lack of sleep and food. The water dripping through his cell. The illnesses. The total lack of communication with any human being other than his torturers. Then the brief moments where they reversed the process and lavished food and rest upon him for a day or two to make the lack even more noticeable. Then they would kick the door open and take it all away and begin the torture anew.

But they let him keep the picture. He now knew why. To remind him of another life and to quicken his breaking under their control. But it had worked the opposite way. The picture gave him strength. There was life out there. Or so he had thought. So he had thought for those eight long years.

Kuzumi leaned back in his wheelchair. The Russians had wanted information. They had seen the blast from Genzai Bakudan. They had known of the program from their own spies. They wanted the secret of the atom. But Kuzumi had never spoken. Never said a word. No matter what they did. For eight years. The Russians got their secrets to develop a bomb elsewhere and when they finally exploded their first one, Kuzumi was no longer valuable in that capacity.

The Society saved him. The Russians no longer needed the secrets in Kuzumi's head. A bullet in the brain would have been par for the KGB men who controlled his fate. But the Society made Kuzumi valuable to the Russians through a discreet Red Chinese agent. They offered money, minerals, and other valuables for the wreck of a body that Kuzumi was. There was a discreet exchange of man for treasure on one of the small Kuril Islands that were in dispute between Russia and Japan.

Kuzumi never walked again. He was returned to Hokkaido. And found out the strength he had drawn from the picture was long gone. So he had embraced the Society that had saved him with all his heart and soul, knowing that never again would he open a space in there for another human being.

Kuzumi took the picture and refolded it. He put it back in the box. The Russians had gone through great lengths for eight years trying to unlock the secret of Genzai Bakudan. Now, what were the North Koreans after and how much of a price were *they* willing to pay?

CHAPTER 6

SAN FRANCISCO
MONDAY, 6 OCTOBER 1997
10:45 P.M. LOCAL

"... and on top of all that, you didn't get paid."

Lake removed the special satellite phone from his ear and looked at it for a second, then put it back. "At least I didn't kill everyone this time," he said.

"Thank God for little favors." Feliks's voice dripped sarcasm. "Where are your friends now?"

Lake looked out the grimy windshield of the battered Bronco II. He'd checked the homing device as soon as he'd got back to his hiding place and tracked down the bug he'd planted in the Ingram. It had led him to this section of the San Francisco port. He'd parked behind a large abandoned Dumpster with a clear view of the trawler the electronic device told him the Koreans—or, more accurately, the guns the Koreans had stolen—were on board. He relayed that information to Feliks along with the name of the ship: *Am Nok Sung*.

"It's flying the South Korean flag," Lake added. He'd stolen the Bronco II two days ago from the outer parking lot of the airport after making sure its parking ticket had just been issued that morning. It wouldn't be missed for several days and Lake planned on dumping it sooner than that.

"I'll run the registry on the ship," Feliks said. "I don't understand why the South Koreans would be running an operation in the United States."

"There's no love lost between the Koreans and the Japanese," Lake said.

"Do you think they might be connected to the event the other night?" Feliks asked.

"I don't know," Lake said. "There's no indication they are except that they went to the Patriots to get weapons, but they could have picked that information up anywhere."

"What do you think they have planned?"

"I don't have a clue," Lake said, a little tired of the questioning. "That's why I'm sitting here watching them."

"Let's not get some friendlies killed with weapons we sold," Feliks said. He paused. "I've got the registry information on the *Am Nok Sung* coming up on the screen right now. It might be flying the South Korean flag, but it's registered in Nigeria. That's a pretty common practice to save on registration fees."

"Who registered it?" Lake asked. A burst of static rippled through the phone and he pulled the phone away from his ear for a second.

"That will take a while," Feliks said. "We found the message that recruited Starry and Preston on the Internet. I'll have a copy put in your drop, but it's not much help. It simply gives them an agency to call and leave a message with their own number. We checked the agency and the drop was paid for in cash. No one remembers who placed it. It was discontinued after two weeks."

"A dead end," Lake said. He was surprised at that. The computer whizzes at the Ranch should have been able to do more. Unless, of course, whoever had placed the message was as smart as they were. Which pointed beyond the Patriots, who weren't exactly known for their collective IQ level.

"We're scanning the Internet, looking for any other similar messages in case whoever sent the first one sends another to get it done right this time."

Not likely, Lake thought. He was beginning to respect whoever was pulling the strings here.

"By the way," Feliks added, "who fired the other shots last night? The ones that saved your butt?"

"I don't know." Lake had been asking himself the same question all day. He knew it meant one of two things: either he was being followed or the Koreans were being followed. He'd used all his skills earlier in the day when he'd stolen the Bronco and gone to the meet site to make sure he wasn't followed, so that left the latter as the only viable possibility. He told Feliks that.

"Well, if you don't figure out what these people are up to in the next couple of days I'm going to have to tip off the ATF and have them recover the guns," Feliks said. "That will also take care of our Korean problem."

"They're moving," Lake said.

"Excuse me?"

Lake watched a party of six men wearing long tan raincoats walking down the gangplank off the trawler. "The Koreans are moving," Lake repeated. "I'll send you a postcard when they get to their destination. Out." He turned off the satellite phone and watched. He had no doubt that each man had a MAC-10 hidden under his raincoat.

The men moved to the end of the pier and turned to the east, following the waterfront. Lake started the engine and began following at a considerable distance; his direction finder told him that one of the men was carrying the MAC-10 with a bug in it, so he didn't have to keep them constantly in sight.

In the crane control room, Nishin also waited until the men were out of sight, then he carefully climbed down. He had spotted the Bronco II when it had pulled in. He now regretted his decision of the previous evening to save the gun dealer; the man was turning out to be a nuisance. Nishin assumed he wanted his money, although how he had found the North Koreans' ship concerned Nishin.

Nishin slid into the darker shadows and followed the band of Koreans. He watched as they broke into the first two cars they found parked and hot-wired them. As they drove off, Nishin quickly broke into another car around the corner and did the same.

Not very subtle, Lake thought as he watched the Koreans steal an old model Ford LTD and a newer Camaro. They'd simply broken the glass on the driver's side, unlocked the doors, and climbed in. They at least had the expertise to smash open the steering column and get the engines started.

He followed the two-car convoy southeast along Columbus Avenue. He noticed a black pickup following farther back and made a note to keep an eye on it. What he did not notice, because it was out of sight, was the white van four blocks back, following the entire procession.

Directly ahead, Lake could see the bulk of the Transamerica Pyramid filling the night sky. Columbus Avenue ended at the base of the pyramid and the Koreans turned to the half-right, going down Montgomery Street. The black pickup was still following.

"One big happy family," Lake muttered.

The procession continued until they were on I-80, heading for the San Francisco–Oakland Bay Bridge. The toll was only for westbound vehicles and traffic this time of evening was relatively light. Glancing in his rearview mirror, Lake could tell that the black pickup was holding its position. The two stolen cars were ahead in the far-right lane and scrupulously staying at the speed limit. They were on the lower level of the bridge, along with all the other eastbound traffic.

Lake didn't like his position between the Koreans and whoever was trailing. He was too close to the Koreans, and there was a good chance they would detect his presence.

He didn't want to take a chance, though, and go behind the pickup, since he didn't know who was at the wheel of that vehicle. For all he knew there were other Koreans in it.

They approached Yerba Buena Island, the midpoint for the four-and-a-half-mile bridge complex. If the Golden Gate Bridge wasn't so near, the Bay Bridge would perhaps be better known to those outside of the San Francisco area. Finished within a few months of its more famous sister in 1936, it had two levels, with westbound traffic on the top five lanes and eastbound on the bottom five. A quarter million cars a day crossed the bridge, and its partial collapse in the 1994 earthquake had caused massive commuter problems for the Bay area.

The bridge actually consisted of two major sections. The western, which Lake was coming to the end of, consisted of two suspension bridges, attached in the middle by a central concrete anchorage which was sunk deep into the center of the bay. The eastern part of this section touched land at Yerba Buena Island, bore through a tunnel in the island, then hit the other section of the Bay Bridge, which was a cantilever bridge built on over twenty piers leading into Oakland.

Lake passed under the last tower of the western suspension section. He was a hundred feet behind the Camaro, which was right on the bumper of the LTD. Both cars slipped into the mouth of the tunnel and Lake kept his distance. He glanced in his rearview mirror; the pickup was also keeping its place.

As Lake returned his attention to the front, he automatically pulled his foot off the gas pedal. The brake lights on the Camaro were bright red in the tunnel ahead. Lake heard the squeal of rubber as the Camaro spun about. A car in the other lane narrowly avoided collision, swerving out of the way. Lake slammed his foot on the brake as the headlights of the Camaro fixed on his windshield.

He halted but the other car didn't. The front bumper of the Camaro smashed into the left-front grill of the Bronco

II, jolting Lake forward against his seat belt, then his head snapping back, bouncing against the headrest. The Camaro pinned the Bronco against the wall of the tunnel, the right-front side of the truck hitting concrete.

Two men jumped out of the Camaro, MAC-10s at the ready. Lake ducked before they fired, the bullets shattering the windshield above him, showering him with broken glass.

He unbuckled his seat beat and slithered between the front seats into the back where the backseat was down. Bullets continued to stream by over his head. He added a few rounds of his own with the Hush Puppy, shooting out the large window in the right corner of the cargo bay.

Lake gathered himself and dove out through the opening he had just created. He bounced off the right wall of the tunnel, grunting as he felt pain jar through his shoulder. Hitting the pavement, he rolled, pistol at the ready, peering underneath his Bronco. He could see the legs of the Korean on the near side of the Camaro. He fired twice, both rounds hitting the man in the ankle, tearing his leg out from under him. Lake fired again at the prone figure, this time a head shot, killing the stunned man instantly. All of four seconds had elapsed since the accident and the only noise had been that of the collision and the bullets shattering glass.

Now, there was the sound of another car coming to a hurried halt and Lake took a chance, popping his head up over the side of the cargo bay he had just come out of to see what the tactical situation was. He expected the LTD to be there, disgorging more gunmen, but was surprised instead to see the black pickup twenty feet away and a man leaning out the passenger side, a silenced Steyr automatic rifle in his hands. The man hosed down the second Korean, blowing blood and guts all over the right side of the Camaro. Lake froze an image of the man in his memory: Asian, more Japanese features than Korean, short and thin, and from the way he handled the gun, a professional at the job of killing.

Lake's visual inventory was brought to an abrupt halt as the man turned the smoking barrel of the Steyr in his direction. For the second time Lake dove for cover as bullets tore chips out of the concrete above his head. Lake fired underneath, but the man was inside the pickup and all Lake could shoot at was the tires.

The firing suddenly ceased and Lake heard a vehicle accelerate away. He carefully edged his head around the rear of the Bronco. The pickup was gone. Two smashed vehicles and two dead bodies. He watched the pickup disappear down the tunnel to the east.

"Fuck," Lake said, standing up and dusting off broken glass from his clothes. There was a bottleneck of frightened motorists in their cars to the west but no sign of police yet. Lake reached into the front of the Bronco and pulled out his homing device. There was nothing else in the truck that could identify him.

Lake brought the muzzle of his weapon up as a white van wove its way through the halted cars and raced up to him. He had a perfect sight picture on the driver who leaned over and threw open the passenger door. "Get in!" the man yelled.

Another Japanese, Lake noted, keeping his weapon steady. He heard sirens in the distance.

"Get in!" the man repeated. The sirens were getting closer.

Lake hopped in, keeping his weapon trained on the driver. The man took off, heading west. They passed through the tunnel and out into the night air on the other side of Yerba Buena Island, onto the eastern section of the bridge.

"I don't see them," the driver said, peering ahead.

"And you are?" Lake asked.

The driver's attention remained focused ahead. He appeared to be young, somewhere in his mid-twenties by Lake's best guess. He wore gold-rimmed glasses and a very nice dark gray suit. Lake pressed the barrel of his pistol into the side of that suit and repeated his question. "Who are you?"

"Yariyasu Araki," the man replied.

Lake spared a glance out the windshield. There was indeed no sign of either the pickup or the LTD. "And you are with?" Lake asked.

"Japanese CPI," the man said. "I assume you are with a United States government agency," he added.

"Why do you assume that?" Lake asked. He knew what CPI was: a secret arm of the Japanese government, the Central Political Intelligence, a cousin to the Ranch, formed after the Tokyo gas attacks a few years back. Its mission was to keep track of Japan's fringe groups. The covert world was a small one, and despite all the secrecy the various agencies had an idea of each other's existence on a level unknown even to their own governments.

"I intercepted your recent satellite communication phone conversation with what appeared to be your boss," Araki said.

Lake was impressed. The Ranch's equipment was top-notch and the satellite phone was supposed to be totally secure.

"Also, you were following the Koreans," Araki continued.

Lake wasn't sure whether to take Araki for what he claimed, but since Lake had the gun in the man's side, he wasn't overly concerned at the present moment about the veracity of the other man's claim. With his right hand, Lake flipped open the cover on his direction finder and turned it on.

Araki glanced over as they descended into Oakland. "You have a fix on them?"

Lake nodded. "They're northeast."

Nishin stayed with I-80 as it turned to the north and ran along the bay.

"Coming up on due east," Lake reported.

Nishin took the University Avenue exit and, first chance

he had, pulled into a parking lot. "Do you mind?" he asked, pointing at the gun which Lake still had poking into his side.

"Actually, I do mind," Lake replied, keeping it in place. "I have no proof you are who you say you are and I just had two different groups of people shoot at me for no reason that I know of. So forgive me if I'm not exactly in the most friendly mood."

"I understand your concerns about my identity," Araki said. His English was precise and each word was enunciated clearly. "But you must know that I do not carry an identification card. I am working in your country on a mission of deep concern to my own country."

"Pretty weak," Lake said, checking the direction finder. The small dot indicating the Koreans had stopped a few miles to the east. "Unfortunately, I really don't have the time to have a deep discussion with you about all this. There's some people I have to catch up with."

Araki nodded. "The North Koreans."

"They're from the North?" Lake wasn't too surprised. "What are they doing here?"

"I don't know," Araki replied.

"Why are you following them, then?"

"I am not following them," Araki said. "I am following a man who is following them."

"The Japanese guy with the Steyr AUG," Lake said.

"Correct."

"And who is he?"

"That is my concern," Araki said.

"He tried blowing my head off back there in the tunnel," Lake said. "That makes it my concern. Also, bud, in case you haven't noticed, you're in America now. I could have your ass thrown in jail."

"As you threw me in jail, would you also admit to selling the Koreans those weapons last night?" Araki asked in a level voice.

Lake pushed the barrel harder into Araki's side, evoking

a surprised grunt of pain. "Don't fuck with me, son. I could also just make you disappear."

"I imagine you could," Araki said. Lake could see him swallow, trying to control his fear. The man was doing a reasonably good job of remaining calm, but Lake sensed that Araki wasn't a seasoned agent. He didn't have the hard edge that men in the world of covert operations gained after only a few years in the field—if they survived that long. Of course, he could also be better than most and a good actor. That made Lake wonder exactly what Araki's role here was.

"We need each other," Araki said.

"Why do I need you?" Lake said, checking the direction finder one more time. The dot was still stationary.

"I want the Japanese man," Araki said. "You want the Koreans. But I do not think you know what the Koreans are up to. I do not know what Nishin—that is his name—is up to, other than the fact he is following the Koreans also. There are many unanswered questions. Two minds can answer them better than one. I have access to my agency's resources, which are quite extensive. Remember, the enemy of my enemy is my friend."

Lake snorted. "You sound like fucking Confucius."

"Confucius was Chinese," Araki began. "I am—"

"Yes, Confucius was Chinese," Lake interrupted. "Confucius, originally known as Kung Chiu, born 551 B.C., died 479." He removed the gun from Araki's side and holstered it. "Personal virtue, devotion to family, most especially one's ancestors, and to justice—all are tenets of his teachings." Lake tapped the direction finder. "In the interests of justice, let's track these little shitheads down."

Araki was staring at Lake. He turned the key, restarting the engine. "Yes. Let us go."

They drove up University Avenue. The dot on Lake's screen remained stationary. "I'd say they are about three or four miles, dead ahead," Lake said.

* * *

At the university, Nishin watched as the four remaining Koreans parked the LTD. His own lights were off and he'd kept a more discreet distance behind ever since the gunfight in the tunnel. Obviously the Koreans had spotted the American gun dealer and in their usual abrupt manner had decided to stop him from following them. Nishin was disappointed that he had not been able to kill the American, but at least there were two less of the enemy to deal with. More importantly, whatever the North Koreans were after now must be the key to their mission, otherwise they would not have caused such an incident to prevent someone from following them.

Nishin glanced around. The University of California at Berkeley was not unknown to him. It had a reputation as a center of liberalism and protest that Nishin had heard of in his time working underground in the States during his training. The campus was practically deserted this time of night, but Nishin knew there must be some type of campus police and he kept an eye out for patrol cars as he parked the pickup truck behind a building, across the street from the lot where the Koreans had parked.

He quickly ran across, keeping the four men in sight. He had the Steyr tucked in to his side, a fresh magazine in the chamber. The Koreans walked up to the side door of a large academic building and opened the door, disappearing inside. The name on the building, Wellman Hall, meant nothing to Nishin.

Nishin paused outside the door, then decided to move along the outside wall and find another way in. He found a door two hundred meters farther down and cracked it open. He was in a short corridor. Moving forward, he peeked around the edge, toward where the Koreans had entered. There was no one there, but he could hear noises, as if someone was moving something heavy about. There was a light on every twenty feet, giving a faint glow to the hallway.

He got to his knees and peered around the next hallway.

A Korean, MAC-10 at the ready, stood guard outside a door, forty feet away. Nishin sat down, back against the wall and became perfectly still.

Araki drove the van into the west entrance of the UC-Berkeley campus.

"Close now," Lake said. He continued giving directions as they wove through the campus, until he spotted the LTD parked outside one of the buildings. "There she is."

Araki drove farther down the street and parked the van in a position where they could observe the car.

"Any ideas why they would be here?" Lake asked. He pulled his gun out of the holster and replaced the magazine with a fully loaded one, Araki watching the action.

"No."

"So who is this guy Nishin that you're following?"

"He is a member of the Black Ocean Society."

"A ronin," Lake said.

The comment earned him a surprised look from Araki. "You know of the societies?"

"A little," Lake said. "They're your version of our Patriot groups or militias. Bunch of wackos running around so far right of right that they aren't even on the map board anymore."

"But our societies have been in existence for many years," Araki said, "while yours are a recent phenomenon. The Black Ocean dates back well before World War II. You used the term ronin," Araki continued. "That is what an agent of one of the overseas societies used to be called. I suspect your knowledge is deeper than you are willing to admit."

"I ain't admitting anything," Lake said. "And you still haven't told me much about Nishin."

"I do not have much to tell other than some of his background. As I told you earlier, I do not know why he is here in the United States, but there is no doubt that it is not for a noble reason."

Lake thought about it. Could there be a connection between the Japanese societies and the American Patriots? While seemingly far-fetched on the surface, the concept held intriguing possibilities if one looked deeper. Starry and Preston on the bridge with the paint sprayer. The part-Japanese man in the boat below. Most curious. Lake pulled back the slide on the Hush Puppy, insuring a round was ready in the chamber.

Nishin heard someone cry out what sounded like an order, but he couldn't make out the words. Boots pounded on the tile. Close to the floor, Nishin looked around the corner. The four Koreans were running toward the door, one of them holding a cardboard box in his arms. Nishin sprang to his feet and the second they were out the door, he sprinted after them.

"There!" Araki cried out.

Four men were hurrying across the lawn toward the LTD.

"They've got something," Lake noted.

"What now?" Araki asked.

"We—" Lake paused as another figure came out of the building. "Shit!" As the last figure raised the Steyr automatic rifle and opened up on the Koreans, Lake kicked open the door to the van.

The man with the box tumbled down, papers spilling out. The other three Koreans dove for cover behind some abstract concrete sculptures that decorated the lawn. Two kept up an effective covering fire as the third collected the box. The gun battle was played out in silence, the flashes of the weapons the only indication that things were amiss on the lawn in front of Wellman Hall.

"Police!" Lake called out from behind the security of his open door. "Freeze where you are!" He was too far away for the Hush Puppy to do much good.

One of the Koreans fired a half a magazine in the van's

direction, the other kept the Japanese man pinned down near the building and they beat a hasty retreat to their LTD. Fortunately MAC-10s weren't much more effective than the Hush Puppy at ranges over twenty-five meters and the bullets passed by harmlessly.

The Koreans worked as effectively as any elite infantry squad Lake had ever seen. The Japanese man with the Steyr retreated back inside the building and out of sight. As the LTD roared out of the lot, Lake made a quick decision.

"Drive up to the body," he ordered Araki as he regained his seat inside.

"What about Nishin and the Koreans?"

"We can find the Koreans again. Right now, we need to do some cleaning up."

Araki did as Lake requested, parking at the curb, fifteen feet from where the body lay facedown in the grass. Lake lifted the man and carried him back to the side door of the van, ignoring the blood that was staining his clothes.

"What are you doing?" Araki asked as Lake dumped the body into the back.

"Cleaning up the scene of the crime," Lake said. He turned and walked back to where the body had been.

"Why?" Araki asked, this time accompanying Lake.

"We left two bodies back there in the tunnel, that's enough publicity for one evening. No one heard this here. I don't hear sirens yet, so there's a good chance no one saw it. The less that gets in the news, the better." He scooped up the loose papers that were on the grass. "When the sprinklers come on in the morning, it will wash away the blood. No one will ever know." He picked up the MAC-10 the man had been carrying and added that to his load.

They got back in the van. Araki started the engine and they drove off the campus. Lake turned on his direction finder and cursed.

"What is the matter?" Araki asked.

Lake picked up the MAC-10 he had recovered. He unscrewed the back of the pistol grip and held up a small metal object. "A one-in-eight chance and of course I end up with my own bugged gun."

"They will go back to their trawler," Araki said confidently.

"So you were watching there, too," Lake said.

"I did—" Araki began but caught himself. "I followed Nishin to the trawler."

"Uh-huh," Lake said.

"What are we doing with the body?" Araki asked.

"Drive to the Golden Gate National Recreation Area," Lake said. "I know where to dispose of it."

"Aren't you worried about the Koreans getting away?"

"Aren't you worried about Nishin getting away?" Lake asked in turn. He didn't wait for an answer. "The Koreans are going back to the ship, like you said. That ship isn't going anywhere this morning. You can't just pull up anchor at one in the morning and sail away. They have to file a request and get permission from the harbormaster to leave port. The Coast Guard would be on them in a heartbeat if they didn't and I don't think they want that to happen."

"You've checked on that?" Araki asked.

"They haven't got a departure slot," Lake confirmed.

"What about whatever was in the box the Koreans stole?" Araki asked. "Won't someone at the university report that?"

Lake picked up the handful of papers. "That's who *I'm* going to talk to first thing in the morning, after we get rid of the body."

CHAPTER 7

SAN FRANCISCO
TUESDAY, 7 OCTOBER 1997
1:30 A.M. LOCAL

The body hit the water with a splash and the chains wrapped around it took it instantly out of sight. Lake walked from the pier back to the van and sat down in the passenger seat. They were parked on the shoreline, just east of the south part of the Golden Gate, near the point where Lake had come ashore the previous week after spoiling the gassing plot. It was a calm place, the only sounds that of foghorns off to the west and the gentle lap of water on the shore. The Coast Guard Station was farther up the shore, well lit, but otherwise looking very quiet.

Lake took a cigarette out of his pocket and lit it, ignoring Araki's look of distaste. Lake inhaled deeply, then let out a cloud of smoke. "Okay, so we're here together," he said, "but I still don't know whether you are who you say you are and even if you are who you say you are, whether I ought to be sitting here with you."

"I understand your concerns." Araki said. "I have similar concerns. I do not know if you are truly an agent of your government and, if you are, whether I should also be sitting here with you."

"I don't give a fuck about your concerns," Lake said without raising his voice. "I've got the home-court advantage here, which means you play by my rules." He reached inside his windbreaker and pulled out his satellite phone. "I'm going to bounce this to my higher-up and see what he has to say about you."

"I do not think that is a good idea."

"Why?" Lake was punching in the numbers to the Ranch.

"Because this situation might be harmful to your country and mine, and if we keep it between us, no extra harm is done. I believe we can handle this ourselves. If you call your supervisor, then this is out of our hands."

Lake pushed the off button and folded the phone shut. He thought of Feliks looking at him at this very spot, giving him grief for killing all three men at the bridge. If he told Feliks that there was an agent of CPI here in San Francisco, Lake knew that the long hand of the Ranch would clamp down on all operations. The Japanese material that had been found in the van on the bridge, combined with Araki's presence, would send red flags flying. It would also slow things down. Lake knew that the freighter wasn't leaving in the next twelve hours, but it could leave as early as this evening. The Ranch was efficient, but it wasn't that efficient. They could lose this whole operation. The bottom line for Lake, though, was that he would lose his operational control. Already he'd had Feliks here once and Randkin here on another occasion. If they wanted to run the show, then they should be the ones getting shot at, Lake reasoned.

"All right," Lake said. "We'll work this together for now."

"What about the papers?" Araki asked. "What do they concern?"

Lake looked at the top piece of paper in the glow of the overhead light. It was a Xeroxed page covered with Japanese writing. He handed it to Araki. "Make yourself useful."

Araki scanned the page. "It is dated 1945. From the heading it appears to be a document of the Imperial Navy, detailing supply operations in the China Sea."

"That's something to kill over?" Lake wondered out loud.

Araki was thumbing through the rest of the few pages the Koreans had abandoned in their haste. "They are all Japanese naval documents, dated 1945. Some are about operations; some about logistics; some concern personnel assignments. There are several orders detailing ships to conduct certain missions. There is no readily apparent pattern."

"Why would these be at UC-Berkeley?" Lake asked.

"Most likely there is a historical archive in the building," Araki said. "At the end of the war, you Americans took whatever wasn't destroyed that could be of intelligence value."

"Why would the Koreans be interested in such documents?" Lake asked.

Araki was silent for a few moments as he read, then he glanced up. "I do not know. Obviously they are interested in something concerning the Japanese Navy in the last year of World War II."

Lake felt stupid asking obvious questions, but he was at a loss with this development. "Why is Nishin following the Koreans? What does the Black Ocean Society have to do with this?"

Araki explained the role the societies had in Japanese culture and the strong influence they had exerted in politics, particularly during the war. "It is something difficult for Americans to understand," he added. "For example, in 1943, the head of the Black Dragon Society made a radio broadcast directly to your President Roosevelt and to Churchill also, threatening the most dire of consequences if the Allies did not unconditionally surrender.

"It is little spoken of or understood in the West, but much of the problem the Allies had trying to negotiate with my country near the end of the war stemmed from the fact that the secret societies and the military exerted such strong influence. Even though there were many in the government who wished to negotiate a surrender, they were unable to counter the weight of the societies until finally the Emperor himself had to make a radio announcement after Hiroshima and Nagasaki, which before that time was unheard of.

"That is why," Araki continued, "my unit was formed a few years back when it appeared that secret societies were again rearing their head. The extremists who were behind the Tokyo gas attacks were much more radical than the traditional societies, but the fear of a repeat of events that happened prior to and during the Second World War was so great that those high in the government did not want to take a chance."

"That's all nice and well," Lake said, "but it brings us no closer to explaining what is so important about these papers to both the North Koreans and the Black Ocean Society."

"As you said," Araki pointed out, "you must go and ask someone at the university about the papers. Maybe you can find out then."

"You drop me off where I tell you, then you stake out the trawler," Lake ordered. "I'll get over to the university as soon as people are awake there."

Nishin was as frustrated as Lake, but for a very different reason. For the third time the American arms dealer had interfered. The North Koreans had whatever they had come for and were safely back on their ship. From his perch, Nishin could see guards walking the deck of the trawler, Ingrams hidden under their coats.

He knew the Genoysha would not be pleased. He had failed. Nishin very seriously contemplated boarding the ship on his own and recovering the box, but his duty passion was tempered by the bitter training he had experienced. The odds were that he would be killed and then the mission would most certainly be a failure. The ship was not yet at sea; there was hope yet.

Nishin knew he needed help and there was only one place he could get it. With great reluctance he climbed down off the crane.

TUESDAY, 7 OCTOBER 1997
9:10 A.M. LOCAL

The campus looked very different in the light of day. Lake felt old as he walked among the crowds of students strolling to and from class. He had exchanged his blood-stained clothes of the previous evening for a fresh pair of jeans, a bulky white sweater with a turtleneck, and a faded sports jacket over the sweater. The Hush Puppy rode comfortably under his arm inside the jacket.

He also felt the irritable presence of the satellite phone in his coat's inside pocket. He hadn't called Feliks with the results of the previous evening, which he knew would not go over well. The report of the two dead unidentified Korean men had been on the third page of the San Francisco paper this morning and Lake knew it was a short matter of time before someone at the Ranch connected the bodies, the MAC-10s found near them, and the stolen Bronco II.

On another front, Lake believed Araki was an agent of the CPI, but even if Araki wasn't, Lake felt confident he could deal with the man. He also believed that Araki had not told him the full story, but that was to be expected. Lake hadn't told Araki everything he knew either. The thing that bothered Lake about this situation was that what he did know was greatly overwhelmed by what he didn't know.

North Koreans; Japanese secret societies; a Japanese special government agent; the Patriots' lurking presence in the San Francisco underworld—all these things troubled Lake. Beyond the fact he didn't know what most of those people were up to, he didn't know why they were doing what they were doing in most cases. Motive was the most critical factor in trying to outthink one's enemy, and here he didn't know that either. He hoped he could gain some answers here.

Just inside the west entrance a large board showed the campus layout, with a large "you-are-here" arrow orienting Lake. He retraced the route they had taken last night in his head and found the building he was looking for: Wellman Hall. It housed the history department, which fit with the type of documents the Koreans had stolen. Before he went there, though, Lake made a detour to the library and spent a half-hour doing some reading. Then Lake walked to Wellman Hall and went in the large double doors in the center. A glass case held a listing of all the offices in the building and Lake studied it.

There were only names, no areas of study listed, so Lake headed for the main office of the history department. Opening the door, he was greeted by a student behind the desk. "Can I help you?"

"Do you have someone here who is working on material dealing with the Japanese Imperial Navy in World War II?"

The student frowned. "I really don't know. Dr. Harmon might be able to help you. She's the Twentieth-Century Pacific Areas Study specialist."

"And where might I find Dr. Harmon?" Lake asked.

"Room one forty-two."

"Thank you." Lake exited the office and walked down the corridor. Room 142 came up on his right and he lightly rapped on the opaque glass that made up most of the top half of the door. There was no answer, so he tried the handle. It turned and he cautiously stepped in. He was in a small foyer, about six feet long. A door was to either side of him, one half-open, the other locked. He could hear someone talking to his right, behind the half-open door. Lake peered around the corner as he tapped on the doorframe.

Lake paused. A woman was seated behind a massive wood desk which was covered with mounds of paper. She appeared to be in her mid-thirties, with long thick black hair cascading over her shoulders and bright green eyes that fixed him in the doorway as she talked on the phone. Lake prided himself on telling a person's ethnic background at a glance, but he wasn't sure with Harmon. He thought she might have some Asian blood based on her facial features, but her skin was dark, as if she had Mediterranean ancestors in her past. Whatever the combination was, it was unique and intriguing. Beyond her looks, Lake picked up a definite sense of purpose and competence, which he found a little surprising. He was used to that feeling when around others in the covert community—men and women who had something extra, beyond the norm, knew they had it and didn't have to tell anyone.

"I'll get back to you," she said, her voice low and firm. She put the phone down and stood. She was tall, perhaps two inches shorter than Lake, and slender. She wore a gray pants suit and no jewelry. "May I help you?"

"Are you Dr. Harmon?"

"Yes."

"My name is Lake," he said, extending his hand. She took it with a firm grip, then let go.

"Is that a first name or a last name?" she asked, sitting back down.

"It's just a name," Lake replied, a bit off-guard.

Harmon laughed, the sound coming from deep in her throat, and Lake slid a couple of inches off his emotional center of gravity. "What can I do for you, Mr. Lake?" She pointed at a chair facing the desk and Lake gratefully sank into the leather.

"I'm interested in information concerning the Imperial Japanese Navy during the last year of World War II."

"For what reason?" Harmon asked, steepling her fingers.

"I'm writing a book," Lake said, "about fleet operations that year."

"For what purpose?" Harmon asked.

"Excuse me?"

"Why are you writing a book about the operations of the Japanese fleet in 1945?" Dr. Harmon amplified. "By that time in the war, most of the Japanese fleet had been destroyed. That which wasn't destroyed was hiding in port, trying to avoid the onslaught of the American carrier forces."

"To be more specific," Lake said, "I'm interested in one ship in particular. The *Yamamoto* went down in April 1945." Lake was using the information he had in the forefront of his brain from the sidetrip to the library. "It was the greatest battleship of the war, larger than either the Germans' *Graf Spee* or the *Bismarck*, yet little has ever been written about it."

"Little has been written about the *Yamamoto*," Harmon said, "because it didn't do too much damage and *its* end was rather unglorious. As you well know," she added.

"Yes, but I'm still interested in the topic," Lake said.

"Well, we do have quite a bit of material from the Imperial Naval archives," Harmon said. "It was gathered by U.S. Naval intelligence at the end of the war and brought back to the Naval Air Station at Alameda. It sat there unopened for decades until I went over and started looking through it about eight years ago. I forwarded some of it to the National Archives. Some of it I brought here when they shut the air base down four years ago and were going to just destroy it. I took as much as I had room for." She reached behind her and pulled a thick three-ring binder off a bookcase.

While she looked in it, Lake checked out the rest of the office. There were the usual diplomas on the wall behind her. He noted that several of the official papers were written in Japanese. There was a picture of Harmon standing alone with Mount Fuji in the hazy distance behind her. Another of a much younger Harmon with a man who appeared to be her own age at the time and an older woman taken in a park. The old woman was seated on a bench, Harmon and the other man behind her, a hand on each shoulder. The man was outfitted in a military dress uniform. A Marine. Lake noted that.

"I'm not sure if I have anything specifically related to the destruction of the *Yamamoto,*" she added as she flipped open the binder. "But on the other hand, I haven't been able to go through one-tenth of what I recovered from Alameda. This binder has the index for what I have gone through and filed."

"Well," Lake said, backtracking on his flimsy cover story, "the material I'm looking for doesn't necessarily have to all deal with the *Yamamoto.* I'm also interested in any Japanese naval operations near what is now North Korea."

Harmon paused in her reading. She closed the binder and rested her hands on top of it. "I don't think you're writing a book. I've written a couple of books myself and been published. One thing I know is that an author has to have a very clear idea of the theme of his work, especially when writing a historical work. I think you're just fishing for some specific information which may or may not have anything to do with writing a book. If you would be more honest with me, perhaps I could help you better."

If I was more honest, Lake thought, you might not help me at all. UC-Berkeley was not exactly the place of choice for a government agent to go looking for information. However, he didn't feel that he should so easily place Dr. Harmon into an antigovernment position. After all, there was the picture of her with the Marine.

"Where do you keep your material?" Lake asked.

Harmon looked at him, her eyes boring into his for several long seconds. "You haven't answered my question. This university pays my salary to teach and do research. It does not pay me to answer questions for any person who happens to walk into my office. Do you have any identification that you can show me, Mr. 'It's-just-a-name' Lake? What do you do for a living?''

Lake slumped in the leather seat, feeling the back of his head touch the headrest. He'd been doing undercover work for a long time now and he'd assumed many different personas. He didn't have the time to be very creative here, nor was he backstopped by the Ranch on any cover he might come up with that would make Harmon cooperate. He looked once more at the picture over her shoulder where she was with the Marine and decided to gamble. An old hand at the Ranch, teaching him covert operations, had told him that when in doubt, the truth always worked the best. Especially if the truth couldn't be verified by the person you told it to. Then all they had was a story.

Lake steepled his fingers. ''Okay. Here's the situation. I'm actually an agent working for the government under deep cover. Last week I stopped some terrorists trying to release a biological agent to infect the city of San Francisco. Last night I followed some foreign agents to this campus and they broke into this building. They left carrying a box with some materials in it. The man carrying the box was killed—not by me, but by someone associated with the Black Ocean Society from Japan, which you might have heard of—and he dropped the box. The other men, North Koreans, escaped with the box, but I was able to retrieve a few documents they left behind.'' Lake reached under his sweater and pulled out a few pages which he handed across the desk to Dr. Harmon.

Harmon didn't look at the documents. She stared at Lake. ''I'm supposed to believe that?''

''If you don't believe that,'' Lake replied, ''then believe my story about writing a book. I can assure you onc of them is true.''

''How come there weren't a whole bunch of police here this morning? How come I haven't heard of this man being killed?''

"Because they all used silencers and I took the body away," Lake said. "Did you read in the paper or hear on the news about two men being killed on the Bay Bridge last night?"

Harmon nodded.

"Those two were Koreans. They tried stopping me from following them here."

"You killed them?"

"One of them," Lake answered. "The other was killed by this fellow from the Black Ocean."

"This is unbelievable," Harmon said, shaking her head. "I've seen more plausible stories than this on TV."

Lake sat still, letting her make up her own mind.

"You don't seem like you have the greatest sense of humor," Harmon finally said. "I don't know you well enough to know about your imagination." She glanced at the documents. "These look like they're from the records I've got here." She tapped long fingernails on the paper. "What government agency?"

"I can't tell you that," Lake said. "But I can tell you it's not the CIA, FBI, or associated with the military."

"And why should I help you?" Harmon asked. She held a hand up. "And please don't give me any patriotic speeches. I saw you looking at the picture. That's my younger brother. He's stationed in Okinawa and it was one of the saddest days in my life when he joined the Marine Corps, but he seems to like it and his life. But it's not mine. So I ask you again: Why should I help you?"

"Because it's interesting," Lake said. "There's a puzzle here and it involves material you have. I need to solve this puzzle and I think you would find it intriguing to help me solve it. It might be fun."

"Fun?" A half-grin crossed Harmon's face. "That's the last reason I thought you'd give me." The grin disappeared. "But if people have died, as you say, wouldn't it also be dangerous?"

"They got what they wanted here," Lake said. "There's no danger to you."

Part of the grin came back. "Okay, I'll play along for a little bit, Mister Secret Agent Man. I've got nothing to lose and this will make a good story to tell at a party. What do you need to know?"

"Have you ever heard of the Black Ocean Society?" Lake asked.

"Yes, I've heard of the Black Ocean Society. Anyone who has made any in-depth study of Japanese history in this century has heard of it." She put the documents down. "Now, why do you expect me to believe your story?"

Lake shrugged. "I don't have expectations of other people because I don't control them. I only have expectations of myself. I've told you the truth; what you choose to do with it is up to you."

"Why would North Koreans break in here? What were they looking for?"

"I was hoping you could help me with that," Lake said. "That's what I'm here for. Perhaps if we went to where you keep these documents, we can find out what they took."

Harmon stood. "Follow me."

They didn't have far to go. Lake was right behind her as she pointed at the other side of the small foyer. "This door doesn't appear to have been broken open," she commented.

"Excuse me," Lake said. He pulled an ATM card out of his wallet and pushed it in between the door and the frame. Sliding it down he pushed the latch back and the door swung open.

"Point taken," Harmon said.

She flipped a light switch and a set of metal stairs going down appeared. Her low-heeled shoes clattered on the metal as she went down. At the bottom, there was another door, this one with no lock. She pushed it open and turned on another switch. It lit fluorescent lights on a low ceiling.

Rows of metal racks rose from the pitted concrete floor to the ceiling. Cardboard boxes filled the shelves.

"We're in the basement," Harmon said. "This used to be the coal room. When they modernized the building about fifty years ago, this room was abandoned. I opened it up five years ago for storage. I'm sure I'm violating some fire code, but I have to make do with what is available."

Lake looked around. "How would someone know this room existed? That records of the Japanese fleet would be kept here?"

"I've published quite a few articles on the subject," Harmon said, "which was why I thought you were a legitimate researcher at first. Anyone who does any sort of checking would find out that I have access to all this. In the academic world we don't hide our sources. By the way," she added, "I *would* like to know which government agency you represent?"

"A multijurisdictional task force," Lake answered. He looked down. He could see boot prints in the concrete, coal, and plaster dust on the floor. "The North Koreans made those last night."

Harmon looked at the marks. "Which jurisdiction of the multi do you come from?" she pressed.

"You are insistent, aren't you?" Lake replied.

"Please don't answer my question with a question," Harmon said. "When a student does that, I give them so much grief they never do it again. It's the sign of a mind that refuses to make a commitment to an answer, be it right or wrong."

Lake was following the footsteps in the dust. The Koreans had gone down every aisle. He was looking for an empty space on the shelves. Some of the boxes were labeled on the end with dates. He was passing 1943 at the present moment. "I am the multi," he said. "I'm so multi, I don't exist."

"If you're so super-secret," Harmon said, "why did you tell me that you were an agent?"

"Because it doesn't matter," Lake replied. "You have a name"—he smiled—"just a name, and you know my face. That and fifty cents gets you a cup of coffee."

"You told me what happened and what is going on with the Koreans," Harmon said. "You also told me that you killed someone last night. Isn't that supposed to be secret, too?"

Lake paused where several booted feet had paused. He had just walked past several dozen feet of 1944. "Hell, Dr. Harmon, I don't know what's going on, so I have no problem telling you. You figure it out or you tell someone who can figure it out, more power to you. Of course by then it will all be too late."

"Too late for what?"

"I don't know," Lake said, "but I suspect my North Korean friends will be setting sail for home this evening. If I don't find out why they were here before then, there's not much I can do about it." He pointed. "Was this the way you left it?"

A dozen boxes had their tops ripped off, loose papers were scattered on shelves.

"No."

"What's missing?" Lake asked.

Harmon had carried her binder with her and she opened it, checking it against the shelves. "Most of the boxes I only labeled by date. I didn't have a chance to cross-reference the majority by message and document type." She was counting to herself and Lake remained silent. "Forty-five dash sixteen is missing," she finally said.

"Which is?"

"A box containing Imperial Navy documents from August and September 1945."

That fit with the papers Lake had recovered from the lawn the previous evening.

"So," Harmon said, "why do the North Koreans want

documents concerning the Japanese Imperial Navy from August and September 1945?''

''You tell me,'' Lake said.

''I don't know what was specifically in the box,'' she said, leading him toward the door. ''Therefore I can't extrapolate based on data I don't have.''

''In other words, you don't have a clue,'' Lake said.

''Do you?'' she shot back as she locked the door.

''Not yet. Why do you have all these documents?'' Lake asked.

''I have a Ph.D. in history and I teach here,'' Harmon said as they reentered her office. She sat back down behind her desk and Lake reclaimed the leather chair. ''My area of specialty is Pacific Studies, mid-twentieth century. The biggest event of that time period was World War II. Every academic has to find their niche. Some pick their niche then go around accumulating source material. I had the general area and when I found out there was a treasure trove of source material about the Japanese navy during World War II so close at Alameda, it didn't take a sledgehammer for me to see what area I should specialize in.''

''Since all we know is a rough time period,'' Lake said, ''why don't we focus on that?''

''August 1945 was the end of the war,'' Doctor Harmon said. She closed her eyes and ticked off each item as she said it. ''The key events of that month in the Pacific were the atomic attacks on Hiroshima and Nagasaki; on the eighth of August the Soviet Union declared war on Japan; numerous conventional air strikes were conducted against Japanese mainland targets, primarily the cities of Tokokawa, Yawata, Hikari, Nagoya and Toyama with the last air raid coming on the fourteenth of August; the U.S. and British fleets conducted air strikes from carriers in the vicinity of Tokyo; on the fourteenth of August the Emperor made a broadcast to the people telling them that they must 'bear the unbearable'; the fifteenth of August is what we call VJ Day; by the eighteenth of August the Russians overran most of Manchuria; and on the twenty-seventh of that month the Allied Fleet anchored in Tokyo Bay in preparation for the surrender which was signed on the second of September."

She opened her eyes. "As far as the Japanese fleet goes, there wasn't much happening that month."

Lake leaned back in the chair, feeling the comfort of the soft leather. He knew Feliks would have a cow if he found out Lake was talking to a civilian like this. But he found talking was helping to clear the fog all the events of the past week had put over everything. "Let's try to connect the dots. This is 1997. You've got the North Koreans, the Black Ocean Society, and the Japanese government all looking for some document concerning Imperial Fleet operations in August or September 1945. A document that is so important that several people have already been killed trying to recover it."

He was watching Harmon's face and he noticed something he'd noticed before when he'd mentioned the Black Ocean Society: a flicker of recognition. Lake waited while the doctor picked up a letter opener in the shape of a samurai sword and lightly ran the edge of her thumb along the blade.

"There *is* something," she said. "Or perhaps I should say there may be something."

"Yes?"

"When you mentioned the Black Ocean Society and North Korea, something I'd read about once clicked. It's kind of outrageous, but your story right now is kind of outrageous so . . ." Her voice trailed off.

"Tell me," Lake prompted.

Harmon stood. "I'll have to show you what I'm talking about."

"Where are we going?" Lake asked.

"The library."

They walked in silence across the campus, each lost in their own thoughts. Lake felt a buzz in his pocket as they neared the library. "Excuse me," he said to Harmon as he pulled his phone out. He hoped it wasn't Feliks calling for an explanation of the last several days. It wasn't. He recognized Araki's voice: "Nishin has left his surveillance post."

"What are you doing?"

"I'm staying with the ship," Araki said. "I believe Nishin must return here."

"Any sign the ship is leaving?"

"They've filed with the harbormaster to depart between 2000 and 2200 this evening."

"All right. I'll be there as soon as I can," Lake said. He pushed the off button.

"Something up?" Harmon asked as they continued their walk and entered the library.

"No."

"Uh-huh," she said. They went down a flight of stairs to a room with several computer desks set up before stacks of magazines and newspapers.

"We've got everything over a year old on CD-ROM," Harmon explained as she sat down in front of one of the computers. Lake pulled a chair up next to hers. "We have almost every major city newspaper in here. I'm doing a search for a newspaper article I read once. I think it was dated 1954 or 1955."

"Which newspaper?" Lake asked

"I don't remember."

"Then how—" Lake began, but Harmon shushed him, her fingers typing two words into the database search: HUNGNAM. It produced one hit in reply.

"Wait here," Harmon said. She was only gone a minute before she returned with a CD inside a plastic case. She pushed it in and hit the ENTER key. A faded picture of a newspaper page appeared on the screen. "The *Oakland Tribune*, dated 14 May 1955," Harmon said. "Read it."

VETERAN RECALLS JAPANESE SECRET BASE

As the dust from the last battles of the Second World War was still settling, Major Frank Harlan, an investigator for the Naval Intelligence Service, NIS, found himself in what we now know as North Korea, in a race with Soviet Russian agents to uncover the mysteries of a secret Japanese base. The same base that Marines retreating from the Chosin Reservoir just a few months ago apparently stumbled across.

"Our orders were to grab anything that might be of significant military value, be it man, machine or document," Harlan recalls from the porch of his South Oakland house. "I'd already been in mainland Japan for two weeks after the formal surrender was signed. I was sent to Hungnam, a coastal town on the east side of the Korean peninsula, because prisoners we interrogated in Japan indicated that a major industrial complex was there. I flew over on a Navy PBY and landed in the harbor."

Located there on the Sea of Japan, the town was indeed a major industrial center with dozens of factories dotting the valley floor. Harlan knew something was strange about Hungnam from the moment his plane came into sight of the city.

"The harbor was devastated," Harlan said. "I'd heard that the Russians [who were occupying Hungnam and all of the northern part of Korea] had a tendency to pound the hell out of an objective when taking it, and that had certainly happened there. The entire town facing the water had been knocked flat. A few boats had been tossed inland several hundred feet and there was no way I could figure out how that had happened. A small island in the center of the harbor looked as if it had been pounded with a sledgehammer. According to the prewar charts I was using, the island was less than one-third its original size and what remained was totally stripped clean of any life."

It wasn't until a month later that Major Harlan came

up with a possible answer. But in the meanwhile, his two-week stay in Hungnam was less than profitable. "The Soviets followed me everywhere and they weren't friendly. There were parts of Hungnam totally off-limits to me and we were not allowed to speak to any natives. I had no doubt that they were doing the same thing I was, except on a much greater scale. While I was there I watched them totally dismantle two ammunition factories, rivet by rivet, load the parts onto rail cars and ship them back to Russia. They were stripping the place bare."

The devastation in the harbor weighed on Harlan's mind, though. He noted it in his official report which he filed upon returning to his unit in Japan, suggesting perhaps that the Russians had used some new form of massively powerful conventional munitions.

"Then, after I was back in Japan, I was sent on a mission to Nagasaki," Harlan remembers. "As soon as we came over the city, I immediately realized that what I had seen in the harbor at Hungnam was the same thing: the result of an atomic explosion. I knew it didn't make any sense, but I couldn't deny what my eyes saw. I was hesitant about making a report about my suspicions, but I did my duty and noted it. I never heard a word back. But a little checking on my own turned up the fact that just after I left, the Russians had made Hungnam and the area around it totally off-limits to foreigners."

Harlan's story might have been lost to history if it wasn't for a story he read in this paper eight weeks ago that prompted him to call this reporter. On the 12th of March, the *Tribune* ran a special story about the 1st Marine Division and the retreat from the Chosin Reservoir.

As Marines were evacuated from Hungnam, several recalled discovering a strange installation on the hillside of the valley. They were in no position to investigate further, but the report prompted Major Harlan, now retired from military service, to remember his own brief visit to the same town.

"I don't know if there was an atomic explosion at Hungnam near the end of the Second World War," Harlan says, his eyes looking out of the water of San Francisco Bay, "but what I saw points to it. Lord knows what the Japanese were working on there. I just thank my lucky stars that if they did succeed in making the bomb, they never had a chance to use it against us and we got them first."

Lake got to the end of the article, then looked up. "You've got to be joking with me. How come no one's ever heard of this?"

"Ah, now who's the one with the outrageous story?" Harmon asked. "Except I didn't make this up," she added, pointing at the computer screen. "I do agree that this story seems too outrageous given the last fifty years of reconstructive historical perspective, but it's not so far out if you simply look at the facts."

Harmon leaned close and spoke in a low voice. "I've thought about this ever since I read the article. I found it when I was doing some research on the Black Ocean Society. Although not as publicly notorious as some of the other societies during the war, the Black Ocean covertly wielded tremendous technological and industrial power. The valley that Hungnam is at the mouth of was indeed, as Major Harlan notes in the article, one of the manufacturing linchpins of the Japanese Empire and very few people know about that. It was developed in the thirties by a member of the Black Ocean Society. I was cross-referencing on Hungnam when I found this article.

"At first, I didn't really believe it, but I did allow myself to consider it as a possibility and the more I think about it now—given what you've told me is presently going on—the more I believe it might be true.

"Consider the facts. The way history is perceived now, every major power *except* Japan tried to develop atomic weapons during World War II. The German attempt is well documented along with the Allied commando assault into Norway to destroy their source of heavy water.

"The British and French deferred to the Americans because we were the ones with the industrial and scientific capability to get the job done and they were too busy fighting the war to work on the project. But even so they were spying on our efforts so they could develop their own programs as soon as they were capable.

"The Russians weren't scientifically capable because of the war but they had a strong espionage interest in the Manhattan Project. Yet we all believe the Japanese didn't even consider making a bomb. That's a bunch of bull," she added without much rancor. "Anyone with even the most basic understanding of history would know that they would have most certainly been interested in such a weapon's potential and they would also have had no hesitation about using it.

"People always like to think that one side or the other is better in a war. What they forget is that people are basically the same everywhere. Generals are the same. Armies are the same. And scientists are the same. There is no moral high ground in war."

Lake remained silent, watching her. From her initial reaction in the office, her mood had certainly changed.

"Let me explain where I'm coming from," she said. "You asked me what my area of expertise was and I wasn't specific. I'm currently writing a book on Unit 731. Have you ever heard of it?" She didn't wait for an answer, even though Lake indicated negatively.

"After conquering Manchuria in the thirties the Japanese set up Unit 731 at Pingfang ostensibly to operate a water-purification plant for Japanese troops occupying China. But that was a cover for the real purpose of the unit, which was to test biological warfare weapons."

That clicked something in Lake's head as he remembered the red glass jar in the van on the Golden Gate, with Japanese characters written on it. Were the ghosts of World War II weapons programs rising again to threaten the new world order across the Pacific?

"The ultimate aim was to build a bomb that could win the war; to a certain extent the article refers to an atomic bomb. But a biological bomb was much more within the means of what the Japanese could actually accomplish quickly. They developed at least a half-dozen variants of porcelain bombs to carry various plagues. Of course, to develop and then make sure their various plagues worked, they had to test them on the intended victims: human beings."

Lake remained still, allowing Harmon to talk under the quiet hum of the library activity. "To find the most lethal variant of each disease, the scientists of Unit 731 had to deliberately infect prisoners, then dissect them while alive, without anesthesia, to withdraw the culture to begin their new batch. Thousands of people were killed in such a manner." Harmon shook her head. "So you can see why I do not find the idea of the Japanese military and secret societies working on an atomic bomb so farfetched.

"Of course," she added with a grim smile, "the Allies were also working on biological and chemical weapons. Particularly after the losses they took seizing the first islands from the Japanese. In the hopes of reducing their own casualties, the Allies tested blistering agents on Australian soldiers who volunteered."

Lake wanted to keep things on track. He knew academics had a tendency to go off on their own specialized tangents, although he might have to get back to her on the Unit 731 thing. "But the article says there were reports the Japanese actually detonated a bomb in Hungnam. I find it very difficult to believe that such a thing could be kept secret for the past fifty years."

"Consider the situation," Harmon said, swiveling in her seat to look directly at him. "The project is said to have been conducted at Hungnam, which is on the Korean peninsula. During the war, that area of the world received very little scrutiny from Allied forces. Hungnam faced the Sea of Japan, which until the very end of the war was totally controlled by the Japanese. It was also out of range of Allied bombers until the last year. Even then, despite the fact that there were tremendous amounts of industry in that valley, it was never attacked by Allied bombers because intelligence failed to designate it as a target. The Japanese managed to keep the entire place shrouded in secrecy.

"When the war ended, it was the Russians, not the Western Allies, who took over North Korea. In fact, while the Russians formally declared war on the ninth of August, it's widely known that Russian forces, particularly paratroop forces, were already seizing key Japanese installations several weeks prior to that date in an attempt to capture both buildings and material intact.

"Any evidence of a Japanese atomic program in Hungnam would have fallen under Russian jurisdiction." She pointed at the computer screen. "I found out from a *New York Times* article that the Russians actually shot down an American B-29 flying in the area of Hungnam near the end of August 1945. They apologized and said there had been a misunderstanding, but the Russians seem to have an extensive history of shooting down planes flying in areas they don't want them in. My question would be, if there wasn't an atomic program in Hungnam then what else could be there of such importance?"

Harmon was excited. "If the Russians did find something in Hungnam of the Japanese atomic bomb program, this could help explain how the Soviets managed to develop their own bomb so quickly after the end of the war. Everyone claims the Russians were able to detonate their own bomb because they stole much of their needed intelligence from the U.S., but that's always been very controversial. What if they used the Japanese scientists and information they recovered from Hungnam?

"I know for certain that the Japanese scientists from Unit 731 that the Russians captured were imprisoned at the end of the war. They were tortured by the Russians, who wanted to find out what they had learned from their experiments. Many of these men died in captivity and the survivors were released almost a decade after the official ending of the war. Who's to say that the atomic scientists weren't also captured and tortured to reveal their work?"

She tapped the screen. "The article also says that American troops during the Korean war *did* find the remains of some sort of secret installation but they weren't able to investigate. And of all the places on the face of the Earth that you would want to hide the remains of a secret base, North Korea is the number one choice. It has the most closed society on the planet. No one goes in there. No one comes out. We can't even keep track of the North Korean nuclear program now, never mind find out if the Japanese might have had one there over fifty years ago."

"How come you never checked all the documents you have," Lake asked, "to see if you could verify this story?"

"Because I had no connection between the Imperial Navy and the story," Harmon replied. "I still don't. *You're* the one who mentioned the Black Ocean Society and *that* was the connection to this story, not the Navy. This newspaper article was the only source material and, technically speaking, the way we historians look at information, it's secondary source material, not primary."

"Wait a second," Lake said. "What's the connection between the Black Ocean Society and Hungnam?"

"The industrialist who first developed Hungnam was one of the key members of the Black Ocean Society," Harmon replied. "If the Japanese military did something in Hungnam, you can be damn sure the Black Ocean was involved also. But I would say it was most likely the other way around: the Black Ocean was involved in the program and the military was brought in to join it."

"What about the report this Major Harlan filed?"

"If it still exists, it would require a hell of a lot of work to find and would really add very little in the way of proof to the article itself," Harmon said. "I didn't pursue this because it sounded farfetched and because there was no avenue to pursue. No proof."

"There must have been something in the box the North Koreans took," Lake said.

Harmon ceded that point. "They must have known what to look for. But what they found might not be proof. Perhaps they were looking for some other information to point them *to* proof." She removed the CD-ROM disc from the computer and returned it.

Lake thought about it. He didn't know exactly how the revelation that the Japanese had had an atomic bomb program during World War II would affect the current world order, but he had no doubt that it would not be good. That was motive enough for all that had happened the last several days. He wondered if Araki knew anything about this.

Harmon came back and indicated for them to leave. Lake followed her out of the library deep in thought. By the time they had returned to Wellman Hall, he had gone full circle and come back to the start line, wiser but still in the same place. "I have to get that box to find out what's going on," was his conclusion.

Dr. Harmon agreed. "At least then we'll know what's important and maybe that will tell us why it's important."

"I'd prefer if you wouldn't inform anyone about my visit here," Lake said.

"I won't," Harmon said. "Besides, as you told me, what can I tell them?"

"Thanks."

"Will you be back?" Harmon asked. "You promised me that you would fill me in on what's going on. That's my price for helping you."

Lake paused and looked her in the eyes, feeling out the edges to the question. "Yeah, I'll be back. I'll let you know how it turns out."

"Thanks. And be careful," she added as he swung the door shut.

11:45 A.M. LOCAL

"For a box of old papers?" Okomo was not impressed. They were seated on top of the Japan Center, inside the cocoon of the Yakuza's protective black glass.

Prior to coming here, Nishin had called back to Japan from a pay phone using the card and special number Nakanga had given him. His boss's instructions had been simple: Stop the North Koreans. Use any means necessary.

The only means Nishin had at his disposal, or hoped he had at his disposal, were under the control of Okomo, and the old man had listened to his story of the North Koreans with little patience. "You do not know what is in the box? It could be nothing."

"The North Koreans consider it something worth dying over, Oyabun," Nishin said, keeping his voice flat.

Okomo spit out a laugh. "The life of a Korean is worth nothing to me." The Oyabun was using a gold toothpick, working on his teeth. He spit something to the side. "I don't like you," he added. "I don't like your organization. Why should I help?"

"The friendship of the Black Ocean Society can be a very valuable thing, Oyabun," Nishin said. He had to grit his teeth to keep from adding his next immediate thought: And the enmity of the Society was a very dangerous thing. He felt the point of the ice scraper on the skin above a ridge of stomach muscle.

"Besides," Okomo said, "the docks are not mine. At least not on that side of the bay where their trawler is anchored. It would be bad for business for me to interfere where my arm is not supposed to reach."

"We can take the ship after it departs the harbor," Nishin said. "At sea, outside the twelve-mile limit. Surely your arm can reach that far. And there will be no trouble from the law, American or otherwise, in international waters, Oyabun."

Okomo stood. "Wait here." Nishin watched the old man walk to a door at the rear of the room. The doors slid open and he was gone. He was back in less than a minute.

"It might be possible," Okomo said. "But it would require a ship and men. Very expensive."

"We will pay you two million in American dollars for your assistance, Oyabun."

Okomo looked at Nishin impassively. Nishin felt like he was in a fish market, trying to bargain with an old lady over some moldering carcass. "Three million."

"Four million with a bonus of one hundred thousand dollars to the family of any man killed or seriously injured," Okomo finally said.

Nishin inclined his head, indicating acceptance of the terms.

SAPPORO, HOKKAIDO, JAPAN
WEDNESDAY, 8 OCTOBER 1997
9:00 A.M. LOCAL

When Nakanga informed him that the Koreans had gone to the University of California at Berkeley, Kuzumi had felt a cold chill run down his spine. He ordered Nakanga to have Nishin stop the Koreans at all cost. As Nakanga left the room, the blue phone on his desk rang. Kuzumi picked it up. The voice on the other end was mechanical, the result of being scrambled and digitized to prevent interception and decryption.

"The box contains Japanese naval records from August 1945."

Kuzumi relaxed slightly.

"I am not sure exactly what records," the voice continued.

"It will be taken care of," Kuzumi said. "What about the Americans?"

"The lid is still on."

"All right. We must ensure it stays on." He turned the phone off.

Kuzumi flicked a switch which ensured he would not be disturbed, then he closed his eyes and thought.

So strange that the Koreans should go to UC-Berkeley where he had worked so many years ago. He was relieved that they were only after documents from the war. He knew that records of his presence there in 1939 might exist, but there was no way the Koreans could connect that with him now. He was supposed to have died in 1945. The only person who knew he was still alive and the Genoysha of the Black Ocean was Nakanga.

When he had been returned from the Russian camp, Genoysha Taiyo had assigned Nakanga to care for him and look after him, cutting Kuzumi off from all other outside contact. Then he had been given a new identity and brought back into the fold, working in the super-secret inner circle of the Society. To all it had long ago been reported that he had died at Hiroshima in 1945.

Kuzumi's left eyebrow twitched, the only sign that that thought had evoked a strong emotion in him. Because he felt he ought to have died at Hiroshima. His son had.

When Genoysha Taiyo had confronted him about Nira's pregnancy and subsequent childbirth, Kuzumi had been shocked, yet secretly elated that he now had a son.

He knew he would have been killed over the issue if it wasn't for the fact that the Society needed his atomic expertise so badly. Leaving a child in a foreign country, one that Japan would soon be at war with, was not the most secure action an agent could have done. The possibility for blackmail, or at least attempted blackmail, was high. Also, the illegitimate child threatened Nira's position working at the university. But because Nira continued to work for the Black Ocean and they did not doubt Kuzumi's loyalty, initially Genoysha Taiyo had not considered the boy to be a problem. But then war came in December 1941, and Nira was in enemy territory with their son.

His Sensei explained it to him. Since the situation was unacceptable and Kuzumi was too valuable for action to be taken on him, another course of action must be implemented. Kuzumi had felt fear then. He knew what the Society was capable of and he feared that they were going to kill his son.

But the Genoysha had an idea, his Sensei explained. "We will bring your son here. He will become part of the Society."

Kuzumi felt tremendous relief at hearing those words. He soon found out that the Black Ocean was in contact with an extensive spy network run by the Spanish called "TO," Japanese for door. The Spanish relayed information through their embassy in Washington to Madrid, where it was forwarded to Tokyo. This was the way Nira was able to update them on the status of Lawrence's work on the electronic process for U-235 separation, the part of the Manhattan Project that was being conducted under his direction. It was also how the Genzai Bakudan project was finding out other essential information that helped keep the project moving.

The TO network could also move people. In April 1942 they picked up Kuzumi's and Nira's son, James, and took him south, across the border into Mexico. They loaded him onto a Mexican fishing boat which rendezvoused with a Japanese submarine in the South Pacific.

Kuzumi had met his son at dockside upon his arrival. He promptly renamed his son Sakae after his own father and also because the American name would have brought him untold grief among the other children at the Society Homeplace school. Kuzumi spent every available moment with him, although with the pressures of the project there wasn't much of that. He was able to send an occasional encrypted letter back to Nira through the TO network, telling her how Sakae was growing. Unfortunately, he was not allowed to send her any pictures. His major desire became to finish work on Genzai Bakudan in order to help bring about a quick end to the war.

But the project progressed slowly. On the thirty-first of May 1942, in San Francisco, Nira watched the American battleships *Colorado* and *Maryland* pass beneath the Golden Gate Bridge under a full head of steam heading west, not knowing that they were already too late to join the American fleet which was massing off of Midway in response to having broken the Japanese secret code and anticipating their assault on that island. Kuzumi was in Japan, still working on theoretical problems with designing an atomic weapon. He and the other scientists were wrestling with how to separate out U-235 from the uranium deposits they had and what the critical mass would be that they would need.

It was work that took years rather than months. And the Battle of Midway had changed the complexion of the war. The Americans were now on the offensive. The year 1943 saw the tide decisively swing toward the United States and the Imperial forces were on the defensive in every area of the Empire. But those defeats, ironically, also gave impetus to progress in Genzai Bakudan. As the armed forces, particularly the Navy, were defeated in conventional combat they directed more resources to the Genzai Bakudan project as a way to regain their superiority over the Americans. There was also the sobering realization that the war was going to last much longer than anyone on the Imperial Staff had expected. Therefore a long-term project such as the atomic bomb was more feasible now.

By late 1943 the Genzai Bakudan project had gathered enough uranium for the needed experiments, no small feat by itself. It had required sending agents out throughout the Empire and commandeering ships and submarines to bring the material back.

Kuzumi remembered those difficult days: convincing

men in uniform to bring back small quantities of an ore most had never heard of, while at the same time tackling the numerous other problems the project faced.

As the pile of uranium grew, they then faced the problem of separating out the U-235. Nira reported from San Francisco that Professor Lawrence was separating out about a quarter of an ounce of U-235 each day using a cyclotron. The problem for Kuzumi was that there was only one cyclotron in Japan and to convert it to producing U-235 would have meant they couldn't use it for the other experiments they needed to conduct for the project. He turned the search elsewhere.

Kuzumi almost had to laugh now at how little they knew back then. They settled on a method called thermal diffusion, which had been perfected in Germany, which meant they had easier access to some of the information on it.

Slowly but surely, though, they overcame each obstacle. Kuzumi turned from his desk and opened his file cabinet and pulled out his wooden box of memories. Digging through he found an old photo that had stayed in Japan when he went to Korea. It showed a group of men in white coats standing in front of blackboard. The best and the brightest from all the universities in Japan, and Kuzumi, young as he was, had been in charge.

By the beginning of 1945 they were past theory and into trial and error with the different components that would make up a bomb. But the sands in the hour glass were running even quicker. The first American heavy bomber attack on Japan had occurred on the fifteenth of June 1944. In February of '45 the Americans captured Iwo Jima and were just over three hours from Tokyo by air. Death and destruction from above became a daily diet for the Japanese.

The loss of power hamstrung the program. B-29s destroyed the power grid feeding the Rikken, and Kuzumi was forced to face the reality that they could not finish the bomb in Japan. He went to Genoysha Taiyo and explained the situation. Taiyo made the decision. The entire project was moved to Hungnam, across the Sea of Japan, where there was plenty of power flowing from the reservoir at Chosin.

Kuzumi gritted his teeth as he remembered packing the labs and equipment for the move. It cost them almost two months in time. In the end the delay probably cost them the war. The worst for Kuzumi was that he had to leave Sakae. The Black Ocean Society was preparing for the eventual U.S. invasion by dispersing its assets and personnel. The Homeplace school was shut down.

Kuzumi gripped the arms of his chair. At the time it had seemed the logical thing to do: Send Sakae to stay with his own parents. So he had said good-bye to his son and departed for Hungnam. Little would he have guessed that he would not return to Japan for over eight years and never see his son again.

In prison the Russians had told him little of what had gone on in the outside world. He had been told that Japan had surrendered. That the war was finally over. And to torment the scientists, Kuzumi in particular, they told him of what the Americans had done to end the war. Of the atomic bombs that had been dropped and their targets.

For eight years Kuzumi did not know whether his son had lived or died in the atomic attack. He also did not know what had become of Nira. When he was flown back to Sapporo by the Black Ocean after being released by the Russians, Nakanga took him directly in his wheelchair to this very room to meet Genoysha Taiyo.

Taiyo had stood upon Kuzumi's entering the room, a very great sign of respect, especially as Kuzumi could not stand himself. Kuzumi remembered the words as if they were being spoken now, drawn back out of the walls that had absorbed them so many years ago.

"I have been told of your concerns in reference to your son and your wife. I regret to inform you that your son perished in the atomic attack on Hiroshima. There was no sign of him or your parents after the attack. Your family house was completely destroyed.''

Kuzumi had prepared himself for this. His face had betrayed nothing, although he felt the knife of truth cut the thread of hope he had held onto for so many years. Hope that had kept him alive in the dark hole of his cell and through the torture sessions.

''Your wife is also dead. As best we have been able to determine, she committed suicide after learning of the attack on Hiroshima and your son's death.''

The second blow had landed on a dead heart. ''Did she know of my imprisonment?'' Kuzumi had asked.

''We informed her in the last message that we know she received that your plane had gone down and you were missing and presumed dead. In the same message we replied to her request about your son, confirming that he was lost.''

Poor Nira. Even now Kuzumi could well imagine her grief receiving two pieces of news in one message. Grief that she would have had to have borne alone among a country full of enemies. Grief that she could tell no one about.

''How did she die?'' he had asked.

''We have a report that she jumped from the Golden Gate Bridge. The body was washed out to sea.''

All gone. All he had left was the Black Ocean. And now it was threatened. He looked at the wooden box that held all his memories. What had the Koreans found in their cardboard box? What memories were they delving into?

CHAPTER 8

SAN FRANCISCO
TUESDAY, 7 OCTOBER 1997
9:48 P.M. LOCAL

The proper papers had been filed and all was in order. The *Am Nok Sung* was cleared to leave San Francisco Harbor any time between 2200 and 2400 local time. The ship was 20,000 tons, less than mid-sized as oceangoing ships went. The forward deck consisted of several large hatches leading to refrigerated holds for the fish. At the rear a three-story bridge complex rose up, overlooking the ship.

The *Am Nok Sung* actually had a complement of twelve men on board whose only job was to indeed conduct fishing operations to maintain the ship's cover and sail the ship. A platoon of North Korean Special Forces made up the rest of the crew. Minus the two men they'd lost on Yerba Buena Island, whose identity baffled San Francisco police, there were still sixteen combat-hardened men left on board.

They only had seven MAC-10s between them for firepower, but a black belt in a Tae Kwon Do was a requirement for every member of the North Korean Special Forces. When getting ready to depart on this mission it had been a most difficult decision to not bring their own weapons on board the ship. The platoon commander had demanded that he be allowed to bring weapons, but the overall mission commander in North Korea had overruled him. The American customs officials had too good of a record. A platoon of soldiers on board a ship with hidden weapons would have been a most unfortunate discovery. Thus, when the ship had come into port, customs had found nothing other than a very strange-looking crew; but there was nothing illegal about that.

There was a twenty-ninth man on board, neither soldier nor crew, who answered only to the platoon commander. This man was a linguist, fluent in English and Japanese, and he was currently locked in a room on the second floor of the ship's bridge tower, three-quarters of the way back on the deck. The bridge and radio shack were one floor above him while the main quarters were one floor below. The twenty-ninth man, Kim Pak, had the box that so many people were now interested in sitting on the desk in front of him. He was going through it, one document at a time, reading carefully, looking for a couple of key items.

In the center of San Francisco Bay, Nishin stood on the bridge of an old tugboat, watching the *Am Nok Sung* through a set of night-vision goggles. He could see the crew moving about the deck of the trawler.

"They will be leaving shortly," Oyabun Okomo said. "We must follow until they clear the inner shoals." He nodded toward the man standing inside the bridge at the wheel. "My friend Captain Ohashi says he will be able to follow with all lights off. He knows these waters quite well."

"How will we get on board?" Nishin asked. "Oyabun," he added after getting no immediate response.

"Leave that to me," Okomo said. "You are paying but I command." The old man smiled. "My men will make short work of those Korean pigs on board."

Nishin glanced down at the deck of the tugboat where two dozen Yakuza toughs armed with automatic weapons waited. He had fought the Koreans at the university and fort. He'd seen what they'd done in the tunnel. They had been disciplined and professional. He knew it would not go as the Oyabun thought it would. That was fine with Nishin. Because in the end, he preferred no one, North Korean or Yakuza, came off the trawler alive.

Lake grabbed the duffle bag out of the back of Araki's van. "How'd you arrange for the chopper?" he asked as they walked down a set of stairs to the concrete landing pier built out over the harbor. A four-seat Bell Jet Ranger sat waiting, blades slowly turning.

Araki smiled and pulled out a small piece of plastic. "MasterCard Gold Card. No credit limit. I have promised the pilot a very generous bonus if he ignores whatever he sees tonight."

"Your government treats its agents better than mine," Lake said as he slipped into the back seat while Araki sat in the right front seat next to the pilot. He put a set of headphones on and pulled the boom mike in front of his lips as the blades increased velocity and the skids lifted.

As they swooped over water, Lake began emptying the contents of his duffle bag on the back seat.

The *Am Nok Sung* rounded the northeast side of the San Francisco peninsula and the Golden Gate Bridge hove into view. Fog was beginning to swirl about the top of the towers, slowly descending. The trawler slipped underneath the arch of the roadway.

Screws picked up speed. Going with the current, the *Am Nok Sung* was making good time, as was the tugboat that followed unseen. Point Bonita was several miles off to the right, not visible as the fog cut visibility down to under three miles.

"You can pay me all you like," the pilot of the Jet Ranger announced, "but the fog rules out here. I can't go any lower."

The *Am Nok Sung* had been lost to sight just before going under the Golden Gate. They knew it was down there somewhere and by using navigational charts they could guess at the course which would follow the main shipping channel, but they couldn't be sure of the speed.

"Any bright ideas?" Lake asked from the back seat. He was ready. He had a parachute on his back, a helmet with night-vision goggles attached on his head, a silenced MP-5 Heckler and Koch submachine gun strapped across his chest, and a wet suit on under all the gear. He'd gotten all the equipment from the Ranch drop site prior to meeting Araki. He was ready, but the weather wasn't cooperating.

"Actually," Araki said from the front seat, "I do." He pulled his metal briefcase up and flipped open the lid.

"What's that?" Lake asked, peering over the back of Araki's seat.

"Direction finder," Araki replied.

"You put a bug on the trawler?" Lake was impressed.

"No," Araki said. "I have a bug in Nishin."

"*In* Nishin?" Lake repeated. That brought two questions to mind and he asked the most immediate first. "Is Nishin on board the trawler?"

"No, but he will be soon. I intercepted some of his communications. I know he was in contact with the local Yakuza and they are providing him with assistance. They are following the trawler on board a tugboat. When they stop the trawler, this computer will tell us where both are. I am sure they will wait until the boat is outside the twelve-mile limit."

Lake had to wonder at the extent of Araki's intelligence net. The man knew more of what was going on than Lake did, and this was Lake's turf. He asked the second question. "How did you get a bug in Nishin?"

"It is a long story," Araki said. He turned and looked at Lake with a smile that didn't reach his eyes. "I must be allowed to keep some of my organization's secrets."

"Right," Lake said, leaning back in the seat. He looked

at the rear of Nishin's head as the man directed the pilot, keeping them in the air above the position the computer told him was Nishin's location. Lake wondered if he had underestimated his Japanese counterpart. Lake could tell they were steadily moving to the west, out to sea, but all he could see below was a wall of white fog.

"Nishin is directly below us," Araki announced, tapping the screen of the small computer on his lap.

"What's our altitude?" Lake asked.

"Six thousand feet," the pilot answered.

"Get us up to ten thousand," Lake said. "How far out to sea are we?"

Nishin was working his computer. "I put us seven miles from the Golden Gate."

"The fog's not as thick this far out," the pilot added.

Lake leaned over and looked down. There were patches of clear below. He could see the dark surface of the ocean here and there.

"Look!" Nishin said. "There, ahead. The *Am Nok Sung*."

Lake followed Nishin's finger. The running lights of a ship were visible about a half-mile ahead, then they just as quickly disappeared again into the fog. "Where's Nishin?"

"Directly below. He's closing on the trawler."

"Next opening we get," Lake said, "I'm going down. We can't wait too much longer." He felt the familiar thrill of pending action surge through his body. He checked the MP-5 one more time.

The openings in the fog bothered Nishin. He was afraid they would be spotted. "We must take them now!" he insisted.

"We are not twelve miles out," Okomo said.

"We are close enough," Nishin said. "We wait any longer we will not be able to surprise them."

Okomo pointed a finger forward and Ohashi pushed down on the throttle. The powerful engines increased revolutions and the tug's stubby prow butted its way through the four-foot swell.

"Here," Araki said, handing what looked like a watch back to Lake. "Put this on."

"What is it?" Lake asked, taking it.

"A homing device. I will be able to find you with my computer."

Lake strapped it on his wrist.

"I'm not going to be able to pick him back up," the pilot said, worry over the entire operation showing in the pitch of his voice. He had glanced back and watched Lake rig the parachute and gun and his enthusiasm had waned accordingly.

"You will not have to get involved. I will make other arrangements," Araki said confidently. "There! She's in the clear again."

"I'm out of here." Lake took off the headset. He pushed open the left rear door. Reaching with his feet, he found the skid. Holding onto the side of the doorframe, he stood on the skid, then dove outwards, assuming a perfect exit position, arms akimbo, palms down, back arched, head looking at the horizon. He waited a few seconds, then pulled the ripcord. The chute blossomed open and he quickly grabbed the toggles, to control the square canopy.

He could still see the *Am Nok Sung* on the open patch below and began a long, slow circle above it, descending all the while. As he was watching, a second ship appeared in the opening, less than two hundred feet behind the *Am Nok Sung*, then just as quickly the fog shifted and both were gone. Lake maintained his orientation and went down toward where he thought the ships *would be* when he reached ocean altitude.

Above him, Araki tapped the pilot on the shoulder and directed him to head to a location farther to the west.

"Ai!" Captain Ohashi cried out as they suddenly broke into clear air and the *Am Nok Sung* suddenly appeared a couple of hundred feet ahead. "Full reverse," he hissed into the phone connecting him to the engine room. He rapidly spun the helm several revolutions to the right and the prow ponderously swung in that direction.

Every muscle in Nishin's body was tense as he unconsciously tried to will the tug back into the protective covering of the fog. Okomo barked out a command and the Yakuza on deck trained their weapons on the rear deck of the trawler.

Just as quickly the *Am Nok Sung* was gone again, a line of white floating along its length and then the stern disappearing. Ohashi spun the wheel back right and ordered full thrust forward. "We will be on them in a minute," the captain said.

Okomo turned and climbed down the short ladder to the front deck and Nishin followed. Several of the Yakuza held grappling hooks with knotted ropes attached to them.

Nishin pulled back the charging handle on his Steyr AUG. He put the stock into his shoulder and looked through the scope. Nothing but white ahead. He peered over the weapon.

A black wall appeared suddenly, thirty feet in front of them. Nishin snapped the weapon back into the ready position. The tug slid up to the left side of the ship and hooks were thrown.

A face looked over the side of the ship at the sound of metal hitting metal, and as the Korean prepared to call out an alert, Nishin settled the laser aiming dot on the center of the man's face and lightly squeezed the trigger. A red flower blossomed where the man's face had been and then it was gone. The piece of expended brass fell onto the deck plates at Nishin's feet, the only sound the gun made. The first of the Yakuza were clambering up the ropes.

Lake was disoriented. Not just as to where the *Am Nok Sung* and the tug were below him, but also vertically. He shifted his eyes from looking down to a quick glance at the altimeter on the navigation board strapped on top of his reserve. Four hundred feet above sea level. He was in the middle of a thick white soup with nothing to orient on.

"Shit," Lake muttered. He braked hard, slowing his descent as much as possible, but no matter what he did, he was still going down.

On board the *Am Nok Sung* the translator put the document he had just read in the completed pile and looked at the next one. His eyes froze as he read the heading:

DTG: 1 AUGUST 1945/1000 HOURS TOKYO
FROM: IMPERIAL NAVY STAFF/COMSUBGP
TO: COM/1 24/EYES ONLY
TEXT: PROCEED TO HUNGNAM, KOREA, AT FLANK SPEED TO TAKE ON CARGO. FURTHER ORDERS WILL FOLLOW.

The translator turned the page and there it was: the further orders with the following day's date, time, group. He read down the text of the document and sharply exhaled. He quickly copied the text of both messages onto a piece of paper. He sprang to his feet and ran for the radio room, the paper grasped in his hand.

Nishin was working his way up the right side of the short rear deck, his destination the bridge. Whoever was in charge would be there and he had no doubt that not far from that person would be the documents.

A roar of automatic fire from one of the Yakuza signaled the outbreak of all-out combat on the deck of the trawler. At least they were all on board, was Nishin's thought as he carefully aimed and killed a Korean on the wing of the bridge deck.

Nishin made it to the base of the three-story bridge complex and slowed down, edging his way along the steel wall. He had far outdistanced the Yakuza who were still making their way across the rear deck, embroiled in combat with a handful of Korean soldiers.

Lake heard automatic fire below him and to the left. He pulled on the toggles and steered in the direction of the firing.

The battle became pitched as the North Koreans rallied and fought back ferociously. Their lack of firepower, only seven MAC-10s, was made up for by their training and disregard for their own safety. A hatch swung open in front of Nishin and two Koreans sprang out. He killed the first with a burst from the Steyr AUG. In his dying second the man threw himself onto the muzzle of the gun and Nishin was forced to drop it to face the second man, who was armed with a fire ax.

The man swung and Nishin leaped back, the ax scattering sparks as it hit the side of the bridge tower. Nishin jumped in, grabbing the Korean's arm that controlled the ax and striking a kite blow in the direction of the man's throat. He missed, his hand slamming into the man's collarbone, snapping it.

The ax fell to the deck with a clatter, but the North Korean was far from being done. He snapped a front kick into Nishin's gut, doubling him over. Nishin dropped the standard moves he'd been trained on and growled as he butted his head forward into the man's stomach, wrapping his arms around the man's waist. He lifted him and slammed him back against the wall. Again. Shifting slightly he did it a third time and the Korean screamed as the handle for the hatch ripped into his back, tearing through skin and muscle.

Nishin stepped back. The Korean was caught on the handle, but he was still alive, writhing in agony, trying by force of will to lift himself off the metal hook, but his feet could get no purchase, dangling six inches off the deck.

Nishin slipped past the man, ducking the dying blow the Korean threw at his head. Inside, a set of stairs beckoned to Nishin, heading up toward the bridge.

Lake had his feet and knees tight together, just like the jump masters at Fort Benning used to scream through megaphones at novice airborne students to do as they drifted toward the ground on their first jump. The firing was much closer now, but the fog was just as thick. Lake glanced at his altimeter: one hundred feet.

He cocked his head. He could hear the throb of a ship's engines in between staccato bursts of fire. He rotated his elbows in to protect his face and kept his knees slightly bent.

Something passed by, about twenty feet in front of him. A ship's crane. He pulled in the last inch of slack in the toggle lines and then he touched down on steel decking, grateful for the deceleration of the square canopy that made his landing so soft. He kept on his feet and ripped open the canopy release assemblies on the front of his shoulder. He popped open the small steel loops inside. The parachute hadn't even settled yet and he was out free of it. The chute drifted over the side of the ship and disappeared.

Lake unhitched the MP-5 as he looked about. He was on the forward deck, standing on top of one of the large cargo hatches. All the firing seemed to be coming from the rear. Lake began making his way to the stern.

Quantity was prevailing over quality. Surprise also was a factor with a third of the North Koreans having died before they realized they were under attack. The platoon commander screamed commands from the open windows of the bridge, rallying his forces, with their final defensive line being the island the bridge was on.

He gave instructions to the ship's captain, then went to

the radio shack at the back of the bridge. It was a small, windowless room with half its space taken up by a sophisticated communications array.

"What are you doing here?" he demanded, seeing the translator sitting at the small table, rapidly typing a message into the encryption device.

"I found it!" the man yelled excitedly. "You will not believe what it says." He thrust the piece of paper he was copying off of in the platoon commander's face.

"You have radioed this information?" the commander asked.

"Not yet," the translator said. "I just finished typing the message into the encryption machine."

"Good," the commander said. He pulled out a double-edged knife from its sheath.

"What are you—" The translator never finished the sentence as the commander slammed the blade to the hilt into the man's chest.

The commander shoved the body aside and sat down at the radio. He began checking the equipment to make sure it was properly set.

Nishin pushed open the door to the room on the second floor and stepped in, muzzle of the AUG leading. The room was empty and he turned to leave when he noticed the box sitting on the small table in the center of the room. Stepping over, Nishin confirmed it was the box stolen from the university the previous evening. There was no time to investigate further. He had to make sure the Koreans were finished first. He went back out, closing the door behind.

Lake surprised two men locked in combat on the left side of the bridge tower. He killed them both with a short burst from his MP-5. There were several other bodies scattered about, both Korean and Japanese. Lake could hear firing coming from above him and he knew that was where he had to go.

* * *

Nishin cleared the bridge with one sustained, silenced burst from the Steyr AUG. He leaped over a body and kicked open the door at the back of the bridge. A man sat by the radio, his hands on a computer keyboard, a body at his feet.. Nishin fired, his bullets slamming the man up against the radio console, blood spraying the machinery.

Nishin rushed over but he saw he was too late. Two words flashed on the computer screen: MESSAGE SENT.

There was a paper in the man's hand. Nishin knelt and carefully pulled it out of the dead fingers that clutched it. He stuffed it inside his shirt. He checked the numbers on the digital displays of the radio, committing them to memory.

There were voices speaking behind him in Japanese. He re-entered the bridge. Oyabun Okomo was standing with a handful of surviving Yakuza, several of them sporting wounds.

Okomo pulled a body off of the bridge controls and grimaced. "We are sinking."

His words caused Nishin's trigger finger to pause just a millimeter from pulling back. He looked about. The ship was listing slightly to the right. Three more Yakuza entered the left side of the bridge, weapons at the ready. Nishin removed his finger from the trigger.

"The captain opened the seacocks to scuttle the ship," Okomo explained, slapping the control panel. "They are jammed. We cannot close them. We must get to the tugboat before it is too late."

"We have achieved what we came for," Nishin agreed. He would get the box on the way out. They all turned for the stairs.

Lake heard the voices one flight up. There was no more sound of gunfire. He edged open a door, the muzzle of his MP-5 leading. An empty cabin with a couple of bunks and a small table. On the table a cardboard box stood unattended. Lake slid into the room and checked. The box was the one that had been stolen from Harmon's archives. A folder was open on the table top, Xeroxed pages pressed flat about halfway in. Lake quickly shut the folder and stuffed it into the box. He pulled a couple of plastic garbage bags out of his wet suit and wrapped them around the box, sealing each one with duct tape.

He could feel the ship angling over to starboard. Lake estimated about a ten-degree list, getting worse very quickly. Since he had heard no explosion he had to assume someone was scuttling the ship. He worked faster.

As he sealed the last bag, Lake heard footsteps clattering on the metal stairs outside. A head poked in the door and Lake greeted it with one round from the MP-5 right between the eyes. He could see two men behind, but the door swung shut before he had a chance to shoot again.

Pieces of skull and gray brain matter exploded into Nishin's face from the Yakuza in front of him who had looked in the room. He flattened against the bulkhead. He had had just a glimpse into the room, but that had been enough. The American gun dealer again! What was he doing here and why was he with the box? The man was wearing a wet suit, which indicated he had gotten on board the ship after it left the harbor, even though they hadn't seen anyone board. Nishin checked the magazine on the AUG. He was going to finish this meddlesome round-eye once and for all.

Okomo was on the other side of the door and held up a hand as Nishin reached for the door handle. "Leave whoever is in there. The ship will be down soon. We must go! Now! We do not have time for this." The Oyabun's voice brooked no dissension. Nishin was tempted to kill the old man then and there, but there were too many of his henchmen about. Now was not the time.

Recovering the box was not essential, Nishin knew.

Making sure no one else would ever recover it was. If the ship went down, that would be sufficient.

Nishin grabbed a fire ax and slid the wood handle through the metal spokes of the hatch's handle. It jammed against the far side of the hatch, effectively freezing the wheel. The American would die with the ship.

They continued on their way out of the bridge castle. As they ran they could feel the trawler listing farther to the right.

The tug was still nudging the right rear of the trawler, although closer to deck level now that the trawler was lower in the water. Nishin grabbed one of the lines that was tied off on the railing and lowered himself hand over hand to the waiting deck.

Lake heard the feet move away, but he continued to wait another couple of minutes, fearing a trap. He tried the door but it didn't move. He tried again, straining against the metal wheel. Nothing. Now he knew the meaning of the Japanese words he had heard but not understood and the sound of wood on metal that had followed them.

Lake ran through the options. He turned about. There was no other door and no portholes in the room. Just metal walls, ceiling and floor. Conduits in PVC pipes disappeared through the ceiling. There were two pipes, each three inches in diameter. Even if he ripped them out he would barely be able to get his arm through, never mind his whole body.

Lake looked back at the door. The metal wheel handle had no exposed screws or nuts that would allow him to remove the entire handle. He grabbed hold and tried turning in the opposite direction from open. The handle moved about an inch then froze. He shifted back the other way an inch. Then again.

The trawler's engines were contributing to its rapid death by pushing water into the openings in the hull. The trawler was still moving forward, albeit slower than before, as it was ten feet lower in the water. Fifty yards to starboard, Nishin was watching the ship go down. He hadn't gotten the box, but that wasn't the important thing—it was going down with the ship and no one had it now. The American, well that was a puzzle, one which he would not have to figure out now.

"We must circle and make sure there are no survivors," Nishin said.

Okomo grunted out some commands to Captain Ohashi and the tugboat began circling.

"I lost sixteen men," Okomo said. He spit. "The Koreans fought better than I expected."

Not as well as Nishin had expected, though. There were still a dozen armed Yakuza on board the tug. His wish to get rid of Okomo and his thugs would have to be forgotten. He needed them to make it back to the safety of land to report the mission's success.

He was concerned about the man he had killed in the radio room, though. The Koreans had managed to send out a message. What had been the message? He hoped Nakanga would know, yet at the same time he dreaded informing him of it. He thought of the piece of paper he had taken off the man at the radio, but he knew he dared not read it in front of Okomo.

A wave crashed over the bow of the trawler. "How deep is the water here?" Nishin asked.

"Eighteen fathoms. Just over a hundred feet," Captain Ohashi said.

A voice cried out on the forward deck. Nishin looked down at a Yakuza who was pointing to the port. Two figures in life vests were struggling in the heavy swell.

A Yakuza raked them with fire from an AK-47, killing both men. "Pull the bodies on board!" Okomo yelled out. "Take their lifejackets off and throw them back for the sharks to have." The Yakuza did as they were ordered. "Another circle," Okomo said. "I want no one alive to tell tales."

* * *

Lake's arms were like pistons as he rammed the handle back and forth in the one inch of slack. He was leaning now, the deck beneath his feet angled at thirty degrees to starboard. There was no give yet in the wood on the other side, but there were no other options. Perspiration poured down his neck, seeping into the collar of his wet suit, joining the sweat that was already soaking it.

There was a loud crashing sound and the ship paused in its forward momentum. Lake didn't stop, his arms moving back and forth.

''One of the forward cargo hatches just went,'' Captain Ohashi said as the sound reverberated through the fog. ''It won't be long now. The water will get to the engines soon.''

They had circled the trawler twice now and found no other survivors. The bow of the trawler was now completely underwater. As the ocean cascaded into the forward hatches, the ship dipped farther down until everything was under except the bridge castle, angled over to the right, sinking down a couple of feet a second.

''Let's go home,'' Okomo ordered.

Ohashi spun the wheel about and pointed the prow of the ship toward the Golden Gate. Nishin turned and watched, his last sight the top of the bridge of the trawler disappearing and nothing left on the surface. Then the fog swallowed up the tug.

Lake had listened to the engines sputter and stop a couple of minutes ago. At least the list wasn't getting any worse, staying steady at about thirty-five degrees to starboard. But he could hear hatches blowing out and water tearing through bulkheads under his feet. The ship was dying and he didn't have very long before he matched its fate.

There was the slightest give in the distance the hatch moved freely, perhaps an extra quarter inch. Lake's arm muscles were screaming in pain from the exertion of the constant movement. He laid on the floor and jammed his back against the floor as he used his feet to kick the handle, then his arms to pull it back the inch and a half, then he kicked again. He fell into the new rhythm even as he heard water sloshing in the hallway on the other side of the door. The seal on the door wasn't perfect as water under pressure slowly began to seep in around several spots on the frame as the water filled the corridor outside.

The PVC pipes exploded, sending shards of plastic through the room. Seawater spurted through where they had been. Lake shook the spray out of his eyes and turned his head. The level in the room was going up at an inch every five seconds. Slower than the ship was going down, he estimated, based on how quickly the water had filled up the passageway on the other side of the hatch.

The arc of movement on the handle was getting slowly larger, now almost two inches. As water crept up around his chest and threatened to cover his head, Lake had to stand and go back to just using his arms. As his muscles worked, his mind calculated. There were three variables. The wood holding the door shut was the key one. If it didn't give before water filled the room, nothing else mattered. If it did, then there was the question of inside pressure versus outside water pressure. The ship was probably all underwater now and the pressure outside was greater than that in here. Lake wondered how deep the ocean was at this point. If they went down over a hundred feet, he could forget everything. There was no way he could make it out of the bridge complex and then make it to the surface from that depth.

The water edged up around his hips and continued sliding up his body. Lake had tied off the trash bags with the document box in them to his weight belt and the box thumped against his back as he continued to work the handle.

As the water reached his neck, Lake's hands slipped off

the handle. He quickly regained his grip and continued. Three inches now.

"Goddamn!" Lake hissed. The thing had to give! He accidentally sucked in a mouthful of seawater and tilted his head up to spit it out. He stood on his toes and took a deep breath, then squatted, completely submerged and gave one great shove. Four inches but that was all.

Lake let go and floated to the air trapped in the upper-left corner of the room and took another breath. He felt the ship settle and come to a halt, still angled down and to the right. Lake didn't know it, but the keel was down at over a hundred feet, but the height of the ship itself and the bridge tower put his depth at just about sixty feet below the ocean's surface.

Lake dove down to the handle and gave three shoves before he had to swim back to the air pocket. It was about four feet by three feet by fourteen inches deep. Lake visually marked a spot on the wall before he dove back down for another try. When he came back for more air, he noted that the pocket had lost two inches. That gave him about four or five more tries before he was out of air. At least the pressure on both sides of the door would be equal now, which was a slight consolation.

Lake dove down and grasped the handle. He pulled it up, then slammed it down. Up again, then down. He felt something give. Excitedly he spun the handle and was rewarded with the door swinging open. The way out beckoned.

Lake turned and swam up to his air pocket, which was now less than six inches in depth. He tilted his head back and his mouth was just below the ceiling as he sucked in several lungfuls of air.

Taking one last deep breath, he turned and dove for the door. He shot through and turned left up the outside corridor. The door to the left railway was open and Lake was out in the open, then he slammed to an abrupt halt, his waist jerking him. He twisted and looked. The garbage bag had caught on the railing and he was anchored to the ship. His hand grazed down his side and pulled out his dive knife. Just as was about to slice through the offending plastic and free himself he halted. He reached down and grabbed the railing with his free hand. Dropping the knife, he pushed on the bag and freed it. Then he finned for the surface. Looking up, Lake could only see dark green. He had no idea how deep he was.

He reached and grabbed the knobs of his life preserver and popped them. The water wings inflated and accelerated his race to the surface.

Lake trailed a steady stream of bubbles out of the corner of his mouth as he'd been taught to do by sadistic instructors so many years ago in the water outside of Coronado, California, just a couple of hundred miles to the south of here.

But he realized he'd never been as deep as this as he ran out of air to blow out. He felt his chest spasm, then he involuntarily opened his mouth and seawater came in, filling his mouth, leaking down his throat into his lungs. Lake spasmed, doubling over, no longer swimming, his body fighting to expel the foreign substance filling his lungs, but no matter how much he retched out, it was just replaced with more water.

Lake felt unconsciousness from lack of oxygen coming and he was looking forward to the relief from the pain in his lungs when he burst to the surface. He retched again, water and vomit pouring out of his mouth and air making its way in as he gasped. Lake's insides felt like they were being torn apart as he coughed and hacked at the same time trying to suck oxygen in.

After several minutes of agony, he could breathe somewhat normally and he lay on his back and looked up. The fog was dissipating and the ocean around him was empty. There was a three-foot swell and an occasional wave lapped over his face.

Lake knew the currents around here were not favorable.

He was caught in the great surge of water coming out of the Golden Gate and pushing out to sea. He lay on his back and began finning to the east, even though he knew it was futile; the outward current was much stronger and quicker than his leg strokes.

Lake reached across his chest with his left hand and pushed a button on the side of the homing device that Araki had given him. Now he was going to find out how trustworthy his expedient partner was.

CHAPTER 9

SAN FRANCISCO
WEDNESDAY, 8 OCTOBER 1997
2:00 A.M. LOCAL

"I want the rest of the payment credited to the same account before close of business today," Okomo said. The wounded were being carried off the tug to dark cars parked on the otherwise deserted pier. They were being whisked away to doctors who owed the Yakuza a favor.

"You will be paid," Nishin said, deliberately omitting the title of respect he had so grudgingly been forced to use the last several hours. He no longer needed the old man and would be glad to be done with all of this.

"That includes the payments for the dead," Okomo growled.

"Yes, yes, I will include the blood money."

"Some of those wounded may die of their wounds," Okomo added.

Nishin again felt he was in the fish market dickering with some old hag. "Sensei Nakanga will contact you in two weeks. Let him know if there are more dead. But do not count bodies that are still breathing, old man, or you will face the wrath of the Black Ocean."

"Ah, the puppy growls," Okomo said with a short laugh.

"But you do not have very long teeth," he added. "Remember, you are not out of reach of my arm yet."

Nishin turned his back on the Oyabun and walked off the tug. He headed for the first phone booth he could find. Stopping at it, he reached into his pocket and pulled out the piece of paper. There were two messages on it, from the dates, obviously copied from messages in the box.

Nishin ran his eyes down the first one.

DTG: 1 AUGUST 1945/1000 HOURS TOKYO
FROM: IMPERIAL NAVY STAFF/COMSUBGP
TO: COM/1 24/EYES ONLY
TEXT: PROCEED TO HUNGNAM, KOREA, AT FLANK SPEED TO TAKE ON CARGO. FURTHER ORDERS WILL FOLLOW.

Then he read the second one and his heart felt an icy hand surround it. He now understood why the North Koreans had been so willing to die.

With shaking fingers he dialed the phone number he had memorized and was gratified to hear Nakanga's voice answer after the second ring.

"Yes?"

"It is Nishin." He knew that the Society's phones were secure. The chances of this pay phone being tapped were not significant enough to be considered a threat.

"Yes?"

"The target has been destroyed."

"With the papers?" Nakanga asked.

"Yes."

"Any problems?"

"There was a radio transmission just prior to the target being destroyed."

There was a sharp intake of breath on the other end. "We will check on that."

Nishin related the frequencies and radio data that he had memorized. "I also have the content of the message," Nishin said.

"Go ahead."

Nishin read both messages. When he was done, there was a long silence, then finally Nakanga spoke. "I will have to speak to the Genoysha about this. Remain there. Await further orders."

"There is something further."

"Yes?"

Nishin told Nakanga about the American arms dealer and how he had been on board the ship.

"Was he there to collect his payment?"

"He was in the room with the box of documents," Nishin said. "I do not believe he would have been there simply to collect a few thousand dollars."

"Then he was not simply an arms dealer?" Nakanga asked.

"I do not believe so."

"You are sure he died with the ship?"

"Yes. There were no survivors."

"You must try to find out who this American worked for. How much he knew and how much he told those he worked for." The phone went dead and Nishin slowly put the receiver down.

The man who Nishin was concerned about in death was actually very much alive at the moment. Lake's legs had settled into a smooth rhythm that he knew from experience was propelling him at three knots through the water. The only problem was that he estimated the current he was swimming against was about six to eight knots which meant he was going farther out into the Pacific at three to five knots an hour.

The option of turning and swimming with the current,

while it would certainly go with the flow, was unacceptable because no matter how fast he swam, Lake didn't think he'd be able to make it to Hawaii; alive at least.

If Araki had chartered a boat, which Lake assumed he had done, the CPI agent would be heading out here and the less distance he had to go, the quicker he'd pick Lake up. That is if Araki was looking for him.

There was always the possibility that he'd get picked up by a passing ship, Lake consoled himself with as he swam. He was in the shipping lane for San Francisco Harbor. There was a chance something would pass by, in which case he could use the flare strapped to his left calf.

Lake became aware of a strange hissing noise that he'd never heard before. He twisted about, treading water, but in the darkness could see nothing. But he felt that something was different in the waves around him. He focused on his hearing because it was the sense that had alerted him. There was still the faint hissing noise, but now there was also the sound of waves splashing against something solid. As another swell lifted him, Lake looked about.

He blinked. A large black form in the shape of an inverted V, with the points in the water, was silhouetted against the night horizon about fifty feet away. Lake watched the ship as it got closer. He'd never seen anything like it. With its sharp angles and flat surfaces, the thing it reminded him of most was the F-117 stealth bomber. Lake couldn't hear the throb of conventional engines, just that hissing noise.

A brief burst of red light showed on the right front. A man's figure was briefly outlined, then the light was out.

"Lake?" Araki's voice called out.

"Here!" Lake yelled.

A rope ladder was thrown down the slick skin of the ship. Lake turned on his stomach and swam over, grabbing hold of one of the rungs. As he pulled himself up, he was surprised to feel that the hull surface wasn't metal, but rather some form of hard rubber. He climbed up the side to where Araki was waiting on a small indentation. The hatch opened once more, bathing them in red light, and Araki led him inside, quickly shutting the hatch behind.

Lake looked around. He was in a large room, obviously the bridge of the ship based on the equipment and amount of activity. Several men in uniform, all Japanese, were watching various screens that showed the sea outside and monitoring computers that gave them readouts. There were no windows and all was lit in the red glow that had come out the hatch.

"Impressive, isn't it?" Araki said.

"What is it?" Lake asked.

"The pride of the Japanese Maritime Self-Defense Force. A stealth surface ship. You saw the outside. It has an inverted triangular hull with a propulsion unit in each leg. This is the bridge. Weapons systems, crew quarters, and supply areas are behind us. All sides of the ship are inclined at angles designed to defeat radar, including missile lock-on systems such as that used by the Exocet."

Lake had heard that the U.S. Navy had experimented with a design such as this and then discarded it in favor of the more traditional ships they were used to. "How does the propulsion system work?" he asked. No one in the crew had come over; they all seemed to defer to Araki, which Lake found interesting.

"Seawater is taken in, put under pressure, and pushed out the rear. Very quiet and efficient and undetectable by sonar outside of five hundred meters away."

"Weaponry?" Lake asked as he unbuckled his belt.

"Surface-to-air and surface-to-surface missiles fired from closed hatches along the top rear deck. Two subsurface torpedo tubes, one on each propulsion pylon."

Lake untied the garbage bags from his belt. "How did you get this here?"

"This way," Araki said, gesturing toward a hatch. "I have some dry clothing for you."

Lake picked up the garbage bag and allowed himself to

be led to a small stateroom. Araki handed him a dark blue jumpsuit.

"I don't suppose you have any cigarettes?"

Araki shook his head. "There is no smoking on board. The captain is very particular."

Lake peeled off the top of his wet suit. "So, how did you get this here?"

"I told you that my government considers this mission very important. I was assigned the appropriate assets to get the job done."

Lake pulled on the jumpsuit. He noted that Araki was looking at the garbage bag.

"How long have you been in the area?" Lake asked. The relief of being rescued had not yet registered on his emotions; he didn't have time for that. It would have to wait for later when he was alone.

"I just arrived here. I picked up your signal and homed in on it." Araki took the homing device from Lake and put it in his pocket. "I assume you got the documents," he added, pointing at the garbage bags.

"I got them," Lake said.

"And Nishin?"

"Nishin got away."

Araki nodded. "I have his signal heading back to San Francisco. I was hoping it was a signal from a dead body."

"No, last I heard, he's very much alive," Lake said.

"You heard?"

"I heard his voice through a hatch just before he left the trawler."

"The North Koreans?"

"The trawler went down. I assume all the North Koreans are dead." Lake related the story of what had happened on board the *Am Nok Sung*, from his jumping out of the helicopter to being picked up by Araki.

Araki picked up with his end of things. "I had the helicopter take me to the Farallon Islands, which are about twenty-one miles outside of the Golden Gate. I was dropped off on a small islet where I had arranged for this ship to be nearby on station. I contacted the captain on my satellite phone and he picked me up with a rubber dinghy. We headed toward your beacon as quickly as possible."

"What now?" Nishin asked.

"Let's find out what all the fuss is about," Lake said. "Do you have a knife?"

Araki produced a stiletto from inside his right boot, something Lake noted for future reference. Lake slit through the layers of garbage bags until he uncovered the document box, somewhat battered for its recent journey but dry at least.

He put the box on the bed next to him and pulled off the lid. He found the bound group of papers that had been on the deck and let it fall open to where the pages were bent. "What's that say?" he asked.

Araki sat on the other side of the box from Lake and leaned over.

"Date, time, group, 1 August 1945. 1000 hours. Tokyo. From the Imperial Navy Staff—there's some letters here, C-O-M-S-U-B-G-P."

"Commander Submarine Group would be my guess," Lake said.

"To," Araki continued, "C-O-M, slash, I-24. Eyes only."

"Commander of whatever I-24 was," Lake interpreted. "It must be a submarine if the orders are coming from the commander of the submarine group."

Araki nodded. "Submarines had the *I* prefix to identify them from surface ships during the war."

"The rest of the message," Lake prompted.

"Text. Proceed to Hungnam, Korea, at flank speed to take on cargo. Further orders will follow." Araki looked up. "That's it."

"Cargo," Lake said, rubbing the stubble of beard on his chin. It snapped into place. "That means this submarine, I-24, took something out of Hungnam before the end of the war. The Koreans must be looking for it. Whatever it is I assume it would give them proof that the Japanese atomic bomb program existed.''

''I have been thinking about that,'' Araki said. ''To be frank, I find it hard to believe. I have never heard even the slightest rumor about such a program during the war.''

''I find it hard to believe also,'' Lake said, ''but it's the only explanation that fits what's going on right now.''

Araki frowned. ''Do not blind yourself to possibilities. Maybe this is all a setup to make us believe there was a program. There may be no proof. Maybe the North Koreans are simply doing this to raise a flicker of suspicion which the media, if it gets a hold of, will fan into a raging fire.''

''It doesn't make any difference,'' Lake said. ''We still have to pursue this as if it were true. This message is real, so let's stay with that. This sub must have come in and taken something out. Maybe the scientists behind the project.''

''It says cargo,'' Araki said.

''People can be cargo,'' Lake replied.

Araki shook his head. ''I don't think so. The Japanese word used is specific for inanimate objects. That's not to say people also weren't taken on board, but from what I read here, the primary purpose of this order is for the sub to pick up something.''

''Perhaps all their data,'' Lake said. ''It would make sense that they would want to save as much information as possible before destroying the base.''

''The date of this message is 1 August 1945,'' Araki said. ''That is two days before Hiroshima was bombed and several days before Nagasaki was bombed.''

''They might not have known the end was near then,'' Lake said.

Araki ceded that point. ''The home islands were preparing for a great defense. Before the bombs were dropped, it was thought the war would last another year at least.'' Araki flipped over the page. ''Perhaps we can find the further instructions and—'' His voice choked and he paused.

''What's the matter?'' Lake said, snapping up straight on the bed, sensing the dramatic mood change in his fellow agent.

''Date, time, group, 2 August 1945.'' Araki read the deciphered words in a flat monotone. ''1745 hours. Tokyo. From the Imperial Navy Staff, Admiral Sakire, Fleet Commander. To COM, slash, I-24. Eyes only.''

''Text. Pick up Genzai Bakudan at Hungnam. Follow orders of Agent Hatari, Kempei Tai. Proceed to primary target, Code Name Cyclone. Secondary target, Code Name Forest.''

''What's Genzai Bakudan?'' Lake asked.

''An atomic bomb,'' Araki whispered.

Lake blinked. ''They had another bomb and they put it on the sub?''

''And they had a primary and secondary target,'' Araki added.

''Great,'' Lake said. ''Just fucking great.''

A long silence descended as both of them considered the import of this message. Lake was the first to break the silence. ''So where's Cyclone and where's Forest?''

Araki couldn't answer that, not that Lake expected him to. He was still processing this startling piece of information. Lake changed direction. ''So where is I-24 now?''

Araki was thumbing through the message in the bound group. ''I'm looking for any further transmissions to the submarine.''

''Obviously they didn't succeed,'' Lake noted.

''But if this is true then there *is* a bomb out there with 'made in Japan 1945' stamped all over it,'' Araki said.

''Probably at the bottom of the Pacific,'' Lake said.

''This can never be made public,'' Araki said.

''Why not?'' Lake asked, even though he knew exactly why not. He wanted more information from Araki, and while the man was still unsettled over the shock of this discovery, it was as good a time as any. "It's over fifty years ago, for Chrissakes."

"Do you know what public opinion in your country will be if it is found out that the Japanese had atomic weapons at the end of World War II? And they issued orders launching an atomic assault against a target?"

"It'll even the score card," Lake said. "Except we did it right."

Araki didn't smile. "This is no time for humor."

Lake hadn't exactly meant to be funny. He didn't have much sympathy for Araki. "They didn't contemplate it, as you said, but they actually did it. They ordered this submarine to conduct the mission. Kind of knocks you off the old atomic moral high ground, doesn't it?"

Araki's fingers feverishly flipped pages and his eyes were scanning.

"We may be pole-vaulting over a mouse turd here," Lake said as he slowed his racing mind and considered the situation. "The explosion in the harbor at Hungnam may have been the bomb they loaded onto this sub going off prematurely or even on purpose to prevent it from falling into enemy hands."

"Maybe," Araki acknowledged, "but we can take no chances. If I-24 is at the bottom of the Pacific, we must find out where and make sure it is never discovered."

"I doubt that—" Lake began, but Araki cut him off.

"Listen to this! It is a message from the Imperial Fleet Commander, to the commander of I-24, dated 10 August." Araki looked up. "That is the day Japan radioed the Allies and said they were willing to negotiate a surrender." He looked back down. "The text of the message reads: Change course. Abort attack on primary target, Cyclone. Proceed to secondary target, Forest, at flank speed."

The first two words of the text struck Lake. "They were at sea for over a week when that message was sent. They'd already been to Hungnam and were on their way to the primary target. So much for the explosion in the harbor being I-24." Lake pointed at the folder. "Anything in there that says what happened to the I-24?"

Araki went through the rest of the folder. "There's nothing further."

"Great, just fucking great," Lake said.

"Look at the bright side," Araki said. "If we don't know, the Koreans don't know either. And we have the documents."

"I don't think we're going to get off that easy," Lake said. "What if the Koreans know what Cyclone and Forest are the code words for? That will give them an idea of where to look."

"We need to check into that," Araki agreed, "and also see if we can find out the fate of I-24."

"You contact your government and take me back to San Francisco," Lake said. "I know someone who might be able to help me find out about the code words."

SAPPORO, HOKKAIDO, JAPAN
THURSDAY, 9 OCTOBER 1997
8:20 P.M. LOCAL

Cyclone and Forest. Kuzumi had the intercepted and decrypted North Korean message on his desk, probably before the North Koreans did. The Black Ocean had access to better technology than even the Japanese government did since most of it was invented by companies that the Society had a hand in controlling or developing. Anything they gave to the government to use, they first had to insure that they had something better made that could defeat it.

Kuzumi stared at the text of the old messages. When the second message had been sent, he had already been taken prisoner by the Russians. He did not know the destinations those two words were the code for. Since the Navy had sent the message, it was likely that the codes were originated by the Navy. He would have to check on that.

What he did know was the atmosphere in Hungnam leading up to that message being sent. In March 1945 there had been little hope that they could make one bomb, never mind two. What little uranium they had scraped together had been used in experiments or lost to American submarines in shipment from Japan to Korea. It was the Germans who had come to their aid.

In early April the Germans decided to mount a special mission to Japan, one that showed the desperate straits the Third Reich was in at the time. Two specially modified submarines, the U-234 and the U-235, were assigned the mission. Kuzumi had found the numbers most interesting and considered it at the time to be a fortuitous stroke.

The two U-boats were modified mine-layers and among the largest submarines constructed in the world. Almost three hundred feet long and weighing in at 22,000 tons, they were ideally suited for their role as underwater cargo vessels. And into those two submarines, the Third Reich packed some of its greatest secrets and assets to be sent to Japan to continue the fight as the Russian juggernaut rolled down on Berlin.

The Germans loaded the plans for their two jet aircraft, the Messerschmitt 262, which made an appearance in the skies over Europe just before the end of the war, and the 163 Komet, which never became operational. They also added in samples of jet fuel and directions for making more. There were various other items, but of special significance to the Genzai Bakudan project was the twelve hundred pounds of uranium that was packed into special metal containers and put on board the U-235. A Japanese liaison officer from their embassy in Berlin was on board each submarine.

The two submarines departed Germany on the twelfth of April, paused briefly in Norway, then headed for the Atlantic to begin their long journey. Their route would be through the English Channel, south through the Atlantic, around the Cape of Good Hope, into the Indian Ocean and then to Japan. The odds of both ships making it that far were very low.

The two subs were not in communication with each other, but did have contact back with Germany. By the time they made it out into the middle of the Atlantic, Hitler was dead and the war in Europe was over. In Hungnam, Kuzumi remembered hearing the news and believing it spelled the death knoll for Japan also. Now the Allies could focus all their destructive energy on Japan.

On the tenth of May, Admiral Doenitz sent a broadcast to all U-boats, ordering them to surrender and giving directions about where to go. The captain of the U-234 complied, sailing west to the United States. The Japanese officer on board committed ritual suicide. The ship was boarded by an American crew and brought into Portsmouth, New Hampshire, under heavy guard and tight security.

U-235, however, did not surrender. No one knew what had happened to it. That is until it showed up in Hungnam Harbor on the eighth of June. Kuzumi could clearly see in his mind that day as the strange submarine surfaced and was challenged by a patrol boat. The excitement as the flag was unfurled from the conning tower. The uranium was taken off and immediately put into production. The U-235 took on food and fuel, then turned back to sea, disappearing forever, most likely destroyed by the Americans who thought it was a Japanese submarine.

The Genzai Bakudan team worked nonstop, Kuzumi remembered, toiling over the parts of the project, trying to bring it all together in the cave on the hillside overlooking the valley where most of the components were produced.

The intelligence forwarded by TO from Nira and other agents in the United States indicated that the Americans were progressing on their Manhattan Project. In early May it was reported that the Americans had exploded a small batch of uranium with TNT as a preliminary test. Kuzumi had been glad to get the results of the American test since Genzai Bakudan could not afford that luxury; there simply wasn't enough uranium to be spent in such a manner, even with what the Germans had brought.

Then in July there was the rumor that the Americans had actually detonated an atomic bomb in the middle of one of their vast deserts. Security had been so tight that no Japanese or TO agent had been able to confirm or deny the rumor. Even Nira did not know. Kuzumi believed it was true and told the Genoysha that. By that time Genzai Bakudan was in its final stages. They had one bomb assembled. Kuzumi wanted to test it. He was overruled by the Navy. They only had enough uranium to make two bombs. They could not waste one on a test. He was ordered to complete the second one.

Kuzumi had recommended that they use the one bomb anyway. Attack an American carrier task force off the coast with it. Again he was ignored. There were fears the bomb would not work and would be captured. There were also fears that the bomb *would* work and that the retaliation unleashed upon Japan would be even more devastating than the current state of affairs. There was concern that if the Americans had successfully tested a bomb in July, that they then might have a stockpile of atomic weapons and detonating the one Genzai Bakudan had could bring a rain of American-made atomic bombs onto Japan.

So Kuzumi was frozen out of the decision-making process on how the bombs were to be used and spent his time putting together the second one. And that was why he had no idea where Cyclone or Forest was and where I-24 was now. But now as Genoysha he could find out. Of that he was sure.

CHAPTER 10

SAN FRANCISCO
WEDNESDAY, 8 OCTOBER 1997
11:30 A.M. LOCAL

Lake waited in the small foyer outside Dr. Harmon's office. Araki had had both of them dropped off from the stealth ship at a deserted pier several miles south of San Francisco along the rough coastline there that he obviously had scouted out at some earlier time. A van was parked at a shopping center a mile inland and Araki had the keys. Lake had had Araki drop him at one of his bolt-holes in a motel where he'd caught a couple of hours sleep before taking the BART to the campus.

Lake could only continue to marvel at the extent of the CPI's operation. If nothing else came of this, Lake decided, he would have to alert Feliks to the capabilities of their Japanese counterparts and the ease with which they moved in the United States and the waters just off the coast. At the very least, Lake mused, as he heard the click-click of a lady's heels come down the hallway, he might get a Gold MasterCard.

Dr. Harmon graced Lake with a smile as she opened the door. "Well, look what the cat dragged in," she said. "You don't look like you had the most restful night."

"I didn't," Lake said. He pointed. "I found your box and brought it back."

"Where did you find it?" Harmon asked as she unlocked the door to her office.

Lake followed her in. "I don't suppose you have any coffee?" he asked.

"I can make a pot," she replied, turning to one of the bookcases and uncovering an old coffeemaker from behind a pile of books.

"Do you mind if I smoke?" Lake asked as she came back in with a pot full of water.

"Only if I can join you," she said. She took the offered cigarette. "This building is tobacco-free, as all the buildings on campus are; but no ever really comes in here, so I think we can get away with one or two." Her eyes narrowed. "Your hands are shaking."

That surprised Lake. He looked down. His hands *were* shaking.

"What happened?" she asked.

With the hiss of the water shifting through the coffeepot in the background, Lake began the story of the previous evening. He kept out many of the details, but quickly gave her a sketch of events from taking off in the helicopter to being rescued by Araki, the discovery of the messages to I-24, and being brought to shore.

When he was done, Harmon was shaking her head. "I don't know whether to believe you or think that's the most outrageous story I've ever heard."

"I don't have any proof—" Lake began, but he paused as she raised a hand.

"I believe you," Harmon said.

"What?"

"I said I believe you. I believed you yesterday and I believe you today."

"Why?" Lake asked.

Harmon smiled. "Let's say it's my own woman's intuition."

"I don't think that's enough to—"

"Would you stop?" she said. "You just can't keep questioning everything and everyone."

Lake blinked as she took both his hands in hers. They felt wonderfully warm. Her eyes locked into his. "You're alone, aren't you? All alone?"

Lake was so taken aback that he answered honestly. "Yes."

"Well, right now you're not," she said. Then he saw her own shoulders twitch and she withdrew her hands and the warmth was gone. "I'm a historian after all," she added. "I know that very strange things go on all the time—the old truth-is-stranger-than-fiction line. I'm just glad you made it out alive."

To that Lake had no reply. He was just looking down at his hands, remembering the feeling of hers.

"Let me see the messages," Harmon said, breaking the silence. Lake handed her the file and flipped it open to the first one. He then pointed out the second and third ones to I-24.

"They must have been in dire straits to use the words 'Genzai Bakudan' openly in the second message," Harmon noted. "That was a mistake."

"Any idea what Cyclone or Forest are the code words for?" Lake asked.

"Not off the top of my head," Harmon replied. "The U.S. Navy in World War II broke the Japanese encryption code early on. But code words for specific locations such as these are different.

"In late May 1942, U.S. Navy analysts were intercepting and decrypting quite a bit of traffic that indicated that the Japanese were preparing a major operation. They could decrypt everything, including the code word of the intended target: XXXX. The problem was, like us, they didn't know where XXXX was. They suspected it might be Midway Island, but the Japanese plan was so complex with so many different feints and maneuvers, it was hard to tell.

"So the code breakers devised a simple plan. They had the American forces on Midway send a radio message in the clear that they knew the Japanese would intercept. The message seemed quite innocent, simply stating that the water desalinator on Midway had broken and certain repair parts were needed.

"A couple of days later, they intercepted a Japanese message to the fleet at sea. When it was decoded, it said that XXXX's water desalinator had broken. Thus the U.S. Navy knew that the main Japanese thrust was aimed at Midway."

"Pretty ingenious," Lake said. "The only problem is that we're fifty years too late to be sending any messages using these code words." He looked at the map of the Pacific on the wall behind her desk. "Do you have any idea what would be a priority target for a Japanese atomic bomb that late in the war?"

"For an atomic weapon delivered by submarine?" Harmon mused out loud. "My first guess would be the Allied fleet. By the time of those messages Okinawa had been taken and the home islands were under constant air attack. The Japanese were waiting for the final amphibious assault. Their number one threat was the Allied invasion fleet."

"And where was that in August 1945?" Lake asked.

Harmon stood and stabbed her finger at the map. "Here. The Ulithi anchorage."

Lake had expected an answer such as Pearl Harbor or Manila. "I've never heard of Ulithi."

"Most people haven't," Harmon said. "It's in the Caroline Islands, centrally located between the two thrusts the U.S. was making toward Japan; from the sea, island hopping, and MacArthur's through the Philippines.

"Actually there's not much land at Ulithi, which is why I think it would be a perfect target for a submarine-launched atomic attack. Ulithi is basically a series of atolls surrounding a deep-water anchorage. The Navy desperately needed such an anchorage in this part of the Pacific from which to stage their forces. They learned a bitter lesson in December

1944 when a typhoon hit Task Force 38, sinking three destroyers and damaging numerous other ships. That's the typhoon that the *Caine Mutiny* was based upon. I'd say there's a possibility that the Cyclone code name might reflect the fact that TF 38 sheltered at Ulithi right after the typhoon."

Lake frowned. "I don't think it would be that easy. Code names are usually decided upon by some staff wienie sitting behind a desk and aren't supposed to have any relationship to whatever it is they are the code name for. Usually there's just a list of words and the staff officer is just supposed to use the next one on the list."

"Sounds like you know something about this," Harmon probed.

"So what was at Ulithi in August 1945?" Lake asked, ignoring her comment.

"In August 1945 most of the invasion fleet was gathered there in the anchorage preparing and refitting for the assault on Japan. Several carrier task forces were conducting operations against the mainland, but the troop transports, supply ships, and quite a number of combatant ships would have been there. Destroying the ships at Ulithi and making the anchorage unusable due to radioactivity would have severely set back the American invasion timetable for probably a year. Since the invasion was planned for '46, that means it would have to be put off to '47.

"It's hard to say whether the American public would have stood for two more years of war," Harmon added. "There was a great outcry over troops being shipped from Europe to the Pacific theater. If the Japanese could have destroyed the fleet at Ulithi, they might have been able to sue for peace."

Lake looked at the map. It made tactical sense. The Ulithi anchorage wasn't that far from the Sea of Japan. "How would they do it, though?" Lake wondered. "Would they sneak in at night and try to offload the bomb?"

Harmon shook her head. "I think that whoever armed

the bomb would still be with it when it was supposed to go off. I think they would put it on a midget sub that they would launch to conduct a kamikaze attack.''

''So we're back to the original question,'' Lake said. ''Where's the bomb now?''

''We have to find out what happened to I-24,'' Harmon said. ''And there's something else.''

''What's that?''

''I said that I think Ulithi atoll would be the primary target for the Japanese bomb if they wanted to stop the Allied fleet. But the second message diverts the I-24 from the primary target to the secondary one, Forest.'' She was looking at the map. ''So where's Forest?''

''That's your province,'' Lake said. ''Let's see if we can't track down the fate of I-24 and then maybe we can get a line on Cyclone and Forest.''

''To the basement,'' Harmon said.

''To the basement,'' Lake echoed.

Nishin wasn't worried about Cyclone or Forest or I-24. That was Nakanga's province. Nishin's orders were to find out who the American was and who he worked for. He wasn't glad he hadn't killed Okomo as he headed toward the Japan Center, but he did realize that he had let emotion almost cause him to commit actions that now would have been detrimental to the success of the mission.

He still needed the Yakuza, much as he didn't want to admit it. The same guard was waiting in the restaurant foyer and without a word he led Nishin up to the enclosed roof after searching him.

Okomo did not look like he had spent the night at sea and fought a pitched battle with North Korean commandos. He was seated at the head of his table, underlings lining the table on either side. ''You would be dead right now if your friend Nakanga was not so efficient. The money is in my account. What do you want? Our business is done.''

''I need information.''

Okomo just stared at him. There were glares from the others around the table.

"Oyabun," Nishin reluctantly added.

Okomo was still silent.

"The North Koreans got their guns from an American. He met them at Fort Point to make the exchange, but they did not pay him. They tried to kill him, but he escaped. I need to find out about this American, Oyabun." Nishin didn't add the information that the American had gone down in the *Am Nok Sung*. That would pique the Yakuza's interest too much. "We will pay."

"Of course you will pay," Okomo said.

Nishin stared into the flat black eyes of the old man. He tensed his stomach muscles, feeling the reassuring presence of the ice scraper poking into the flesh. The old man was dangerous, perhaps more dangerous than Nakanga knew.

"I will inform you when I find something out." Okomo waved a hand dismissing him. Once Nishin was gone, Okomo slowly walked back to the rear elevator to make his report.

It was hot down in the basement of Wellman Hall. Lake's shirt was soaked with sweat as he hauled boxes to the old wood desk that Harmon was seated at. She was scanning documents from January 1945 on, searching for any other reference to the code words Cyclone or Forest. Since Lake couldn't read the Japanese text, he was reduced to being the errand boy. He didn't mind. It gave his mind a chance to relax and unwind from the stress of the past several days. And he could also watch her without her knowing. He found himself mesmerized by the way the scant lighting reflected off her face and glowed through her hair. Her eyes flickered back and forth over the paper, then she glanced up, catching him watching and smiled, and he looked away. She returned to reading.

Lake was also glad to be in the basement because it meant his cellular phone wouldn't ring. He had now been out of touch with Feliks and the Ranch well past when he should have checked in.

As he deposited another box on the desk, Harmon looked up. "What happened to your neck?"

Lake was surprised at her directness. People rarely asked, not so much because of politeness, but because Lake tried to always project an image that discouraged people from asking him questions.

"It's a long story," he said.

"I can listen and read at the same time. You have nothing else to do," she added.

Lake sat down on a metal folding chair on the other side of the desk. "I'll make it a short story. It happened a while back. Do you remember when that plane with all those troops coming from the peacekeeping mission in the Sinai crashed in Gander and they were all killed?"

Harmon nodded. "Yes. The official cause, if I remember rightly, was ice on the wings."

"Yeah, that was the official story, but there were some who thought it was a bomb that destroyed the plane. And someone in our government thought they knew who might have planted that bomb. And someone in the chain of command felt that action in retaliation ought to be taken."

"Revenge?" Harmon asked, shutting one file and opening another.

"No, not really. More along the lines of keeping the scales even. You hurt me, I hurt you. With the logical extension that the other guy then will think twice before hurting you again. So I was on the team that was picked to do the hurting back."

"Were you with the same organization that you're with now?" Harmon asked.

"No. Back then I was in the SEALs. Naval Special Warfare Unit Two, stationed in Coronado, California. They selected a squad from my platoon. Six men. I was the leader. We trained with some Agency guy who then picked two of us: me and my chief NCO, Rick Masters. The CIA man then briefed us. Our mission was to infiltrate into a certain country, which I will leave unnamed—and kill the man who had supposedly been the mastermind behind the bomb plot.''

Harmon arched her eyebrows. ''Did they have any proof?''

''They didn't show us any,'' Lake said dryly.

''So the government . . .'' Harmon's voice trailed off.

''Yes,'' Lake said, ''the U.S. government really does shit like that. How do you think we've managed to keep terrorism from our shores for so long? You don't scare the bad guys by being nice. You scare them by being meaner than they are.''

''So did you succeed in being mean?'' Harmon asked. She had stopped reading. All her attention was on Lake.

''Yes.''

''And the scar?''

Lake had been debriefed about the mission, but he had never told anyone outside of official channels about it. He wasn't sure why he had even answered her question about the scar. This entire mission seemed out-of-sorts. Too many pieces that didn't seem to fit other than the fact that Lake had stumbled across them. He wasn't a big believer in coincidence. The events of the last several days he could handle piecemeal as they came up, but the cumulative effect was overwhelming. Being here in this dark archive basement seemed like a refuge from all that. Especially with Peggy Harmon sitting across from him.

He knew there was no evidence to prove what he was saying. It was just like everything else he had told her. And he felt a need to talk, to let out the darkness that had been in him for so many years.

''Rick and I infiltrated the target country after locking out of a submarine,'' he said.

''Lock out?''

''The sub stayed submerged,'' Lake said. ''Rick and I went in to the escape hatch, it filled with water, then we opened up the outer hatch and swam away. We were using rebreathers so we could stay under for quite a while and didn't have any bubbles coming up to the surface. We swam in, landed, cached our gear, and made our way to the target."

"You make it sound so simple."

"It sounds simple, but it wasn't," Lake acknowledged. "The swell was almost six feet at the surface and our rebreathers required that we stay within ten feet of the surface. That meant we caught the surface effect quite severely. It was pitch black and we were fighting a cross-shore current. We were lucky to make it ashore at the right place. We had to cross the beach, cut through a fence—they have a fence along the entire shoreline there—and move inland a couple of hundred meters before we could hide our rebreathers."

Lake remembered the adrenaline rush more than anything else. "I was only five years out of—" He paused. He couldn't tell her about the Naval Academy. That would give her a way of finding out who he was. And just as quickly as he thought it, he felt a sharp twist of disgust with himself and the life he was leading. Always the deception. "I was only five years in the Navy. This was my first live mission. Rick had been shot at before—he was a twenty-year man, so I followed his lead, even though I was the ranking man."

That was an understatement, Lake knew. Rick Masters had been his mentor for two years, ever since he had joined the SEALs. They'd taught Lake a lot in SEAL school at Coronado, but the real learning had begun the first day he'd shaken the hand of the grizzled old veteran who was the team's senior noncommissioned officer. In the SEALs the man with the most experience commanded, not the man with the most rank on his shoulder. It made the unit better.

"Our target was living in a small house not too far in from the beach at a camp where they trained people like him. Rick led the way using the information the CIA had given us. We found the building where our target was supposed to be sleeping. It was guarded by two men. We killed them with silenced pistols.''

That had been the first time Lake had ever killed or used a Hush Puppy. Kneeling in the dark, feeling Rick's hulking presence at his side, the older man whispering out a three-count and both firing at the same time. The two guards crumpling to the ground, their brains splattered against the cinder-block wall behind them. There was no time then to think or feel about it. That would come later, and by the time later came there was much more to think and feel about.

''We went into the building fast. It was one story, only three rooms. The target was sleeping in the back room.'' Lake's voice had gone flat. He was reciting it just as he had in the debriefing. ''He was just sitting up when we kicked open the door to his room. We both fired and killed him. We immediately left the building.

''Everything had gone exactly as planned up to that point. Then it went to shit. The hole in the fence must have been found. We had tied it back together with fishing line so it wouldn't be so obvious, but one of the sentries must have spotted it. Then they had followed our trail to the cache site. There were six men standing right where we'd left the rebreathers. They weren't exactly expecting us to come up. They were too excited over finding the gear. We weren't expecting them to be standing there. It was one big jug-fuck.'' Lake shook his head.

''We came tearing down this ravine and there were these guys. Rick just started shooting and I followed suit. They fired back and it was like World War III. We hit four of them and the other two went to earth right on top of our gear. We heard other guards yelling in the distance and these two guys were guiding them in.

''Rick grabbed me. He yelled in my ear for us to forget the gear and head for the beach. So we did a left-face, scrambled up the slope of the ravine, and then made our way shoreward in the next ravine. The guys back at the cache site were still shooting; we could see their tracers flying through the sky.

"We came to the fence, except not at the point where we had cut the hole. That was about two hundred meters farther up the beach and we could see flashlights up there. So we used our wirecutters and went to work where we were. But by that time the sentries were out in force. A squad came up the fence from the south and spotted us. They opened fire and hit Rick in the initial burst. He went down. I fired over his body and made the bad guys take cover."

Lake finally paused in his story and looked at Harmon. She was perfectly still, as if any movement on her part might derail his memories, but he was into it now. He felt the gun in his hand, jerking from the recoil as he fired at muzzle flashes. Rick lying at his feet, the sound of surf pounding, the crack of bullets flying by. If there had been any other expression on her face, any movement on her part, he knew he couldn't go on. But there was something about her that drew him in and the story out.

"Rick was alive. I grabbed him and pulled him away from the fence, then I used a satchel charge to blow it. No more time for niceties. I just pulled the activating cord and threw it at the fence. It blew and there was a gap. I grabbed Rick and threw him over my shoulders."

Lake didn't add that Rick demanded that Lake leave him. That the older man had insisted that he be left behind to cover Lake's withdrawal. That he knew his wounds were too severe to make it back to the sub. For the first time since he had joined his SEAL team, Lake had ignored his senior NCO.

"I ran across the beach." Lake shrugged. "I don't know why I wasn't hit. I wasn't exactly setting a world record in the fifty-yard dash with Rick on my shoulders. I hit the water still running. When I was waist-deep I realized I was in a little bit of a predicament hauling Rick. I quickly took the safety lines from around my waist and hooked it into his, but I couldn't swim like that. So I looped it around my neck."

Lake touched his scars. "I finned with my legs and pulled with my arms as hard as possible to get out of range from the shore. By then the rope had dug in to my skin so far I couldn't get it out so I just kept it there. I swam for six hours to get to the rendezvous site. My biggest concern was that the blood from Rick's wounds and my neck would attract sharks."

He didn't add in the agony of the rope ripping into the flesh and then the salt water washing over it with each stroke. The rope buried into the torn and swollen flesh, sliding back and forth just a little bit each time. The shifting from swimming on his back to his stomach then back again to use different muscles, each move tearing new flesh around his neck.

"The sub was at the rendezvous spot even though we were late. They surfaced and pulled us in." Lake let out a deep breath. "Rick was dead."

When Lake didn't say any more for a minute, Harmon finally spoke. "I'm sorry."

"I kind of knew he was dead shortly after leaving the beach," Lake said. "He was too hard core of an old cuss to just be towed along like I was doing. I didn't ever stop to check, though."

"But . . ." Harmon's voice trailed off.

"But why didn't I leave him if he was dead?" Lake asked.

Harmon nodded. "He must have slowed you down. What if the submarine had not waited and left your pick-up point?"

"I couldn't abandon him dead or alive," Lake said flatly. He pointed at the box on the desk. "Enough chitchat. Let's get back to work."

"I had to know," Harmon said. She stood and walked behind him. Her hands reached up and she lightly touched his neck, her long fingers tracing the knotted flesh.

"Know what?" Lake was caught off guard, still feeling the resonating effects of telling her what had happened so many years ago and the unexpected pressure of her hands.

"Know who you were. Are," she amended.

"Why?"

"Always the questions," she said with a low laugh. She withdrew her hands and walked back around the desk and tapped the paper in front of her. "So I could decide if I should tell you what Cyclone and Forest stood for."

Lake slowly sat down and waited.

"I have an earlier Japanese message," Harmon continued. "It tracks the American Task Force 54 in January and February of 1945. TF 54 had six battleships, five cruisers, and sixteen destroyers in it, so the Japanese were very concerned as to its whereabouts. In the beginning of 1945 it was at both Cyclone and Forest, according to these decoded messages sent out to the Japanese fleet commanders. Since *I* know from history where Task Force 54 sailed to and from in those days, I know what Cyclone and Forest stand for."

Lake continued to wait. The mood in the basement had changed. It was growing colder and darker.

"Cyclone is Ulithi, as we guessed. Task Force 54 sailed from there to conduct a preliminary bombardment of Iwo Jima between the sixteenth and eighteenth of February. The battleship *Tennessee* was damaged in the action."

Lake's mind was racing one lap ahead. "So Forest is Iwo Jima!"

Harmon doused that with one word. "No." She was looking down at the piece of paper in front of her.

"Well?" Lake finally insisted.

"Task Force 54 sailed from Forest before arriving at Cyclone or Ulithi. Forest is the Japanese navy code word for San Francisco."

SAPPORO, HOKKAIDO, JAPAN
WEDNESDAY, 8 OCTOBER 1997
3:20 A.M. LOCAL

San Francisco. Kuzumi was not surprised at the piece of paper Nakanga had carried in from the intelligence section. It had not taken them long to go back and dig up the code words.

It made sense. San Francisco was the most important port on the American west coast. Most of the war supplies and ships that were thrown into the war against Japan flowed out of the Golden Gate in 1945. But there were other very important factors to be considered when looking at that city.

San Francisco from April through June of 1945 had been host to the inaugural meeting of the United Nations. If Japan wanted to strike back at the world that was bearing down on the Empire, there was no more symbolic target than San Francisco. Even by late August there still were representatives from almost every country other than the Axis powers present in San Francisco working under the fledgling auspices of the UN to develop a new world order.

Nira had to have known. That was the first thought that popped into Kuzumi's head. Was that why she killed herself? When the mission failed, as it obviously did? With her husband declared dead, her child killed in the blast at Hiroshima, and the final mission of the Genzai Bakudan a failure, had she finally given up? Kuzumi thought about it for a few moments and decided it was most likely what had happened. It was what he would have done. He silently mouthed a prayer to the Sun Goddess for his dead lover and his dead son.

And why had Genzai Bakudan failed? Even though he now knew I-24's final destination, he still didn't know where I-24's journey to that final destination had been interrupted. Where did the ship and the bomb rest? Kuzumi could still see the second bomb as clearly as if it were yesterday.

Unlike the American bombs, the Genzai Bakudan had been rectangular shaped. Having decided that they could never make one light enough and small enough to be carried by an airplane, the engineers under Kuzumi's direction had seen no need to develop it with a traditional bomb shape. The rectangle had worked best. It had been over eight feet long by five on each side. They had waterproofed the second one and set it for remote detonation using a radio controller on a specific frequency and amplitude. It had weighed in at over eight thousand pounds when completed.

They had packed enough batteries around the detonator that— Kuzumi stiffened in his chair. They had packed enough batteries that if the submarine was resting on the ocean floor in cold water, there still might be enough juice left for the detonator to fire.

But could it still work after all these years? Would the uranium have decayed past the functional point? Would the metal case have sprung a leak? His scientific training answered each question as it came up. Kuzumi knew the bomb would still be functional unless— He thought about the journey the ship had taken. Most likely the bomb would be sitting in such deep water that the entire casing had been crushed by water pressure. The Pacific was the deepest ocean in the world, and if the journey had been interrupted anywhere between Hungnam and San Francisco it would be lost forever. That is what he had been told had happened to the I-24.

Yes, Kuzumi decided, the Koreans were fishing and their quarry was buried beyond the current capability of any present technology to recover even if it was found.

But then why did he feel so uneasy?

CHAPTER 11

SAN FRANCISCO
WEDNESDAY, 8 OCTOBER 1997
11:30 A.M. LOCAL

"So where's I-24 now?" Harmon asked. They were in her office, having departed the dark basement after finding what they were looking for and putting everything back in place.

The audacity of the Japanese plan was still sinking into Lake's mind. "That's the million-dollar question."

"It must have gone down between Hungnam and here," Harmon said. "I guess we'll never know what happened to it. One of those mysteries of history."

"What makes you so sure it went down, Doctor?" Lake asked.

"Call me Peggy," she said. "I think we know each other well enough to dispense with the formality, although you weren't exactly formal or informal when you came in here with your name."

Lake nodded. "All right, Peggy. What makes you so sure it went down?"

"Well, no one reported it captured," Harmon said. "I

think we would have heard if a Japanese sub had been captured with a nuclear weapon on board.''

''Don't be too sure of that,'' Lake said. ''Bigger things than that have been covered up.''

''Like what?''

''Let's stay with the problem we have,'' Lake said. ''I think an atomic bomb is big enough for us to deal with right now. I think it is possible that the sub was captured. The last message was dated what, the tenth of August, right?''

''Right.''

''So when did the war end?''

''VJ Day was celebrated on the fifteenth of August. That's when Emperor Hirohito made his broadcast saying that the Japanese people must bear the unbearable.''

''Okay.'' Lake walked to the world map tacked to the wall on the side of the room. ''Do you have a calculator?''

Harmon handed one over.

''The I-24 departed Hungnam around the third of August according to those messages, heading for Ulithi.'' He started punching into the calculator. ''They would have to sail south down to the east China Sea. Then they get a message diverting them from Ulithi to San Francisco. Start heading due east at flank speed.

''Let me think. A World War II sub; say ten knots surfaced, about the same on batteries submerged. Distance''—his fingers were flying over the keys—''we're talking over six thousand miles. Let's say six thousand, five hundred miles from Hungnam to San Francisco. On the tenth they would have been . . .'' He grabbed a pen and started writing. ''Sixty-five hundred miles is about fifty-six hundred nautical miles. Moving at ten knots, you make two hundred and forty nautical miles every twenty-four hours. On the tenth they were sixteen hundred nautical miles out. About here.'' He tapped the map. ''On a line between Guam and Iwo Jima and on course for Ulithi.

''So they get the third message and change course

slightly and head due east. On the fifteenth they are another twelve hundred miles east, near Wake Island. Still twenty-eight hundred nautical miles from San Fran. Another eleven or twelve days of sailing ahead. They would have reached here about the first or second of September.''

''The peace was signed on board the *Missouri* on the second of September,'' Harmon noted.

''So I think it's very likely that the I-24 surfaced and surrendered to Allied forces somewhere around Wake Island in the middle of August.''

Harmon shook her head. ''They would never have surrendered.''

''Okay, then, they committed hara-kiri, or whatever it's called, and dove to the bottom of the Pacific when they found out the war was over and they'd lost,'' Lake said.

''That's much more likely than surrender, especially considering the cargo they were carrying,'' Harmon said.

''Well, at least we know it didn't make it here,'' Lake said.

''How do you know that?''

''There was no big boom in San Francisco Harbor in 1945 last I studied my history.''

''Maybe it didn't work,'' Harmon said. ''Maybe it's at the bottom of the harbor.''

''The one in Hungnam worked. At least that's the information you showed me,'' Lake said. ''I would assume this one would have worked. Thus it never made it here.'' Lake pointed at the file folder that had contained the original messages to I-24 that was sitting on her desk. ''You say there are no further messages to I-24 after they were ordered to divert to Forest, which we now know is San Francisco?''

''I didn't find any.''

''Don't you think that's a bit odd?''

Harmon shrugged. ''I don't know.''

''I mean, don't you think someone high in the Japanese command would have realized that they had a sub with a nuke on board heading to blow the crap out of San Francisco while they're in the middle of suing for peace? Don't you think someone would have said, well, whoa, wait a second, let's call that bad boy back?''

''I do think that would be logical,'' Harmon said. She tapped the folder. ''But there's no further message to the I-24.''

''Very odd,'' Lake said. ''The submarine most likely was operating under radio listening silence, but that only means they wouldn't transmit. They would have still been able to receive messages at night when they ran on the surface recharging their batteries.''

Lake felt his pocket buzz. He wished they had stayed in the basement. Feliks was the last person he wanted to talk to right now. He pulled his portable out and flipped it open. ''Lake.''

He recognized the voice on the other end immediately. ''Araki here. I have been trying to get a hold of you for the past hour. Why do you not answer your phone?''

''I was underground,'' Lake said.

''Underground?''

''Why were you trying to get a hold of me?'' Lake asked.

''It is not over. I have received some information from my headquarters,'' Araki said. ''They intercepted a message from Pyongyang to another North Korean trawler already at sea. It is a spy ship just like the *Am Nok Sung*.''

''And?''

''The message ordered the ship to immediately proceed to San Francisco.''

''Maybe they're trying to find out what happened to the *Am Nok Sung*,'' Lake said.

''Maybe. But the message also told them to conduct a search for radioactive material. Now, why would they do that?'' Araki asked.

Because they know where Forest is, Lake realized. He didn't know how they had found out, but he knew they had. And they were going to follow the path the I-24 had taken.

"Can your people keep tabs on that trawler?"

"Yes. It is well east of Hawaii, so it will not take them long to get here. Perhaps two days, maybe even less, since we don't have an exact fix on it yet. I suppose you are not going to tell my why they are heading this way right now, are you?" Araki asked.

"Not right now. Meet me here on the campus at three. I'll explain then." That would give Lake time to figure out what he was going to do and how much to say.

"I will see you at three, then?" Araki repeated.

"Yes." Lake closed the phone.

"Nothing, right?" Harmon asked with a slight grin.

"No, actually it was something," Lake said. He explained that another North Korean trawler was headed this way, with orders to search for radioactive material.

"So the Koreans must know about where I-24 was supposed to go," Harmon said when he was done. "Maybe they're taking a shot in the dark that the I-24 made it close to San Francisco."

She poured them both another cup of coffee. "Again, I don't think the I-24 surrendered," she said. "It would have been against the nature of the crew and officers. No matter what you say, I think we would have heard something if a Japanese submarine carrying an atomic weapon had been captured at the end of the war."

"The other factor to consider," Lake said, "is that if it did surrender, then the Koreans can look for it all they want and they'll never find it. So let's assume it didn't. You said the most likely course of action for the sub was for the captain to take it down for a mass suicide."

"That was my initial thought," Harmon said, "but the more I think about it, the more I believe that the I-24 might have kept on going no matter what. I don't think the captain of the submarine was in charge. Remember that the commander was supposed to follow all orders of"—she flipped through message flimsies—"this fellow Agent Hatari, of the Kempei Tai.

"The Kempei Tai was the Japanese military's secret police during the war. But it's just as likely that this Hatari fellow was an agent of the Black Ocean. They often used the Kempei Tai as cover, especially when they had to deal with the military because a Kempei Tai agent on special assignment, no matter what his rank, could order any senior regular military officer to do as he said. I believe that the I-24 may have pursued its mission to the end."

Lake wondered why she was following this train of thought that they'd already derailed once. "But there was no explosion," he pointed out.

"That doesn't mean that the I-24 didn't make it to San Francisco or somewhere close by," she said. "It just means that the bomb didn't go off. The North Koreans are the ones who triggered this whole thing in the present day," she added. "*They're* coming to San Francisco again. I have to believe that they have access to more information than we do."

Lake thought about it. If the I-24 was down in deep water, it was probably lost forever. The Koreans had the same messages he did and they were sending a ship in this direction. Maybe they knew something more, like Harmon said. Or maybe they were just gambling that the I-24 had gone down in shallow water and could be found. Either way, Lake couldn't afford to ignore the situation.

"Do you have any suggestions?" he asked.

Harmon smiled. "As a matter of fact, I do. During World War II San Francisco Harbor was protected by a submarine net. It stretched for three miles across the main channel entrance from the St. Francis Yacht Club at the Marina to Point Sausalito."

She sketched on a pad. "It was inside of the Golden Gate because the currents were too strong there. Two ships serviced the net, anchored on either side of the thousand-foot movable part. They each had winches on their prows which could move the net. One pulled it open, the other pulled it shut. If the I-24 was going to launch a midget kamikaze sub attack, they would have to have considered how to breach that obstacle. Perhaps they planned on sneaking the midget sub through along with a ship passing in. Of course," she added, "by September 1945, the net might have been left open all the time."

"This is all fine and well," Lake said, getting a little tired of all the history lessons, "but what—"

Harmon held up a hand. "The important thing is that the maritime defense forces had the whole harbor and its approaches wired for sound. They had a hydroacoustic listening station at Fort Miley. The duty personnel kept a log of all contacts. I suggest we go take a look and see if anything was heard around the first or second of September."

"Where would those logs be?" Lake asked.

"Follow me," Harmon said, grabbing her jacket. She paused, then put her arm through his. "Change that to 'please come with me.' "

The Chain Drive was empty this early in the afternoon. Nishin had watched it for the past hour from across the street, making sure he had the area memorized. Okomo had called his room two hours ago and told him he could find out more about the American arms dealer from a man named Jonas, who owned this establishment. It would simply be a matter of extracting the information.

Nishin slipped across the street and opened the scarred wooden door. The interior was dark and he stepped aside from the door and stood still, allowing his eyes to adjust to the lack of sunlight.

"What do you want?"

The voice came from the only other occupant of the room, a large bearded man who stood behind the bar. There were numerous bottles laid out in front of him and he had a clipboard in his hand.

"Are you Jonas?"

"Who wants to know?"

Nishin checked out the rest of the bar. "I will assume you are Jonas, since I was told Jonas owned this place and there is no one else in here."

"Yeah, I'm Jonas. Who the hell are you?"

"I am looking for someone," Nishin said. Now that he could see better, he was looking around the room. He could see the various posters on the walls.

"I don't run a phone book. This is a bar."

Nishin could see that the man's right hand was hidden behind the bar. Nishin walked forward and took a stool directly in front of Jonas. "Then I would like a drink."

Nishin had been briefed about the American Patriots. Extremists who fought against government control. Nishin thought the entire concept quite ludicrous in the country with the laxest society he had ever seen. If you couldn't do it in America, you couldn't do it anywhere. The Patriots didn't have any higher agenda. In his opinion, they were only fighting against something, not for anything. The Black Ocean had the Sun Goddess and the Emperor. To fight negatively like these men did was doomed to failure.

"What kind?" Jonas asked.

"Saki."

"We don't have that piss-water here," Jonas replied. "Why don't you take your act down the street?"

"You are not very hospitable for a man whose occupation is hospitality," Nishin said. He noted that Jonas's right hand was still below the bar. "I will take whatever beer you have on draft."

Jonas stared at him, then reluctantly grabbed a mug with his left hand. He paused, then turned toward the taps. That was what Nishin was waiting for. He swiftly leaned over the bar and grabbed the sawed-off shotgun that Jonas had hidden there.

"Hey!" Jonas yelled. He froze as Nishin pointed the twin large bores at his midsection.

"I have heard that such weapons are illegal, even here

in America,'' Nishin said. ''But it is fortunate that you have this.'' He ignored Jonas's confused look. ''Because I am interested in meeting a man who would deal in such weapons as this. Indeed, I am searching for even more sophisticated weaponry.''

''I don't know nothing about any kind of man like that,'' Jonas growled.

''Ah, but this says differently,'' Nishin said, wagging the end of the gun slightly.

''I did that myself. The gun's legal at full length. I cut it. Any fool can do it with a hacksaw.''

Nishin ran the fingers of his left hand over the end of the bore. ''This was not done with a hacksaw. This was professionally done.'' He shrugged. ''Be that as it may, I do not wish to further waste my time. I am looking for a man who sold eight silenced Ingram MAC-10s to some Koreans a few nights ago.''

Jonas folded his arms over his chest. ''I don't know what you're talking about.''

Nishin gave a deep sigh, then tossed the shotgun to Jonas, who, startled, reached out to catch it. As he did so, Nishin was vaulting the bar, both feet smashing into Jonas's now exposed chest, staggering the bigger man against the back of the bar. Bottles fell and crashed, the shotgun clattered to the floor, and Jonas doubled over trying to catch his breath.

Nishin drew out the modified ice scraper. He grabbed the hair on the back of Jonas's head and pulled his face up. He jammed the point of the ice scraper into the bartender's neck. ''Who was the gun dealer? What was his name?''

''Fuck you,'' Jonas hissed.

Nishin realized he had miscalculated. He had usually found that large men broke easily once you gained the upper hand. He stepped away and scooped up the shotgun, putting the ice scraper into his pocket. Jonas was leaning against the back of the bar, trying to control his breathing, wincing from the pain of broken ribs. Nishin grabbed a large towel from under the bar and wrapped it around the end of the shotgun.

"What are you doing?" Jonas asked, his eyes following Nishin's every move.

Nishin didn't reply with words. He aimed at Jonas's left leg and fired one of the barrels. The towel muted the noise of the blast so that it wasn't heard outside of the bar, but it didn't slow down the pellets that ripped into Jonas's left knee. The joint buckled and Jonas was down, cursing in pain.

"Fuck you! Fuck you!"

Nishin stepped over Jonas's prostrate form and aimed at his groin. "Who was he? You know I will fire again since I already have once."

"Oh, shit," Jonas groaned. "You're fucking crazy."

"I just want some information," Nishin said. "I think I have been most reasonable up to a point."

"I got protection, man. I'm fucking protected!" Jonas screamed.

"I am not interested in your American gangsters or their protection," Nishin said.

"Not the mob, you dumb fuck. I got friends in the feds. The government. They'll be on you like shit on stink."

Nishin found that interesting. "Really? And who exactly are your friends?"

"Fuck you!"

Nishin glanced at the door. At any moment someone might wander in. He got back to his original purpose. He jammed the end of the muzzle into Jonas's groin. "The name of the gun dealer?"

"Lake," Jonas spit out.

"Lake?"

"Yeah, as in a fucking large body of water. Lake. That's all I know. That's the only name he uses."

"Who does Lake work for?"

"He's a freelancer," Jonas said, his eyes still mesmerized by the ripped end of the towel on the end of the shotgun and the smoke curling around the barrel. "He sells guns to whoever has the money. He's been hanging around the Patriots, working with some of them, but he doesn't work for anyone as far as I know."

"Is he a Patriot?"

"Not a member of any group I know, but he seems to support the cause."

"Where can I find him?" Nishin asked.

"I don't know."

"You must have had a way to get in contact with him," Nishin insisted.

"I've got a phone number. It's a hall phone. Sounds like some cheap flophouse. Sometimes he's there, sometimes he isn't."

"The number?"

Jonas recited the seven digits.

"Does this Lake work for your government?"

Jonas shook his head. "Hell, no. He sells guns. I'd know if he were undercover."

"I think you are very stupid," Nishin said.

"Fuck you," Jonas spit out.

"Is there anything else you can tell me about this man Lake?"

"He'll kick your ass," Jonas said. "I hope you do run into him."

"I already have," Nishin said. "And I'm here. He's not. Do *you* work for the government?" Nishin asked. "For your friends who protect you?"

"I got friends," Jonas repeated. "They help me out, I help them out, but I don't work for them. But you mess with me, they'll mess with you."

"Yes, so you've said, but unfortunately they are not here now to help you. And now is the important time for you, isn't it?"

"Fuck you," Jonas said, his hands covered in blood as he pressed down on his injured leg. "You'd better just get your ass out of here while you can."

Nishin didn't reply with words. He raised the muzzle of the shotgun slightly and fired.

"The hydroacoustic system was linked together and terminated at Fort Miley," Harmon explained as she drove. "But they all answered to a central command that controlled the harbor defenses."

"They were really worried about San Francisco being attacked?" Lake asked as they crossed the Bay Bridge. He noted the site of the gun battle from the other night showed little sign of it as they went past, other than some chips in the wall of the tunnel where bullets had struck.

The question put Harmon in her element as historian. "San Francisco was the most tempting target on the West Coast for the Japanese. After Pearl Harbor people here were very worried about getting attacked. No one knew what the Japanese had planned. You have to remember that in 1941 and early 1942 it seemed like the Japanese were invincible and everywhere. It was a very dark time. The list of Japanese successes was quite long: first Pearl Harbor; then Wake Island fell two days before Christmas; Hong Kong fell on Christmas Day; Singapore and seventy thousand men surrendered in February; the Philippines and Bataan; China; Burma; it went on and on.

"As far as the West Coast goes, I do know for certain from my studies that on the night of December 17, a Japanese submarine surfaced outside the harbor and then remained on station up until Christmas before being ordered back to Japan. In fact, an entire Japanese submarine group operated off the West Coast in those early days, sinking quite a few ships. There was one sub for every major port from Seattle down through San Diego and they were supposed to surface and expend all their deck gun ammunition on Christmas Day before heading back to Japan. For some reason the order was rescinded just before Christmas and the subs went back to Japan without incident.

"The U.S. Navy fortified the harbor quite extensively.

I've already told you about the submarine net. They also built defenses against surface ships. Heavy guns were put in at several places. The Navy had shore-mounted 16-inch guns powerful enough to shoot thirty miles out to sea. That's far enough to fire beyond the Farallons, a group of islands off shore."

Harmon and Lake were now driving north on Van Ness, following Route 101 through the city. "The Navy also put in an extensive minefield. All of these defense systems were headquartered at Fort Scott, which was in the Presidio. That's where we're headed right now. I've got a friend who can give me access to all the war records from HDSF at Fort Scott."

"HDSF?" Lake asked.

"Harbor Defense, San Francisco."

Route 101 turned left onto Lombard Street. Lake felt a buzz in his pocket and pulled out his portable. He had no doubt who it was. He turned toward the window and activated the phone.

"Yes?"

"I thought we lost you." Feliks' voice came through clearly, as if he were sitting in the back seat.

"I'm still kicking," Lake said.

"But some Koreans aren't, from what I understand," Feliks said. "Seems there was a bit of gunfight in the tunnel on the Bay Bridge a couple of days ago. Two KIA and several vehicles shot up. Two silenced MAC-10 submachine guns were recovered by the police. The guns were sterile, but you and I know where they came from." Feliks didn't pause. "And there's the matter of no confirmation of a weapons drop that was supposed to be made *last* night. I would assume said drop was made early because some of said weapons were in the hands of the two KIA who are also as sterile as the guns. All that the SFPD has from the autopsies is a racial makeup by the coroner saying they are of Korean ancestry. No ID, no record, no nothing. So who are they?" Feliks asked abruptly.

"North Korean commandos," Lake said.

"North Korean commandos," Feliks repeated. "How curious. What's even more curious is that I haven't heard a damn thing from you for quite a while. Start talking."

Lake had wrestled with answering that question for the past twenty-four hours. He did as good a job as he could of encapsulating the events of the past twenty-four hours, leaving out the presence of Araki and Harmon's help. It took him four minutes, during which Feliks didn't interrupt once. When he drew to a finish, Lake waited.

"This is all about a Japanese atomic bomb from World War II?" Feliks asked.

"Yes, sir."

"If I didn't have these reports of bodies being found, I'd think you had gone nuts. In fact I think you probably have gone nuts."

"I'm only telling you what I've discovered," Lake said.

"It sounds very farfetched. How do we know this isn't all a setup to embarrass us?"

"We don't know," Lake said. "But I didn't think we could take a chance that it's for real."

"*You* didn't think *we* could? Who authorized you to think for me?" Feliks snapped. "I run things around here, in case you've forgotten."

"I am authorized to act on my own initiative," Lake argued. "That's the whole point of—"

"Enough!" Feliks cut him off. "The North Koreans could just be pawns. You could be playing right into the hands of whoever is behind this."

"I—" Lake didn't get past that first word before getting cut off again.

"What action are you taking now?"

"Nothing," Lake said.

"Nothing? Then why didn't you report in?"

"I just found out this information," Lake said. "I was working on a report when—"

"Bullshit! You don't have a clue what you're doing.

You're stumbling around in the dark, tripping over things. I do the thinking and I do the planning! But I can't do a goddamn thing if my operatives do not keep me informed and if they go off on their own all the time."

Lake was surprised. He'd expected Feliks to be upset, but he'd never heard his superior curse before.

"I'm putting you on suspension as of this moment," Feliks continued, his voice cutting through the phone like a whip, causing Harmon to glance over even though she couldn't hear the words. "We have had a major incident involving weapons that you moved without final authorization. You also did not inform us that you had moved the weapons. What if a bunch of civilians had been killed in this gunfight you had on the Bay Bridge? There was no way we could have had damage control prepared for that since we thought the guns were still in the drop site."

Again Feliks didn't wait for an answer. "And if there is any truth to this story you've just told me, who the hell do you think gave you the right to withhold that information?"

Lake assumed that was a rhetorical question, so he remained silent.

"You are to take no further action until I arrive on the scene. At that time you will brief me fully, then you will return to the Ranch for further disciplinary action. Is that clear?"

Lake clenched his jaw. "Yes, sir."

"By the way," Feliks continued, "what was the name of your contact there with the Patriots? The one in the bar?"

Lake was confused by the change in direction. "Jonas."

"That's what I thought. Well, your friend Jonas is dead. Intelligence just picked that up off the San Francisco Police Department internal wire while checking on your little excursion in the tunnel the other night. Someone shotgunned a knee then his head. Any idea who?"

"No."

"Well, you don't know too goddamn much, do you, in

your own backyard there? Sounds like you've managed to screw things up royally.'' Feliks changed tack again. ''I just checked and we have a satellite that can eyeball the inbound North Korean trawler,'' Feliks said. ''How did you find out about it?''

''From frequencies I lifted off the first trawler,'' Lake lied.

''Uh-huh,'' was all Feliks said. ''You hold in place. I'll be there this evening.''

The phone went dead and Lake stared at it. How had Feliks learned about Jonas getting killed if it had just happened a short time ago? He knew the Ranch was tied in to the San Francisco Police Department computer, but Lake also knew that if the Ranch computer was alerting about Jonas's death, that meant the Ranch was double-checking on him, and he didn't like that one bit. He didn't buy Feliks's line that they had picked it up when checking on the incident in the tunnel.

''Trouble?'' Harmon asked. They were on the Presidio now, driving along a tree-lined winding road.

''Yes,'' Lake said. He understood Feliks being upset about his breach of normal operating procedures the past two days, but the extent of the reaction seemed extreme. A field agent normally had quite a bit of latitude in conducting operations. But, then again, Lake had to imagine that if he were in Feliks's position and he received information about a possible Japanese atomic bomb lost in the ocean somewhere, he might be a bit perturbed also. Lake was surprised at how detached he was from any effect Feliks's orders had on him. It was as if it didn't really matter. This thing was a lot deeper than Feliks's anger.

''Can you talk about it?'' Harmon asked.

''I'm being relieved,'' Lake said.

''Relieved?''

''I'm not supposed to do any more work on this case until my superior gets here and I can brief him.''

''Too late,'' Harmon said. ''We're already here. You'll

have to be relieved after we leave because I'm not making this drive again and I'm not going to be involved in this any more than I am already.''

They were in front of a pre-World War II–era building with a red tile roof. Harmon led the way inside. After talking to her friend, she led Lake to a small unoccupied office. ''Wait here. I'll be right back.''

Lake didn't have much time to reflect on his suddenly terminated career, because she was back in less than two minutes with several large canvas-covered books. She thumped them down on the desk. ''HDSF logs for August and September 1945. Shall we?''

''You look, I need to think for a minute,'' Lake said. As Harmon flipped through pages, he unfocused his eyes and slowed his breathing. He felt like he was sitting on a dock jutting out into a large lake. He could see the surface, but what was underneath was hidden from his view. Lake knew that bodies of water held all sorts of hidden threats and treasures. There were forces at work here that he couldn't even begin to understand. Fifty-two years was a long time for things to simmer under the surface.

Harmon's voice intruded on his dark thoughts. ''September the second, 1945, 2027 hours in the evening, hydroacoustics picked up an initial possible submarine contact nine miles out from the Golden Gate, just south of the main channel.''

Lake leaned forward in his chair as she pointed at a small map of the harbor.

''The station that first picked it up was here, on the south peninsula at Hydrangea. Since the war was over, there was no special concern about it being an enemy contact,'' Harmon said. ''The minefield had already been deactivated and the sub net was no longer in service.''

''So the harbor was wide open,'' Lake noted.

''Yes.''

''Is that our boy?'' Lake asked. ''Did the I-24 make it here?''

"I think that may be it," she said. "There's no record in here of any American submarine that was supposed to be in the area. The duty officer specifically notes that. But since the war was over, no alert was issued and no further action was taken."

Harmon tapped the old duty log. "The station tracked the contact in to three miles off the Golden Gate where there's a semicircular shoal called the Potato Patch. Then something strange happened. They heard nothing for a half hour, then the submarine apparently went back out to sea, but the log says there was an echo going in toward the harbor."

Lake frowned. "An echo? What do they mean by that?"

"I think that the initial contact was the I-24," Harmon said. "Remember I told you that they would most likely have a smaller submarine on the deck of the I-24, a midget sub? I think the echo is that midget sub which would have carried the Genzai Bakudan or at least towed it to the target."

Lake looked down at the map. He remembered the current he had faced several miles out to sea from the Golden Gate. From his SEAL training he knew quite a bit about hydrography and he also knew something about seagoing craft. He'd seen pictures of Japanese midget subs, such as the one that was beached on Oahu shortly after the attack at Pearl Harbor.

"I think a midget sub would have a hell of a hard time trying to make it in the Golden Gate, even from only three miles out," Lake said. "The current there is very powerful and a midget sub doesn't have the greatest engine or an unlimited supply of power. Also, one of those old-style nuclear bombs must have weighed a hell of a lot."

"Maybe that's where it all fell apart," Harmon theorized. "They sent out the midget sub and it got caught in the current and pushed back out to sea, lost forever."

"They wouldn't be that stupid, would they?" Lake mur-

mured. Why couldn't the damn sub have just disappeared in the mid-Pacific, he thought to himself.

"Excuse me?"

He was still looking at the map. "I mean they would have known about the current and all that. They were sailors, for Chrissakes." Lake's frustration and anger at the recent phone call and events was seeping out of him, water flowing over a high dike of discipline and self-control. "Something's not right about this." He slapped the table top. "Shit, nothing's right about anything."

He drew his finger across the map to the narrow gap between the peninsula of San Francisco and Marin County to the north. "You said the harbor was basically undefended after the war. The mines were deactivated and the sub gate was open all the time. They would have expected that. So what happened to the mini-sub? Where is it resting?"

Harmon was turning pages in the log, looking for any more information. "Here's something," she said.

"What?"

"The U.S.S. *Honolulu*, a cruiser that was departing the harbor after overhaul, picked up a small sonar contact that coincides with this echo. They tracked it until they lost it at—" There was a sudden intake of breath that caused Lake to look up from the map in concern.

"What's wrong?"

"They tracked it until they lost it against the southern tower of the Golden Gate Bridge." She looked up from the log. "The midget submarine with the second bomb is at the base of the Golden Gate Bridge."

CHAPTER 12

SAN FRANCISCO
WEDNESDAY, 8 OCTOBER 1997
1:05 P.M. LOCAL

"So why didn't they explode it?" Lake asked.

Harmon was seated now, staring at the logs in front of her as if they might suddenly jump up and bite her.

"Maybe it didn't work," she said.

"The one in Korea worked," Lake said, remembering they'd already had this conversation. "There's no point dwelling on that right now. The key issue is, was this contact really a midget sub and, if it was, is it still down there?" The answer came to him even as he asked the question. "Yeah, I think that contact was it and I think it's still down there."

"Why?" Harmon was rousing out of her shock and closing up the logs.

"It makes sense to me now. They knew the midget sub could only stay down so long and make it so far against the current with its batteries. If they could just make it to the mouth of the harbor, they could anchor it against the base of the southern tower. The northern one is connected to land, but the southern one stands alone in deep water. Then with the bomb tied off there, they could blow it at any time. Imagine taking out the Golden Gate? Not only that, but the blast would have hit the headquarters for the HDSF right here at Fort Point and the adjacent areas in the Presidio.'' Lake remembered the other night and the paint sprayer on top of the bridge. ''And the prevailing winds would have carried the fallout right over San Francisco.''

''You really think it's still down there?'' Harmon asked.

''Yes. I think that's what the North Koreans are hot after and has the Japanese scared shitless.'' Lake had a feeling that Araki might even know this and had withheld this little piece of news. Or perhaps Araki had been using Lake as bait on the hook he was using to fish for the bomb's location.

''What are you going to do about it?'' Harmon asked.

''I don't know at the moment,'' Lake said. ''I have to think about it.''

''Well, while you ponder that,'' Harmon said, ''I do have to get back to the campus.''

Lake checked his watch and nodded. ''I have someone I'm meeting there at three.''

Harmon drove out of the lot and headed back to Berkeley. She glanced over at Lake a couple of times. He knew she wanted to talk, but he was deep in thought.

''You're troubled,'' she finally said.

''Well, we just discovered that there might be an old atomic bomb tied off to the base of the Golden Gate Bridge,'' Lake said. ''I'd say that might be cause for concern.'' He sighed. ''I feel like I'm only seeing part of what's going on here. Sort of like an iceberg—most of what's happening is hidden from me.''

''I've been thinking the same thing,'' Harmon said tentatively. ''There's some aspects of this that bother me beyond the idea that there might be an atom bomb sitting at the base of the bridge.''

''Such as?'' Lake asked.

''The end of the war. I've been analyzing it with the added perspective of the Japanese having an atomic bomb.

Asking myself how that would have affected things that happened."

"And what have you come up with?" Lake asked.

"It might explain some things that have puzzled historians, especially recently. Under the Freedom of Information Act, quite a bit of material on World War II has become unclassified and open for researchers to study. One of my colleagues recently published a book based on some of this information. He uncovered documents that indicated that the Japanese and the Russians were conducting secret negotiations in June of 1945. They were going to split Asia between them. That would allow the Japanese to redeploy their Kwantung army in Manchuria—over a million troops—back to Japan to face the American invasion. My colleague stated that the documents he had access to said that the Soviets had very seriously considered the proposal.

"When I first heard of that, I thought it was almost as ridiculous as the story of a Japanese atomic bomb," Harmon said. "I saw no reason for the Soviets to negotiate for what they could, and did, seize by force. But putting the two together, I see now that maybe the Japanese did have something to offer the Russians. Maybe they offered to split Asia between them without a fight *and* throw in the secret of atomic weapons at the same time. The Russians were already splitting up Europe at that time and looking ahead to their next enemy—the United States."

"Jesus," Lake said. He was staring at Harmon as they negotiated the streets of San Francisco. "Do you think that's possible?"

Harmon's hands were gripping the steering wheel tightly. "I think it is. I think the dropping of our bomb on Hiroshima put an end to that, but I think the Russians would have been very tempted to get the secret of the atom from the Japanese and might have been willing to pay a very high price for it. It might also explain why the Russians were so keen on occupying and keeping North Korea after the war was over."

Lake felt a splitting headache, centered right between his eyes. They were turning onto the Bay Bridge, leaving San Francisco behind. "I don't know, Peggy. This whole thing is so far beyond me, I can't even begin to see all the angles and edges to it. Is anything the way it was in the history I was taught in school, or is it all just a bunch of lies and cover-ups and double-dealing?"

"Depends if you want to look at the world as a good place or a bad place," Harmon said.

"No," Lake disagreed. "There is a truth under it all."

"There may be, but it's a truth no one will probably ever know. Even if you can find out exactly *what* happened, you can never be sure you know the *why*. And it's the why behind an action that is key. That's the trouble with being a historian."

"But I'm not a historian," Lake said. "I can try to find out." He looked out the window at the water of the harbor below. "I can most certainly try to find out," he whispered.

He felt her right hand slide over and touch his forearm. It slid down his arm until she had his hand. "I'll help you as much as I can," she said. She wrapped her fingers in his and they made the rest of the trip like that in silence.

"I believe I am getting tired of seeing you here," Okomo said.

Nishin was tired of coming to the Japan Center. He felt like he was tied to the Yakuza's coattail for information, but this was their country, not his. "I need to find where a phone number is."

"You come to me for something as simple as that?" Okomo shook his head. "Have you never heard of a reverse directory?"

Nishin remained silent, not wanting to admit he hadn't. He longed for this mission to be over and to be back in Japan where he understood the environment in which he worked.

''The number?'' Okomo asked, his voice dripping with disgust.

Nishin repeated the number Jonas had given him and one of the men at Okomo's side spoke into a phone. A few seconds later he wrote something down on a piece of paper and handed it to the old man. Okomo looked at it, then folded it and tossed it at Nishin's feet. ''There is the location of your phone. Is there anything else you need? Perhaps someone to wipe your chin after you eat?''

Nishin slowly bent down and picked up the paper. He locked eyes with Okomo.

''Take him out of here,'' the old man said, not blinking. Two Yakuza grabbed Nishin's elbows and hustled him to the staircase. As soon as he was gone, Okomo slowly walked to the elevator to his rear. It slid down into the earth and when the doors opened to the dim red light he stepped forward, head down.

''Nishin is going to the gun dealer's last location.''

The voice that came out of the shadows behind the desk was no more than a rasp, a whisper of what might have once been something more. It was old, but beyond that little could be told of the owner of the whisper. Only Okomo of all the Yakuza was allowed down here. ''That is no longer important. The North Koreans have a trawler en route. It will arrive much sooner than I expected.

''The gun dealer's superior is the one we want to be here and he is coming. Direct Nishin further so that he is where we want at the right time and most importantly so that word gets back to his superior that the stakes have risen and that time is short. Hold your men ready. As we planned, the clouds are gathering and the storm will break very soon.''

Okomo bowed at the waist. ''Yes, Oyabun.''

Lake briefed Araki as succinctly as possible about all they had found out, leaving out the detail of the bomb's location. He felt that since the bomb was in American water, that was more his concern than Nishin's. They were seated on a bench outside Wellman Hall, the sun shining brightly down on them. Students passed back and forth on the walkways all around.

"So the bomb might be here?" was the first thing Araki said when he was done.

"Yes," Lake answered, feeling like he wasn't holding too much back from the Japanese agent. For all he knew, Araki knew exactly where it was. "Somewhere off the coast. Maybe within three miles of the harbor."

"And that is why the Koreans are coming," Araki said. "This is very bad news."

Lake frowned. "How would the Koreans know that, though? It wasn't in the records that we found."

"Maybe they have other information," Araki said.

"What about the trawler?" Lake asked. "When is it due in?"

"Sometime after midnight and before dawn at its present course and speed."

"And your stealth ship is still off shore?" Lake asked.

Araki gave a half-smile. "Perhaps."

Lake had had enough. It was Feliks's problem now. He stood up. "I don't know what's going on and it's no longer my jurisdiction. I'm done with it."

"What do you mean?" Araki asked, surprised at his sudden movement.

"I've been relieved. My superior is coming here to take over the entire case."

"You did not tell him about me, did you?" Araki asked, concerned.

"No. But I'm done with it, so you're on your own."

Araki stood. "It was good to work with you."

"Yeah, right." Lake turned and walked away. After turning the corner, he went into a side door of Wellman Hall. Harmon was in her office, waiting for him.

"How did it go?"

Lake settled down onto the old battered couch next to a bookcase. "I told him what he needed to know but not about what we just found out. If nothing else happens, at least the Japanese will stop the Koreans from recovering the bomb.''

''Why not tell Araki where the bomb is and let the Japanese take care of it? They put it there,'' Harmon said, ''why not let them take it away?''

''I don't know,'' Lake said, rubbing his forehead.

Harmon came over with a mug of fresh coffee and sat down, handing it to him. ''How are you feeling?''

''Beat,'' Lake said, taking a sip, then leaning his head back against the wall.

Harmon put a hand on his forehead and gently pressed down, her fingers strong and firm, massaging from the center around to his temples, then again.

Lake slowly felt himself relax, the stress of the past weeks receding for a little while at least. He felt her lean closer, her breath on his neck, her side pressing up against him. He opened his eyes and turned his head, looking into her eyes so close. He cradled her head with his hands and drew her to him. He felt her lips on his, then was briefly startled as her tongue snaked out, ran around his lips, then darted inside his mouth and just as quickly was gone.

Lake turned, sliding his hands down until he had his arms around her waist, then he stood, easily lifting her. Her legs wrapped around his waist, her skirt sliding up around her hips. ''I—'' he began, but she quieted him with a finger to his lips. ''Not a word.''

He pressed her back against the wall between the bookcase and couch. She reached down and unbuckled his belt. It was awkward but their sudden passion overcame each obstacle, unzipping, pushing aside, until he slid into her.

Lake felt her mouth on his neck, her teeth biting. He pulled his head back slightly and tried to see her eyes, but they were closed. She leaned her head back and it thumped lightly into the wall with each stroke he made. She didn't seem to notice but he did. He carried her over to the desk and laid her down on top of the message folders from the Japanese Navy in World War II.

"What if one of your students walks in?" he softly said to her, leaning over, nibbling on her neck.

"They'll get the thrill of their life," she whispered in return.

"What about—" Lake paused.

Her eyes opened. "God, ever the practical one. I'm on the pill. Now shut up." She punctuated the sentence by grabbing the collar of his windbreaker and inducing her own rhythm over his. Lake shifted his own body, feeling the flow of her body under his, the pressure of her hands, the pace of her breathing.

Nishin looked around the hotel room. It was as bare as a room he would have occupied. He'd searched it thoroughly, although there wasn't much to search. An empty dresser. A bed with one sheet on it that looked like it had never been slept in. An empty closet. An empty medicine chest. If Nishin had not confirmed that the phone number Jonas had given him was the pay phone down the hallway, he would have thought no one had been in here in days.

He walked over to the grimy window and looked out on a debris-filled alley. The room was on the second floor and a fire escape was right outside. It was exactly the type of room Nishin would have chosen.

There were footsteps in the hallway. Nishin drew his 9mm and slid across the room so that he would not be seen as soon as the door opened. The door swung wide open and an Asian man wearing a leather jacket and a black watch cap stepped in. Nishin drew a bead on the back of the man's head.

"Do not move or you will die," Nishin said in English.

He was surprised when the figure answered him in fluent Japanese. "I come from the Oyabun. He had more information about the man you are seeking. The man from this room."

The barrel of the gun didn't waver. Nishin wondered why they couldn't have told him this when he was at the Japan Center. "Go ahead."

"He is an agent of the American government who spies on the Patriot movement. He works for an organization called the Ranch, which is headed by a man named Feliks."

"Why wasn't I informed of this earlier?"

"I am relaying a message for the Oyabun," the man simply said.

"Anything else?"

"That is the message."

"Go."

Nishin left via the fire escape on the chance that the Yakuza might be waiting for him below. He hurried to the first pay phone he could find and called in what he had just learned to Nakanga.

SAPPORO, HOKKAIDO
WEDNESDAY, 8 OCTOBER 1997
1:05 P.M. LOCAL

"The American government had an agent on board the North Korean trawler that was sunk," Nakanga said. "He perished with the ship when it went down, but the man was aware of the North Koreans and the break-in at Berkeley, so we must assume that the American government knows something."

Genoysha Kuzumi watched his chief sensei without expression or comment.

"The American's name was Lake and he worked for a secret organization called the Ranch. His superior's name is Feliks. I do not know whether that is a code name or not. This information was given to Nishin by the Yakuza. I do not know where they got their information from. We do have a file on the Ranch and a man named Feliks," he added, but he didn't seem overly happy about that piece of information.

Kuzumi looked at Nakanga's hands. They were empty. He felt great irritation. "Where is the file?"

"There was just a file folder, Genoysha. There was nothing in it. It is among the old records. We do not know when it was started or what happened to the material in it."

Kuzumi stiffened. Only the Genoysha could permanently remove material from the intelligence files and he knew that he had not done so. That meant it had been done before his time. Genoysha Taiyo must have hidden or destroyed the material. It also meant this went back many years.

Nakanga hurried on. "The second North Korean trawler will arrive in the vicinity of San Francisco after midnight, local American time. About eleven or twelve hours from now."

"Why is it heading there?"

"I do not know, Genoysha. Perhaps to recover something from the sunken first trawler."

I do not think so, Kuzumi thought. Not if it was equipped to search for radioactivity. There was much Nakanga did not know, that Kuzumi was getting from his own source. The American named Lake had not perished. The Koreans were on the trail of Genzai Bakudan itself. It was all bad news, but inside the dark cloud of this information there was something that thrilled Kuzumi: to think they had made it so close with Genzai Bakudan!

Kuzumi's mind had been racing ever since receiving the news about I-24. He cursed Taiyo even more. What had the man held back from him? The only thing Taiyo had ever told him about the second bomb was that it had been lost at sea en route from Hungnam to Japan. Obviously that was a lie.

Kuzumi stiffened. He could see clearly the first Genzai Bakudan, lying in the entranceway to the cave, ready for its journey to the dock. The second bomb right behind it.

He had done the final preparations on both bombs himself. The thought that sent chills up his spine was the realization that he had prepared the two remote detonators for the I-24 bomb. One had been taken by an agent of the Black Ocean a week prior to the bomb's departure. Kuzumi remembered the man now, and he remembered asking him where the detonator was going.

The man had not answered him other than to say that he was working under direct orders of the Genoysha. He had left the cave, the detonator in a black leather bag, such as that carried by doctors, and gone to the airfield to fly out. Kuzumi had never heard what had happened to that detonator. But now that he knew what had happened to the bomb, he knew what had happened to the detonator.

The bomb was designed to be towed by the midget sub to its location. It would then be left in place. They would have to wait on final orders for detonation and the proper timing. The crewman would either leave or die with the submarine, but he could not survive underwater for more than a day or so. There was enough air in a midget sub for that long. So they must have prepared another way to detonate the bomb at the target with the remote.

It was very plain to see now. It was what Kuzumi would do if he had to make such a choice. The remote detonator had been sent to America through the TO network and Kuzumi knew whose hands it had ended up in: Nira's. Why had she not detonated it? Had it malfunctioned, or, as was more likely, had she been stopped from finishing the mission?

Was there more to her "suicide" than Taiyo had let on? What had happened? Had the Americans stopped her? Why was the file on this American organization missing? Kuzumi saw plots within plots and he saw the death of the woman he had loved a half a century before at the center of a typhoon of deceit. The question was: Who had been the architects of all this? For the first time in his life, Kuzumi turned his head and looked at the painting of the Sun

Goddess that hung behind the desk and he was uncertain.

Kuzumi's fist slammed into the teak desktop, startling Nakanga, who had been waiting patiently for further orders. "Make preparations for travel," Kuzumi ordered.

Nakanga inclined his head, indicating he understood the order. "Where am I to go, Genoysha?"

"You are going with me." Nakanga's head snapped up, his eyes wide in disbelief. "To San Francisco."

"But, Genoysha! You cannot—"

"Prepare for travel." Kuzumi's voice left no room for argument. "We leave immediately. How long will it take us to arrive in San Francisco?"

"By our fastest jet, it will take us nine hours, Genoysha."

"Then we may arrive before the trawler?"

"Yes."

"Make the arrangements, quickly."

Nakanga paused in the doorway. "And Ronin Nishin, Genoysha? What should his orders be?"

"He is to do nothing."

"But what about the Korean ship? Should it not be stopped?"

"I have already made arrangements for that," Kuzumi said. "Now, no more discussion. We must leave immediately."

CHAPTER 13

SAN FRANCISCO
WEDNESDAY, 8 OCTOBER 1997
8:23 P.M. LOCAL

Lake had spent the rest of the day at Harmon's apartment. They had a more slowly paced, but no less passionate, replay of what had happened in her office. They had not spoken until his portable had buzzed. It was a call from Ranch Central with orders to meet Feliks at ten on the Embarcadero. Lake had been waiting for the call. At that time he could unload the information about Genzai Bakudan and be done with it. If only it was that simple, he thought to himself.

"What are you going to do?" Harmon asked, her head resting on his chest, her fingers playing along his stomach.

"I have to meet him. He'll chew my butt, get an update on everything, and then I'll be out of here. He'll have to deal with the little problem resting at the base of the south tower."

"Where will you go?"

"I don't know," Lake said. "I might even be fired, in which case I guess I'll have to look for a job."

"I know a job you could have right now," she said, her hand straying lower.

The phone call and impending meeting with Feliks had made an intrusion on the quick wall her presence had built up for him. Reality still was out there and things were happening. There were still all the unanswered questions.

"There's something I need to check before I meet Feliks. Can you give me a lift?"

"Certainly." She stood up and walked across the room. Lake watched her for a few seconds before he started pulling on his own clothes. Her body was neither voluptuous nor model-thin, but rather lean with smooth, long muscles flowing under the skin.

Lake had never met anyone quite like her. Her strange aura of purposefulness disconcerted him. He had not expected what had happened in the office, but it did not surprise him. Very rarely did he feel something when he encountered a woman, but on rare occasions there was a chemical attraction. He also knew that the stress of the past few days and the lurking danger of his mission had pushed both their emotional drives into hyper.

"Where are we going?" Harmon asked, pulling on a pair of jeans.

"A bar," Lake said. "I want to play a hunch."

She threw on a sweater and they walked out into the cool night air. She drove a red Chevy Blazer and Lake gave her directions. When they pulled up at their destination he could see that the Chain Drive was closed, police tape crisscrossed over the doorway.

"This doesn't look good," Harmon said.

"Don't worry," Lake said. "I'm not going in there. Wait here for me," he added. "Keep the doors locked. I won't be more than an hour."

"Be safe," she said.

Lake went around the back of the bar to an old set of wooden stairs. He climbed them and quickly picked the lock on the door at the top. Lake made sure the shade was pulled on the single window before turning the overhead light on. He was in a one-room apartment above the bar. There was no sign the police had been in there, indeed there was no sign anyone had been in here other than Jonas since the last time Lake had been up here, about four weeks ago to conclude a deal.

He looked around. A battered sofa sat at the foot of a double bed, both facing a TV. The coffee table was covered with Patriot literature. Clothes were scattered on the floor. A few empty beer bottles sat next to the sink.

Lake began searching the room as he'd been taught at the Ranch, working top to bottom in a clockwise, descending spiral, foot by foot. He wasn't sure what he was looking for but he was following his instincts. Someone had killed Jonas. Feliks had known about it within a couple of hours. Something wasn't quite right and he hoped the room revealed a clue as to what that something was.

It did. It took Lake forty-five minutes to work down to the level of the outlets and he unscrewed them one after another. Removing the cover on the one underneath the window revealed that the connection box had been gutted. There were two items in there and Lake removed both. The first was a thick roll of money wrapped in plastic. The outside bill was a hundred and Lake estimated there were at least a hundred of those in the wad. He pocketed it.

The second item was a top-of-the-line cellular/satellite phone. Lake held it in his right hand as if he were weighing it. Then with his left he pulled out the Ranch-issue phone from his pocket. The two were identical.

Nishin slowly hung up the phone. Do nothing? He did not understand. What about the second trawler? he had asked. Do nothing, Nakanga had hissed at him.

Nishin walked the streets, his eyes unfocused, his mind trying to accept his orders. Perhaps Nakanga did not understand the situation? Perhaps I did not explain it well enough, Nishin thought. Nakanga had sounded distracted and somewhat confused. Perhaps there is something else going on that is causing Nakanga to lose perspective on this mission, Nishin reasoned.

Nakanga was his Sensei, but there was a higher authority that Nishin owed allegiance to. The Koreans must be stopped. That had been his orders when he had departed for this mission and if there was a second trawler, that one too must be stopped. The Genoysha himself had said that protection of the existence of the Genzai Bakudan program was of the highest priority.

Nishin had walked to the Japan Center without even being conscious of it while he had struggled with his new orders. He walked into the restaurant and encountered the same man standing in the small hallway.

"What do you want?" the man said when he saw Nishin.

"I must see the Oyabun," Nishin said. "There is a matter of utmost urgency."

The guard spoke into a cellular phone, then jerked his head. "Follow me."

After going through the next door, Nishin was searched and relieved of his 9mm pistol. The man patting him down missed the ice scraper again. They went up the metal stairs to the roof.

Nishin could tell something was up. There was quite a bit of activity with numerous men moving about. Okomo was talking to the captain of the tugboat, Ohashi, when Nishin was brought before him. He found that curious. Perhaps Nakanga had already called here asking for help in stopping the trawler. "What are you doing here again?" Okomo asked. "My man gave you the information you needed."

"There is another North Korean trawler headed this way," Nishin said. "I assume Nakanga has called you and—"

"You assume incorrectly," Okomo said. "However, *we* need you and it is most courteous of you to present yourself to us, rather than make us track you down.'' He made a gesture and the guards on either side grabbed Nishin's arms, immobilizing the nerve centers in his elbows. A third guard crossed his wrists over each other behind his back and slid two plastic cinches over his hands.

Nishin was confused by Okomo's words and actions, but his training took hold. Nishin flexed the tendons in his wrists just as the man pulled the cinches tight, thus keeping the blood flow from being cut off and allowing him a little bit of mobility. What did the Oyabun mean by saying that he had fulfilled his role and that they needed him? Nishin wondered. He knew better than to ask though.

''Release me,'' Nishin said. ''You cannot cross the Black Ocean and not—''

''Shut up!'' Okomo snapped. ''I have no further desire to listen to your Black Ocean prattle. You are a very stupid man who has been brainwashed by those who are smarter than you. You are nothing but a tool and no longer a useful one at that. Do not give us any trouble because we only need your body, whether it is living or dead, it doesn't matter to me, but it is easier to move alive.''

He waved a hand. ''Take him to the boat. We will dispose of this Black Ocean trash appropriately—in the ocean, once he has completed his final task.'' Okomo found that amusing and gave a quick bark of laughter.

''But where are you taking me?'' Nishin struggled helplessly in the guards' hands.

''To Genzai Bakudan, of course,'' Okomo said.

''You know of the bomb!'' Nishin was stunned.

''We not only know about it, we know exactly where it is,'' Okomo said with satisfaction in his voice. ''Move!'' he snapped at the guards. ''Get him to the boat!''

The two guards lifted Nishin off his feet and hustled him off the rooftop.

* * *

"Are you sure it is from your organization?" Harmon asked, looking at the portable phone from Jonas's apartment in Lake's hands.

Lake took out his own and put them side by side on the console between the two of them. They were identical. "These are made to government specifications. They aren't available on the civilian market because of their scrambler ability. It also has no serial number, which is a requirement of equipment that my organization uses."

"And your organization is?" Harmon asked.

"It's called the Ranch. I don't really have time to get into that right now."

"What does it mean that Jonas has a Ranch phone?" Harmon asked.

That was the question Lake had been asking himself and he didn't like the potential answers. "I don't know for sure," he said, checking the number on Jonas's portable. He looked at his watch. "We need to get to the meet. I want you to drop me off a couple of blocks away."

"You don't think it will be dangerous, do you?" she asked as she started the truck up.

"I don't know what I think anymore," Lake said. He was running the area of the meet through his mind. "Park at the South Beach Yacht Club," he said. "I'll walk the rest of the way."

They made the drive in silence, each lost in their own thoughts. Lake was starting to put pieces together, various events that he had participated in since joining the Ranch and he wasn't enjoying the picture his new perspective was showing him.

"How long do I wait?" Harmon asked as she pulled into the parking lot for the yacht club.

"Until I get back, or I call you on the portable, or two hours go by."

"And if two hours go by and you haven't come back and you haven't called?" she asked.

"Go home and forget you ever met me," Lake said.

"I can't do that," she said, stopping the truck.

"Then, remember me and remember me well," Lake said.

Harmon grabbed his arm. "This isn't the time for humor."

"I'm sorry," Lake said. He turned to her and kissed her lightly on the lips. "I don't know what's going to happen and I don't want you to get caught up any further in this. No matter what, I'll get back in contact with you. All right?"

"I suppose that will have to do. Be safe," she added, giving him one last kiss.

Lake wasn't certain what to say in turn, so he returned the kiss, then jumped out of the truck and began walking swiftly to the north. As his feet hit pavement, he pushed thoughts of Peggy waiting for him out of his mind and began to focus on what was coming up.

As he got closer, he had the distinct feeling that he was being watched, something that had not happened last time when he had met Randkin here. Of course, Feliks would not have come here alone. Security personnel were standard whenever the number one man at the Ranch went traveling, but it didn't make Lake feel any more comfortable. The up ramp for the Bay Bridge loomed directly overhead. Several piers beckoned off to the right and Lake could hear the gentle lap of water on rotting wood and concrete. Where there wasn't pier, there was a concrete retaining wall built at the water's edge.

"You're late." The familiar voice echoed in the dark.

Lake turned to the shadows across the street and Feliks appeared out of them, a darker shape, his white hair standing out. He wasn't alone. Two men wearing long black raincoats flanked him. They walked up to Lake as if to sniff him, then took up flank position, about ten feet off on either side. Feliks took Lake's right arm in his hand and nudged him toward a deserted pier. "This way."

Lake allowed himself to be guided. They walked along

until they were out of sight of the Embarcadero. The sound of traffic overhead on the Bay Bridge sounded loud above their heads.

"I'm very disappointed in your recent performance," Feliks said. He pulled out his cigarette case and lit up. Lake noted that he ignored offering him one and remained quiet.

"You have broken quite a few rules and shown poor judgment," Feliks continued.

"Is there a point to this?" Lake said.

"I want whatever information you have about this Genzai Bakudan situation that you haven't given me," Feliks said.

"I briefed you fully on the phone," Lake said. The two guards had shifted position, both making sure they would have clear shots of Lake without Feliks being in the way. Each had his right arm under his coat, no doubt resting on the handle of a weapon as Lake had been taught at the Ranch school.

"Oh, come, come," Feliks said. "You know I am not stupid so do not treat me that way. Your story was full of holes. I want those holes filled. For example, who got you the information about the Japanese fleet during World War II? How did you figure out where Cyclone and Forest were?"

"I went to the library and looked it up," Lake said.

Feliks was now just a shadow with a glowing red tip in the center of his face. "I thought I could count on your loyalty."

"I am loyal," Lake said. "My oath is to defend the Constitution and this country from all enemies, foreign and domestic." He remembered swearing that oath for the first time on the parade field at Annapolis so many years ago as a young seventeen-year-old plebe. Even at the Ranch, despite the cynicism and covert angle, they worked under the same oath. Or, Lake amended his thoughts, at least they were supposed to.

"The Constitution and the country," Feliks repeated.

"Very nice. You also are legally bound to obey orders. So again, tell me all the parts you left out of your report to me."

"I've told you all," Lake said.

"You're lying," Feliks said. "You don't lie well. Oh, I know you can keep your cover well and lie within the confines of a mission, but when it comes to doing it on your own, you just can't cut it."

"I suppose you can," Lake shot back.

"When I feel it is necessary and serves the higher good," Feliks said.

"Who determines the higher good?" Lake asked. He felt like he was walking on ice, pushing his foot ahead slowly and testing whether it could take his weight.

"I do, of course." Feliks tapped the ashes off the end of his cigarette. "I take responsibility, something most people, particularly politicians, don't want to do. Because I take responsibility, it is up to me to determine the rightness or wrongness of each course of action. Of course, it's not as black and white as all that, but I make do." His voice changed abruptly. "Now, I want the information you've withheld."

"Why'd you have Jonas working for you?" Lake suddenly asked, taking a leap across the ice.

"The Patriot bar man who was killed?" Feliks asked.

"You just said I shouldn't treat you as if you're stupid," Lake said, "so don't act the part either. And you have no need to lie to me anymore. You know exactly who I'm talking about. I just found over a hundred thousand dollars in cash and a Ranch phone in his apartment."

"He did occasional work for us," Feliks said with a shrug. "He thought he was working for the CIA. Another poor fool."

"Why wasn't I informed of that? It was in my operational area." Lake was seeing the ice he had jumped over cracking and sinking into darkness. He couldn't go back now.

"You are told what you need to know to do your job. No more. Having both you and him and others reporting in ensured that I was getting the complete picture. One of the most dangerous things in my job is to trust only one source."

Lake stared at Feliks. He'd never personally liked the old man, but Feliks had been an efficient boss who'd taken care of Lake when he'd needed help on missions. "So you're the only one who knows all and decides what the higher good is?" Lake asked.

Feliks threw away his cigarette. "I'm wasting time with you. Even if you know more that you've told me it's no longer important. The Korean trawler will be outside the harbor by two in the morning. It will be dealt with and this entire matter finally closed."

Lake folded his arms across his chest. "What do you mean by 'finally'? Why are you so concerned about this?"

"It's my business to be concerned about security threats to our country," Feliks said.

"No." Lake shook his head. "I think it goes beyond your job and that you're personally concerned about this matter."

"I know much more about this then you will ever know," Feliks said after a pause. "You really don't understand the way things work in the real world, do you?"

Lake was tense. He kept the two guards in his peripheral vision while he stayed focused on what Feliks was saying and, just as importantly, what he wasn't. "Why don't you tell me?"

Feliks ticked off two fingers as he spoke. "Knowledge and the ability to make decisions. Those are the key to everything. I have both traits, which makes me a rare commodity in this world. You have neither. You've only known what I've wanted you to know. And you were given orders to carry out, which negates your ability to make decisions. So you're nothing."

"Then why are we having this conversation?" Lake asked.

That gave Feliks a momentary pause, then the old man smiled, his teeth glinting in the light reflected off the harbor surface. "You think you're so damn smart, Lake. I've run you on ops for years and you've done a good job, but you can train a dog to do a good job. You don't know shit. Yeah, I was running Jonas, but not just him. Who the hell do you think controls most of the Patriots?"

Lake stared at Feliks, listening to words he should be surprised to hear, but somehow he wasn't. He was glad he hadn't given up Genzai Bakudan's location now. It was all he had to negotiate with. Of course, he didn't think that Feliks was going to do much negotiating.

"Who was it that said," Feliks continued, " 'Keep your friends close but your enemies closer'?"

"That's attributed to Genghis Khan," Lake answered.

"Don't you think you can determine the outcome of a chess game much more easily if you play both sides, rather than just one?" Feliks continued.

"So you've been running the Patriots?" Lake asked.

"That's a bit strong. Actually, it would be nice if I had them completely under my thumb, but that's not possible. First off, we didn't invent them. They came into being and we slid in and took up some of the reins. Enough so that we could keep a lid on them and also have a good intelligence network inside of their operation." The smile was still on Feliks's face. "Plus it looks rather good for us to have such a perfect record stopping their terrorist acts. It's rather easy to stop acts that you instigate. Sort of what was done with other groups like the Black Panthers in an earlier time."

"You're a fucking traitor," Lake said.

"No, that's not true," Feliks said. "There are always going to be people who are going to join an organization such as the Patriots, so we must allow such an organization to exist. One we know about, otherwise they will start one we don't know about until it's too late. Then, as a natural progression, an organization such as the Patriots is going to do something. We just make sure they do what *we* want them to do. We direct which way they go so that way we can control the outcome. Remember what I said, knowledge and the ability to make decisions? It works on everything."

"The incident on the bridge? Starry and Preston? Were they working for you?"

The smile left Feliks face. "No, I didn't set that up."

"So your knowledge is lacking, isn't it?"

"By tomorrow morning I'll know everything I need to know," Feliks said.

"You didn't instigate that, though, so perhaps things are not only getting out of your range of knowledge, but also your range of control?" Lake pressed. "Maybe someone else has the knowledge and is making some decisions?"

"Sometimes damage control is necessary when there is an accident," Feliks said.

"That was no accident I stopped," Lake said. "It was a setup."

For the first time, Feliks had no answer.

"What's the connection between the Patriots and Genzai Bakudan?" Lake asked.

"There is none," Feliks said.

Lake snorted. "Maybe, maybe not, but you don't really know, do you? What else don't you know?" Lake pushed on. "You can't very well make your great decisions without these pieces of knowledge, can you? That's why you want what I know."

"You should be more concerned about what *you* don't know," Feliks said with a trace of anger in his voice.

"So what don't I know here?" Lake asked.

"You don't know anything," Feliks almost yelled, then got his voice under control. "You think Genzai Bakudan is something you just discovered? You think I was surprised to hear about it during your report? Hell, I first heard the term in 1944, before you were even born. The Ranch was dealing with this back then and it will finally deal with it now."

Lake felt his heart rate accelerate. "What happened back then?"

Feliks had half-turned away. His voice was low as if he were talking to himself. "Deals were made and broken, that's what happened."

His voice firmed up. "All that hoopla a few years back about Truman and the decision to drop the bomb? That crap about the *Enola Gay* display at the Smithsonian? The Japanese and the revisionists all whining about what a terrible thing it was, us dropping the bomb on Hiroshima? Hell, not only would revealing the existence of the Genzai Bakudan project change all that, but how do you think people would react if it was discovered that Truman was informed of the Japanese atomic bomb program at the same time he was told of the Manhattan Project, right after Roosevelt died? And that the day he made the decision to drop the bomb on Hiroshima, it was after being briefed about I-24?"

"So why wasn't this made public?"

"It couldn't be in the interests of national security. You think your little discoveries now are so damn important, they aren't anything!" Feliks said, his voice disgusted.

"Do you know where Genzai Bakudan is?" Lake asked.

"No, but no one else does either. The key is not the bomb, the key is stopping those looking for the bomb. The bomb was lost long ago. It's at the bottom of the Pacific."

"You don't sound so certain," Lake said. "Why are the North Koreans heading here? That means the bomb must be here."

"The bomb never made it here," Feliks insisted. "The Japanese scuttled I-24 several hundred miles off the coast in deep water."

"How do you know that?"

"Because that's the deal we made with the sons-of-bitches!" Feliks snapped.

Lake was momentarily stunned. What the hell was Feliks talking about? "Who did you make a deal with?" When Feliks didn't answer, he tried another question. "Then why is this second North Korean trawler coming here?"

"Because they're like you," Feliks said. "They don't know shit and they're blundering around in the dark, hoping to hit a jackpot. They probably know San Francisco was the target for the second Genzai Bakudan, so they're hoping it's around here somewhere."

"Maybe they know more than you," Lake said. "As you just said, there are gaps in your knowledge." Lake realized that Feliks didn't know the bomb was at the base of the bridge. He also realized that whatever deal had been made so long ago, maybe neither side had completely kept their part.

Feliks's thumb rasped on his lighter and a small flame illuminated his face as he lit another cigarette. In the brief glow, Lake could see that the old man's face was drawn tight. "This all should have been finalized a long time ago," Feliks said. "I don't know why it's come alive again, but in the morning I will have finished it."

"Not with my help," Lake said.

"I didn't plan on that. I just hoped you might be smarter than I thought and played along."

"It isn't a game," Lake said.

"It is when you're winning," Feliks replied.

"The final move hasn't been made yet," Lake said. If Feliks truly believed Genzai Bakudan to be at sea, then that meant there was something else at work here that was beyond both his and Feliks's knowledge. "And I don't think you're winning," Lake added. He knew he was a dead man. No matter what the emotion, Feliks was too much of a professional to have just told him the information he had if he hadn't already decided to kill Lake.

Feliks rolled his eyes. "Oh, give me a break with the dramatic statements. It's over for *you.*"

Lake smiled. "No, it isn't. Remember what you said? Knowledge and the ability to make decisions? Well, you just gave me some knowledge."

"It won't do you much good," Feliks said.

"Don't be so sure." Lake was moving even as he said the second word. He hit the closest guard with a spinning back kick, his boot smashing into the side of the man's head. Lake flowed with the kick falling onto the ground on top of the guard, gripping the body and rolling it on top of him as the other guard instinctively began firing.

The guard's body took the first two rounds, then Lake was over the edge of the pier, falling into the water, still holding the body. As he splashed in, the cold water took his breath away. He allowed the dead weight of the guard to take him down. Then, when he could just barely make out the surface above, he let go and began kicking with all his might due south through the water. In SEAL school he'd had to swim forty meters completely underwater without equipment. Here he broke that requirement, going almost half the length of a football field before he carefully surfaced and looked about.

He could hear Feliks yelling and several vans pulling up on the pier, disgorging Ranch security men. Flashlights were licking the surface, but Lake edged in along the waterfront and continued south without being spotted.

THE PACIFIC OCEAN
WEDNESDAY, 8 OCTOBER 1997
9:15 P.M. LOCAL

The *Han Juk Sung* was a sister ship to the *Am Nok Sung*, built along the same lines. Its real job was espionage under the cover of being a fishing trawler. At the present moment it was steaming at flank speed due east, directly toward San

Francisco harbor. On board were a squad of navy frogmen with specialized equipment for picking up radioactivity underwater.

Kim Pak, the commander of the frogmen and ship, had initially been very unhappy with his mission. Originally it had been vague and generally consisted of "turn your ship and head toward San Francisco as quickly as possible and turn on your equipment." That was the first message. Then had come the second which told him what he was looking for: an atomic weapon aboard a World War II Japanese submarine. That got the adrenaline flowing. He didn't allow his mind to dwell on the possibilities that message conjured.

Of course it was a big ocean, Pak reflected. They were sixty miles off the coast in the main shipping channel heading for San Francisco Bay. His underwater sensors ranged out to one mile on either side for a bomb of World War II make. His current plan was to brush right up against the twelve-mile limit and then— He paused in his thinking as his second-in-command came hurrying up with a radio flimsy.

"Sir, we have been given a definite location for the bomb!"

"From who?" Pak asked.

"High command in Pyongyang. They do not say how they got the information."

"Coordinates?" Pak asked as he turned to the chart.

His executive officer read off the numbers. "Longitude 122 degrees, 31 minutes west. Latitude 37 degrees, 48 minutes north."

Pak took a ruler and drew two lines. Then he stared at the point where they bisected. He looked up at his XO in disbelief. "It cannot be! We cannot go there!"

The XO waved the message. "We are ordered to go there and recover the bomb, sir!"

Pak stood straighter. "Then we will. Tell the men to

prepare to dive in . . ." He did some calculations. "In three and a half hours."

"Yes, sir." The XO leaned over and looked at the chart. The two thin black pencil lines crossed another solid black line printed on the chart. "I do not understand," the XO who was not a sailor said. "What is this?" he asked, putting his finger on the spot.

"That is the Golden Gate Bridge," Pak said. "To be more exact, the coordinates for the bomb indicate it rests right next to the southern tower for the bridge."

CHAPTER 14

SAN FRANCISCO
WEDNESDAY, 8 OCTOBER 1997
10:22 P.M. LOCAL

Lake shook like a dog, spraying water all over the concrete sidewalk. He jogged down the street, as much from a need to rush as to keep warm. He came to the corner across from the Yacht Club and came to an abrupt halt. Peggy Harmon's Blazer was gone. Slowly he walked across the street to the spot where it had been parked. There was no broken glass, no sign of a struggle, nothing to indicate why she had left.

Lake looked about. Had the police come by? Feliks's men? But there was no reason they should know anything about her or that she would be parked here. Unless I was followed, Lake realized. He didn't think he had been and he had checked continuously, but he had no doubt that the Ranch could probably put surveillance on him that he couldn't spot.

Lake shook again and less water came off this time. He reached into his coat and pulled out the Ziploc bag holding his portable phone. He punched in the number for Jonas's portable. After it rang eight times without answer he reluctantly pushed the send again and dialed Peggy's home number. He didn't expect an answer and he didn't get one. Then he tried her office. Slowly he pushed the power-off button.

Lake spoke to the empty parking lot, feeling as abandoned as the empty tar. "Damn, Peggy, I hope you're all right." He'd gotten her into this and now he didn't even know where she was to get her out of it.

Turning the phone back on, Lake dialed the cellular number that Araki had given him. Again the phone rang with no answer. "Damn," Lake muttered. He wished now that he'd told Araki where the bomb was. At least then the Japanese would take care of it. He dialed in a different number and got the Ranch automated switchboard. He punched in a three code extension. This time the phone was answered.

"Randkin here."

"Randkin, it's Lake. I have a question for you."

"Reference?" Randkin was all business. Lake knew he was used to being asked all sorts of strange technical questions at strange hours.

"The atom bombs we used in World War II at Hiroshima and Nagasaki," Lake began, then stopped to think how he could phrase the question.

"Little Boy and Fat Boy," Randkin filled in.

"Excuse me?" Lake was shaken out of his thoughts.

"That's what they were called. Little Boy was dropped on Hiroshima, then Fat Boy on Nagasaki."

"Okay," Lake said. He knew he didn't have much time. He was surprised his phone hadn't been cut off by Feliks yet, but he figured that the man had a lot on his mind at the present moment. "If one of those type atomic weapons had not been used, say it was stored somewhere for all these years, would it still be capable of functioning?"

"What do you mean stored?" Randkin asked.

"You know, just put somewhere and left."

"Have you found something we should know about?" Randkin asked.

"Just answer the damn question," Lake snapped.

''Well, those were actually two very different types of bombs,'' Randkin said. ''Little Boy was a uranium fission bomb while Fat Boy was more advanced, using plutonium.''

''I don't want to build one,'' Lake said, looking about the deserted streets. ''Just tell me, would one still be functioning after all these years? Would it go off if you pushed the right button?''

''Maybe,'' Randkin said.

''Maybe?'' Lake repeated. ''What are the odds?''

''That's hard to say. There's so many variables. The biggest question I would have is what is the firing mechanism? Electrical or explosive? If it's electrical, then—''

''I don't know what the triggering mechanism is,'' Lake cut in. ''So you're telling me it's possible such a bomb could go off if fired?''

''Those early bombs were made very simply,'' Randkin said. ''There's not much—''

''Yes or no,'' Lake cut in.

''Yes.'' There was a pause. ''You've found one, haven't you?''

''Not yet,'' Lake said, snapping shut the portable and putting it back in the Ziploc bag.

Standing perfectly still, Lake closed his eyes and thought. Priorities. Options.

''Fuck you, Feliks, I don't think you know shit,'' Lake muttered as he slowly opened his eyes and looked to his right at the boats berthed in their slips at the Yacht Club. He spotted what he was looking for three lines over. A thirty-four-foot boat, capable of taking the heavy swell of the ocean with its powerful engines. More importantly, it had an entryway and ladder off the rear that scuba enthusiasts had built into boats for ease in entering the water.

Lake hopped on board and checked the cabin. As he had hoped, he found a set of scuba tanks and a regulator stowed in one of the lockers below decks. He checked the bleed and the tanks were about two-thirds full. He carried them up on deck and set them down.

The ignition was easily hot-wired. Lake untied the lines and stowed them as the engine warmed up. He peeled off his clothes until all he was wearing was the wet suit he'd had on underneath. The stainless-steel Hush Puppy was strapped to his shoulder. A double-edged commando knife was on his hip, while a dive knife was on his right ankle.

Pushing the dual throttles ahead, Lake eased out of the berth and made his way into San Francisco Bay. He could see the lighted arc of the Bay Bridge above and ahead. As soon as he was clear of the docks, he edged north five hundred meters from the shore until he could see the pier he had jumped off of. There were several vehicles parked there with the lights on. Lake killed the engine and rolled on the swell, all lights off, waiting. Finally, he could hear car engines start and a convoy left the pier and headed north along the Embarcadero.

Lake restarted the boat and pushed the throttle wide open. The bow slowly settled down and the boat hissed across the water at forty knots as he kept pace.

Nishin was tied to the right side of the tugboat's bridge by a length of chain looped through the cord tying his hands together. He had about a foot of slack from the steel piping that made up the handrail for the stairs on that side of the bridge.

A dozen Yakuza armed with automatic weapons were scattered about the prow of the tug. Ohashi was on the bridge, his hands on the controls, Okomo by his side. The engine was running but the boat wasn't moving. They were still tied to the pier by one rope, waiting.

A red Chevy Blazer pulled up and a woman got out. Nishin watched as she stood on the edge of the pier next to the gangplank, not looking down at the tug, but back along the dark length of concrete. He couldn't make out much about her except she was tall and slim.

A pair of headlights cut the darkness, silhouetting the woman. A limousine pulled up to her position. She opened the back door and Nishin twisted, trying to see who was getting out. He could make out a figure shrouded in black. He stood on his toes, and then the side of his head exploded. All he could see was red as he dropped to his knees, kept from falling off the boat by the chain.

"If I want you to look, I will tell you," Okomo hissed in his ear. "If I want you to breathe, I will tell you." The old man's gnarled hand grabbed Nishin's chin and twisted his head. "Do you want to know why I even have your worthless carcass on board?"

Nishin tried to blink blood out of his eyes. "You fear the wrath of the Black Ocean, you pig."

Okomo laughed. "You are so stupid. I have you here because you have a transmitter in you. We picked it up when you came calling the first time at my headquarters. We do not only check for weapons, we check for electronic transmissions when you walk through the corridor just before the stairs. At first we thought you were trying to record our conversation, but when my electronic experts analyzed the data, they said it was a beacon." He shook Nishin's head. "Did you know you were bugged?"

Nishin was stunned. "No."

"I didn't think so. It is inside you. We scanned you the second time you came. It is located in your left buttock. That is why you are here. Because we want whoever bugged you—and we think it is your own people in the Black Ocean—to follow us. We do not fear the Black Ocean. In fact, the more of the Black Ocean that comes here, the better. We want everyone to be here for the end."

Okomo let go of the chin. "You had best start praying, Ronin. Pray to your Sun Goddess because you do not have much time left." Okomo walked away to greet the visitor who had gotten out of the limousine.

Nishin shook his head, ignoring the pain, blinking, trying to get the blood out of his eyes. He curled in a ball around the railing and slowly he reached under his shirt until the fingers of his right hand closed on the ice scraper taped there. With small rocking motions he began to free the scraper.

"Ahead one quarter!" Kim Pak ordered. All lights were out on board the trawler, a violation of international sea law, but Pak knew that his ship's presence here in United States waters was already a violation of law and there would be many more laws, American and international, broken before this night was over.

The fog was coming in and for that he was grateful. He could hear the foghorn on the Southeast Farallon from his right rear. He could also just make out the lights on the top of the two towers of the Golden Gate Bridge directly ahead, but there were tendrils of fog beginning to reach up that high also.

Pak took another sounding to his right front and checked the chart. He identified Mile Rock, a lighthouse/foghorn poised on top of a single rock sticking out of the ocean and, checking it against the sound from the Farallons, he plotted himself five miles out from the bridge. There were no other ships showing on his radar, which was not at all unusual for this time of night. Normal entry into the port was made in the daytime.

A quarter mile off the port stern another ship shadowed the *Han Juk Sung*, unseen by eyes because of the fog and by radar because of its shape. It had been there ever since the trawler had passed through the outer banks. As the North Korean trawler slowly moved forward, its shadow stopped keeping pace and rapidly moved forward, water spraying off of the twin hulls. The ship made little noise though other than the sound of water rushing by.

Pak spotted the trailing ship first and that was the last thing he ever saw. The inverted V shape of the hull was new to him, but the lack of any lights and the black coating over the skin of the ship told him that this wasn't a chance encounter. As he yelled a warning, a bright light flashed out from the apex of the V and Pak's warning changed to a shrill scream of pain. His eyes burned as if acid had been thrown in them.

Pak collapsed to his knees, both hands over his damaged eyes. Other crewmen who had been caught by the burst of high-intensity laser also were blinded and in agony. Those who weren't blinded caught on quickly and looked away from the source of the light which allowed the stealth ship to slide up next to the *Han Juk Sung* unopposed. Men clad in black and armed with silenced submachine guns fired grappling hooks across the small space between the two vessels, immediately grabbing onto the ropes and climbing across. They wore special night-vision goggles to be able to see in the dark and protect them from the laser.

The man wielding the laser on top of the stealth ship continued to visually suppress the Koreans until the assault party was on board, then he shut it down. Next to him, the captain of the ship and Araki watched and listened to the attack with satisfaction. It was all over within thirty seconds. It was a much simpler and more efficient assault than that by the Yakuza on the first trawler.

Every Korean on board was dead. The chart and all records of radio transmissions were seized and brought back. The commandos opened the sea valves, and for the second time in as many days, a North Korean intelligence ship went down off the Golden Gate.

Araki and the captain looked at the chart from the trawler. The intersection of lines at the south tower of the Golden Gate caught their immediate attention.

"This is where they were headed," the captain said.

"Take us there," Araki ordered.

The captain obeyed without question and the stealth slipped forward in the fog as the last of the trawler disappeared under the waves.

* * *

Lake eased up on the throttle until the engines just purred, pushing the boat through the water. He was within four hundred yards of the Coast Guard station, southeast of the Golden Gate. The convoy was pulling into the station.

The fog was pouring through the ocean gap between Marin County and San Francisco, but it was still clear where he was. He shut down the engine and cocked his head listening. Car engines were turned off and doors began slamming. A voice was giving orders. There was an eighty-foot cutter tied up to the dock and lights began going on aboard the ship as men carried gear up the gangway. Lake waited patiently as he heard the sound of the cutter's engine begin to rumble.

The Coast Guard cutter slowly began moving away from the pier. Lake started his own engine. Wherever Feliks was going, he was going also. He would soon find out how much Feliks knew about the fate of Genzai Bakudan.

Eighty miles from the Pacific Coast, the specially designed and constructed tilt-jet plane that the Black Ocean used for high-priority covert missions was coming in over the wavetops at six hundred miles an hour.

In appearance, the jet looked like the experimental American V-22 tilt-rotor Osprey, with the major difference being that instead of propellers on the wings there were two jet engines. This allowed the tilt-jet to fly at airplane speeds, twice the speed of the Osprey. Like the Osprey, it could hover and land like a helicopter when its wings were rotated from the horizontal through the vertical.

The tilt-jet was being developed by a company controlled by the Black Ocean under a Japanese government military contract. It was highly classified and still supposedly in the "testing" stage, but the Black Ocean had been flying this prototype for the past two years. Its unique features made it most valuable for entering foreign countries where there were no prying customs officials.

In the rear, Kuzumi had spent an anxious flight, his mind

going over all that he had been told by his various sources, trying to make sense of it. The fact that it didn't make sense convinced him that his decision to come to America to personally take charge was the correct one. The stakes with Genzai Bakudan on the table were simply too great.

"We will be landing here," Nakanga said, holding a map in front of the Genoysha. The point he indicated was in the Presidio at the south end of the Golden Gate.

Kuzumi remembered the place from his days at UC-Berkeley. "That is a military post," he said.

"It is now a national park," Nakanga said. "It will be deserted at night. I have not been able to get in contact with Ronin Nishin to meet us—" He paused as Kuzumi held up a hand and took the map from him.

"I will make arrangements for our meeting. It is not Nishin who I wish to speak to."

Nakanga frowned but didn't say anything. "Yes, Genoysha."

"We must not be discovered," Kuzumi warned.

"We are under the airport radar. We will not be detected." Nakanga paused. "Sir, with all due respect, I believe I should know what is happening in order that I might serve you better. Who are we meeting?"

Kuzumi looked up from the map. "You will serve me by doing as I order."

Chastened, Nakanga left the rear cabin to go back up front.

"Hurry," ordered Okomo, "we must beat the Koreans to the bridge so we can lie in wait."

"We will get there before them," Captain Ohashi calmly said. "It is right ahead. Prepare your men."

Okomo yelled out to the Yakuza gathered on deck and two of them began putting on wet suits and scuba tanks.

Still curled up off the edge of the bridge, Nishin continued to work feverishly to free himself. His hands were bleeding from cuts he had inflicted upon himself from the ice scraper. It was awkward holding the handle with just the edge of the fingers in his right hand and he nicked skin as much as he hit rope.

He had not seen any more of the woman and the figure in black. They must be in the room below the bridge. The tug was churning through the water, the deck plates vibrating from the thrust kicked out by the powerful engines. He could feel the chill air blowing across his skin, and looking down he could see the dark water of the harbor almost ten feet directly below.

"There is the south tower!" Ohashi said as he slowed the tug and turned the wheel.

The tower disappeared into the fog, the roadway 210 feet above not visible. Above that, the tower rose to over 746 feet above the surface of the water. Below the surface, the tower extended down over 100 feet into the mud and then bedrock.

At water level, the tower was perched upon a concrete and steel pier surrounded by a circular concrete fender. The pier base was over 65 feet thick. The concrete fender around it was 155 feet high, going from the bedrock below to 10 feet above the surface of the water. When the bridge had been constructed in the '30s, the fender had been built by first extending a pier from the south shore, over a thousand feet away to the proposed location. Divers were sent down and blasted through 20 feet of mud into the bedrock.

The wall was built up to its present height, then the water inside was pumped out, allowing the engineers to build the pier base inside the hollow and now dry interior. The tower was then built onto the base. A reinforcing iron frame and rock fill had been placed around the pier base after the tower had been completed and then water had been let back in to allow the entire thing to settle.

The Yakuza tug was dwarfed by the size of the pier base and fender. Warning lights flickered along the top of the fender, telling ships to keep away. The tug's engines had to fight the swift current to keep steady, just a few feet away from the pitted concrete wall.

As Nishin continued to work on the rope, he wondered how the Yakuza knew the tower was where the Koreans would head. He also wondered who had put the bug in him. It indeed could have been done by the Black Ocean to keep track of him. Certainly they had the opportunity during his training to do such a thing. But he was also afraid it might have been done by someone else.

Regardless, he could wait no longer. The massive tower was just off the port side of the tug now. Everyone on the bridge was focused on that side as the two men were done putting their scuba tanks on. The first of the two slid over the side and into the water, holding a powerful light in one hand and a six-foot-long hooked piece of metal in the other. Nishin saw the purpose of the piece of metal as the man hooked into a crevice in the concrete ship fender to hold himself in place against the strong current.

The first diver had disappeared under the swirling water and the second one hooked into place. Suddenly Nishin understood where they were going and why they were going there and that kicked in an extra jolt of strength to his sawing.

The last strand of rope parted under the plastic point of the scraper. Nishin swiftly stood, grabbing the chain and sliding it through so that he was free.

"Hai!" One of the Yakuza on the bridge spotted him and came running. Nishin slammed the ice scraper into the man's chest, pulled it back out, turned, and dove from the bridge to the water below, gulping in a deep breath as he went down.

He hit the surface and went under. Nishin finned hard, feeling the hull of the tugboat with his free hand, the scraper in the other. He could feel the current tearing at him and he knew he had only one chance to survive. He followed the curve of the hull, feeling barnacles attached to the metal tear at his free hand as he remained oriented.

The keel of the boat slipped by. He put both feet against the side and pushed off toward the hulking presence of the tower fender. He smashed his head into concrete, then scrambled his free hand along the pitted surface, tearing fingernails, searching for a hold.

His fingers slipped into a vertical crack and he was no longer moving, ten feet below the surface of the water. There were lights being played along the water above him and he imagined the Yakuza there had their weapons trained all around the boat, waiting for him to surface. He twisted and looked about, tucking the scraper into his waist. He could see the underwater glow of light from one of the lamps to his left and slightly down. Nishin's lungs were burning as he pulled himself down and in that direction.

Nishin spotted the top diver, just ten feet below him. He was uncertain whether he could make it but he had no choice. Hands pouring blood from cuts and scrapes he pulled himself down with every ounce of energy left in his body. The diver was unaware of his presence as Nishin closed the gap.

Nishin pulled out the scraper from his belt, turned head down in the water and pistoned the last part of the distance with his legs. He looped his left arm around the man's neck as he jammed the point into his back repeatedly.

An explosion of bubbles from the man's mouthpiece and blood from the wounds filled the water. The man couldn't let go of the metal hook or he'd be swept away, but by not letting go he couldn't defend himself against Nishin. By not solving that Catch-22 in time the diver died. Nishin dropped the ice scraper and grabbed the hook with that hand. Then he ripped the regulator out of the slack mouth and took a deep breath, tasting the man's blood on the mouthpiece and not caring. He gasped in several mouthfuls of air.

Nishin pulled the tanks off the man's back. He also took the man's mask, putting it on and then clearing it with air from the regulator as he'd been taught. The light was dangling by a safety cord from the limp wrist and Nishin appropriated that. Then he took off the man's weight belt and, with difficulty, strapped it around his own waist. He also took the man's dive knife. Before he tucked the knife under the weight belt, Nishin slammed it into the man's chest twice, once in each lung. He then pulled the dead diver to his chest to make sure all the air was out of them. When he let go, the body floated away at neutral buoyancy.

Looking below, Nishin could see the first diver was a faint glow about twenty to thirty feet away in the murky and pitch-black water, unaware of the struggle that had just occurred above him. Using the hook, Nishin began to follow him down.

''He was swept away by the current,'' Captain Ohashi said.

Okomo cursed. The body of the Yakuza Nishin had killed was still lying on the floor of the bridge, a pool of blood underneath him. There had been no sign of the Black Ocean man surfacing. Yakuza lined the rails, weapons at the ready.

Ohashi pointed out to the west. ''He will die many miles out to sea. No swimmer can fight this current.''

Okomo spit. ''All right. Pull us away. Let us leave this open for the next ship, whoever that might be, to park.''

The tugboat slowly slid away into the fog, crossing the Gate directly under the unseen span of the bridge until it was just offshore, where the northern tower was built on the edge of the land. Hiding in the shadow of that tower, they would remain unseen by radar, yet be close enough to get back to the southern tower when necessary.

Nishin soon found the rhythm of sliding the hook down a couple of feet and pulling himself after it, then repeating the maneuver. He found it so well that soon he was only a few feet above the first diver who appeared as nothing more than a dark figure in the cone of light put out by Nishin's light.

As he got closer Nishin decided on a course of action. He slid his hook down and then over the diver's when it was paused. That locked the man in place. He looked up and Nishin smashed the butt of his knife into the other man's mask, shattering the glass. The man flailed about, blinded. Nishin slipped the knife under his arms and slashed his throat. Blood squirted out into the light of the lamp.

The man let go of his hook and tried to kick for the surface, but Nishin reached out and grabbed hold of his weight belt, keeping him in place. Blinded and dying, the man offered little resistance. When there was no more movement, Nishin insured that the diver's hook was jammed in place in a crack in the concrete, then he slipped the other end under the diver's weight belt, holding him in place. Then he continued his journey down.

Occasionally he could see steel bars sticking out of the concrete or loops of metal where the workers sixty years ago had made an underwater scaffold. His entire world consisted of the slightly curving concrete wall in front of him and the inky blackness all around. Nishin could hear his breathing and he forced himself to slow the rate down. He had no idea how deep he was and he tried to remember what he had been taught in the fast and furious dive classes he'd been given as part of his training. He'd never had to use the training before, but he did remember that there was a definite limit to how deep he could go and how quickly he could resurface. He had to assume that since the two Yakuza had planned on going down here with the same equipment, that it was safe for him so far.

He spotted something and froze, then relaxed. The bottom, a brown, dirty spread of streaked mud pressing up against the concrete fender. Nishin went down the last few feet and stood, his feet sinking into the ooze. From the way his bubbles were blowing away, the current was not quite as swift here, but it was still strong.

Nishin looked left, then right. Which way? He chose to the right. Using the hook to keep himself from being washed away, he made his way around the base of the fender, his feet kicking up swirls of mud that were quickly swept away.

He made forty feet when he saw something ahead. With each step, the shape materialized out of the dark—a short blunt metal cigar-shape, half covered in mud. A conning tower was in the center bearing the rising sun of Imperial Japan. The sub was canted over on its right side, pressed up against the tender at a sixty-degree angle.

Nishin's feet clanged on metal as he clambered up the steel slope of the forward deck. He could see the cable for the submarine's anchor stretched into the mud. Another cable came off an eyebolt on the deck and was looped around an exposed steel rod from the tender.

Nishin reached the conning tower, but his gaze was drawn to the rear of the sub where two steel cables led back into the darkness. He adjusted the light and in the glow he saw a rectangular metal object at the end of the two cables. The mud was pressed up against the bottom half, but the top half was kept free of debris by the strong current. There was no mistaking the Japanese script written on the steel: GENZAI BAKUDAN.

CHAPTER 15

SAN FRANCISCO HARBOR
THURSDAY, 9 OCTOBER 1997
12:09 A.M. LOCAL

"Negative radar contact," the young rating called out from his chair on the left side of the bridge.

Captain Carson, the Coast Guard officer in charge of the U.S.S. *Sullivan*, looked over at the man who had identified himself as Agent Feliks. Upon boarding, the man had flashed both a badge and a set of documents indicating he was a very-high-ranking federal officer and that Carson was to obey his every order. "Course, sir?"

Carson, being a cautious man, had called his higher headquarters to check on the papers and received verification. Apparently this Feliks fellow was high up in the dark world of government intelligence. Carson had had DEA, CIA, and FBI operatives on board the *Sullivan* at various times, so he didn't find this so odd. The Coast Guard was the branch of the government assigned with policing the nation's waterways and coastlines, so whenever any other government agency needed to operate in that area, they called on the Coast Guard.

It had taken Sullivan twenty minutes to gather a crew together and get the ship ready. They had pulled out of the

Coast Guard station five minutes ago and would cross under the Golden Gate in another couple of minutes.

"There's a North Korean trawler out there," Feliks said. "We need to track it down and my men will board."

Carson looked down at the dozen men dressed in black, wearing body armor and carrying machine guns that crowded his forward deck. His own crew was at battle stations, the forward five-inch gun manned and ready, along with four .50-caliber machine guns located about the ship. "My radar man reports negative contact," Carson said.

"It's out there," Feliks insisted. "We had positive satellite contact up until the fog rolled in an hour ago." He put the tip of a finger on the chart on the table in the center of the bridge. "Right here."

"It's not there now," Carson said. "We'd pick it up."

"Then it's hiding."

Carson looked across at his executive officer, then back at Feliks. "You can't hide from radar on the surface of the ocean, sir."

"Could it have turned and gone out of range?" Feliks asked.

"If it was here," Carson touched the chart, "an hour ago, then it would still be in range of our radar even if it turned around and headed west at flank speed."

"Then it's around here somewhere. What if they're hugging the shore?" Feliks asked.

"They might be able to hide in shore clutter, but . . ." Captain Carson didn't complete the sentence. He had long ago learned to let these visitors on his ship make their own decisions and take responsibility. The minute he gave an opinion, responsibility started to shift.

"It's out there," Feliks said with certainty.

"Yes, sir," Carson replied.

"Then let's get out there and find it."

"Yes, sir."

* * *

Two hundred yards behind the *Sullivan* Lake could just barely see the stern running lights of the Coast Guard ship through the fog. He could hear foghorns all around, blasting out their warning at different notes and pulses so they could be identified.

He flipped open the navigational book for the West Coast that was in a small drawer next to the controls and flipped through it. He found what he was looking for: there was a foghorn on the south tower and north tower of the Golden Gate. He read the code for the south tower: two short blasts, one long, three short. Repeated every thirty seconds.

Lake cocked his head and listened. Finally he heard it, almost due south. He was near the bridge, and even as he realized that, he could hear the echo of traffic on pavement above his head. He couldn't see the bridge, but from the noise he knew he was directly below it. And that meant the *Sullivan* was heading out to sea.

"You don't know shit, Feliks," Lake said for the second time this evening. He spun the wheel of his boat hard left and turned south.

Adjusting for the strong seaward current, he headed toward the foghorn on the south tower. Within a minute he spotted the warning lights on the tower fender. Lake circled around the massive concrete fender. There were no ships.

There was a metal ladder leading up to the top of the fender for servicing the lights and foghorn. Lake eased up to the ladder, then quickly jumped up on the prow of the boat and tied it off. The current immediately swung the boat around and pressed it up against the concrete, ruining the paint job as the swell slammed it back and forth. That was the least of Lake's worries right now. He grabbed the scuba gear and began rigging. He was glad that the dive locker also contained a head lamp that strapped on above the face mask. Last, but not least important, Lake took the Hush Puppy out of its holster. He inserted a muzzle and chamber plug into the gun, waterproofing it.

Fully equipped, Lake walked to the rear of the boat and opened the dive gate. He walked off and into the water. He was instantly pressed up against the fender and, like a mountain climber in reverse, he began climbing down, his fingers searching out holds in the surface, his feet pushing him down. It was disorienting work being upside down, but Lake kept his focus close in, using his rising bubbles and the slight curve of the fender to keep himself oriented.

A hundred feet below, Nishin was shivering, sitting in the cold metal interior of the midget sub. It wasn't just the cold water that was knee deep on the inside that caused his condition. The mummified body of a disemboweled man was directly across from him in the cramped space of the sub. On the body's chest was the tattoo of the Black Ocean and the dagger still sticking out from his stomach where it had finished its diagonal cut, had a handle carved with Black Ocean symbols.

Nishin had entered the sub through the conning tower, which was simply a double hatch. He'd opened the top hatch to find the inside of the tower flooded and another hatch at his feet. He'd closed the top hatch, then opened the bottom, the water falling inside. He'd carefully lowered himself into the darkened interior. He'd checked the air and found it breathable after all these years. The suicide of the only crewman helped explained that—he had not waited for his air to turn bad.

The inside was small, about eight feet long by four wide and five high and crowded with instruments. The midget subs weren't designed for comfort and could hold a maximum crew of two. The rear half of the submarine was taken up by the engine. The angle the sub rested at canted everything inside at sixty degrees from horizontal. There were rudimentary controls near the front and two metal seats. There was no window, just a small periscope.

Nishin propped the underwater light on a shelf. He looked around for any record of what had happened. Why had the submarine stopped here and why hadn't the bomb been detonated? He could see a metal box in the corner near the body that had warnings all over it. He picked it up. There was a metal cover that he opened. A faded red knob rested underneath, set into a long slot. The Japanese word next to the knob said SAFE. The word at the bottom read FIRE. It was the remote detonator for the bomb. There was a dial with a listing of a range frequencies. Nishin closed the cover.

Searching further, Nishin found the ship's log jammed on top of a metal box next to the body. Opening it, Nishin immediately went to the last entry. Written in shaky Japanese it explained what he had found:

2 SEPTEMBER, 1945

With the guiding hand of the Sun Goddess behind me I have reached the objective as ordered. I was released four kilometers from the target as arranged. The current was as strong as we feared but staying low to the bottom allowed me to arrive at the south tower of the American bridge although it used almost all my battery power as also expected.

I exited through the hatch using the rebreather and secured the submarine to the tower. The bomb is still attached to the submarine and seems to have made the journey intact.

I am tempted to use the remote control to detonate the bomb myself. We could see in the I-24's periscope the cloud that rose above Hungnam right after we left. We could feel the shock of the explosion in the submarine even though we were many miles distant and submerged. I have no doubt the bomb will destroy the bridge. I would prefer to go further into the harbor and strike at a military target but my orders directed me here.

I do not understand why the primary target of the

American fleet was canceled and we were diverted here, but I believe that the Genoyshu knows what is best and my wonderings and questioning must stay with me.

I also do not know why I was told not to detonate the bomb; that it would be taken care of by another. What if this other person is delayed or stopped? I am here now. I can do it. But duty must come first. I obey.

I am wet and cold and I will be dead soon. If this is found, please excuse my ramblings. I do not question my orders, but a man who is about to die should be allowed to speak to the paper freely. If you find me, you will know I did my duty as I was ordered to.

However, I know there is another detonator and I believe that this submarine, my body, and all around will cease to exist soon, if the Sun Goddess smiles upon our homeland.

I have no family so to the Society I say my farewells. I will do as I must to end my life. I do not wish to allow the cold or lack of air to kill me. It is not the brave way.

Hatari.

Black Ocean.

Nishin looked up at Hatari. He had committed hara-kiri in the traditional manner, pushing the knife in, then slicing across his abdomen. To do it required tremendous strength of will. To do it alone, on the chance that the wound would not be immediately fatal and not having a person acting as second to behead you in that case, took even more courage. Nishin bowed his head toward his long-ago comrade and said a prayer to the Sun Goddess. Then he noticed that there was a folded page further in the log. He turned to it and uncreased the page. In the slant of the characters and the angry way the pen had been pressed into the page, Nishin could tell the mood of the man who had written it.

I could not kill myself right away. I wanted to wait, to experience the final moment when the bomb explodes. Yet it has been eight hours since I arrived here.

I have been betrayed! I have tried the detonator. It does not work. I opened up the back. It is not functional! Perhaps the frequency they gave me is the wrong one. They did not trust me. Why? Why?

It is as I feared. I had heard rumors that the Genoysha was negotiating with enemies of Japan. With the Russians at least. Maybe with others. What was my purpose in bringing this weapon here if I was not to set it off? That question bothered me as I crossed the ocean and I thought of the second detonator. But I trusted in the Sun Goddess, the Society, and the Genoysha. But I am here now, at the target, with a detonator that cannot work. I have been betrayed!

If you find this, then know that I die alone and I die bravely. Braver then those who sent me here. I curse them!

Nishin read that page, then reread. He looked at the detonator and checked the screws on the back. It was obvious from the way the metal was scratched that it had been opened.

Now it was Nishin's turn to question his mission. Why had he been sent here to stop the Koreans and then told to do nothing when the Koreans were coming again? Why had the Yakuza turned on him? Why did he have a tracking device inside of him? How did the Yakuza have so much information?

As he sat down against the cold wall of the sub, across from Hatari's body, Nishin was no longer praying. He was thinking.

* * *

Lake came across the body of the diver hooked onto the metal pole. He looked at it for a second, noted the stab wounds, then continued.

A mile and a half to the west of the Golden Gate, the *Sullivan* and the stealth ship slid by each other less than eight hundred meters apart, neither aware of the other's presence. On the bridge of the stealth, Araki was watching the small computer screen on his ever-present laptop.

"The reading is weak," he said. "Distorted."

The captain of the stealth had tracked homing devices before and was familiar with all the possible readings. "That is because the man you are seeking is underwater."

"Get me there," Araki ordered. "Prepare the swimmer-delivery vehicle and my dive gear. Now!"

The captain looked at the digits on the clock above the control panels. "Sir, if we are to make—"

"Do as I order!" Araki yelled.

The captain was not happy, sailing about blindly in the fog. He could not turn his own radar on because it would cancel out the ship's invisibility. Reluctantly, he ordered the engine room to increase thrust.

In the shadow of the north tower, Okomo and Ohashi had watched the *Sullivan* go by on their radar screen. There had been a slight image just after that, as if a small boat was out there but it had quickly disappeared.

Okomo checked his watch. His divers had another half hour of air. Then he was going to have to go back for them regardless of whether anyone else showed up or not. He went to the floor below the bridge to inform his passengers of that.

Just to the south of the drama being played out on and in the waters of the Golden Gate, the tilt-jet was slowing as the wings rotated from horizontal to vertical. Looking out the window, Kuzumi could see that they were very low over the ocean, perhaps thirty feet up. He could see a line of white in the darkness ahead: breakers hitting the shore.

Kuzumi could tell that Nakanga was very nervous. Kuzumi had not filled him in on what was going to happen, but he knew there was very good reason why that was so. It was because Kuzumi didn't know what was going to happen. He was playing this by ear. He just wanted to be within earshot to do something once he did find out what was happening.

CHAPTER 16

SAN FRANCISCO HARBOR
THURSDAY, 9 OCTOBER 1997
12:48 A.M. LOCAL

Lake was like a spider on the fender, arms and legs holding to the concrete, his head pointing down. He looked at the midget sub and the object it had towed in the glow of his headlamp for several moments. He knew that whoever had killed the diver caught on the pipe had to be around here. His gaze flickered over the dark terrain and saw nothing moving or hiding. In the sub, Lake thought. He crawled down, then onto the sub and up the conning tower. From the way the rust and dirt had been disturbed he could tell that the handle had been touched.

Lake considered the situation. With only one entrance, and that one being an airlock, there was no way to get in without whoever was inside knowing he was coming. That made them even, Lake thought, as he turned the handle for the outside hatch. As he cracked it, an air bubble burst out. Lake slid in, pulling the hatch shut behind him and securing it.

He looked down at the handle at his feet. If the person inside didn't want him in, all they had to do was jam it. He grabbed it and twisted. It turned freely. The hatch was designed to open in and the moment he loosened it enough, it fell open with an explosion of water into the sub. Lake followed, the Hush Puppy at the ready.

His feet hit the side of the compartment and slid out from under him. Despite losing his balance his hands were working on the Hush Puppy, drawing back the slide, which ejected the chamber plug making it ready to shoot.

Which Lake didn't do as he came to a halt half against the floor and wall, the muzzle of the weapon steady on the other occupant of the submarine. Who had an old-style Japanese pistol trained in reverse parallel to Lake's aim.

"Nishin," Lake said, spitting out his regulator after seeing that the other man was breathing the sub's air.

The Japanese man raised an eyebrow. "How do you know my name?"

"An agent of your government has been following you," Lake said, his grip still steady on the gun. He didn't dare take his eyes off the other man, but in his peripheral vision he could see there was a body next to Nishin.

"Was he following me using a bug inside my body?" Nishin asked.

"Yes."

"Ah." Nishin was staring at Lake. "Your name is Lake. You are the American gun dealer. Except that is your cover. You really work for an organization called the Ranch."

"How did you know that?" Lake asked.

"I was told so by the Yakuza."

Lake was surprised that the Yakuza would know about him and the Ranch. Of course, he imagined that Nishin wasn't too thrilled about having a bug in him. He also realized that he really didn't know why Nishin was here.

"Now that we've been properly introduced," Lake said, "what now?"

He knew he could kill Nishin with a pull of the trigger. And the odds were the other man would be dead before he could pull his own trigger. Of course he also knew that Nishin could have done the same at any moment also. But

Lake had a feeling that Nishin held some of the pieces of this mystery and Lake wanted answers more than he wanted another body. Why Nishin hadn't fired yet, he didn't know.

"I do not know," Nishin said. "I should kill you, I suppose. But there is information that you have that I desire. A compromise perhaps?"

Lake didn't trust Nishin and he knew the other man didn't trust him. But they were currently in a lose-lose situation. They were both professionals, which meant they both knew that if they had wanted to kill the other, somebody would be dead right now. Nishin lowered his weapon and Lake followed suit.

"Who is that?" Lake said, finally looking at the mummified body. He grimaced as he spotted the hand on the knife and the slashed midsection. It was fortunate it was so cold down here or else the air inside of the submarine would have been foul. The body had dehydrated and the flesh was brown and wrinkled.

"The operator of this ship," Nishin said. "A man named Hatari."

Lake pointed at the box next to Hatari's body. "Is that the detonator for the bomb?"

Nishin laughed, which surprised Lake. "It is supposed to be," Nishin said. "But it is not functional."

"After all these years it . . ." Lake began, but Nishin cut him off.

"I know it should not work after all these years, but it was not functional in 1945," he said. He picked it up and tossed it to Lake.

"How do you know that?" Lake turned it over in his hands, looking at it, then he stuck it under his weight belt.

Nishin held up a leather-bound book. "The ship's log. Hatari tried to detonate the bomb. Nothing happened."

Lake remembered Feliks's boasting about deals being made and broken back then. What the hell was this all about?

Nishin must have seen the look on his face, because the

Japanese man tucked his gun into his pants. "Hatari was betrayed. I am beginning to believe I might also be betrayed." He tapped his left buttocks. "Someone put this bug into me without my knowledge. Things are most strange."

Lake had to agree with that. "I think I have been betrayed also." He felt like he was talking to Harmon again, letting out information and thoughts that his training said he shouldn't but the circumstances and his gut instincts told him he should. Nishin was a killer, but so was Lake.

Nishin didn't seem at all surprised by Lake's worry. "I have been a fool. I have been told that by a Yakuza Oyabun and I am beginning to believe he is right."

You're not alone, Lake wanted to say. Was Feliks right? Was he just a stooge who followed orders? Was Nishin one also? Had Hatari been in the same situation in 1945? Lake slid the Hush Puppy into his holster.

"There are many people after this bomb," Lake said. "I think we—"

"What do you mean 'we'?" Nishin snapped. "I am not one of you. I am Japanese and that is where my allegiance lies. I am Black Ocean and that is where my allegiance lies. I might be a fool and not know what is going on, but I must be loyal. This man"—Nishin nudged Hatari's shoulder—"was betrayed, but he was also Black Ocean and he died like a man. I will do the same if it is necessary." Nishin's hand strayed to the butt of his gun.

"The bomb will still be here even if you kill me," Lake said. "What do you plan on doing with it?"

"One thing at a time. I will think of that when I am done with you," Nishin said.

"How about if we do this together?" Lake said. "You don't want anyone to find the bomb and I don't want anyone to find the bomb."

"I do not think—" Nishin began, but he paused as a metal thud reverberated through the interior of the submarine. They both looked up as if they could see through the metal skin and spot what had caused the noise. Both had instinctively drawn their guns.

"A visitor," Lake said.

"Your people?" Nishin demanded, the gun focused right between Lake's eyes.

"For all I know it could be *your* people," Lake replied as he swung the hatch he had come in back up and wheeled it shut.

"It cannot be my people," Nishin said. "It might be your CPI friend and *his* people. They are well equipped."

"I guess we'll find out shortly," Lake said. He moved across the sub to Nishin's side, ignoring the other's gun. They both watched, waiting to see what wild card was going to be played into their standoff. From the sound, Lake guessed that someone with a submersible vehicle had come down. He figured that meant either Araki's or Feliks's men, the two agencies that had the technology.

He could hear the outer hatch opening. He glanced at Nishin, but the other man's face showed no emotion. The outer hatch closed. Then Lake could see the inside wheel turning. It shot open with a gush of water and Lake blinked, keeping his gun focused on the figure that dropped in.

It was Araki dressed in a full-body black wet suit. "Lake!" he called out as he got his bearings. He had a submachine gun in his hands, which he brought to bear on Nishin.

"Hold it, Araki!" Lake yelled. "Don't shoot!"

"He is Black Ocean!" Araki cried out. "He must die!"

Lake didn't bother to argue further. He kicked, knocking the sub out of Araki's hand. "Damn it, just hold on a second!"

Out of the corner of his eye, Lake saw Nishin taking aim. Lake clamped down on Nishin's gun hand, his thumb jammed into the gap between the hammer and the chamber, preventing it from firing. "Will both of you just hold on a goddamn minute?"

Araki drew a knife. He slashed and to Lake's astonishment the blade flew at his face. Lake felt the blade cut into his cheek and slide along as he ducked, parting flesh and sending jolts of pain to his brain. In one smooth movement, Araki reversed the blade and the blade slammed into Nishin's left shoulder. It was out just as quickly, a spurt of blood coming from the wound.

Lake and Nishin both let go of Nishin's gun and scrambled out of the way of Araki's knife, a blur of steel flitting back and forth between them. Nishin feinted forward and the blade went toward him. To Lake's astonishment, Nishin caught the blade in his hand and grabbed hold. Lake didn't waste thc effort. He slammed an open palm on the left side of Araki's head, knocking the agent against the steel wall, out cold.

Nishin slowly opened his hand. The knife had cut through skin and tendons to the bone. Blood flowed freely. Lake grabbed a rag and wrapped it around Nishin's hand to stop the bleeding.

"Jesus," Lake muttered as he worked. "I don't know why he was so damn trigger-happy."

Nishin was holding the knife that had cut him in his undamaged hand and looking at it with a strange expression on his face.

"What's wrong?" Lake asked.

"I recognize this steel," Nishin said. "This blade."

"What—" Lake began, but Nishin leaned forward and before Lake could stop him, he had the tip of the blade inside the collar of Araki's wet suit.

"Now hold on," Lake said.

Nishin ignored him, slicing neatly through the rubber down to Araki's navel. The material peeled back to reveal an intricate tattoo on Araki's chest. Of a sun rising over a black ocean.

"He is not CPI," Nishin said, throwing the knife to the floor with a clang. "He is Black Ocean."

"But . . ." Lake began, then shut up as he collected his thoughts.

"I do not know him," Nishin said, answering one of the questions that flittered across Lake's brain.

"He was the one who was tracking you," Lake said.

"Of course," Nishin said. His voice was quiet, introspective as if he was talking to himself. "The Society could have put a bug in me while I was unconscious when they worked on me after my last mission."

"Why?" Lake asked, looking down at the man who up until a minute ago he had believed worked for the Japanese government.

"I do not know," Nishin said. "I was ordered to back off and not pursue this matter any further. He must not have expected me to be here."

"What a shitpile," was Lake's less than elegant summation of their situation. But it was all he could think of.

"As you were saying," Nishin said, "what do we do now?"

Lake looked at Araki, then at the hatch. "Let's see what kind of ride we have."

Nishin nodded. "But first . . . ," he said as he reversed the knife and slammed it into Araki's chest. The body twitched once, then was still.

Lake stared at him. "Why did you do that?"

"He was going to kill both of us. There is no point to keeping an enemy alive."

Ohashi picked his way through the fog very slowly. They could hear the blasts from the south tower foghorn slowly grow stronger. Visibility was less than twenty feet. The Yakuza on the forward deck held their weapons at the ready.

"Anything on radar?" Okomo asked.

"We have the same one contact to the west," Ohashi replied. "The ship that passed through earlier."

"What is it doing?"

"It's circling, as if it was waiting."

Okomo gripped the bottom edge of the open window that

faced forward. Where was everyone? Where were the North Koreans? The Black Ocean? The Americans? The CPI? One of those four must be to the west, but where were the other three?

Okomo had ordered Ohashi forward to pick up the two divers a few minutes ago. He waited until they could just make out the base of the southern tower. Ohashi's hands moved smoothly over the controls, holding their position.

"They are not here," Ohashi said, a most unnecessary comment, Okomo thought angrily. He checked his watch. The two men would be out of air in five minutes. They should have surfaced and waited, holding on to the fender, ten minutes ago.

"We wait," Okomo ordered.

The second hand on Okomo's watch swept around. Then again. After four more minutes, he had to accept what the empty concrete fender told him. "I will be back," he informed Ohashi as he turned.

The captain's voice halted him. "That contact to the west is coming back. It will be passing under the bridge in twenty minutes. They might have picked us up coming across."

Okomo nodded to indicate he understood, then headed below.

"How could we have missed it?" Feliks demanded.

"It was in the radar shadow of the Golden Gate and the north shore," Captain Carson explained.

"Is it the trawler?"

Carson looked over his radar operator's shoulder. "It's small. I don't think it's the trawler."

"What about underwater?" Feliks asked. "The North Koreans were moving a submarine in this direction."

"Sonar?" Captain Carson called out.

"Negative contact, sir," the operator reported.

"How long until we sight the radar contact?" Feliks asked.

Carson stared at him for a few seconds, then answered. "Visibility is down to maybe twenty-five feet. If we see a ship, we'll ram it."

"Then what do you suggest?" Feliks snarled. "I have to find out who that is under the bridge."

"I suggest we track the ship and stay close by," Carson replied calmly. "Sooner or later the fog will burn off. Then we can see what it is."

"Great," Feliks muttered. "Just great."

If he could have whistled, Lake would have, but the mouthpiece from the scuba gear prevented that. The swimmer-delivery vehicle, or SDV, that Araki had ridden down was top-of-the-line equipment. About twelve feet long with double propellers, it was only three feet high, which meant it had very shallow draft. It was of the "wet" type, which meant that the place for the crew was not watertight. Lake looked in: there was room for two men side by side on their stomachs in the crew compartment. The double screws meant that the engine was probably very powerful, driven by banks of batteries in a watertight compartment in the rear. The SDV was held to the midget by a steel cable running from its front to an eyebolt on the midget's deck, just forward of where the bomb sled was attached.

Lake looked up as Nishin swam out of the hatch of the midget sub. Lake pointed at the SDV and Nishin came over. Lake pointed at the cable, then back at the bomb sled. He could see Nishin's face through his mask; it squinched up in confusion for a second, then cleared as the other man understood what Lake wanted to do. Nishin nodded. Lake pointed at his chest, then into the SDV. Then he pointed at Nishin, then the cable. Nishin gave a thumbs-up, international diver talk to indicate he understood.

Lake slid into the driver's place. Looking around, the controls were not much different than the SDVs he had been trained on in the SEALs. There was even a place for

Lake to hook his regulator in to breathe air off tanks on the SDV and conserve his own back tanks.

Lake powered up the SDV. The twin screws churned behind him as he got the feel of the controls. They were quite simple. Two levers, each of which determined power to a screw. That handled speed and turning. Then a shorter lever above those two that controlled a single horizontal stabilizer that was behind both propellers. That controlled attitude, which determined whether the sub went up, down, or remained at constant depth.

Lake looked out the Plexiglas window to his front. Nishin was holding onto the anchor cable, waiting. Lake signaled for him to release the cable, which he did. The current immediately grabbed hold of the suddenly free SDV and Lake manipulated the controls. It took him a few seconds to get the feel and in that time they were swept fifteen feet away from the midget and the sled.

Lake eased them back in, Nishin dangling at the end of the cable like a hooked fish. He maneuvered until Nishin was hanging right over the sled. He held in place while Nishin hooked the cable onto the front of the bomb sled. Then Nishin released the two cables that had anchored the sled to the midget.

Nishin swam up and entered the SDV, taking his place next to Lake. Pushing the center lever up slightly, Lake then increased power to both screws. For several moments nothing happened. Lake pushed the levers forward until they couldn't go any further. Water churned in the rear but still nothing. Then slowly, with a cloud of mud, the sled began moving. For the first time in fifty-two years, Genzai Bakudan was on the move again.

CHAPTER 17

SAN FRANCISCO HARBOR
THURSDAY, 9 OCTOBER 1997
12:48 A.M. LOCAL

"We've got a contact!" the sonar man announced. "Heading nine-five degrees. Depth nine-zero feet and climbing."

Captain Carson hurried over to the sonar, Feliks right behind him. The lines on the screen were an incomprehensible jumble to both men. The *Sullivan* was in the main shipping channel, about a mile west of the Golden Gate Bridge, moving toward the harbor.

"What is it?" Carson asked.

"Small," the sonar man said, one hand holding the headphones, the other playing with knobs. "Very small, sir."

"Where is it?" Feliks asked.

Carson turned and led him to the table behind the wheel. He pointed on the chart. "Nine-five degrees from us is here. Near the bridge and just to the south of the main shipping channel." Carson turned back to the radar man. "What's the contact's heading? Is it moving?"

"It's moving, sir. Heading . . ." There was a pause, then, ". . . heading is six-zero degrees."

"Heading into the harbor, somewhat north," Carson interpreted.

"Follow it," Feliks ordered. Then he remembered something. "What about the other ship? What's it doing?"

Carson checked with radar. "It's starting to move in that direction also."

"One big party," Feliks muttered.

"Oyabun, we have picked up an underwater contact moving away from the base of the tower." Despite the cool air in the cabin, sweat was standing out on Okomo's forehead as he made his report. "I have ordered Captain Ohashi to follow on the surface."

The figure Okomo addressed was seated in the shadows in the corner of the room and did not respond. The woman standing nearby stepped into the light. "Could it be the Korean submarine?" Peggy Harmon asked.

"I do not believe so," Okomo replied. "The contact is very small. More likely it is an American submersible. Or perhaps one from the CPI or Black Ocean."

"From the Coast Guard cutter?" Harmon asked.

"I do not know." Okomo was keeping his eyes on the third person in the room, not Harmon.

That person finally spoke, the voice so low, Okomo had to lean forward to hear it. "Could it be the midget submarine?"

Okomo had not considered that possibility and he was momentarily thrown off guard. "I do not know, Oyabun. I do not think it would still be capable of functioning after all these years."

There was a noise that might have been laughter and the figure held up a metal box in an age-withered hand. "I have been told that with the right frequency this detonator will still work. I have been told Genzai Bakudan will still work. Why not, then, the submarine?"

To that Okomo had no answer.

"Leave us," Harmon snapped.

With a bow, Okomo scuttled out of the room.

Nakanga was standing on the other side of the cabin, waiting for further orders. The phone at Kuzumi's elbow buzzed and he picked it up.

"The SDV is moving to the east," the voice on the other end said succinctly in Japanese. "There are also two surface contacts. I believe one of them is a U.S. Coast Guard cutter. I do not know what the other one is."

Kuzumi was surprised that the SDV was moving to the east, but he didn't bother asking why Araki was doing that because there was no way the man on the other side could know why. Araki was simply supposed to recover the bomb back to the stealth ship which was to the west.

"Follow," Kuzumi ordered the captain of the stealth ship. It was the prototype for a model that he had sold to the Japanese Navy. The government thought the ship had been disassembled. Like many other projects completed under government contract, it went into the Black Ocean arsenal.

Kuzumi turned the phone off. "Tell the pilot to be prepared to lift off."

The current was fighting the SDV and keeping its speed down to less than five knots. Lake was giving more power to the right screw, pushing them slightly to the north. Nishin had been still for a while, but now he picked up a board that had been lying inside and wrote on it with the marker that was clipped to it. It was the only way people inside could communicate with each other and part of the standard equipment for the SDV. Lake glanced over at the message:

WHERE?

Nishin wiped the question off and handed the board to Lake. Locking the controls, Lake took the marker and wrote the answer.

ISLAND. SECURE BOMB.

Nishin took the board and looked at it. It was the best idea Lake could come up with. Actually, what he didn't bother to write was that he wasn't sure how exactly he was going to secure the bomb. He had considered taking it out to deep sea and dumping it, but that would only reinvent the problem they had just encountered, leaving it out there for the next person to find.

His major goal right now was to get the bomb away from the bridge and also to get away from the ship that had launched the SDV. Lake knew that the SDV had not come alone. Lake had a very strong feeling that the SDV came from Araki's stealth ship, which had rescued him just a few days ago, and it would be sitting out to the west. It wasn't much of a plan, but given the circumstances, it was the best he could come up with under short notice.

He didn't have an exact idea where he was. He was working on instinct and educated guesswork. The headlight on the SDV lit up the next thirty feet of ocean and the scene never changed: inky water in a cone of light.

Lake knew from the instrument panel that he was at a depth of fifty feet, but that was all. From the speed of the SDV, subtracted by the speed of the current, multiplied by time elapsed, he estimated that they had already covered about a mile from the bridge.

Nishin shoved the board back into its slot, which Lake took as acceptance. Not that Lake thought the other man had any choice. Lake tried to remember what San Francisco Harbor looked like. He knew the Navy had a base at Treasure Island, but that was also close to the Bay Bridge, which wasn't the smartest place to bring a nuclear weapon.

Then he had it. There was another island almost straight

in from the bridge and it was deserted. The perfect place to bring the bomb up and call for help.

"Let's be real careful now," Captain Carson called out to his bridge crew. Carson could have told Lake his estimate was wrong. The *Sullivan* was less than a mile out from the Golden Gate. Carson could hear the Mile Rock foghorn to the south, not too far away. Close enough for him to worry about seeing it suddenly loom out of the fog. There were numerous other shoals and rocks out here, off of the main channel.

Carson checked his electronic eyes one more time. The sonar contact was another half mile to the west of the Coast Guard ship. Checking radar, he could see that the surface contact was between his ship and the underwater vessel, a quarter mile to the west of the *Sullivan*. They were all fumbling around in the dark, to what end he wasn't sure.

He went back to stand behind his radar man. Feliks joined him. "Any idea where we're headed?" Carson asked.

"No," Feliks said.

"Would you mind telling me what we're following?" Carson asked.

"Yes, I mind very much," Feliks said. "It's classified."

"Can you give me an idea—" Carson began, but the scream of one of the forward lookouts cut him off.

"Ship off the port bow!"

Carson saw it, less then thirty feet away, a black shape. He had a moment to wonder why radar had not picked it up, then he was screaming orders.

"Full reverse! Hard left rudder!" Even as he spoke he knew it was hopeless. Ships didn't have brakes and they didn't stop quickly. Mass in motion in the water tended to keep moving in the same direction for a while. The thirty feet disappeared in four seconds. In that time Carson registered that the other ship was of a type he had never seen before. Shaped like an inverted V with sloping black decks.

There were no running lights lit, a violation of sea law, Carson thought as the bow of the *Sullivan* hit the sloped left-front side of the other ship.

The weight of the cutter and its specially constructed bow, designed for cutting through small ice fields, combined with the slope of the side of the other ship, led the *Sullivan* up onto the side of the other ship, then something gave. The sound of tearing metal and the clang of the *Sullivan*'s collision alarm filled the night air, echoing into the fog.

Carson ran to the right side of his bridge and looked down. The severed rear half of the other ship was listing in the water, going down quickly. He ran over to the left side. There was nothing there. The front half must have been pushed under the keel of the *Sullivan*. The grinding sounds continued as the *Sullivan* slid over the remains of the stealth ship. Then there was only the collision alarm.

"Prepare for rescue operations!" Carson cried out. He leaned over the voice tube to the engine room. "Continue reverse until we come to a stop."

"What do you think you're doing?" Feliks demanded.

Carson ignored him. "Damage control, all sections report in." He listened as the various parts of the ship called back. It appeared that the other ship had take the brunt of the damage. The *Sullivan*'s bow was slightly crumpled but they weren't taking on any water.

Feliks waited until he could be heard. "We have to continue after the underwater contact."

"We can't leave the scene of an accident." Carson was indignant. "There might be survivors in the water. That's the international law of the sea."

"I don't give a goddamn about the international law of the sea," Feliks hissed, leaning in close. The bridge was shuddering from the power of the engines in full reverse, still trying to stop the ship. He gripped Carson's arm. "There may be a Japanese nuclear weapon on board this contact we're tracking. A nuclear weapon that had been delivered to destroy San Francisco. That ship we just ran over was from the Japanese government trying to recover that bomb. I really don't have too much sympathy if there are any survivors. We would have had to fight them for the bomb anyway.''

''I can't leave men in the water,'' Carson said obstinately.

''I'm ordering you to continue pursuit.''

Carson shook his head. ''I have a higher law that I must obey as a seaman.''

''I'll have your ass,'' Feliks growled.

''You very well may,'' Carson said, ''but after I check for survivors.''

''What is that?'' Okomo demanded as the sound of metal tearing echoed through the fog.

''It sounds like a ship hitting something,'' Captain Ohashi said.

''I thought you said there was only one radar contact,'' Okomo said.

Another sound, a jarring clanging soon filled the air. ''That is a ship's collision warning alarm,'' Ohashi said. ''There must have been a collision.''

''The underwater contact?'' Okomo demanded.

''Heading slightly north of east,'' Ohashi replied.

''Any idea where it's heading?''

Ohashi looked at his chart. ''If they keep their same course, they will hit here.'' His finger tapped an island.

''Take us there!'' Okomo ordered.

Feliks watched the surface contact move east. The crew of the *Sullivan* had not picked up any survivors from the stealth ship, but Captain Carson, to Feliks's extreme displeasure, was keeping them circling in the same spot, still looking.

Feliks checked the chart. There were so many directions the ship could go in once it made it into the harbor, he was going to lose them soon. He walked out to the bridge wing where Carson was looking down at the water.

"We have to . . ." Feliks paused as his eyes were caught by something. He tapped Carson on the shoulder. "Can you launch your helicopter?"

Carson nodded. "It's all set. The crew is on board in case we need them."

"You stay here and search," Feliks said. "I'm taking the chopper."

Kuzumi threw the phone down in disgust. There had been no reply from the stealth ship for the past five minutes. Piling that on top of Araki's course change to head east, and things were not looking good. He had a sudden foreboding about what was going on. Perhaps Araki was no longer driving the SDV.

Araki had been his ace in the hole to keep a personal eye on this whole operation. Kuzumi had long ago found that it was very profitable on high-risk operations to put a deeper-cover operative on an operation that a regular operative was sent on. It was redundancy in the system, an engineering term.

Kuzumi pulled a small computer out of the sideboard next to him and turned it on. He tapped into the keys, pulling up the code for the bug in Nishin. The image came on the screen very faintly to the north. Kuzumi overlaid a map of San Francisco on top of the dot. Nishin was in San Francisco Harbor, to the east of the Golden Gate. Kuzumi followed the dot to the right. He turned to Nakanga. "Tell the pilot to take off."

"Where are we going?" Nakanga asked.

Kuzumi held up the map. "Alcatraz."

CHAPTER 18

SAN FRANCISCO HARBOR
THURSDAY, 9 OCTOBER 1997
1:20 A.M. LOCAL

Time to go up and take a peek, Lake thought as he pulled back on the center bar. The SDV glided up against the current, the Genzai Bakudan buffeting its way less smoothly ten feet behind the propellers.

The gauge on the instrument panel showed their ascent. Forty feet. Thirty feet. Twenty feet. Lake could begin to feel the effect of the swell above. Still nothing but dark water ahead, the headlight piercing it for thirty feet. The engine of the SDV was struggling now against both the outgoing current and the weight of the Genzai Bakudan.

Ten feet. Lake felt the bow lurch up, then they were thrown down, nose pointing almost straight to the bottom. He pulled back hard and the next swell lifted them up, then the cables from the sled snapped taut, slamming both Nishin and he around on the inside. They were on the surface, bouncing about.

Water broke over the Plexiglas nose. Lake peered ahead. He could see a flashing light directly in front, less than a quarter mile away. A short, white line of breakers crashing on rock was directly below the light. Lake pushed the lever forward, moving the stabilizer, and they went down again. He descended to twenty feet and held at that depth where the surface effect wasn't that strong. He edged forward, slightly more power going to the right screw.

He drove the SDV by feel, keeping the depth constant, edging farther right when the turbulence of the water against the rocky shoreline grew stronger. Soon he could feel the turbulence more to the right than in front, which told him he was moving along the north shore of the island. Lake edged in, remembering the tour he'd gone on to Alcatraz during his time in the city. The U-shaped jetty for the island was built on the north shore. One part of the U was the shore, the other a wooden dock on pilings and the opening facing to the west. If he played his cards right, he should come right up to the center of the jetty and be able to tie up there.

Of course, Lake also realized, his hands tense on the controls, if he was too far out he'd miss the jetty altogether and if he was too close they'd hit the rocky shoreline. He wasn't sure how much power was left in the batteries of the SDV, but his experience with similar vehicles in the SEALs told him there probably wasn't that much. If they lost power, the weight of the bomb would pull both it and the SDV down to the bottom.

Lake took a glance over to the left. Nishin was lying there, his face inscrutable behind his mask. Looking at the Black Ocean agent, Lake again had to consider that if he did make it into the jetty, then what?

Captain Ohashi had his hands on the helm as the Alcatraz lighthouse, the first lighthouse built on the west coast of the United States, drew closer on the port bow. The sonar contact was breaking up in the "shadow" of the island.

Ohashi knew the harbor intimately and he knew that the only place that any kind of craft could put to shore on Alcatraz was at the jetty on the north side. He increased speed and aimed the prow off his ship just offshore the east end to round it and come in to the jetty from that direction.

The tilt-jet circled as Kuzumi stared at the computer screen, then out the window. "He is right below us," he told Nakanga.

Nakanga didn't ask who, remaining silent, waiting for the wishes of his Genoysha to be known.

"He is going to land on Alcatraz," Kuzumi announced as the dot that reflected the bug inside Nishin merged with the northern side of the island. "Tell the pilot to put us down there."

From the Coast Guard helicopter, Feliks could see that the tugboat was closing on Alcatraz. He, and the pilot, were startled when a strange aircraft swooped by them and descended toward the island.

"What the hell was that?" Feliks demanded.

"I don't know, sir," the pilot replied. "I've never seen anything like that before. I didn't see any markings."

Feliks glanced about the cabin. He could only fit two of his men on board. He turned his attention outward and was impressed when the wings of the plane that had just gone by began rotating and it started to settle onto Alcatraz. Just like the Osprey that Congress had killed, he thought, except with jets. He knew that there was a craft like it on the drawing board in the U.S. government's black budget but no operational models. That left only one country on the planet with the technology to make such a craft.

"Follow them!" Feliks ordered.

Lake spotted the jetty two seconds before the front of the SDV hit it. He slammed both levers all the way into reverse, then cringed as the Plexiglas bounced off the wood piling that had suddenly appeared. The glass cracked but since the inside of the SDV was already exposed to the water it didn't make any difference. He braced himself and waited, then felt the slam from the rear as the sled with Genzai Bakudan on board hit them from behind.

Lake hit the emergency button on the lower-right side of the control panel and two large water wings rapidly inflated on either side of the vehicle. They were on the surface in four seconds. Genzai Bakudan slowly settled to hang below the SDV.

The swell inside the protection of the jetty was not as great as that in the harbor. Lake and Nishin slithered out of the SDV and each took a nylon line in one hand as they attempted to make the jump from the bouncing SDV to the jetty wall. Both jumped on an upswell. Climbing up to the top, they tied off their lines to metal cleats

''Where are we?'' Nishin asked, looking up at the imposing structure of the abandoned barracks building next to the jetty. A road ran from the jetty to their right, to a sally port that had a drawbridge and controlled access to the old prison proper. To the left, a large open area was bounded on the left by the sea and to the right by a steep slope leading up to the old military parade ground. On the high ground above them lay the big house of the abandoned prison and the lighthouse, whose light flashed above their heads every few seconds.

''Alcatraz,'' Lake replied.

''There is no one here?'' Nishin asked.

''Not at night,'' Lake said.

''And now what do you have planned?''

To that question, Lake had no immediate answer. He'd had to concentrate on driving the SDV here, so he really hadn't had a chance to consider future courses of action. At the very least, he felt, they weren't tied off on the southern tower of the Golden Gate anymore.

''I guess I'll try to get in contact with someone who can take care of the bomb,'' he said.

''It would not be good for the Black Ocean if the existence of this bomb is made public,'' Nishin said. ''Could we not destroy it ourselves? Dismantle it somehow?''

"I don't think . . ." Lake paused and cocked his head. Both he and Nishin turned and watched a large tilt-jet plane come to a landing in the open area fifty yards away.

A door in the side of the plane opened and two men armed with submachine guns jumped out. A third man came out, extending a long platform. Then that man went inside and came back out, pushing a man in a wheelchair.

"Ai!" Nishin cried out. "It is my Genoysha. The head of my Society. The man pushing him is Nakanga, my Sensei."

Lake had the Hush Puppy in his hand, Nishin a knife. Not exactly a good firepower ratio against the two men's subs. The four men began moving across the open area toward them, the two guards slightly in the lead, the butts of their weapons tucked into their shoulders, muzzles pointing at Lake and Nishin.

They came to a halt fifteen feet away, the guards on either flank, Nakanga directly behind the Genoysha's wheel-chair.

"Ronin Nishin, you have done well," Genoysha Kuzumi called out.

Lake glanced over at Nishin, but he couldn't tell anything from his face.

"Have you recovered Genzai Bakudan?" Kuzumi asked.

"Yes," Nishin said.

"More company," Lake said as a helicopter flashed overhead, searchlight illuminating the scene. Everyone paused and watched as the chopper settled down beyond the plane. The side door of the chopper opened and four men jumped out of it.

Lake recognized the figure of the lead man immediately. "My boss, Feliks, is here too," he whispered to Nishin.

Nishin didn't say anything in reply.

Feliks and his guards moved toward Lake and Nishin, circumventing the Japanese party. Lake and Nishin were at the point of a triangle, the Black Ocean Genoysha at another and Feliks at the third.

''One big happy party,'' Lake called out. It was silent except for the sound of the surf pounding the island now that both the tilt-jet and helicopter had shut down their engines.

''Do you have the bomb?'' Feliks asked.

''First I think introductions are in order,'' Lake replied. ''My name is Lake. I work for the Ranch, which works for the U.S. government.'' Lake stabbed a thumb at his partner. ''This is Nishin. He works for the Black Ocean Society.'' Lake pointed at the Japanese group. ''Nishin tells me that over there is his Genoysha, or head, of the Black Ocean.''

''Do you have the bomb?'' Feliks demanded.

Lake knew there was no use denying it since he had taken it as far as he could. ''Yes, we have it.''

Feliks then turned toward the Black Ocean people. ''I believe we can resolve this once again with—'' He paused as a powerful searchlight raked across the jetty.

Everyone on land turned and watched as a tugboat pulled up to the outside of the jetty. A cluster of armed men poured off the boat, forming a skirmish line on the wood dock. Several figures climbed off the boat behind them, then the entire party moved forward.

Lake froze as he recognized a tall, slender figure in the rear of the new group: Peggy Harmon, her arm supporting an older woman dressed in a long black coat.

The Hush Puppy was forgotten in Lake's hand. There was enough firepower in the immediate vicinity to make Swiss cheese of Nishin and him, but that wasn't what preoccupied Lake's mind at the moment. He suddenly realized this was all a setup. It had to be. It couldn't have been coincidence that brought him to Harmon's office and her here now. And Feliks and the Black Ocean Genoysha. Underneath that strategical analysis, though, was his profound disappointment in Harmon and even more so in himself for being so easily deceived and set up.

* * *

Lake was not the only one experiencing strong emotion. As the people had gotten off the tug, Kuzumi had also realized all these individuals coming to this location at the same time could not be coincidence. There had to be a hand behind it and he knew it wasn't his, which was what concerned him the most.

He didn't recognize the people from the tug, although Nakanga had whispered in his ear that the old man with them was the Oyabun of the San Francisco Yakuza.

"The young woman?" Kuzumi asked.

"I don't know, Genoysha."

Kuzumi squinted. He could not make out the features of the older woman on her arm. The night combined with a dark shawl obscured her face.

"I am glad you could all make it," the old woman said, and Kuzumi felt his heart tremble. It could not be—but he knew it was.

"Nira!" he cried out from his wheelchair.

The old woman slowly walked forward until she was a few feet in front of Kuzumi's wheelchair. She pulled back her shawl and looked hard at him. There was no doubting it now, Kuzumi knew. Fifty-six years had passed but he could still see the features of the young woman he had loved and who had fathered their son.

The others on the jetty were mute spectators to the reunion, all waiting to see how this played out and affected their own futures.

"Kuzumi! They told me you were dead," Nira said.

Kuzumi felt a stab of pain that she did not step forward and bridge the gap between them. He held up a hand. "Nira!"

"You didn't die in the plane crash, then," Nira said, almost to herself. "How did you escape the Russians?"

"The Society traded for me."

"And you didn't try to get in contact with me?"

"They told me *you* were dead," Kuzumi said. "That you had jumped from the Golden Gate Bridge."

Nira laughed, but there was no mirth to it. ''All these years,'' she said, ''and it was you ruling the Black Ocean. When did you become Genoysha?''

''In 1968.'' Kuzumi's hand was growing tired, extended as it was, yet still she did not close the gap.

Nira's voice grew firmer. ''As you can tell I did not jump from the bridge, although your predecessor sent someone to throw me from it. Unfortunately for him, by that time I had friends who protected me and made it seem I was dead so that they would not send another.''

Kuzumi lowered his hand. He should have known he'd been deceived by Taiyo. As Genoysha he had never trusted anyone with the truth, why should he have expected the Genoysha before him to be any different? The burning question was why? What had happened so many years ago that led to this group being gathered here with the last Genzai Bakudan?

''I did not know,'' Kuzumi said.

''No, you didn't,'' Nira said. ''But I believe that you would have done the same since you are now Genoysha.''

''I do not understand,'' Kuzumi said. ''What happened?''

A new voice cut in. ''I had a deal with your predecessor,'' Feliks called out. ''You need to get on your plane and go back home,'' he said to Kuzumi. ''I don't know who you are, lady, but you can go home, too.''

Nira slowly turned. ''Yes, a deal. I would like to know what the deal was since I was one of the pawns to be sacrificed by that deal.''

''You people are so naive,'' Feliks said. ''It's ancient history and it's going to remain that way.''

''I want some answers,'' Nira said. ''That is why I arranged for all of you to come here.''

''You arranged?'' Feliks said. ''You—''

''The Patriots, your man''—Nira nodded toward Lake—''killed on the bridge were paid for and given their mission by me. They didn't know that, but they didn't have to. I knew they would draw the Ranch in. And once I had the Ranch drawn in, I knew the words 'Genzai Bakudan' would draw you in, Mr. Feliks. I know your name. I know you worked with Genoysha Taiyo to stop Genzai Bakudan from working.''

She turned to Kuzumi. ''And the Black Ocean. I wanted you here, too, although I did not know you were the Genoysha, Kuzumi. Through my underworld sources I alerted the North Koreans to the location of the cave in Hungnam you told me about. I fed them information to keep them going, like dogs on a leash after you destroyed the cave. I directed them here to steal those documents. Documents my daughter has studied for many long years to find out if the I-24 really made it here and if the midget submarine had actually launched. She only found that out last year. Since then I have been planning this reunion.''

''Your daughter?'' Lake said.

Nira kept her attention on Kuzumi. ''Yes, my daughter. I remarried after the war. An American. He was a good man and I needed him to keep my place in society even as I used the contacts I had made working for the Black Ocean to work my way into the Yakuza of San Francisco. *I* am the Oyabun!''

''You may be Oyabun, but I've got a couple of platoons of men headed in this direction right now,'' Feliks said. ''So I think—''

''I do not care what you think,'' Nira snapped. ''I am in charge here.''

''Says who?'' Feliks asked.

Nira turned to Kuzumi. ''The frequency for the detonator for Genzai Bakudan?''

Kuzumi had those numbers imprinted in his memory. He told her.

Nira held up a hand and in it was a small metal box. Lake recognized it as a twin to the one in the submarine. She turned a dial on the front. ''I had the special code transmitted and now I have the proper frequency. I control Genzai Bakudan."

"That thing won't go off," Feliks said, but Lake could hear a little bit of uncertainty in his voice.

"I think you'd better call Randkin and check on that," Lake said. "When I asked him, he said there was a good chance the bomb would work."

Feliks looked about, then settled on Nira. "What do you want?"

"The truth," Nira said. "I knew one of you would have it." She pointed at Kuzumi. "Obviously he is ignorant of what happened since he was a captive in Russia at the end of the war and Taiyo told him nothing but lies. So you must know the truth."

Feliks shook his head. "What good would that do now? It's all worked out for the best. Let it go."

"It is my life!" Nira shouted, startling everyone with such a powerful voice in such an old body. "My life. My son's life." She snapped her head around to Kuzumi. "James is dead, isn't he? Or was that another lie fed me?"

"I am sorry to tell you that our son is indeed dead," Kuzumi said.

Nira turned back to Feliks. She held up the remote. "Tell me what treachery was wrought at the end of the war."

"It was not treachery," Feliks said, stung by the word. "What was done was done in the mutual best interests of my country and yours," he added, nodding toward Kuzumi. "Taiyo was a very smart man. You tried to make a deal with the Russians. Give them Genzai Bakudan in exchange for their alliance against us in the Pacific. The Russians laughed at you and took Hungnam by force even before they declared war.

"Then you turned to us. You had one Genzai Bakudan after you blew the one at Hungnam. You knew we had the bomb—make that bombs. Hell, we really didn't need the atomic bomb, we were hitting you with enough conventional ordnance that there would be nothing left of the infrastructure of Japan by the end of the year."

Feliks's voice carried over the sound of the waves hitting the rocks and echoed off the stone walls above them.

"Your Emperor wanted peace, but the military didn't want to surrender. He needed a way out. We had the bomb. You had the bomb. One of the agents the Black Ocean used here in the states, a Spanish man, approached me with the word about Genzai Bakudan. At first, I think Taiyo thought we would be willing to negotiate something more than the unconditional surrender the Allies were demanding if we knew you had an atomic weapon."

Feliks laughed. "He was quickly disabused of the notion, especially since Roosevelt had just died and the war in Europe was over. So it was time for plan two. My superior who headed the Ranch at that time went to Truman and told him about Genzai Bakudan. And that it was en route to attack some Allied target. This was right after Truman was briefed on the Manhattan Project."

Feliks paused, as if thinking of how to say what he was telling them. He shrugged. "So we struck a deal. We dropped the bomb on Hiroshima, you assured us Genzai Bakudan would not be detonated."

"What kind of deal was that?" Nira demanded, her shock representative of what Kuzumi and Lake felt.

"It was a deal that saved Japan from being leveled," Feliks shot back angrily. "Do you know what would have happened if that thing"—he pointed at the jetty—"*had* gone off? Yeah, you would have taken out the Golden Gate Bridge and then what? You didn't have any more and we knew that. You think the United States would have said, Gee, we're sorry after five years of war and let's have a truce? Didn't you see how we reacted to Pearl Harbor? If you had detonated Genzai Bakudan, it would have been genocide. There wouldn't be a Japan today. There'd be just a bunch of lifeless lumps of land in its place."

"And Nagasaki?" Kuzumi asked. "Was that part of the deal too?"

"That was *your* problem. The Emperor still couldn't get the military hotheads under control. So we helped him convince them."

"That is why the frequency this was set on," Nira said, "was the wrong one."

"Correct," Feliks said. "Taiyo kept that frequency as the final control over Genzai Bakudan."

"And why they tried to kill me and get the detonator back," she added, almost to herself.

"Right."

"All these years," Nira said. She looked at Kuzumi. "You knew none of this?"

Kuzumi shook his head. "I was in Russia. When I returned I was told that the I-24 which carried Genzai Bakudan had been scuttled at sea and you were dead."

Nishin spoke for the first time. "The detonator in the submarine was on the wrong frequency, too. Hatari thought he was betrayed."

Kuzumi spread his hands. "I did not know."

"But you did," Nira said, staring at Feliks. She raised her empty hand and pointed at Feliks.

"It was necessary," Feliks said. "It was the right . . ." He never finished the sentence as a black hole suddenly appeared in the center of his forehead. The back of his skull exploded out and the body flipped back onto the gravel. The two Ranch guards were also shot, their bodies crumpling under the impact of several rounds each.

"It was treachery all around," Nira said. "There was no honor in it." She reached out the same hand that had signaled Feliks's death to Kuzumi and took his hand. "I am sorry that we have lost all these years."

At the jetty Lake glanced at Nishin. Lake walked forward to Nira and Kuzumi. "What now?"

Nira's face still held some of the beauty it had once glowed with. She smiled and handed Lake the detonator. "It is all yours. Peggy told me that you were a man that could be trusted. Do what you will with the bomb. Sink it at sea like it should have been long ago." She turned to Kuzumi. "We must leave. It will be dawn soon and people will be coming."

Kuzumi nodded. "Come with me?" he asked her.

Nira tapped her daughter on the shoulder. "Take the men back. I will get in contact with you later." She took Nakanga's place and pushed the wheelchair toward the tilt-jet, whose engines were starting up.

"Come with us, Nishin," Kuzumi called out.

Nishin had walked forward with Lake. The Japanese looked at Lake and shrugged. "It is all I know," he said.

Lake simply nodded. Nishin followed the couple, in step with Nakanga.

Lake looked at Harmon. She reached into her coat pocket and pulled out a tape recorder. "You might want Feliks's words. They might help you get reinstated."

Lake took the tape recorder. "You should have told me the truth. I told you the truth about me."

"My mother and I didn't know the truth," Harmon said. "We had to find it out."

"So you lied to get to the truth?" Lake shook his head. "All of this," he added, gesturing at the tilt-jet taking off, Feliks's body, the Yakuza tug, the Coast Guard helicopter that was also taking off. "All of it happened because of lies."

"What are you going to do?" Harmon asked.

Lake felt very tired. "The first tourist boat will be out here shortly. Maybe Feliks's men are coming. The Coast Guard pilot probably has called the police by now.

"I'm going to wait," Lake said. "I'm going to give the bomb to the park police. And I'm going to give them the tape."

"You're going to cause a lot of trouble if you do that," Harmon said.

"All this happened because no one wanted the trouble the truth would cause. Seems like the lies don't do much better than the truth."

"And you?" she added in a different tone of voice.

"And I'm going away," Lake said. He met her eyes for a long minute, then turned and walked away toward the tied-up SDV. Harmon stood still, then quickly walked toward the tub, her men following her.

Soon there was no one but Lake left alive on the island. He strolled over to Feliks's body and reached into his jacket. He pulled out the old OSS cigarette case.

When the first police boat reached the island, Lake was on his second smoke.